DIGITAL DREAMS

Computers are unforgiving creatures, and not terribly bright. You tell a person to do something stupid and dangerous, and you'll get a variety of rude answers: common sense and self-preservation will make them say No. But tell a computer to do something stupid and dangerous, and if its programmers haven't anticipated your request, and made the machine idiot-proof, it'll do it — or at least try to.

Digital Dreams is an all-British collection of original computer stories. They're all brand new, written especially for this collection, by people with strings of books behind them, and there are first stories by new writers. There's SF, and Fantasy, and Horror, and History and Mystery and Murder and Spoof; there are stories about the Arts, and scientific stories; there are stories set in the future, the present and the past. There are stories that will have you giggling on the umpteenth reading, and others that will make you want to weep. And there are stories here, and quite a few of them, that will make you *think*.

ACKNOWLEDGEMENTS

Digital Dreams

Edited by
David V Barrett

NEW ENGLISH LIBRARY
Hodder and Stoughton

British Library C.I.P.

Digital Dreams
  1. Short stories in English, 1990– – Anthologies
  I. Barrett, David V
  823.0108

ISBN 0–450–53150–3

Printed and bound in Great Britain for Hodder and Stoughton Children's Books, a division of Hodder and Stoughton Ltd., Mill Road, Dunton Green, Sevenoaks, Kent, TN13 2YA. (Editorial Office: 47 Bedford Square, London WC1B 3DP) by Cox & Wyman. Photoset by Chippendale Type Ltd., Otley, West Yorkshire.

CONTENTS

Introduction   David V Barrett   7

Bronze Casket for a Mummified
Shrew-Mouse   Garry Kilworth   11

Digital Cats Come Out Tonight   Ben Jeapes   25

What Happened at
Cambridge IV   David Langford   37

The World of the Silver Writer   Anne Gay   53

Forgotten Milestones in Computing No. 7: The
Quenderghast Bullian Algebraic
Calculator   Alex Stewart   67

ifdefDEBUG + "world/enough"
+ "time"   Terry Pratchett   77

The Great Brain Legend   Josephine Saxton   95

The Reconstruction of Mingus   Phil Manchester   111

Twister of Words   Michael Fearn   129

The Mechanical Art   Andy Sawyer   143

Last Came Assimilation   Storm Constantine   159

Virus	Neil Gaiman	183
Measured Perspective	Keith Roberts	189
Where He Went	Paul Kincaid	209
The Coleridge Bombers	Paul Beardsley	229
Dependant	David V Barrett	245
Nad and Dan adn Quaffy	Diana Wynne Jones	259
The Machine It Was That Cried	John Grant	281
The Lord of the Files	Ray Girvan & Steve Jones	317
Speaking in Tongues	Ian McDonald	333

INTRODUCTION

On June 19, 1985, a laser signal beamed from the top of a mountain in Hawaii was supposed to have been bounced off a mirror on the side of a space shuttle, and so back to Earth. Unfortunately, the guy who wrote the program had forgotten to tell the shuttle's computer that the top of the mountain was 10,230 *feet* above sea level; the computer assumed he meant 10,230 *nautical miles*, and for some reason failed to find a mountain top that high above the earth's surface*.

A simple programming error, but this experiment was part of Ronald Reagan's Star Wars project which, if it ever really gets going, will require an estimated ten billion lines of programming. Now *everyone* who's ever written a program knows there is one basic law: It Won't Work First Time. Programs need testing, debugging, rewriting and testing over and over again before they'll work as they're supposed to. As MP Tam Dalyell says, the only problem with the billions of lines of code in Star Wars is we don't have a spare planet to test them on.

Computers are unforgiving creatures, and not terribly bright. You tell a person to do something stupid and dangerous, and you'll get a variety of rude answers: common sense and self-preservation will make them say No. (This is why squaddies are trained in unquestioning obedience – who in their right mind would go over the top

---

* Source: *Scientific American* December 1985. Thanks to Dr Chris Moss of Imperial College, London, for helping me track this down.

to get themselves blown apart?) But tell a computer to do something stupid and dangerous, and if its programmers haven't anticipated your request, and made the machine idiot-proof, it'll do it – or at least try to. I've destroyed files, wiped disks and crashed computers many times, because no one had had the prescience to warn the beast about *this* idiot.

Whether you love them or loathe them, computers are now part of our everyday lives, and you can't escape them. You shove your dirty clothes in your automatic washing machine (controlled by a microchip) and set your video (ditto) to record a film while you go out shopping. You take some money out of your bank's cashpoint (or Automatic Teller Machine) and spend it in your local supermarket where the bar-coded baked beans trigger messages to a computerised stock-control system while the till's producing your bill.

You return home and find the video's recorded some fancy electoral guesswork from the latest opinion poll, and a weather forecast (both computer projections). There are some nice graphics, though – computer-generated, of course.

You can't escape them.

All sorts of details about you are held on computers. Your health record, your academic record, your tax details, your driving licence and insurance records, the number of times you've been overdrawn at the bank, the one time you were late with a hire-purchase payment (or someone else who used to live in a different flat at your address; it has the same effect: you're blacklisted). You might like to know that the National Insurance computer in Newcastle has its own private chatline to the M15 computer in Gower Street, London, according to Peter Wright in *Spycatcher*. If you've ever been a vetted civil servant, an active member of CND or even a journalist, there's a security file on you on a computer somewhere. And I hate to think how *Reader's Digest* and Time-Life Books always know when I've changed address; it never takes long for their special offers to catch up with me.

You can't escape them. How many of us have word processors or educational (i.e., games) computers in our homes? And we bought them down the High Street.

It would be nice to say that all this was forecast in science fiction years ago. Some was, some wasn't. John Brunner talked about computer viruses and self-replicating software worms in *The Shockwave Rider* back in 1975. Arthur C. Clarke had a computer doing some divine counting in 'The Nine Billion Names of God' in 1953, and of course HAL making life and death decisions in *2001: A Space Odyssey* (1968). And Frederick Pohl has a wonderful German-accented computer psychoanalyst (now we call them expert systems) in *Gateway* (1977).

But SF writers didn't get it all right. For years they would have walkin', talkin' robots, more intelligent and quicker-thinking than mere humans, while a company's accounts were calculated on punched cards by a computing machine taking up half a block. We can do the latter today on a desktop PC costing under £1,000; the former is somewhat further away.

Digital Dreams is a computer short-story anthology with a difference. Previous books have been largely American collections of reprinted stories, re-treading the old, familiar, stale ideas. *Digital Dreams* is an all-British collection of original stories – original in both senses. They're all brand new, written especially for this collection, and they're all new, bright, stimulating, exciting, thought-provoking ideas. The sheer quality of the stories you're about to read is way beyond what I had hoped for when I first set out. There are stories by people with strings of books behind them, and there are first stories by new writers. There's SF, and Fantasy, and Horror, and History and Mystery and Murder and Spoof; there are stories about the Arts, and scientific stories; there are stories set in the future, the present and the past. There are stories that still have me giggling on the umpteenth reading, and others that make me want to weep. And there are stories here, and quite a few of them, that will make you *think*.

Most books are a long time a-birthing. This one was conceived at the Milford SF Writer's Conference in September 1986, but it was only after the next Milford, in 1988, that it really began to grow. I want to thank all the people there for their faith and encouragement, and in some cases their stories, especially Neil Gaiman who named the unborn infant very late one drunkenly creative evening when a group of us were tossing story ideas around. Thanks to Humphrey Price at NEL for giving the child a home and for nursing me through my first birth and making it relatively painless. Thank you also to someone who kicked me when I needed it. And thank you most of all to everyone who wrote stories for *Digital Dreams*.

Back in 1968 Christopher Hodder-Williams wrote a terrifyingly prophetic novel, sadly long out of print, about the all-pervasive presence of computers, running amongst other things telephone systems, airline bookings, hydro-electric dams and American nuclear defence; the problems begin when the computers start talking to each other. There's one paragraph of *Fistful of Digits* which has haunted me for two decades, especially as a programmer and later as a computer journalist:

> 'Many people fear computers because they seem to impersonate human beings. But they are wrong. What they should fear is the opposite: human beings who impersonate computers.'

I'm *not* against computers. I *am* against their misuse, and I worry about their effect on people. Sometimes I worry myself to sleep. Sometimes I have Digital Dreams. Thankfully, they're not all nightmares.

David V Barrett

BRONZE CASKET FOR A MUMMIFIED SHREW-MOUSE

Garry Kilworth

Garry Kilworth

Garry Kilworth has been publishing short stories for over fifteen years and considers it his primary writing passion. Now forty-eight years of age, he has published twelve novels, two collections of short stories and some odd poems, as well as three novels for young adults. His most recent book is *Hunter's Moon*, a bestselling novel about the life of a fox. *Midnight's Sun*, a story of wolves, is due to be published in September 1990 by Unwin Hyman. He is currently working on a collection of adult fairy-tales, *Dark Hills, Hollow Clocks*, to be published by Methuen.

I EXPECT YOU'RE wondering what the hell has gone wrong with the world in the last few months. I expect you're asking yourself why all the earthquakes, floods, pestilence, famine, accidents, incidents, tragedies, disasters. Why, you are saying to your neighbour, are the stars going out (one by one); why have the laws of science and nature gone beserk; where have lost bits of the Earth gone to? You needn't ask, because I'm going to tell you anyway. Look on this as something of a confession. I don't think it *really* matters whether I confess or not: Old Nick is warming up a floppy disk for me right now, if I'm not mistaken. You can't do what I did and expect to be forgiven, no matter how many confessions you indulge in. And this is in the nature an indulgence. I've just got to get it off my chest. It all began when I was under the surgeon's knife and my heart stopped beating. In the middle of an operation . . . No, perhaps it's not *all* my fault. He's got to take a bit of the blame.

You see, God has just discovered he likes to use a word processor.

I'm not kidding. Up until now God has been writing it all up by hand, first the old pen and ink, then (a reluctant change) a ballpoint, occasionally using the typewriter when he wanted things clearer in his mind. Writing the story of the world, making it up as he goes along, like any creative author.

Now he's written computers into the scheme of things. It took him a while to get around to trying one himself. Comes of inventing things second-hand, I suppose. I mean, what he does is write down something like ' . . . on the third of October, dah-dah-dah-dah (note: enter year later), Alexander Graham Bell invents the telephone.' Big J doesn't actually invent the thing himself, you understand. I doubt the Old Man even understands how the telephone system works. (Does *anyone* understand how the telephone system works?) He gets one of us to do it and then, later, when he's overcome his prejudices of the thing, tries it out himself. Sometimes he's delighted, sometimes he's not. It's not a generally well-known fact but God can be a bit of a materialist at times. I mean, he likes gadgets and appliances, especially things that revolve at high speed, like kitchen mixers and whisks. He's still a kid at heart, though the rest of him is older than time. Automatic toasters are also a great hit with the Ancient of Days, even though he never eats toast. He likes to see it jump, he says.

What?

Who am I?

Actually there's no reason why you should know me, even if I gave you my name. I'm one of those guys that 'died' on the operating table, only to be brought back to life a few minutes later – and if you think a few minutes is not enough to get an insight into what happens up there, you don't know anything about time my friend. Three minutes of eternity is long enough to get to know the whole shebang inside out.

So, as I was saying, God's into computers. He's also making a mess of what was once a pretty good system. OK, it wasn't *perfect*: things didn't dovetail all the time. But now? Now the whole PLAN is going awry.

How do I know? I'll tell you how I know. Remember the last but one President of the United States, Tom Mishnler? President for exactly four months? No, of course you don't. Know why you don't know? Because God used the erase key on him, that's why. He hasn't had the word processor long and he's been practising with things like that lately. Why do I alone remember Tom Mishnler? Well, the fact is, be it coincidence or what, I 'died' on the operating table just as the Old Man was preparing to wipe out the president, so

I was up there when it happened, looking over his shoulder with the rest of the angels, saints and souls. When he had effectively zapped Mishnler, much earlier than planned, he spun round on his typist's stool (which he *loves* by the way) and asked, 'Who was last up?'

'Me,' says I. 'Couple of minutes ago.'

'OK,' says the Old Man, 'we've got to replace that latent fascist Mishnler, to keep the numbers straight, so you get a second shot. I should erase your memory, but,' he looked at his Longines, 'I've got to cause a tsunami in the Pacific – in fact I should have done it three nano-seconds ago. Don't tell anyone about this place or I'll zap you quick as look at you. Understand?'

'Understood,' I gulped (he's a fearsome-looking fella, is God).

Thus the doctors down below, who had been busy with my body, pumping it full of injections to get the old heart going again, looked up to see a blip on the heart monitor. *Blip, blip, blip*, regular as twenty-one jewel movement clockwork.

'We did it!' they cried, and the intern who had given me the wrong anaesthetic fainted in relief.

Swop one fiction writer for a president.

But did God do right? Ah, there's the rub. God is omniscient, he *knows* all things – but can he remember to actually *do* all things? There's a great difference. He's like the professor who can remember whole chunks of math theory, quote it verbatim, but ask him where his car keys are and he looks at you as if you'd just discovered a cure for cancer.

Like I said, Big J was just playing with the keys, trying out things, that's how you get to know your word processor. Now, an erase key in the wrong hands can be a very dangerous tool. I wouldn't go so far as to say God's hands are 'wrong', but as everyone knows, you've got to start young if you want to be an expert. Get any eight-year-old kid and his dad together, on a home computer, and see which one's the whizz at video games.

God is no eight-year-old. Eight years is a finger-snap to 'I
AM'. God's got socks that are older than my grandfather.

What I'm trying to say is, he's not your flash-brained
whizz-kid.

OK, the answer to the question. *I* think – and this is
purely a personal observation you understand – I think
God erased Mishnler because the president was showing
neo-Nazi tendencies from the moment he entered office.
The guy was beginning to reveal strong fascist policies
and we had already been through all that once. Hitler,
Franco, Mussolini, Papa Doc – God is bored with fascists.
I can see him, chin in hand, when, having just written
Mishnler into office, and seeing what he's doing once
he's there, groaning and saying, 'Not *again*! Where's my
fershlugner erase key?'

Now, this is where the problem lies. Let's go back to
when the Old Fella used pen and ink. If he didn't like Tom
Mishnler then, he would write in his big book, 'Mishnler
snuffs it after four months in office. Heart-attack on the
steps of the White House while he's inspecting a regiment
of Mishnler Youth. Streatham, the vice-president, sworn
in. First black President of the United States. etc, etc.' So,
everyone would remember Mishnler, many would have
seen what they were in for, and heaved a sigh of relief.
'Squeaked through that one,' they would say. 'Better watch
for it in future. We're getting too damn complacent.'

OK, that's the pen and ink job. But what about erase
keys? Ah, that's where the system starts to break down.
It may seem clean and efficient and all that, but what you
haven't got is a continuing script, with all the historical
bits still there, if you care to go back a few pages. The
History of the World is no longer a diary or a journal, so
to speak, but a single chunk of writing, constantly being
revised and re-written. There's not even a first draft lying
around somewhere. It's all pristine copy. So once God
gets used to his erase key, and he decides it's easier
than writing a continuing saga, bang goes the History
of the World. We just sort of do a mark time. With the

erase key comes memory wipe, because once God has done the biz with the magic key, that piece of history no longer exists. It ain't in the big book. It's nowhere.

Or is it?

This is where the second part of the problem comes in.

As I said before, the Almighty, bless his ancient cotton socks, hadn't thought things through. What he hadn't realized was that the word-processing software on his PC contained failsafes for at least the first six files erased from any block. What happens is simple: you erase a file and it goes into a *limbo file*. The device is so new to the Lord of Hosts that he hasn't found out about limbo files yet. Mishnler was still somewhere in his machine, just waiting to get out again, like all the souls in the real Limbo. All God had to do was press a few wrong keys in sequence one day – granted, *unlikely*, but as that great humorist P G Wodehouse once wrote, never confuse the unusual with the impossible – and Mishnler was back in the totalitarian governing business, somewhere on the globe. Don't forget, Mishnler didn't die, as such. He was just erased. And since he wasn't erased completely, he's still there, behind a couple of locked doors.

When I was up top I noticed that God was having a few more terminals put in and my guess was that he was going to train the Archs, Gabriel and his buddies, as computer operators, so that they could transpose the History of the World from book form to computer program. I'm sure some bright recently-dead soul has done the salesman pitch with the Old Man and convinced him that his archives would take up far less room if everything was on disk. Heaven may be infinite but you've still got to walk around or climb over the racks of paper files. I can see the guy now:

'You see, Sir, the *paperless* office is the thing of the future. Get everything on microfisch or disk is my advice. You won't regret it, I can assure you . . . '

Well I can assure both of them that they *will* regret it.

You see, I've done a very foolish, not to say, evil thing.

Fact is, at first I didn't really care whether or not Mishnler got out and began his reign of terror somewhere in the world. Chances are it would be some small republic on an island off South America and the people would end up burning him on a bonfire with chickens tied to his legs, or something of that nature. But I have a personal problem at stake here. I mean, if Mishnler got out and came back, what would happen to me? I *like* being alive. I enjoy the pleasures of the flesh. I'm not saying I'm debauched or depraved or anything. I'm no de Sade or mad Russian monk. I'm no Louis XIV. I'm just your average guy who likes his pint, enjoys a take-away of a Friday, and has a regular girlfriend who is willing to participate, if you know what I mean. Nothing kinky, nothing illegal. You see, I *know* what's up there, and I don't want to go *down*. I'm not ambitious. I'm happy to be a ranker when I go back. Let the keen ones go for sainthood, whatever. I just want to do my job, live my life best as I can, and still enjoy it a little.

Now God did indicate something to the effect that there was a balance of some kind. I don't think he would claim to be neat and tidy, but it seems everything has got its place. If Mishnler were to escape from his hidden file, I might find myself in a nasty traffic accident, in order to make up the number of dead souls.

One day I was wandering around the British Museum, worrying the hell out of this problem, when I found myself in the Egyptian section. I walked amongst the glass cases, in between the sarcophagi, staring moodily at the contents. I was trying to think of some way of screwing up the system in Heaven to take God's attention away from his new toy. You see, nothing ever goes wrong up there, and if I could throw a glitch into the system God might hand over the keyboard to a soul expert in such matters (some new guy who worked for IBM in his mortal years?) and turn his omnipotence to putting his own house in order. No one who knows what they're doing would call a limbo file forward except on purpose, and I was sure I'd be safe for at least my own lifetime.

Suddenly, I stopped, and an idea came to me.

The object that had caught my attention was a tiny metal oblong box labelled BRONZE CASKET FOR A MUMMI-FIED SHREW-MOUSE. You see, the Ancient Egyptians had it right: animals do have souls. They actually deserve the same rites as humans get, whatever the religion. (By the way, there *is* only one bloke up there, whether you call him Jehovah, God, Sun, Moon, Tree or John Frum). During my eternal three minutes I saw every kind of animal-soul wandering around. Wild animals always go to Heaven, though there are one or two of the domestic beasts that go to the other place. This is because they have been warped by contact with some evil human during their lives and animals have a choice too. They can be bad or good. But God doesn't even bother to personally vet (ha, ha,) wild animals, because they operate by instinct and therefore you're extremely unlikely to get a bad one. Yes, they kill, and fight, and bonk each other randomly, but these are all instincts, built in, and uncontrollable. When humans do it, we do it *knowingly*. Apparently there hasn't been a bad wild animal since Noah's ark, and the crocodile in question was forgiven because the circumstances were considered to be mitigating. The croc had, after all, been cooped up for weeks with a lot of other beasts, birds and insects. No, I'm not going to tell you what it did, that wouldn't be fair on the creature now that God's given it a clean slate. Suffice to say that it would have gone up in smoke in one of two biblical cities had it been around at that time and there was no blame attached to the other party because *that* unwitting correspondent, a wallaby, was already dead at the time the act took place.

However, the scheme that unravelled in my mind required that P G Wodehouse adage to work. It is extremely unusual for a wild animal to go bad, *but not impossible*. The archangel responsible for doing the checks had become remarkably complacent about the beasts of the field, and gave them but a cursory once-over, if that. What I had to do was first get myself an evil beast of the field, and secondly, get him into Heaven.

My plan was to get a 'bad' soul up there and screw up the system, so that God and his archminions would have more to worry about than playing with word processors. The Lord and his Band of Angels would know that something was rotten in the state of Paradise, but they would have one hell of a time finding what and where it was, especially if it was *very very small*. Imagine the fuss it would take looking for a tiny bad soul in infinite space and eternal time!

For my purpose, what better trainee than one of those nasty-tempered little mammals, the shrew?

It took me a week to catch the little devil and training began in earnest, straight away. At the end of a certain period of time I had corrupted the shrew completely. Its soul was as black as sin. It would kill at the drop of a hat, that is to say, for gain. It attacked and raped lady shrews out of season, just for the hell of it, and had lust coming out of every orifice. It envied all other creatures, for one thing or another. It collected and hoarded food it would never eat, and would rather the stuff rotted than give it away to some starving brother shrew. It ate all kinds of delicacies, from honeyed humming-bird's wings to pickled bees' livers, always to excess. It drank any kind of alcohol I put in its dish, to the point of vomiting. It was fat, lazy and cruel. It tortured and maimed, sending other shrews into nests far afield, in order to get the edge on its enemies. It would tear the eyes out of jenny wren as soon as look at it.

I assisted it in forming an empire in the wood outside my home, where it gathered slaves to itself, took concubines, encouraged prostitution and graft, made other shrews fight to the death for its own entertainment. It massacred babies and pillaged the nests of birds and voles and wood mice, robbing the rich and poor alike, storing all for itself in huge empty molehills. It was paranoid and was not slow in indicating which other creatures I was to execute, when it felt a plot might be forming against its despotic rule.

It set up an opium route to feed its own habit, getting shipboard rats to smuggle the stuff in from Thailand. It chased dragons and mainlined until its eyes were popping and its tail as stiff as a needle.

It dabbled in black magic, calling forth Mephistopheles with more frequency than did Dr Faustus, selling instead of its *own* soul to the devil, those of yet unborn generations of amphibians, damned by a shrew even before the metamorphosis from tadpole to frog. It scrawled letters in blood on the trunks of trees and hanged infant squirrels for the theft of a single seed. The skulls of innocents were piled high in the woods and the bones of unwary animal travellers were scattered amongst the grasses of my lawn.

It invented tortures unknown to Orientals: tortures de Sade would have given his mistress's eyes to have at his fingertips. There were nights when the screams of the dying penetrated every corner of my garden and days when the vegetable patch was covered in small crosses bearing crucified beasts. Rasputin would have been jealous of the devious ways my shrew found of inflicting pain, its methods of skinning until the nerve ends of the victims were raw. It even found a way to debone a sparrow without killing the creature, so that it collapsed in a sickening splodge of feathers and flesh, and was left to perish slowly like a stranded jellyfish, eyes full of terror.

Towards the end there were genetic experiments going on inside in the wood and many was the time I was awoken to find a nightmare creature, part rat, part fish, part toad, flopping over my kitchen floor and mewling at me as if I were its devilish parent.

When the wicked shrew finally died of an overdose of heroin, I heaved a sigh of relief. The terrible creature's personality was beginning to affect even me: it was beginning to control my life too.

Thus Maurice-the-Unmentionable, as I had nicknamed him, went to Heaven, and as I now know, got in without a second glance at his stained and bloody soul. He slipped quietly beneath the hem of St Peter's garment and into the tranquil place beyond the gates. What I didn't know at the time was that God had updated his system and had a huge, powerful IBM with megabytes coming out of its ears. Not only were the archs putting the History of the World on to this monster, God had ordered them to put all spirits of the dead on it too – all, that is, except for the wrecking crew, down the hot hole.

What happened, I'm sure, is that Maurice went into the archives with the rest of welkin's pure of heart, and the little bastard's soul became, yea, as a software disease, which spread throughout the system and corrupted everything with which it came into contact.

Maurice is a computer virus, and that's why the world is coming to an end, with no hope of salvation for anyone, especially not me.

I hope Satan isn't into writing his own software yet. Some of those video games can be pretty frightening, and I'm sure he's got it all there, Hunt the Sinner or Burn the Iniquitous, one of those garage jobs which made twelve-year-olds into millionaires. I know, I know. Damn Maurice and his little black soul. Damn me, too.

I'm not without my problems down on Earth, either. Ever since Maurice crawled into a corner to die with a smile on his face, the woodland creatures have been gathering outside my house. I believe they want to be sure that his reign of terror is finally over, and won't believe it until they see the corpse. There are mice, voles, small birds, weasels, stoats, squirrels, even a fox and a couple of badgers out there, all burning holes in my house with their eyes. Maurice's intrigue and evil affected every creature in the parish. I guess I owe it to them to show them a carcass.

Maurice has dried out now, to a husk, the way small creatures do. Mummified, I suppose. I've got an empty Benson and Hedges cigarette packet, which is the nearest thing I can find to a bronze casket. I intend putting him in it and laying him out in state on the lawn. The animals and birds can file past and spit on his corpse, or whatever wild creatures do with their dictators. I feel like spitting on the arrogant little shit myself, but I'll let them have first shot.

It's the least I can do.

DIGITAL CATS COME OUT TONIGHT

Ben Jeapes

Ben Jeapes

Ben Jeapes was born in 1965 and studied philosophy and politics at the University of Warwick. He first started writing with intent to be published in the summer after A-levels; after six years of trying, this is his first sale. He lives in Farnborough and works in London for the academic publishing house Jessica Kingsley Publishers.

CONSIDER FEAR. A marvellous thing. It gives wings to our feet, it makes us traitors. It robs the mind of all its powers of acting and reasoning; this is its best feature.

And now consider cats. Take, for example, a farmhouse. A farmhouse from the Middle Ages – no, earlier. After all, the Ancient Egyptians had cats, so we need to go earlier than that. Picture a Sumerian farmhouse.

It has a barn, in which food is stored. The farmers are unhappy, because mice keep eating the food. This is not good, as the farmers will starve. Oh, they are very unhappy.

All is not lost! Enter Felix.

Felix kills the mice and eats them. This is his function. The mice hate and fear him. Unfortunately, they are very much smaller than him and tend to freeze up when he approaches. He can swallow them in one bite.

Does Felix eat all the mice? No, because there are too many. The problem is solved, however, because the mice are too afraid to venture into the barn. They are under control. The application of fear is effective.

I'd never really considered fear *per se* until we moved into Cinnamon Towers. Once it had been a very up-market apartment block, before the Death of the Yuppy. The architect's pride and joy had been the building's fully integrated computer network, which effectively ran every appliance in every apartment exactly to the taste of the occupier. Now the apartments were cheap, the building was running down and the management found it a millstone.

Double apartments were cheaper still, which was great for a newly married couple. Sally and I couldn't afford anything fancy – not until Felixware got off the ground. When we first set up the company (not out of any entrepreneurial philosophy, but simply because we had a deep, abiding horror of even the thought of working for anyone else), we had to give it a name like that, based on our common love for the animals. Our actual association with cats didn't come until later.

It was the management's fault, for getting heavy-handed. We had a respectable ninety-nine-year lease, and we were staying until it suited us to move. We didn't know things would escalate. We were already the proud owners of three cats before things did.

I trace the start of it to a blustery day in March. I had been out doing the shopping, while Sally stayed in putting the finishing touches to our latest pet. When I got back in to the lobby, I could tell at once that the mice were at play. The lights were dim and the air-conditioning was full on (as I say, it was March). The place was a gloomy ice block.

Miracle of miracles, a lift was working. I positioned myself in front of the doors and looked up at the green lights flashing their way down to ground level. The doors opened with a chime and I got in.

It jammed between the third and fourth floors. I gave it a minute, then reluctantly put the bags down to free my hands. I pulled out my portable phone (at least there was no one to see it) and dialled.

'It's me.'

'Hello, dear. Where are you?'

'In the lift. It's jammed between three and four. Can you send Alonzo down?'

'Hang on.' Pause. 'Alonzo's in the basement with the heating. Will Britannicus do?'

'Have to.' Britannicus lacked Alonzo's subtlety, so I sat down.

Ten seconds later the lift jerked itself up violently. I looked up at the ceiling.

"Oos a booful pussy-pussy?' I murmured.

Sally was still busy at the terminal.

'You're just in time,' she greeted me. 'Meet Napoleon.'

Napoleon lurked on the screen in the form of a mass of code, apparently as un-deadly and as un-Jellicle as ever.

'Hello, Napoleon,' I said.

We released Napoleon into a carefully closed system that covered the apartment. LEDs glowed at various points around the main room, some nowhere near any other electrical instrument and others wired up to the coffee-maker, the television, the stereo. Many of these LEDs flickered red, indicating the presence of the mice – the tiny, mischievous, havoc-causing artificial intelligences that scurried about the system, similar in all respects to the hordes that the management had released into the building's own system in a final effort to oust those tenants who preferred to stay.

'Releasing Napoleon now,' Sally reported, and pressed the execute key. The red flashing became more agitated.

The LED on the television glowed green suddenly, and the fuzz cleared to show the latest Antipodean soap opera. I turned the sound down.

The coffee machine spluttered and started to pump out the dark, brown liquid.

The light in the bathroom came on.

'Let's diddle the odds,' Sally murmured, and released some more mice into the television. For a moment the set switched to a different channel and the sound blared out, then the volume returned to its former silence and the picture was again of a quiet Sydney cul-de-sac.

'He gets about fast,' I commented.

'And he's not complacent. Even Alonzo would have been taken aback to find mice in an area that he'd already cleared.'

The test went very well indeed. Napoleon was the best cat yet, combining cunning with killer instinct, and even a touch of sadism. Almost like the real thing, and a far cry from the crude violence of the very first model, the unsophisticated Britannicus. Napoleon had the right unpredictability, the random element, that made the application of fear so much more effective.

It wasn't long before the only red LED was on a small memory module next to the terminal. A green one glowed next to it. The mice were holed up in their refuge, and their nemesis waited outside patiently. You could almost see the tail lash and the ears strain forward, waiting for the least movement.

'You think we can release him into the main system yet?'

'Perhaps, perhaps.' Anyone from the management would have cringed at the glee on my spouse's face. 'And then maybe we can sell him. It's about time we put the cats on the market.'

So, we did the rounds. Several companies expressed a polite interest in our product, if only for the novelty value. I think they had been searching for years for a good way of exposing AIs to the general public, and we were quite optimistic about this one.

Then Sally was asked by Cinnamon's oldest resident, Miss Anderson, to have a look at her apartment's controlling software. It was playing up again.

'Miss Anderson's got the mice.'

'They're reading our mail again.'

We spoke simultaneously as Sally returned to the apartment. My message had the greater news content.

'What do you mean?'

'Take a look.' On the screen was a message from a large software house, expressing an interest in our cats. Nothing in the message showed what kind of cat was being discussed.

'And next . . . .' I said.

A message from the management, apparently uncon-
nected, reminding all tenants of the penalties for having
animals in the building.

'Did Miss Anderson have this message?'

'Of course not. But we can't prove anything, all the same.
The scumbags! Just for this, Britannicus visits them tonight.
The rough, alley-cat treatment.'

Then I remembered what she had said.

'What do you mean, she's got the mice? Alonzo and
Napoleon have both been up there.'

'I know. But mice she has, love. The cats are being
interfered with. Or they're not as deadly as we thought.'

'Could they be multiplying faster than we thought?'

'I really don't know.' I squeezed her hand as she looked
worried. 'We'll have to think about it.'

'Or take advice.'

'You mean . . . ?'

'AI Agony!'

'We have developed three low-level hunter/killer AIs that
operate on the fear principle. Their purpose is to restrict
the activities of an indefinite number of lesser AIs that
are loose in our network. There are too many of these
to be completely annihilated, so we have designed our
own AIs to inspire 'fear' in the enemy. The enemy AIs
thus restrict their activities to the minimum and stay out
of the main systems.

'This approach has proved successful until recently. The
enemy AIs appear to be gaining in confidence and number,
and though our hunter/killers are constantly on the watch,
the situation is worsening. We have checked our hunter/
killers most carefully, but can see no signs of tampering.
Likewise, the enemy AIs are the same as they ever were.

'Please advise.'

An answer was not long in coming.

'Forgive any presumptions in this answer. I have to
make them because of the lack of detail in your query,

presumably meant to avoid clues to your identity. Very commendable.

'If the principle, as you say, is fear, and the system no longer works, could it not be because the enemy is no longer afraid? Or, there is something else in the system that your hunter/killers are afraid of? I suggest you do a careful check of the network to see if there are any AIs of a higher level than your own . . . '

Whoever the management's man was, he was good. I say this out of all respect for the enemy – someone I felt I could get on well with socially. He had the same approach to computers and AIs as I did. It was an art of the mind.

I don't think Sally saw it that way. The cats were my idea, but they were her creation.

'He is going to suffer, that man,' she ranted, once we had discovered what was going on. We were both seated in front of the terminal, looking at the evidence on screen. 'I will not have my cats being tampered with by an outsider. I'll—'

'Hold it, hold it,' I soothed. 'No one said they've been tampered with.'

'But they're—'

'Yes, yes, yes. Look.' It didn't seem the best time to point out that the designer of our new adversary might feel the same way about our instinctive killers being unleashed on his pets. 'I think I see what's happening. Want my theory?'

'I'll get it anyway.'

'Thank you. Now, you've got the gist of it, but not the specifics. AI Agony helped, but it wasn't entirely on the right track, either.'

'Meaning?'

'Meaning, no, they haven't set dogs on our cats. The new AI in the system is of a higher level than the cats, just like the cats are higher than the mice. But the cats aren't afraid of him. They *like* him.'

'So – '

'Can't you see it? Britannicus, Alonzo and Napoleon busy chasing mice. Along comes – oh, call it a human.

What would a cat do? It stops. It rubs up to the human. It sniffs the carpet. It purrs. And it forgets the mice.' Sally thought about this.

'So the mice are still afraid of the cats, but the cats aren't afraid of the stranger? And there's nothing about to challenge the stranger.'

'Correct.'

'Hmmm. Interesting. So, logically, we ought to design something to scare the stranger.'

'Makes sense. But that's your department.'

'Y-e-s . . . got it.'

'Go on.'

'Remember, Napoleon was built on the shortcomings of Alonzo, and Alonzo on the shortcomings of Britannicus. Until the stranger appeared, Napoleon was the best. And yet, ever since this stranger's come on the scene, Britannicus has been the most effective.'

'He doesn't purr at the stranger? He's as antisocial as ever?'

'That's right. The stranger still gets the better of him eventually, though. Britannicus is the alley-cat, but he's still susceptible to humans.' She had that light in her eye that anticipates a fight.

'This doesn't answer the question,' I objected.

'Yes it does. Look, open a new file and call up the specs for Britannicus. I'm going to make some fine adjustments.'

'Right. What name for the file?'

'Bagheera.'

And so it started. Bagheera was, believe me, lethal. We traced his actions on the first night that he was out in the system. We attached him to Napoleon, so he would know his way around. Napoleon headed for a cluster of mice on the roof that were lurking in the cooling towers (the weather was warming up). The mice scattered as he approached and pounced, and before long he was in his element. He really was just like the real thing, with his domesticated veneer swept away by his not-so-vestigial jungle instincts.

Bagheera watched from a distance, as it were, bored. Panthers go for higher game than mice. Then he was distracted.

The stranger – by now we were calling him Clint – sidled up to the scene of the action. Napoleon saw him coming and instantly started to show off, forgetting the mice as he chased his tail, rubbed up against Clint, and generally let his domestic instincts come to the fore again.

Then Bagheera pounced from the sub-system in which he had been hiding. It was swift, lethal and messy. In a flash, what had been a sophisticated structure of code was reduced to a pile of disconnected, helpless subroutines which Bagheera, calmly and methodically, began to absorb. When he was finished, all that was left were a few random signals in the network that could harm no one. Mentally, I held my hat against my chest in respect for the passing of Clint.

The system was clear for a long time, now. The mice continued to run around and the cats continued to deal with them. Bagheera also prowled about, and several times we detected a new Clint in the network which promptly withdrew when Bagheera approached. We gave him a brother, Pink, to help him out and to spread the fear blanket a little. Fear, glorious fear. It worked wonders.

Until the management man tried a new approach.

What comes up the fear scale from a panther? Nothing much, we had thought. Lions, tigers, cheetahs – yes, they may have their own hierarchy out in the wild, but a Big Cat is a Big Cat.

But the management had cottoned on to the fear principle by this time, and we should have guessed they wouldn't be hampered by our own cat-obsession.

There is a creature in the wild that very few creatures will attack, because it is substantially bigger than any of them and capable of defending itself by sheer bulk. It is called an elephant.

The first elephant entered the system six months after

Bagheera's first triumph. Bagheera took one look and fled. The elephant shouldered its way casually through all our defences and wreaked havoc in the lighting, the heating and (we still can't work this out) the kitchen units of every even-numbered apartment. We think it was only a combined charge by Bagheera and Pink together, aimed not at the elephant but at one of the Clints controlling it, that turned it back. We had to think, and fast, of a way to beat this one.

We didn't have the time. We had heard of the Software Riots, but hadn't paid them much attention. Now they were brought home to us.

Apparently, there was contention amongst religious groups concerning AIs. Some maintained that they were the work of the devil and were to be exterminated. Others said they were just as valid as natural intelligences, i.e., us. They should therefore be protected.

The strength of feeling that culminated in the Riots took the government by surprise, and legislation was rushed through. All of a sudden Pink, Bagheera, Napoleon, Alonzo and Britannicus, not to mention the elephants, the Clints and even the mice, were protected species until such time as the government could think of what to do with them. Even to devise a way of bumping off a rival AI was, in the eyes of the law, the same as devising a way of bumping off a bat or a whale. It was considered naughty.

There is now a major ecology flourishing in the network of Cinnamon Towers. The last time we looked, it seemed that some of the Clints were adopting the mice as pets. And some of the cats.

Yes, *some* of the cats. There's more of everything than there used to be. Yesterday, perusing the system, we saw a cat we've never met before, but which had the characteristics of Napoleon and Britannicus. One of those two apparently wasn't what we thought it was.

Unfortunately, *looking* at the system is all we can do. All networks containing AIs have had government-imposed guardian AIs slapped on them. We're not sure what they do, but they're pretty horrific. We tried, when we thought no one was looking, to get our cats out of the system again, but our terminal flipped at the thought. It took one look at the guardian and went catatonic. Perhaps *demons* would be a good name for these newcomers. I don't know.

We also got a message detailing everything that would happen if we even tried to meddle with the system again, before a ruling can be reached by higher authority, and it was very nasty. So, we don't dare.

Now, that really galls.

WHAT HAPPENED AT CAMBRIDGE IV

David Langford

David Langford

David Langford was born in 1953, escaped from Oxford
with a physics degree, and worked (1975-80) as a Ministry
of Defence weapons physicist – an experience misreported
in his satirical novel *The Leaky Establishment* (1984). A
freelance writer since 1980, he has published much SF,
criticism, humour, futurology and computer material. His
awards include the British Science Fiction Association
Award and, four times, the Hugo. Rather than waste
time on sleep, he also runs the software company Ansible
Information.

TO WHOM IT may concern:

There's death in this package. I send it to you because you're considered a dubious risk. Sorry about that; the address appears on this handy list compiled by our security office. What a lot of 'potentially undesirable contacts' there seem to be at this end of the Thames Valley. If one of our staff were seen having a quiet drink with the likes of you, they would have been . . . nudged. Of course, it's impossible to tell how reliably unreliable you are: when I look at List U and see people called Murphy and O'Shea, I can't help wondering whether any real probing was done, whether the computer just threw up its chips in horror at the name.

Well. Perhaps you're honestly outraged at the thought of being branded with a secret smear. I should tell the police if so. You surely won't be the first. My advice in this case is *not* to open the sealed envelope that you found enclosed. (Don't open it yet, no matter what. This is a serious warning.) It's remotely possible that being an officious big-mouth – I mean, of course, a public-spirited citizen – could ease your name into a computer file less innocuous than any list at Cambridge IV.

You could burn all this, of course. But naturally there'll be an investigation, and List U will be part of the information they work with. All right: I hereby announce my intention of making this a random mailing to only a certain percentage of the Listed. Should you be the person I'm aiming for, hide the packet and lie when they come to ask. You have an excellent chance of getting away with it.

The innocent can leave us now.

Still with me? Good . . . but people have already died for what you're holding. Before you even think of breaking the seal, you'll need some background. That isn't wholly true, but this is *my* last will and testament, and I make the rules. You won't be compromised, yet. The background details are harmless. It's the big picture that kills.

(For all I know, you might be on List U simply for sharing a common human quirk with me.)

So let me tell you about the imaginary brain. About the infernal machine and the dead scientists. About the thing that glows in Room C23. All pixels of the big picture.

To begin. Cambridge IV is much nearer to you than Cambridge, as you will have cleverly deduced from the postmark. This is governmental thinking: a Discreet establishment with an IT focus should have an oh so subtly computer-evocative name. Somebody thought of Alan Turing – he of the famous thought experiments, the Turing machine (an abstract universal computer) and the Turing test. He was a fellow of King's at Cambridge, and that's all the connection there is. Or almost all.

A Discreet establishment is one your taxes pay for, but which isn't surrounded by all the rigmarole of guard dogs, armed police, sensor fences and NO PHOTOGRAPHY. The only trace they leave, if they happen to be big enough, is a blank whiteness on Ordnance Survey maps. A good place to work if you like your privacy; not so good when the boat begins to rock, since job security (unlike the other kind) is in short supply at a location that officially doesn't exist.

I'm writing this in my drab green-walled office, three floors up in a non-existent building. The only significant items present are an early graphics print-out looking like a dark and hook-beaked bird, pinned on the wall askew; a frozen bolt of lightning in perspex on my desk; and a bottle of whisky whose level is sinking rather too fast. Why not? The project is at an end.

Cambridge IV funding had been steadily declining for eighteen months. As deputy director I tried to keep it going, fought to keep Whitehall interested in what I told myself could be a vast new insight into minds, brains and computers. Alternatively, the hydrogen bomb of psychological weapons. I snipped at the staffing table like a surgeon determined to prove that a human being can indeed live without limbs, a stomach, one lung, one kidney, half the liver, two-thirds of the brain . . . however that dreary list goes on. I fought endless rearguard actions against the death of a thousand cuts, because I believed in –

No.

I can be honest here. In the beginning I thought Cambridge IV was the biggest damn fool idea since phlogiston. What I believed in was Vernon Berryman, the originator and research leader, and a man in the genius class of Turing himself. Poor Vernon.

Alan Turing committed suicide, they say, in 1954. Do you know why? The climate is supposed to be more liberal today, except in sensitive government establishments. There, entirely legal preferences are entirely *verboten*. If one were different one could be blackmailed. What with? Well, one would lose one's sensitive government job if it came out. Why should that be? Because we can't have people who could be blackmailed occupying sensitive government jobs. And so on, forever.

Dr Vernon Berryman did not commit suicide. He had a regrettable accident. A triumphant accident. A crabbed accountant in Whitehall killed him. I killed him. Each man kills the thing he loves.

More whisky. Let me tell you about the project work.

Ceri Turner was supposed to be the physiological/neurological expert, digging out data about the brain's wiring for Berryman and his mathematical models. Smooth, blonde, heavily perfumed, the sort of overstuffed young woman who gives wet dreams to teenagers. Her legs were quite nice if you liked the type. I was unconvinced about her on the intellectual side (she came from America, where they'll hand a Ph.D to anything that can read, write and sit on its bottom for long enough). Berryman was absurdly courteous, giving her joint credit for papers which were ninety-five per cent his. If his name had been Wherryman I swear he'd even have put hers first.

Between them they constructed a ghostly mental model, and tried to shatter it. 'Only the roughest sketch of a mind,' I remember him saying with that wide lopsided smile. 'Hardly even as complex as a permanent under-secretary.' Turner's whiny giggle always irritated me.

She provided the input, and Berryman worked miracles. I could copy some bits out of 'their' major paper here ... you won't find it in *Nature* or *New Scientist*: the classification is SECRET * BASILISK, named distribution only. It's a sort of miniature honour, a backpat without financial clout, for an establishment as tiny as Cambridge IV to have its own identifying marking. 'Basilisk' is nearer the bone than any allusion to Cambridge, as you'll see. A clue, perhaps, that those who hand out such labels didn't really take us seriously.

Seriously, how much do you need to be told? I could reprint parts of 'On Thinkable Forms, with notes towards a Logical Imaging Technique' here, but if I know you – as naturally I don't – you're a practical person. You're not interested in sitting through twenty pages on the Entscheidungs Problem, Gödel's Theorem, and Berryman's own unnerving theoretical extensions. Instead, there's a little indoctrination chat I know by heart and trot out for visiting dignitaries and purse-string holders. It's as practical as an Armalite rifle. It goes like this:

Kurt Gödel showed that all formal logical systems have flaws: true theorems that can't be proved, shattering paradoxes that won't go away. Alan Turing offered the practical man's version of this mathematical nightmare, with his proof that some problems aren't computable. An ideal machine set to solve them would grind on forever like a government inquiry. Then our very own Vernon Berryman took a boring old analogy – that the human brain is a computer made of meat – and pulled out a wild idea. Suppose Turing's 'computability' has a parallel in human thinkability? What programs can't we run? Berryman went haring off to deduce the logical input which clouds the minds of men.

His big new insight: while the mind can always refuse to accept a problem (didn't yours effortlessly shrug off all those horrible technicalities, a little way back?), the pattern-handling systems of the visual cortex can instantly and willy-nilly accept huge blocks of data from the eye. One picture is less ignorable than a thousand words.

To put it another way, I'd say at this point as I poured out the restorative dose of single-malt, Dr Berryman thinks that with a neural simulation system the size of the Alphanode Plus you saw on the tour, we can find the key to unthinkable images. Computer op-art that takes advantage of the flaws which mathematics says the mind must have. A pattern which compels attention, perhaps, a pattern from which you couldn't easily look away. Runes of power.

And depending on rather careful judgement of my audience (male? reasonably bright? sense of humour? like me or not?), I'd whip out a big card-mounted *Penthouse* nude and watch the sequence. Attention momentarily caught in quicklime; an artificial blink; a studied glance away, with excessive unconcern . . . We're all so predictable. If I was lucky, they'd finish the sequence with a smile.

There, I'm not as ancient and stuffy as you'd expect of a deputy director. I feel I do need to wear a dark suit and waistcoat, but I draw the line at Whitehall's pinstripes. If I hadn't decided otherwise, there'd be years to go before retirement or even the big 6. Not past it at all.

Berryman was thirty-four. They say mathematicians do their best work relatively young. Turing cracked the Entscheidungs Problem in his twenties. I would never have made a fool of myself over Berryman, but . . .

I did, though. I built an infernal machine.

The latest round of ministerial cuts was threatening the Alphanode Plus itself. If we lost two more operators, the shift rota would break down and the wretched machine wouldn't be able to handle Berryman's all-night runs. I saw the argument running on in well-worn channels, downhill: under-utilization, cannot justify continued rental, suggest merger other project, divided leadership not practicable, bye-bye Cambridge IV. I didn't relish defending a set-up where one of the chief so-called scientists had taken to spending half the day flat on a bloody couch, thinking God knows what into the Alphanode simulation.

By then I'd known for some weeks what was wrong with me, wrong or gloriously right. Absurd to tell of it: I passed Berryman in the corridor as he padded off to the toilet in his shirt-sleeves, and something turned over inside me. Narrow-faced and intense, very white skin and very black hair, and the dark shadow of his nipples through the thin shirt. I was married for eight tolerably pleasant years, until May went down with cancer. Nothing in those years ever hit with a lightning-flash like *that*.

One picks at these details, the turn of a head, the curl of a thin finger, and tries to pin down blame. The shifting details explain nothing. It's the big picture that kills.

If Cambridge IV had to shut down, its director would be retired or just possibly transferred, while its mathematical genius carried his hat round half a dozen universities that would love to have him if only they could justify (that damnable word) the project grants. Perhaps the Turner woman would follow. I felt sure she was making eyes at him. Never to pass in a corridor again.

I was very circumspect, very discreet. But I built an infernal machine. (Did a tingle of interest go through you then? Perhaps you're my man.) Nothing intricate; I have the remnants of a science degree, but my fingers are too sausage-clumsy for work like that. No, I travelled first-class — a happy perk of my grade — into the vast anonymity of London, and bought two gadgets from a photographic outfit up the Tottenham Court Road. A cosmopolitan corner-shop in Soho supplied the newspaper, and I lashed out a final £1.99 on a piece of plastic trash from an open suitcase on the pavement. I was insane, of course.

You might as well know the details. Be implicated. The 'Sonic Shutter' is supposed to be for self- and group-portraits: whistle or snap your fingers, and the shutter clicks, the flashgun fires. It had stuck in my mind for its sheer stupidity. Who wants to be captured for posterity with pursed lips or cocked fingers? The flashgun was the cheapest available, and the point about the trashy pink watch was its alarm. Wearing lab gloves, I taped them all together, to give me a delayed flash: but first I took pliers and snapped away part of the flashgun's plastic shell. Now, as any idiot could see, the batteries would stay put only if wedged. My final purchase was an imported Russian-language edition of *Pravda*.

Our pussycat internal security is a joke. Cambridge IV doesn't exist, so prowlers are not expected. Often you can pace alone through hundreds of yards of dead light and air, listening to that feeble roar of ventilation which always makes me think 'corridors of power'. I paid one of my occasional visits to the computer hall, where in an unreal universe of silicon and optoelectronics a ghostly simulation of the human brain was under attack – assaulted by Berryman's image programs, and so far resisting every one. The brain's electrochemical immune system has fended off most of the conceptual viruses evolution can throw at it ... though intangible things can go wrong, can't they? And do.

As always, activity stopped while I poked officiously around. Ceri Turner lay with eyes closed on the interface couch, meditating or some such nonsense while the EEG fed the simulation with her brain rhythms. Her red-stockinged legs were stretched out vulgarly: the idea of *her* as a standard brainwave reference! The operators hunched in resentment over their keyboards, unwilling to catch my eye in case I commented on paperbacks, playing cards, tell-tale crumbs. My package of junk went on to a high, blue bank of power conditioners. I blew my nose (not too loudly) into the handkerchief wrapped round my fingers. That was all. The cleaners would be suspected, but you can't make an omelette, etc.

I *was* insane, of course. I explained to myself with great lucidity that the miserly forces of Whitehall had driven me to turn their own murderous, paranoid logic against them, to jolt them into the notion that an establishment worth sabotaging must be an establishment worth preserving. But perhaps my infernal machine doesn't sound very deadly? Trust me. It was deadlier than I thought.

In a vague spirit of self-improvement, I always skim the computer newspapers sent free throughout the trade (officially we are Amber Data Systems, which is supposed to account for our purchasing pattern). One can pick up some interesting information amid all that tiresome drivel and hype: specifically, the reason why flash photography is forbidden in major computer installations.

Next morning floppy-jowled Symond, our security chief, explained it all to me pompously, with vast technical detail about the intricate electronics that had been employed. 'We're dealing with a dead clever outfit here.' He'd become important for a day, and was savouring it *ad nauseam*. But I won't speak ill of him now.

The misguided saboteur, he said, must have assumed the computer hall had an old-fashioned fire protection system. Electrical fires often start with a brilliant flash, which therefore triggers ... (I nodded my wise nod of total incomprehension.) Had the sensors been connected to old-style sprinklers, the entire computer system could have been soaked and ruined. Even foam or powder would have done the Alphanode no good. Luckily, the saboteur didn't know one important fact. (I contrived another blank nod.) Modern defences, like ours, stop fires in their tracks by sealing all exits and driving out every trace of oxygen with a flood of inert halon.

'So no damage was done?' I said comfortably. The operators, of course, are trained to run like hell when the siren sounds.

'There'll be a manslaughter charge when we catch the bastard.'

For too long I stared blankly at the fossil lightning on my desk.

Afterwards I saw that there was no trap: Symond failed to eye me critically while tossing his thunderbolt, failed to detect the cold shock that curdled my bowels and my thoughts. Through the slow icy churning, I dimly caught the word 'doctor'. Each man kills the thing . . .

Symond bored remorselessly on about unauthorized late-night sessions (yes, Berryman had been driving himself hard), and the picture filled itself in automatically. A visit to collect some print-out or whatever; sirens, panic, a slip and fall in belated haste, a moment's dizzy confusion, and the doors are clamped, the nozzles hissing.

My office is three floors up. If the windows weren't sealed for obscure reasons of air-conditioning, I'd have been ready to jump.

But Symond dropped a new word into my numbness, and crystallized it into something else. The word was 'she'. A doctor can be a Ph.D as well as a D.Phil. Ceri Turner had been running late that night, on into the small hours with one of Berryman's runs, and the idiot woman had tested a private theory that I couldn't have predicted. She died through her own recklessness. I refuse to accept any blame. I had nothing against her, nothing serious. I hoped she and Berryman hadn't had anything between them, because if so I wouldn't be able to be sorry.

Symond departed with hints that there were international ramifications and that he had a Clue. Something whose precise nature he did not care to divulge had been wedged with a significantly printed wad of paper. It would have been a terrible thing, on that morning, to laugh.

What an idea, though! More sympathetic magic than science. It was in her notebook − I have it here now − a pastel thing with flowers on its cover and the austerely scientific heading THINKS. '#136. Input reference-level

brainwave patterns assoc. with forced loss of consc. You
never know. Check med. stores. Quaaludes?'

And with the crazed open-mindedness of Darwin exper-
imentally playing the trombone to his tulips, she'd fed
herself a nice safe dose of lullaby pills on the couch; only,
that night, nothing that blocked out sirens was safe. I had
to listen to Symond being delighted at getting some use
from his outdated copy of *Isolation and Identification of
Drugs*, and offering the remarkable forensic insight that
the Quaalude brand name, just like Turner, was American.
They found her convulsed and ugly, still linked to the
systems. I cannot accept –

I can't forgive her for getting something so nearly right.

So I'd bought us time by the logic of Whitehall, at the
cost of a sacrifice. The investigation pottered on for a while,
the only result being a revised and slightly shorter List U.
They might have found and deported some suspicious
immigrants, or cleared others from all shadow of doubt:
who knows? Funding was discreetly increased. What I'd
done didn't deserve to work, but it had.

Berryman worked on furiously. He had lost much weight;
he said he was sniffing on the track of something new. 'Rich
uncharted seas,' he muttered once. 'Ceri . . . I'm sorry. I
need time.' There was a trace of guilt when he mentioned
her name, as though he and I were accomplices. I didn't
understand that until much later, when I read about the
source of his last insight.

I had to ration my contacts with Berryman, for fear of
being caught staring at the fine silky hairs on the backs
of his hands. Nor could I avoid him: this was no time
to distort the pattern of our days at Cambridge IV, and
perhaps attract attention. For almost the first time in my
life I regretted my middle-class education. At a public
school, I'd gathered, certain overtures are learned. Could
I have picked up a body-language familiar to Dr Vernon
Berryman of Winchester and (like Turing himself) King's?

Time passed. The project reports grew ever more optimistic. In furtive visits to our great corrupt capital I tried

to slake my feelings. The mathematical brain-model took some hard knocks: but in spite of Berryman's frantic, doomed intensity, he seemed no nearer to a real-world version of the simulated success. One of the failed images is still pinned to my grimy office wall: a horrid black thing like half a Rorschach blot, a fractal shape whose outline vaguely suggests a bird. It catches the eye but (despite heroic wishful thinking) never quite compels it.

I remember the weekly Project Working Party meeting at which we solemnly discussed what safeguards should be taken against an 'active' image, one that really did stab into the visual cortex with stunning or paralysing force. The Psychiatric Liaison woman suggested the scrambler glasses used in some perception test. These things were specially made at a frightful price, and we couldn't justify the purchase at that time.

(In the early days of the Manhattan Project, did they ponder on better bullet-proof vests and stouter plate-glass to withstand the new weapon? I wonder.)

I had another clue to where Berryman was going when he said with scorn, 'It's not real mathematics any more. I can't construct an elegant model. Instead . . . You know, like that Appel-Haken proof of the four-colour theorem: they didn't *solve* it, they just clubbed it to death with fifteen hundred hours of computer time. That's my position now.'

Gradually the money supply began to fall off again, not overtly cut but gently eroded by inflation. Three times a day I sighted Berryman and felt the impossible gulf widen between us. Somehow, in our classless civil service, the grades who get deep-pile carpet in their rooms do not by tacit agreement join mere senior scientific officers in the pub.

Other times, I sat at the wide mahogany desk appropriate to my rank and made wild plans. I would put forward the theory of a broad spectrum of response to the image technique. Volunteers would be called for. I would steal equipment from the optics lab that we never used. Trial

viewings of test images would take place under laboratory conditions. Somehow I'd manipulate the volunteer
selection process. My weak-eyed, epileptic subject would
come in for test on a sunny day, wearing polaroid glasses.
Unknown to anyone else, the porthole opening on the
harmless image would conceal a polaroid sheet which
a hidden motor could rotate. Gazing through glasses
and window on Berryman's latest effort, my victim's
field of vision would flicker on and off as the planes of
polarization crossed and recrossed. The blink rate would
be five times a second. *Petit mal.* Berryman vindicated.
Roars of applause.

That was one of my more sensible schemes. I had actually
gone so far as to check that the optics lab had stocks of
polaroid plastic. It was, of course, a mere fantasy. The real
end of Cambridge IV has outdone any of my fantasies.

Each man kills . . .

It happened, I guess, between three and four hours ago.
I can only write the postscript and obituary. Why did we
think that when the human computer tried to tackle a
visual program it could not run, the only result would be
disorientation? We know from our machines that arranging
subtle delays and finite loops is far, far harder than simply
crashing the whole system.

The nastiest of the ironies is that I, put out to grass as a
mere administrator, laid the fuses of catastrophic success
all by myself. Ceri Turner had had a wild theory that
brainwave feedback from drugged sleep would lower the
Alphanode simulation's defences . . . later, when Berryman
analysed the session records, he found something better
than a digitized pattern of sleep. It could be the making
of his career at her expense (and *did* he care for the
woman? Did he?).

The electromagnetic signature of death.

The frozen lightning bolt sits on my desk, a souvenir
from the gigavolt facility at – never mind. Every ranking
visitor got one. Most people think it's some sort of feathery
white seaweed or coral, preserved in perspex. The plastic is

charged to a massive voltage throughout, and an earthed spike driven into the base. When the smoke clears, the forking, fractal paths of the discharge are captured forever. The final lightning-stroke in Turner's mind was caught like that, in silicon and optoelectronics, for Berryman to discover. In words that reek of guilt, he gave her credit for it in his final notes: posthumous credit, of course. Show a scientist a pattern, and he can usually work out how to reproduce it.

'The image of the murderer will appear on the dead man's retina!'

Oh God.

There is a grim scene I remember from Mark Twain's *A Connecticut Yankee in King Arthur's Court*, where knight after armoured knight is felled by an electric fence. A growing heap of death as each hapless paladin touches the conductive armour of the last. This, brought up to date, is the hecatomb now on display in Vernon Berryman's workroom . . . the first fruit of our collaboration. His work is a brilliant success.

The desk faces his door. The hi-graphics monitor is thus not visible until, one by one, the passing project technicians go to find why Berryman is slumped in his chair, and look over his shoulder into the terminal. Only I, on my own regular tormented visit, had the faith to believe in his triumph. Instead of peeping at once, I went away and thought.

It was with closed eyes that I snapped my way through many rolls of the Polaroid (capital P this time) film they use to record EEG displays. This is the other reason why you should not have opened the sealed envelope. It also contains a standard-format diskette holding the last few days' notes and programs. Downloaded courtesy of our user-friendly network. You must know a bright computer enthusiast with your own political leanings, one who can make use of Berryman's graphics algorithms. Tell him to be very careful.

Why? Why all this? Indirectly, I killed Berryman myself. Whitehall killed him too, both through miserable funding (he *might* have viewed his latest, ungrateful pet through the scrambler optics we couldn't afford) and by starting a project which one might say was morally appalling. Before you sneer: these are all quibbles. I don't care about people any more. When I began to care specially, for you know who, the relationship was poisoned by those twisted fears before it could ever give voice. You are my revenge. Afraid of AIDS, are they? As of now there's a psychic AIDS that's no respecter of rubbery protectives.

(I saw Symond there in Room C23. The first flash of insight in his whole flabby life, and it wasn't good enough. He'd put on rubber gloves.)

Open the envelope with great caution. Remember, politicians don't like to fiddle around with mere details. What they want is an overview of the big picture. Send a letter to your MP for me.

Myself . . . A last glass of the pale Glenlivet, for VIP visitors only. A last walk outside Cambridge IV, briefcase bulging with H.M. prepaid envelopes, to the nearby pillar-box in a crowded, sunlit High Street. And finally I'll join the sacrificial victims heaped behind my love like Egyptian servants in a noble's tomb, and before I look into the screen and over the edge I'll touch his hand at last.

THE WORLD OF THE SILVER WRITER

Anne Gay

Anne Gay

Anne Gay has had a handful of short stories published, including 'Roman Games' which was reprinted in *The Year's Best Fantasy II* from *Other Edens II*. Her first novel *Mindsail* was published by Macdonald this year, and she is currently writing another SF novel with the working title *The Brooch of Azure Midnight*. A teacher of Modern Languages, she is also creating a new style of Spanish textbook with Luz Serrano Kettle.

GEMA COULD SMELL insanity on Arlvad's skin.

It was almost the watch of the dead, the time when the night breathes its last and the body is cold. Fatigue gnawed at the will-power that kept her safe and awake, that shrank her in on herself lest she break through the barrier into Arlvad's world. Legs under her as if she were on a raft over a cruel and bottomless ocean, she felt/watched/heard the story her chair was telling her on half-power, and saw –

Arlvad moved.

He slammed down his fist on his chair (he'd been watching the news). He said loud above the painful kaleidoscope of shattered colour, 'How can they *do* that? How can they put a man down just 'cos she said he'd raped her?'

She tried not answering but now that he wanted an audience for his explosion he could suddenly see her through the metaphorical wall that protected his opinions from reality.

He snapped another capsule, inhaled. Higher, straining, his voice forced its way past his fix. 'Oy, you, the tart with the hearing-aid, I'm talking to you.'

Gema tried not to feel her anger or her fear; the bleating of the kid excites the tiger. She tried to find a reply whose contempt wouldn't flay him to violence. An eternal few seconds while she struggled to be super-logical, to explain in calm, simple words –

'The machine found him guilty,' was all she finally managed. And at the same time, not hearing her, he said, 'Bloody typical. What are you, thick or something? Christ, a half-wit could see how unfair it was. But not you. Some geezer's going to be numbed for ten bloody years. She was a prostitute, for Christ's sake. What's one more customer?'

Gema thought, *With a broken bottle? He rammed her with broken glass until her bowel spilt into her womb and he's just one more customer? But Arlvad won't accept that* . . .

'Say something, you stupid cow! You're not on this planet, are you? Living in your own little world. That bloke's going to be frozen for the next ten years for some ugly whore! A guy got sliced right next to me at the Saturday fight but nobody's going to bust a gut to get the gang who did it. What makes women so special?'

Gema's words came slow and solid like iced treacle past the guard on her tongue: 'Then they should – '

'The difference is, men don't go blarting, "Help me, help me!" ' (Gema hated Arlvad's stupid, high sneer of a woman's voice.) 'But your race think they're God's gift.'

He drew breath, triggering the capsule again with his thumb. The faintly-blue vapour had lost its colour before it reached inside his body but that's where it had left its most ineradicable mark. The indigo patch on his thumb might almost have been decorative . . .

Arlvad held the drug in his lungs a moment; Gema took advantage of the pause to say, 'Well I think – '

'Don't bloody interrupt! I don't give a toss what you think. What do you know about anything, anyway? You don't even do a proper job! Just sit in your precious little dark-room all day. You want to keep your mouth shut till you've done seven years on the floor like I have.'

Mistake: she yelled back. Her face twisted with anger (like his), thrust forward, (like his). 'I know enough to say violence is wrong whoever the victim is!'

Arlvad threw the table over. Her glass of mulled wine leaped from its heated element to spin scalding through the air, spears of crimson that lanced like fire on her thigh. Second mistake: she jumped out of her seat with a scream.

Arlvad misread her pain. 'You want violence? I'll show you violence!'

He was between her and the door.

It was only afterwards that Gema realized: in everything he did, he never left a permanent mark on her.

But in the morning he woke her from her cramped and fitful sleep on the air-bed – with coffee and a cuddle. He didn't see the wine on the wall or the shattered glass. He smiled and didn't know what had happened last night, and her skin crawled when he touched her.

His gentle hands dropped abandoned to his sides. He said, 'I wish you wouldn't keep rejecting me,' and the gentle hurt in his face made her want to weep for all that their reality wasn't any more.

They close the door on the dark-room and the last slice of light shrinks and is gone.

Do you know what total silence is?

It's perfect.

But you panic; you find yourself listening for your heart-beat – and there it is – and the silence isn't perfect any more.

Sometimes the silence in this place is a loving refuge of black velvet, but you can't hide for long in silence. Your thoughts go with you: all the emotional encumbrance that makes you wish you were here and then finally it's your turn and you get here and you think *But what's the point?*

Sometimes before you start, when there's nothing, the dead silence is the black weight of a tomb, a whole necropolis pressing you down into the grave. And we all go down into the dark alone . . .

Except . . .

Except here, impelled by the frightening silence, your thoughts spiral and erupt, and the silver radiant ink shoots out, fluid beauty. My fingertips gavotte on the keyboard; my breathing swoops like a barque on the sea, and there, liquescent, the figures dance on the stave.

I (there's no room here for the other Gema, the one whose body carries the pain I leave outside the door) – I love it.

It's laughter distilled in sunlight, joy on the shores of ocean. One of the figures – a man – switches on music (so I have to go back and put the musicom in earlier, another silver squiggle on the malleable glass).

There's quite a gang of them in the world I've made in my machine. I hope they're having a better time than I am. (My laughter and then tears, real, now, invisible but felt in the dark as the wetness spreads hot down my face.) How can you be jealous of a person you've made up? – Practice. (A wry grin; silent whistling in the dark.

More than that. Loneliness, anger, frustration; all the times you think *I should have . . .* but you didn't. But that's the half of my life I try to forget in here. I try to pretend all that's happening to someone else. Don't think of that –)

So, music: I go back and write the music in, glowing symbols on the sound stave, finding snatches of melody in memory, cueing them on the computer. It finds the sounds in its banks, and I print them on to the glass so that there is visual harmony in the dark-room. And in the image-tank my silver world lives.

I play the scene, and replay it, tinkering with it, getting off on it, orchestrating the wind and sky, making the figures smile and dance, eye touching eye with secret laughter; all done in a script like balletic notation, with words – just right – starring the dark.

Because words, the gift of conversation pegged on the sharing of a smile, are all that stop us going down into the dark alone.

Alex (that's what I'll call him, a sound-shape to tell the computer how to encompass all he is of cheerfulness, of stability and caring) – Alex doesn't look anything like Arlvad. I won't let him.

Alex stoops, tall and blond with the sunlight weaving rainbows in his hair, to hum a snatch of melody to the musicom. He looks up to see if she's caught it, the musical reference to their night before. He grins, gamin, and she breaks into a delighted smile while the music blossoms by the sea.

*Once Arlvad used to smile at me like that. Not so long ago
I heard him laughing on the visiphone and for a minute I
couldn't think who it was in our living-room. When did we
stop laughing? — When he —* My heart beats so painfully my
whole ribcage echoes —

Alex. I'll concentrate on Alex. Checking the image-tank,
I know that's not quite how he'd move. I press the eraser
and the ink sucks back into the printer, and there's Alex
back in the position he was in before. Time erased. (*If only
I could go back! All the things I'd change . . .*)

So I search visual references until I see the movement-type
I want and the computer projects it for me, and when the
shape of Alex sums up his exuberance and his grace I
tabulate it, and there he is frozen for a second, that movement choreographed on the glass-sheet, his head flicking
up to see her delight, wanting her to share his pleasure.

Like Arlvad did before there was only him in his
world: sun, centre of his gang at work, lead in his nar-
cotic dreams.

We're all centres, I guess, only sometimes it's nice to
overlap. I think of all the people I'm programming this for,
all the people who'll sit in their chair some night and watch
the happiness I've made for them, men too, though Arlvad
says I don't like men and I'm always putting them down.

Don't have to with Arlvad. He does it for himself. (*And
when did I get this bitchy? I'm sure I never used to be this
way. I used to know —*)

So, Alex. With the song springing bright on the beach,
everyone's happy. Some of them are dancing again, a
woman lugs a small barrel of wine over from the boat,
letting the waves bounce it shorewards. There's plenty
of people to help her, splashing and laughing like kids
with streamers of spray glittering in golden arcs. Stock
characters, more or less. I let the computer handle their
bodies; all I put in is their emotions.

But my heroine: what shall I call her? I get the computer
to try out several names on Alex's lips. His pleasant tenor

voice (so warm!) makes me smile sadly, but when he says 'Astra', he sends a *frisson* through me and I capture her thrill and mine in silver.

God, I love this world. Thank you for letting me make it.

And I rhapsodise about this man, skimming hundreds of scenes the computer-adjunct has taken from real life, because I don't want a puppet. I want Alex to be a real person, a man you might meet at a party or on the steps outside the bank, so I tame my rhapsody. Still, a man would be glad to have him as a friend (I go back and write him a friend), and a woman would be glad to stand near him sharing his body-heat.

At their first kiss, I can't write any more. I tell myself it would be prying, but I don't believe it. It's pain; the jealousy, the regret: *Why me?*

I push back from the monitor and stretch my aching back. My hands on the console shine pale and faint in the light from the image-tank. Just visible on the concave walls of our dark-room, multiple curves reflect the glow: the kettle, the fridge, the microwave. Everything's rounded in here, even the toilet-access and the bed in the hollow of the wall. That's so that none of us hurts themselves blundering round in the dark. Ergonomics. I cling to the word as I go to the loo, get a Martini, eat a pre-packed salad by the radiance of the world I've made. All I've got to hold on to is insubstantial words.

And if any light came in, I'd lose them. They'd smear on the glass-optic scroll. Because I'm still writing this so I can't lacquer them with fixer. That's why, out-side the dark-room, there's a big sign for all visitors to our writers' guild, DO NOT UNDER ANY CIR-CUMSTANCES OPEN THIS DOOR – EMERGENCY PHONE (RED) WILL CONTACT THE WRITER INSIDE SO THAT HIS/HER WORK MAY BE FIXED BEFORE DOOR OPENS. And Winston's on rota in the waiting-room, carving a meerschaum pipe probably, ready to keep anybody out.

I can't put it off any longer. When I ask, the bio-crystal computer tells me it's seven-twenty p.m. I've been here all day and I've only made (I check) forty-nine minutes of programme for an hour slot. Robyn's on tomorrow so it'll be an all-nighter unless I get a move on.

Besides, when I'm late back, Arlvad is worse than ever, jealous of the time I'm not spending on him. (And what if it's one of the days when he's so kind and loving and I'm not there? – Guilt should be outlawed.)

I go back to Alex and Astra, and oh! how their good times hurt me. It's a physical pain, down below the parting of my ribs, and my heart starts its flamenco again and I'm afraid alone in the dark. But that side of life belongs to Gema and I won't mix her up with what I'm doing here. But I'm terrified that her palpitations will turn into a heart-attack and kill me . . . What if I die on my own because there's no one else here?

I won't give in to it.

Now I have to put in the tension and drama. The good guy, the bad guy, the innocent victims swept up in someone else's cruelty. But for me it's just a frame for the real picture: ordinary people who aren't me having a good time on a beach. Weave the threads of plot through like black strands of tapestry criss-crossing the sunny scene.

(Maybe you have to have the bad times so you can appreciate the good? But what of victimology? The fact that some people get mugged again and again because they somehow look like victims? Is that what I'm doing? Somehow making Arlvad take out his anger on me? What have I ever done to deserve this? I must be horrific, evil on a scale like Pol Pot. I loathe myself. But my friends love me, and Arlvad's always used the capsules as long as I've known him. It's just that everyone else takes them only now and again, and you can tell how they're going to behave. With Arlvad you can't tell, who he is from one minute to the next . . . The times I've wanted to hurt myself for being so stupid! How could I have been so thick that I set up home with him? And to stay after it got so bad? (But how could I live on my own? I'm so afraid and I hate myself for being such a wimp.) There is no bottom or top to my depths of self-hatred. I'm shaking again, and the only way I know I'm alive down here in the dark-room is the way my thorax throbs to my clumsy heart-beat.)

But I've got to make all that external, let it belong to Gema. I split myself deliberately. (*Arlvad's mood-swings are fragmenting me.*) But there's a deadline. I've got to get this story finished.

The bad guy arrives, and the bad woman. You can't tell they're the baddies just by looking at them; there are no black hats in real life. They shatter the tranquillity of the jewelled time on the beach. Seagulls (have to put some in earlier) squawk raucously upward to show lives fragmenting and a love-song on the musicom is the counter-point. Guns are waved around, people get hurt. Astra's friend makes a diversion and Arlvad gets the baddie.

Arlvad?

Arlvad the addict? The one I've lived with for seven years?

And I know it's true. Weeping in the dark-room I know that almost everything that's good about my hero used to be true about Arlvad, still is – some days. Friendly, kind, loving, always good for a laugh. It's the drugs. There's something lacking in him that makes him use them to fill the void that I longed (long*ed?*) to fill. He says there's nothing wrong, and then cries and says there is, and forgets he's ever broken down, and takes out his rage on me. I beg and plead and cajole but he won't accept help, says experts know nothing, and there's nothing wrong with him anyway. He holds down a good job, doesn't he? A real job of work, not like my poncing about in the dark-room. So what if there's nothing left of him when he gets back home to me? They all think he's normal. I'm just making a fuss because he acts like a man and I don't like men.

A long time later I drink coffee and it's hot and soothing in my swollen throat. The blue skies in the image-tank hurt my sore eyes and all I want to do is sleep to get away from it all. But I can't. I'm afraid to sleep because I have nightmares in which my heart explodes, and anyway, Robyn's got dibs on the dark-room for tomorrow so I'll have to finish this off tonight. There's the seagulls to put in, and a spot of characterisation for the bad woman right at the beginning of the story, and then the fade-into-the-sunset ending. But I've nearly finished. And it's just as well because it's — bloody hell! It's nearly half-past ten! Arlvad'll go crazy when I get home.

So: the woman. Show her trying to use her credit card and she's way over the limit. And although I start to scroll forward to the end of the story I stop to tinker a bit here, a bit there, and before you know it I've watched the whole thing through, and the scents of the beach-barbecue mix with wine and salt breeze, and in the music-laden dusk (sunset's too trite) there are couples breathing soft and I'm about to finish with a joke and an after-trace of pheromones, and I think I'll put some luminescence on the crests of the waves, but the pheromones will be good because they'll leave the audience happy and with something to do —

The sound-proof door slams open. Yellow light glares in with Arlvad a gangling spider in the oval. He's shouting but I don't hear him. I'm watching the harsh glare swamp my delicate silver writing. The sound blurs, the sunshine and the conversation and the love smear grey on the dulling glass sheets. In the image-tank my world dies. The characters go nova, then there's only a blood-red pulse in the overloaded machine. It's dead. Everything I am is dead. Goodbye Alex.

And now the outside world is here in the dark-room. There's an aural assault, Arlvad shrieking, and past him I can see Winston crawling to the threshold, his nose bleeding on to shattered meerschaum. I can't handle it. I'm numb.

Arlvad twists his fingers through my hair and I'm not numb any more. There's a sharp, tearing pain in my head and it gets worse as I tune into what he's yelling.

'You bastard! You get back home *now!* You told me
you'd be home by nine but you're just like all your race!
Couldn't give a stuff about anybody else. How would you
like to come back home to a cold empty house after ten
hours of grafting?'

I wrench away, and there's a hank of my hair hanging
from his fist and bruises from the chair-arm. They're my
bruises, not Gema's. (Part of me thinks I must remember
the accidental injuries you do to yourself in my next story.)
Now Arlvad's here Gema and I are no longer two separate
people. We're coming together.

Safe on the far side of the chair I say, 'You know you've
not only wrecked my story, you've also broken fifteen
thousand pounds' worth of machine?' and I manage not
actually to shout.

'I couldn't give a flying toss. In fact, I'm glad I screwed
up your stupid writing. All it is is you playing with yourself anyway.'

Walking past him, quiescent (a ploy), I kneel by Winston
and say, 'You all right, man?'

'Oh, fine,' says Winston. 'You?'

Arlvad's bustled past us, accidentally-on-purpose kicking
my back. I was expecting it. I raise a grin and say, 'I'll
live.'

Arlvad's at the outside door yelling, 'Come on, you
stupid tart. Can't you think about anything but yourself?'
I can see the blue stain on his thumb where he's leaning on
the door-jamb.

Safe by Winston I say, 'Why don't you get some therapy?'

Arlvad ignores it and walks out between the subur-
ban shops, but I know he heard. I saw the tight look
on his face.

I smile at Winston and say, 'See you soon.' He nods,
disbelieving.

Arlvad slams the car door and sits angrily revving the
engine.

In the soft May night with the chestnut candles scenting
the air, I walk round the car. I know he can't ram me

because he's parked in a slot facing the bollards on the kerb. Stony-faced, Arlvad stares out of the windscreen.

I think – and the tears stream down my face and I hate myself for crying but I won't soon, I'll be strong one day – I think of my poor broken story.

So he's broken the machine. So he's smashed that story, that silver world.

Arlvad's not expecting it, and to tell the truth, neither am I. To our surprise I've finally found courage.

I slip down a side alley. I hear him drive furiously round the other end of it, and I'm dizzy with physical fear, but then I'm back in the writers' guild and Winston and I lock up and slide over the road to a pub that faces the river. Winston goes to the gents to clean up and incidentally to talk to his girlfriend who works behind the bar, and I'm left alone on the terrace, shivering a little as I watch a breeze fragment the ripples on the oily water. The fear – and its destructiveness – leak away. And when the breeze has passed, the images on the river come together again.

Arlvad may have smashed my silver-writer story but there's a new one. A story of adventure into the real world, where the dangers aren't dealt out by the friend at your side, they're shared. They unite us.

So maybe I once let him dictate my past.

But even Arlvad can't rewrite my future. That's being born now, sweet and gold-glistening with hope, inside my head, perfumed by the river and laved by the love of friends.

FORGOTTEN MILESTONES IN COMPUTING No. 7: THE QUENDERGHAST BULLIAN ALGEBRAIC CALCULATOR

Alex Stewart

Alex Stewart

Alex Stewart is in his early thirties, and has been a full-time writer since 1985. He was the first new writer to appear in *Interzone*, in 1982, with his story 'Seasons out of Time'. He is the editor of *Arrows of Eros*, published in 1989 by NEL. He has also written one pseudonymous novel.

ONE OF THE least known, and, it must be said, least influential of the early pioneers in the field of computing was Thaddeus Q. Quenderghast III, of Nettle Bend, Wyoming. Little is now known about his life, and few records of it remain extant; it has even been alleged by some researchers that his family, in an excess of zeal or embarrassment, destroyed not only his private papers, but every trace of their errant relative they could possibly get their hands on. Or, for that matter, those they couldn't; the mysterious fire at the Nettle Bend county clerk's office in 1897 is widely believed in some circles to have been instigated by members of the Quenderghast family. In the absence of any reliable evidence, and mindful of their propensity to litigation, I tend to the view that it was, indeed, a regrettable accident. Thomas Quenderghast, you may recall, was aquitted on all charges, and his explanation for the eight empty kerosene cans in the back of his buggy ('someone must've put 'em there') readily accepted by the court.

To gain some insight into the course of Quenderghast's researches, therefore, we must rely almost entirely on secondary sources. Though these are few and far between, sufficient tantalizing hints exist to allow us to assemble a speculative portrait of a man who successfully walked the fine line between genius and insanity for many years; the widespread belief among so-called respectable historians that he finally fell off it altogether can safely be dismissed as the petulant sniping of lesser minds.

Almost nothing can be reconstructed of his early life, although it seems certain his peculiar genius was not reflected among any of his immediate family. Indeed, the mere fact of his having been christened Thaddeus Q. Quenderghast the *third* would seem to indicate an innate conservatism on the part of his parents which stands in marked contrast to the visionary nature of their son. The exact date of his birth is not recorded either, the relevant certificate having fallen victim to the fire already mentioned, but was most probably some time around the spring of 1821.

A little more is known about his education, although the tragic gas explosion at the offices of the Nettle Bend School Board left few traces of his academic record. What is certain is that he showed an early and precocious aptitude for some of the more abstruse areas of higher mathematics, solving the four colour problem one afternoon during a finger-painting exercise. His teacher, Miss Gwendolyn Abernathy, later trampled to death by an unexpected cattle stampede down the central aisle of the local millinery store, appears to have encouraged the young Thaddeus in his interest, going so far as to write a letter of recommendation to the dean of the Dodgeson Mathematical Institute at Harvard University on his behalf. Unfortunately this was the university in Harvard New Jersey, rather than its more famous namesake, but the young Quenderghast accepted their offer of a place in the next semester with alacrity.

The disastrous flooding which obliterated the campus in 1903, following the unexplained collapse of the local dam, left few traces of Quenderghast's original researches. It is, however, fairly certain that this is where he first encountered the concepts of Boolean algebra, which were later to have such a fundamental influence on his design for a calculating engine. In this, of course, he was far ahead of his British contemporary, Charles Babbage, who was still wrestling with the complexities of a machine designed to work directly in a decimal base.

It may also have been during his time at the Dodgeson Institute that Quenderghast started corresponding with Ada Lovelace, a noted mathematician of the time, and a close associate of Babbage. If so, it may well have been

Lovelace or Babbage who first sparked his interest in the possibility of building some form of calculating machine.

Certainly there was a considerable exchange of ideas, culminating in a visit to England Quenderghast is believed to have made some time between 1847 and 1850. The date cannot be pinned down with any greater degree of certainty, because Lovelace destroyed all their correspondence shortly thereafter, reportedly refusing to even acknowledge his existence for the remainder of her life. The reasons for this rift must perforce remain conjectural, although an undated fragment from one of Babbage's own papers refers to an 'unfortunate' scene at a dinner party, involving a 'colonial whelp.' If this was indeed Quenderghast, perhaps it raises more questions than it answers.

One thing that is certain is the date of the demise of Quenderghast's father, Thaddeus Q. Quenderghast II, in a bizzare accident involving a pig and a watermelon. On 3 December 1861, Quenderghast returned home to Nettle Bend, the new master of the Lazy Q cattle ranch.

At that time the Lazy Q covered roughly seventy square miles of excellent grazing land, and supported several thousand head of prime beef stock. The practicalities of running such an enterprise must have come as something of a shock to Quenderghast, who had never expected to inherit it; tragically, his older brother, Rickmansworth Runcible Quenderghast IV, had been scalped by renegade Indians the summer before.

Nevertheless, Quenderghast soon came to grips with his responsibilities. In this he was greatly assisted by the timely aid of his younger brother Thomas, their sister Esme, and his brother-in-law Franklin J Spoonbender. Declining Spoonbender's offer to buy him out, and amalgamate the ranch with his own neighbouring spread, Quenderghast threw himself into the business of stock breeding with single-minded enthusiasm.

Whether he had either the time or the inclination to pursue his mathematical interests over this period remains moot. There is little evidence either way; his monograph on self-reflective matricies, drawing on the research of his Dodgeson contemporary Porter Kincaid, was certainly published during this period, but the work itself could easily have been completed some time before. Exact dating of the monograph itself has proven difficult, owing to the unfortunate destruction of the publishers' offices by a freak tornado, which destroyed all the copies before it could be distributed.

By 1863, however, the Lazy Q was financially stable, enabling Quenderghast to devote more of his time to his researches. It was undoubtedly at about this time his old interest in calculating machines was revived.

Accounts of the reasons for this vary, and what little evidence exists is purely anecdotal. It has been said that one of the ranch hands, aware of his employer's interests, suggested in jest that he turn his mind to a way of counting the stock more easily. Others contend that he hoped, it must be said somewhat naïvely, to regain the good opinion of Lovelace and Babbage by vindicating their ideas. Myself, I incline to the view that what drove this wayward genius was the very audacity of the idea, the sheer joy of advancing the frontiers of human knowledge.

Be that as it may, we can be fairly sure the initial impetus for the idea came from a visit to the stock pens. Musing on a problem in Boolean algebra, Quenderghast was apparently struck by the realization that the gates of the various enclosures and the movements of the cattle within them represented these abstractions in concrete terms; gates were either open or closed, and the pens themselves either empty or occupied.

This might have remained little more than idle speculation, but for the intervention of fate in the form of a reunion of the Dodgeson alumni. It was here that Quenderghast renewed his acquaintanceship with Cyrus K Cattermole, an old classmate from the Institute, who had gone on to do much work of little significance in the field of binary mathematics. No record exists as to which of the men first suggested the two disciplines could be interlinked, thus simplifying the creation of a calculating machine enormously; what is certain is that Quenderghast returned to Nettle Bend in a state of extreme agitation, and began work on his machine almost at once.

Viewed from the vantage of hindsight, it was a tremendous undertaking. Over half the total land-area of the Lazy Q was eventually given over to the experiment, and the Quenderghast family fortune, vast as it was, dwindled away almost to the point of bankruptcy. It was presumably at this time the estrangement of Quenderghast from his neighbouring relatives occurred; certainly they were no longer on speaking terms by the late 1860s, when Quenderghast had his first limited success with a two acre pilot project capable of calculating pi to four decimal places.

That this initially encouraging result went to his head cannot be doubted; he was to spend the rest of his life, until fate struck him down in the form of an unusually violent display of ball lightning, in obsessive pursuit of ever more powerful calculating abilities.

Throughout this period he corresponded voluminously with Cattermole, from whose surviving papers the nature and extent of Quenderghast's machine can be inferred with a high degree of probability. Unfortunately none of Quenderghast's original letters survived the meteorite strike which killed his collaborator and effectively demolished most of the town in which he lived, but several of Cattermole's own notebooks had fortuitously gone astray in a portmanteau erroneously delivered to a Mr Silas K Cluttermule of Indian Giver, Idaho, by a disaffected minion of the Boston and Maine Railroad company. The Cattermole notebooks contain relatively little of value, consisting as they do mostly of limericks about an old maid from Nantucket, but one of them devotes several pages to a detailed description of a visit Cattermole made to Nettle Bend some time in the late 1880s.

It appears that by this time the perfection of his calculating engine had become an obsession with Quenderghast, to which all else was subordinate. Cattermole is scathing about the state of dereliction into which the ranch had fallen, and evidently alarmed by the corresponding physical deterioration of his old friend. However the visit appears to have passed off amicably, with Cattermole much impressed by the machine itself.

His description of it is, perforce, somewhat sketchy, but sufficient for its workings to be deduced. I present a condensed version here, with the gaps in Cattermole's account filled in by my own inferences.

Essentially, the machine appears to conform to Quenderghast's original flash of insight by the stock pens so many years before, but played out on the grand scale necessary to perform calculations in a manner strikingly analogous to that of a modern electronic computer. A network of fences sprawled out from the ranch house, covering many miles in each direction, dividing the range into small, self-contained units. Each pen was fitted with gates, controlled from a distance by a system of levers similar to those installed on the railroads of the time for the purposes of switching and signalling. A network of switching towers, each one roughly a mile from its fellows, allowed the gates around it to be opened and closed by a single man. Each tower was fitted with heliograph mirrors, enabling Quenderghast's instructions to be relayed in a special code of his own devising, and the results of the operations thus ordered to be returned to him in a similar manner.

Cattermole describes its operation thus:

'On entering the study my attention was at once arrested by a vast blackboard, some two yards by three, affixed to the wall opposite the window. Upon closer examination it proved to be divided into many squares, miniscule in size, and far too many in number to be readily calculated.

'Observing my evident puzzlement my host merely chuckled, remarking "all will become clear," the while engaged intently upon some task connected with the heliographic apparatus installed by the window. At length, presumably satisfied, he operated it furiously, producing a pattern of flashes unfamiliar to me. He later explained that the system devised by Mr Morse, though admirable for the purposes of common communication, would have been far too slow for the uses he had in mind; therefore he had devised a code of his own, in which each symbol stood for a specific word or calculation to be performed. A complete sequence of these instructions he termed, somewhat whimsically, the "playbill."

'At length he stopped, and stood waiting. In the still summer air I could hear the results of his labours, the clashing of the gates and their controlling machinery, the lowing of the cattle as they took up new positions among the lattice of interconnected pathways.

'Shortly thereafter a distant heliograph began flickering, in the incomprehensible code my friend had devised. He sprang at once to the blackboard, like one possessed, and began dabbing chalk upon it apparently at random. Only gradually I began to apprehend that each flicker of light related in some way to a specific square, which he blocked in with single-minded dilligence. Soon I began to discern the outlines of letters, then words themselves. As the flickering stopped my friend stood back from the board, nodding quietly in satisfaction, and I was able to read the message emblazoned upon it:

GOOD MORNING, THADDEUS.
WHAT DO YOU WANT TO PLAY?

'The rest of that all too brief morning passed in what seems to me now the product of a febrile dream. With the power of this machine at his command, my old friend was able to perform intellectual prodigies which remain to this day beyond my grasp. In all modesty I must own to being no mean mathematician; but the bewildering complexities of the diagrams he formed upon that miraculous blackboard were like nothing I have experienced before or since. It seemed to be some problem of military strategy, in which successive waves of hastily sketched riders threw themselves against a strongpoint defended by a single, mobile cannon. I have since thought long and hard about bringing this miraculous device to the attention of some friends I have in Washington, since, with its assistance, any army must surely become invincible; but I must confess I remain undecided.'

We can only presume that Cattermole kept his silence, since the device remained in Quenderghast's possession until his tragic demise. Of his later researches little is known, but a letter from his sister to their attorney shortly after Quenderghast's death refers to 'vermin' infesting the cellar. It is therefore tempting to conclude that the ever-inventive Quenderghast was experimenting with a miniature version of his creation, in which mice, or possibly roaches, were to be substituted for the cattle.

In any event, after his death the machine was all but forgotten. The ranch was inherited by Thomas Quenderghast, who promptly amalgamated it with the Spoonbender property, and the miles of fencing were torn down to facilitate grazing.

Now nothing remains of Quenderghast's brainchild except for one of the switching towers, which was pressed into service shortly thereafter by the newly-laid Sumpville and Nettle Bend Railroad. Today it stands derelict at the north end of the Nettle Bend switching yards, where it reportedly continues to do sterling work as a makeshift abode for the more discerning of the local indigents.

ifdefDEBUG + "world/enough"
+ "time"

Terry Pratchett

Terry Pratchett

Terry Pratchett is best known as the author of the Discworld books. His most recent book, co-written with Neil Gaiman, is a humorous (of course!) novel about Armageddon, *Good Omens* (Gollancz).

NEVER COULD STAND the idea of machines in people. It's not proper. People say, hey, what about pacemakers and them artificial kidneys and that, but they're still machines no matter what.

Some of them have nuclear batteries. Don't tell me that's right.

I tried this implant once, it was supposed to flash the time at the bottom left-hand corner of your eyeball once a second, in little red numbers. It was for the busy exec, they said, who always needs to know, you know, *subliminally* what the time is. Only mine kept resetting to Tuesday, 1 January, 1980 every time I blinked, so I took it back, and the salesman tried to sell me one that could show the time in twelve different capitals plus stock market reports and that. All kinds of other stuff, too. It's getting so you can get these new units and you go to have a slash, excuse my French, and all these little red numbers scroll up with range and position details and a vector-graphics lavvy swims across your vision, *beepbeepbeep*, lock-on, fire . . .

She's around somewhere. You might of even seen her. Or him. It's like immortality.

Can't abide machines in people. Never could, never will.

I mention this because, when I got to the flat, the copper on the door had that panicky look in his eye they have when they're listening to their internal radio.

I mean, probably it looked a great idea on paper. Whole banks of crime statistics and that, delivered straight to the inside of your head. Only they get headaches from all the noise. And what good is it, every time a cab goes by, they

get this impulse to pick up a fare from Flat 27, Rushdie
Road? My joke.

I went in and there was this smell.

Not from the body, though. They'd got rid of that
smell, first thing.

No. This smell, it was just staleness. The kind of smell
old plastic makes. It was the kind of smell a place gets that
ought to be dirty, only there's not enough dirt around, so
what you get is ground-in cleanness. When you leave home,
say, and your mum keeps the room just like it was for
ten years, that's the kind of smell you get. The whole flat
was like that, although there were no aeroplanes hanging
from the ceiling.

So I get called into the main room and immediately I
spot the Seagem, because I'm trained, you notice things like
that. It was a series Five, which in my opinion were a big
mistake. The Fours were pretty near ideal, so why tinker?
It's like saying, hey, we've invented the perfect bicycle so,
next thing we'll do, we'll put thirteen more wheels on it
– like, for example, they replaced the S-2030s with the
S-4060, not a good move in my opinion.

This one was dead. I mean, the power light was on
and it was warm, but if it was operating you'd expect
to see lights moving on the panel. Also, there was this
really big 4711 unit on top, which you don't expect to
see in a private house. It's a lab tool. It was a dual
model, too. Smell *and* taste. I could see by the model
number it was one of the ones you use a tongue glove
with, which is actually quite OK. Never could understand the spray-on polymers. People say, hey, isn't it
like having a condom in your mouth, but it's better
than having to scrape gunk off your tongue at bed-
time.

Lots of other stuff had been hooked in, too, and half a
dozen phone lines into a patch unit. There was a 1MT
memory sink, big as a freezer.

Someone who knew what they wanted to buy had really
been spending some money here.

And, oh yes, in the middle of it, like they'd told me on the phone, the old guy. He was dead, too. Sitting on a chair. They weren't going to do anything to him until I'd been, they said.

Because of viruses, you see. People get funny ideas about viruses.

They'd taken his helmet off and you could see the calluses where the nose plugs had been. And his face was white, I mean, *yes*, he was dead and everything, but it had been like something under a stone even before, and his hair was all long and crinkly and horrible where it had been growing under the helmet. And he didn't have a beard, what he had was just long, long chin hair, never had a blade to it in years. He looked like God would look if he was on really serious drugs. And dead, of course.

Actually, he was not that old at all. Thirty-eight. Younger than me. Of course, I jog.

This other copper was standing by the window, trying to pick up HQ through the microwave mush. He looked bored. All the first-wave scene-of-crime types had long been and gone. He just nodded to the Seagem and said, 'You know how to fix these things?'

That was just to establish, you know, that there was them and us, and I was a them. But they always call me in. Reliable, see. Dependable. You can't trust the big boys, they're all dealers and agents for the afer companies, they're locked in. Me, I could go back to repairing microswatch players tomorrow. Darren Thompson, Artificial Realities repaired, washing-machine motors rewound. I can do it, too. Ask kids today even to repair a TV, they'll laugh at you, they'll say you're out of the Arc.

I said, 'Sometimes. If they're fixable. What's the problem?'

'That's what we'd like you to find out,' he says, more or less suggesting, if we can't pin something on him we'll pin it on you, chum. 'Can you get a shock off these things?'

'No way. You see, the interfaces – '

'All right, all right. But you know what's being said about 'em. Maybe he was using it for weird kicks.' Coppers think everyone uses them for weird kicks.

'I object most strongly to that,' said this other voice. 'I object most strongly, and I shall make a note of it. There's absolutely no evidence.'

There was this other man. In a suit. Neat. He was sitting by one of these little portable office terminals. I hadn't noticed him before because he was one of these people you wouldn't notice if he was with you in a wardrobe.

He smiled the sort of smile you have to learn and stuck out his hand. Can't remember his face. He had a warm, friendly handshake, the kind where you want to have a wash afterwards.

'Pleased to meet you, Mr Thompson,' he said. 'I'm Carney. Paul Carney. Seagem public affairs department. Here to see that you are allowed to carry out your work. *Without* interference.' He looked at the copper, who was definitely not happy. 'And any pressure,' he added.

Of course, they've always to wanted to nail Seagem, I know that. So I suppose they have to watch business. But I've done thirty, forty visits where afers have died, and men in suits don't turn up, so this was special. All the money in the equipment should've told me that.

Life can get very complicated for men in overalls who have problems with men in suits.

'Look,' I said. 'I know my way around these things OK, but if you want some really detailed testing then I would have thought your people'll – '.

'Seagem's technical people are staying *right* out of this,' snapped the copper. 'This is a straight in-situ report, you understand. For the coroner. Mr Carney is not allowed to give you any instructions at all.'

Uniforms, too. They can give you grief.

So I took the covers off, opened the toolbox, and stuck in. That's my world. They might think they're big men, but when I've got the back of something and its innards all over the floor, it's me that's the boss . . .

Of course, they're all called Seagems, even the ones made by Hitachi or Sony or Amstrad. It's like Hoovers and hoovers. In a way, they aren't difficult. Nine times out of ten, if you're in trouble, you're talking loose boards, unseated panels, maybe a burnout somewhere. The other one time it's probably something you can only cure by taking the sealed units into the hypercleanroom and tapping them with a lump hammer, style of thing.

People say, hey, bet you got an armful of degrees and that. Not me. Basically, if you can repair a washing machine you can do everything to a Seagem that you *can* do outside a lab. So long as you can remember where you put the screws down, it's not taxing. That's if it's a *hardware* problem, of course. Software can be a pain. You got to be a special type of person to handle the software. Like me. No imagination, and proud of it.

'Kids use these things, you know,' said the copper, when I was kneeling on the floor with the interface boards stacked around me.

(I always call them coppers, because of tradition. Did you know that 'copper' as slang for policeman comes from the verb 'to cop', first reliably noted in 1859? No, you don't, because, after all that big thing ten years ago about the trees and that, the university put loads of stuff into those big old read/write optical units, and some kid managed to get a McLint virus into the one in the wossname department. You know? Words? History of words. This was before I specialized in Seagems, only in those days they were still called Computer Generated Environments. And they called me in and all I could haul out of 5kT of garbage was half a screenful which I read before it wiped. This guy was crying. 'The whole history of English philology is up the swanee,' he said, and I said, would it help if I told him the word 'copper' was first reliably noted in 1859, and he didn't even make a note of it. He should of. They could, you know, start again. I mean, it wouldn't be much, but it would be a start. Often wondered what 'up the swanee' really means. Don't suppose I'll ever know, now.)

'Kids use them,' he said. You could tell he wanted to use a word like 'bastards', but not with the suit around.

Not ones like these they don't, I thought. This stuff is top of the range. You couldn't get it in the shops.

'If I caught my lad with one, I'd tan his hide. We used to play healthy games when I was a kid. Elite, Space Invaders, that stuff.'

'Yeah.' Let's see, attach probes *here* and *here* . . .

'Please allow Mr Thompson to get on with his work,' said the suit.

'I think,' said the copper nastily, 'we ought to tell him who this man *is*.' Then they started to argue about it.

I suppose I'd assumed he was just some old guy who'd hooked into one porno afer too many. Not a bad way to go, by the way. People say, hey, what you mean? Dying of an overdose of artificial sex is OK? And I say, compared to about a million other ways, yes. Realities can't kill you unless you want to go. The normal feedback devices can't raise a bruise, whatever the horror stories say, although between you and me I've heard of, you know, *things*, exoskeletons, the army used 'em but they've turned up elsewhere. They can let your dreams kick the shit out of you.

'He's Michael Dever,' said the copper. 'Mr Thompson should know that. He invented half this stuff. He's a *big* man at Seagem. Hasn't been into the office for five years, apparently. Works from home. Worked,' he corrected himself. 'Top man in development. Lives like this. Lived. Sends all his stuff in over the link. No one bothered about it, see, because he's a genius. Then he missed an important deadline yesterday.'

That explained about the suit, then. Heard about Dever, of course, but all the pix in the mags showed this guy in a T-shirt and a grin. Old pix, then. A big man, yes. So maybe important stuff in the machine. Or he was testing something. Or they thought, maybe someone had slipped him a virus. After all, there were enough lines into the unit.

Nothing soiled though, I thought. Some people who are gone on afer will live in shit, but you do get the thorough ones, who work it all out beforehand – fridge stacked with TV dinners, bills paid direct by the bank, half an hour out from under every day for housework and aerobics, and then off they go for a holiday in their heads.

'Better than most I've seen,' I said. 'Neat. No trouble to anyone. I've been called into ones because of the smell even when they *weren't* dead.'

'Why's he got those pipes hooked up to the helmet?' said the copper.

He really didn't know. I supposed he hadn't had much to do with afers, not really. A lot of the brighter coppers keep away from them, because you can get really depressed. What we had here was Entonox mixture, the intelligent afer's friend. Little tubes to your nose plugs, then a little program on the machine which brings you out of your reality just enough every day for e.g. a go on the exercise bike, a meal, visit the bathroom.

'If you're going to drop out of your own reality, you need all the help you can get,' I explained. 'So the machine trickles you some gas and fades the program gradually. Gives you enough of a high to come out of it without screaming.'

'What if the valves stick?' asked the suit.

'Can't. There's all kinds of fail-safes, and it monitors your – '

'We believe the valves may have stuck,' said the suit firmly.

Well. Good thinking. Seagem don't make valves. The little gas units are definitely third-party add-ons. So if some major employee dies under the helmet, it's nice to blame valves. Only I've never heard of a valve sticking, and there really *are* a load of fail-safes. The only way it'd work is if the machine held some things off and some things on, and that's *purpose*, and machines don't have that.

Only it's not my place to say things like that.

'Poor guy,' I said.

The copper unfolded at high speed and grabbed my shoulder and towed me out and into a bedroom, just like that. 'Just you come and look at this,' he kept saying. 'Just you come and *look*. This isn't one of your bloody electronic things. Poor guy? Poor guy? This is *real*.'

There was this other dead body next door, see.

He thought I was going to be shocked. Well, I wasn't.

You see worse things in pictures of Ancient Egypt. You see worse things on TV. *I* see them for real, sometimes. *Nearly* fresh corpses can be upsetting, believe me, but this wasn't because it'd been years. Plenty of time for the air to clear. Of course, I only saw the head, I wouldn't have liked to have been there when they pulled the sheets back.

She might have been quite good looking, although of course it was hard to be sure. There were coroner's stickers over everything.

'Know what she died of?' asked the copper. 'Forensic think she was pregnant and something went wrong. She bled to death. And her just *lying* there, and him in the next room in his little porno world. Name was Suzannah. Of course, all the neighbours are suddenly concerned that they never saw her around for years. Kept themselves to themselves,' he mimicked shrilly. 'Half of 'em afers too, you bet.

'He left her for five years. Just left her there.'

He was wrong. Listen, I've been called in before when an afer's died, and like I said it's the smell every time. Like rotting food, you know. But Dever or someone had sealed the room nicely, and put her in a body-bag thing.

Anyway, let's face it, most people these days smell via a Seagem of some sort. Keeps you from smelling what you don't want to smell.

It began with the Dataglove, and then there were these whole body suits, and along with them were the goggles – later the helmets – where the computer projected the images. So you could walk into the screen, you could watch your hands move inside the images, you could *feel* them.

All dead primitive stuff now, like Edison's first television or whatever. No smell, not much colour, hardly any sensory feedback. Took ages to crack smell.

Everyone said, hey, this is *it*, like your accountant can wear a whole reality suit and stroll around *inside* your finances. And chemists can manipulate computer simulations of molecules and that. Artificial realities would push back the boundaries of, you know, man's thirst for wossname.

Well, yeah. My dad said once, 'Know where I first saw a microchip? Inside a ping-pong game.'

So prob'ly those thirsty for pushing back boundaries pushed 'em back all right, but where you *really* started seeing reality units was on supermarket checkout girls and in sports shops, because you could have a whole golf course in your home and stuff like that. If you were really rich. Really very rich. But then Seagem marketed a cut-down version, and then Amstrad, and then everything went mad.

You see people in the streets every day with reality units. Mostly they're just changing a few little things. You know. Maybe they edit out black men, or slogans, or add a few trees. Just tinkering a bit, just helping themselves get through the day.

Well *sure*, I know what some afers do. I know kids who think you can switch the wires so you taste sound and smell vision. What you really do is, you get a blinding headache if you're lucky. And there's the people who, like I said, can't afford a rollafloor so they go hiking through the Venusian jungles or whatever in a room eight feet square and fall out the window. And afers have burned alive and turned into couch crisps. You've seen it all on the box. At least, you have if you're not an afer. They don't watch much.

Odd, really. Government is against it. Well, it's a drug. One you can't tax. And they say, freedom is the birthright of every individual, but you start being free, they get upset. Coppers seem to be offended, too. But . . . well. Take rape. I mean, you don't hear about it these days. Not when you can pick up *Dark Alley Cruiser* down the rental shop. Not

that I've watched it, you understand, but I'm told the girl's
very good, does all that's expected of her, which you don't
have to be an Eisenstein to work out isn't what it'd be like
for real, if you catch my drift. And there's other stuff, I
won't even mention the titles. I don't need to, do I? It's
not all remakes of *Rambo XXIV* with you in the title role
is what I mean.

I reckon what the coppers don't like is *there's all this
crime going on in your head and they can't touch you for
it*.

There's all that stuff on the TV about how it corrupts
people. All these earnest professors sitting round in leather
chairs – of course *they* never use *their* machines for anything except the nature programmes or high-toned stuff like
Madam Ovary. Probably does corrupt people but, I don't
know, everything's been corrupting people since the, you
know, dawn of thingy, but with afers it stays inside. They
aren't about to go and knock over some thin little girl in
cotton underwear coming back from the all-night chippy,
not after *Dark Alley Cruiser*. Probably can't, anyway. And
it's cheap so you don't have to steal for it. A lot of them
forget to feed themselves. Afers are the kind of problems
that come with the solutions built in.

I like a good book, me.

They watched me very hard when I checked the gas-feed
controls. The add-on stuff was pretty good. You could see
where it was hooked into everything else. I bet if I had time
to really run over it on the bench you'd find he had a little
daydream every day. Probably didn't even properly come
out from under. Funny thing, that, about artificial realities.
You know how you can be dreaming and the buzzer goes
and the dream sort of incorporates the buzzer into the plot?
Probably it was like that.

It had been well-maintained. Cleaned regularly and
everything. You can get into trouble otherwise, you get
build-ups of gunk on connectors and things. That's why all
my customers, I tell them, you take out a little insurance,

I'll be round every six months regular, you can give me the key, I've even got a bypass box so if you're, you know, *busy* I can do a quick service and be away and you won't know I've been. This is personal service. They trust me.

I switched off the power to the alarms, cleaned a few boards for the look of it, reseated everything, switched it back on. Et wolla.

The copper leaned over my shoulder.

'How did you *do* that?' he said.

'Well,' I said, 'there was no negative bias voltage on the sub-logic multiplexer,' which shut him up.

Thing is, there wasn't anything wrong. It wasn't that I couldn't find a fault, there was nothing to say that a fault existed. It was as if it'd just been told to shut down everything. Including him.

Valve stuck . . . that meant too much nitrous oxide. The scene of crime people prob'ly had to get the smile off his face with a crowbar.

The lights came on, there were all the little whirs and gurgles you get when these things boot up, the memory sinks started to hum, we were cooking with gas.

They got excited about all this.

And then, of course, I had to get out my own helmet.

Viruses, that's the thing. Started off as a joke. Some kid'd hack into someone else's reality, scrawl messages on the walls. A joke, like the McLints. Only, instead of scrambling the wage bill or wiping out English literature, you turned their brain to cheese. Frighten them to death, or whatever. Scares the hell out of some people, the thought that you can kill people that way. They act illogical. You find someone dead under an afer unit, you call in someone like me. Someone with no imagination.

You'd be amazed, the things I've seen.

You're right.

You're clever. You've had an education.

You're saying, hey, I know what you saw. You saw the flat, right, and it was just like it was really, only maybe cleaner, and she was still alive in it, and maybe there was a kid's voice in the next room, the kid they never had, because, right, he'd sat there maybe five years ago maybe while she was still warm and done the reality creation job of a lifetime. And he was living in it, just sane enough to make sure he *kept* on living in it. An artificial reality just like reality ought to have been.

Right. You're right. You knew it. I should've held something back, but that's not like me.

Don't ask me to describe it. Why ask me to describe it? It was *his*.

I told the other two and the PR man said firmly, 'Well, all right. And then a valve stuck.'

'Look,' I said, 'I'll just make a report, OK? About what I've found. I'm a wire man, I don't mess around with pipes. But I wouldn't mind asking you a question.'

That got them. That got them. People like me don't normally ask questions, apart from 'Where's the main switch?'

'Well?' said the suit.

'See,' I said, 'it's a funny old world. I mean, you can hide a body from *people* these days, it's easy. But there's a lot more to it in the real world. I mean, there's banks and credit companies, right? And medical checks and polls and stuff. There's this big electric shadow everyone's got. If you die – '

They were both looking at me in this funny way. Then the suit shrugged and the uniform handed me this print-out from the terminal. I read it, while the memory sink whirred and whirred and whirred . . .

She visited the doctor last year.

The girl who runs the supermarket checkouts swears she sees her regularly.

She writes stories for kids. She's done three in the last five years. Quite good, apparently. Very much like the stuff she used to do before she was dead. One of them got an award.

She's still alive. Out there.

It's like I've always said. Most of the conversations you have with most people are just to reassure one another that you're alive, so you don't need a very complex paragorithm. And Dever could do some *really* complex stuff.

She's been getting everywhere. She was on that flight to Norway that got blown up last year. The stewardess saw her. Of course, the girl was wearing environment gear, all aircrew do, it stops them having to look at ugly passsengers. Mrs Dever still had a nice time in Oslo. Spent some money there.

She was in Florida, too. At the same time.

She's a virus. The first ever self-replicating reality virus. She's everywhere.

Anyway, you won't of heard about it, because it all got hushed up because Seagem are bigger than you thought. They buried him and what was left of her. In a way.

I heard from, you know, contacts that at one point the police were considering calling it murder, but what was the point? The way they saw it, all the evidence of her still being alive was just something he'd arranged, sort of to cover things up. I don't think so because I like happy endings, me.

And it really went on for a long time, the memory sink. Like I said, the flat had more data lines running into it than usual, because he needed them for his work.

I reckon *he's* gone out there, now.

You walk down the street, you've got your reality visor on, who knows if who you're seeing is really there? I mean, maybe it isn't like being alive, but perhaps it isn't like being dead.

I've got photos of both of them. Went through old back issues of the Seagem house magazine, they were both at some long-service presentation. She *was* quite good-looking. You could tell they liked one another.

Makes sense they'll look just like that now. Every time I switch a visor on, I wonder if I'll spot them. Wouldn't mind knowing how they did it, might like to be a virus myself one day, could be an expert at it.

He owes me, anyway. I got the machine going again and I never told them what she *said* to me, when I saw her in his reality. She said, 'Tell him to hurry.'

Romantic, really. Like that play . . . what was it . . . with the good dance numbers, supposed to be in New York. Oh, yeah. *Romeo and Juliet.*

People in machines, I can live with that.

People say to me, hey, this what the human race meant for? I say, buggered if I know, who knows? We never went back to the Moon, or that other place, the red one, but we didn't spend the money down here on Earth either. So people just curl up and live inside their heads.

Until now, anyway.

They could be anywhere. Of course, it's not like life but prob'ly it isn't death either. I wonder what compiler he used? I'd of loved to have had a look at it before he shut the machine down. When I re-booted it, I sort of initialized him and sent him out. Sort of like a godfather, me.

And anyway, I heard somewhere there's this god, he dreams the whole universe, so is it real or what? Begins with a 'b'. Buddha, I think. Maybe some other god comes round every six million years to service the machinery.

But me, I prefer to settle down of an evening with a good book. People don't read books these days. Don't seem to do anything, much. You go down any street, it's all dead, all these people living in their own realities.

I mean, when I was a kid, we thought the future would be all crowded and cool and rainy with big glowing Japanese adverts everywhere and people eating noodles in the street. At least you'd be communicating, if only to ask the other guy to pass the soy sauce. My joke. But what we got, we got this Information Revolution, what it means is no bugger knows anything and doesn't know they don't know, and they just give up.

You shouldn't turn in on yourself. It's not what being human means. You got to reach out.

For example, I'm really enjoying *Elements of OSCF Bandpass Design in Computer Generated Environments.*

Man who wrote it seems to think you can set your S-2030s without isolating your cascade interfaces.

Try that in the real world and see what happens.

THE GREAT BRAIN LEGEND

Josephine Saxton

Josephine Saxton

Josephine Saxton is the author of *Queen of the States*, *Jane Saint & Other Stories* and *Jane Saint & The Backlash* (Women's Press). There have also been earlier novels and collections of short stories, often under the erroneous label of Science Fiction, from the late sixties. She is licensed in Traditional Chinese Acupuncture and holds predictably Green convictions.

'I WILL TELL you a tale that a teller told me, when I was young, but even then had a memory for words. First I will tell you how she began the tale, and then a little about the teller herself, for she was a strange one indeed. Even as to you I might seem strange, for those of us who do not travel with a tribe have no marks of kin upon us, and can dress as we please.

' "She woke as if struggling upwards through thick mud, although the analogy did not occur to her. This was in the days before mud, when the world was all dwellings, neat, clean, stacked. You have heard many times of that world, and who knows but what it was a real place. I tell it as it was told to me, more or less, but all who listen to stories know that something is increased with every telling, that is the way with the truth. Stoke up the fire, for dogs love a night-time story, when the ears of humans are bent towards the past." She had come and sat amongst us, placing her stringed drum and her bag of healing arts bedoodahs beside her, and after we had fed her and given her a big pot of beer (ah, thank you, your brewing is excellent), she continued her story.'

Having got the attention of her audience, a tribe of gatherers camping by the shore, Kyrie the teller, a woman of no age although her hair was white, passed on the tale again.

'The teller was an old woman, her accent slightly Black Country, her features a mix of races. Her eyes Asian, her lips and hair African, her skin a dark gold and her build that of a plump and strong European. Typically English in fact, and a wanderer as they mostly are, but like myself of no tribe. I was in the group of field-makers that night, and glad of the entertainment. We'd been harvesting rice all day and I was dead tired and cold, but not big enough to get right by the fire. With one ear out for a pack of dogs, as I hope you all are too, I hunched up and paid attention. Even to hear of someone waking up in a dwelling, neat and clean, was something wonderful to me, as doubtless it is to your hungry minds and bodies. I'd heard several stories before about earlier times, before the New World, where you could bathe in hot water behind closed doors, and your dinner came ready cooked out of a hole in the wall, just by pressing a button. Maybe it was all true, who knows? Anyway, I'm passing it on to you because not far from here is a place, said to once have been a great centre for the whole brain of the Old World. Right underneath the earth, far below the mossy concrete, all broken and heaped about, so people say, it is still alive and only needs finding and mending, and the Old World will appear again, complete with all its magic and comfort!

'Now, I don't understand a half of what that old woman put into her story, but she spoke so clearly and with such authority, we believed each word as she spoke it, and I remembered it all, for like all tellers, I love words as precious objects. Some words you use all the time, and these are for every day, but other words are so strange and marvellous you want to use them on special occasions, just to hear the sound, and get the mind wondering what they might mean. Take a word like "astrolabe" for example, or "horticulture", or "perimysium", what lovely words are those but who knows what they mean? Not I for one. I collect them, cherish them, store them up and bring them out to gloat on, as others might with their pots and pans and bits of clothes. So that's how I can tell them to you, and you will make of them what you like.'

A sussurus of impatience mingled with the sea breeze as it passed its chill through the group of listeners, for they had become interested in the woman waking up in a dwelling, and not in all the byways of the telling, and the pauses and decorations of philosophy. But this kind of thing had to be borne, for storytellers know their own worth and can indulge how they like. Kyrie, with her long hair in many braids, her bright rags wrapped around her strong body, smiled to herself, perhaps thinking of how history repeats itself. She was welcome anywhere, with her bag of healing tricks and her stories, so could do as she wished. She'd been given a good supper of fish baked in seaweed, and mushrooms and flat bread and now as much beer as she needed to oil the wheels of her mind. And when the audience had settled, she felt one particular pair of eyes upon her, intensely burning into her mind from the back of a group. The gaze belonged to a young girl, a thin, strong child with no ailments, who had come to watch the treatments with silent interest. Kyrie met her gaze for a moment, and it did not flinch. There sat one who thought deeply. Kyrie smiled and looked back into the fire, to find the thread of her tale.

She took time out to cough and get herself more comfortable, and continued her story.

'So there, as I said, was a woman from the long ago, waking up in a dwelling, just opening her eyes, not feeling too well that day, all alone in her bed which was covered in sheets woven so fine you'd think no human hand could make them, and indeed this was the case, for then, everything was made by machines. This was a woman such as you don't see these days, with hair as smooth as running water, and skin without a blemish. She was a hundred years old and yet you'd think to look at her she was no more than twenty, for they had ways of staying young and lovely then. And one of those ways was to look after their health in every detail every day. Every detail mind, and how do you think they did that?'

Kyrie scratched amongst her locks, drinking her beer and waiting for effect. To her audience, to whom disease and a short life were normal, even the thought of living to a hundred, let alone being beautiful, was a marvel. It was not possible of course, but then, if you challenged all the things which storytellers said, there would be no story at all.

'Well she used the computer of course, for every human living then had a personal branch of the Great Central Brain – the one which lies buried somewhere even now – and all you had to do was check out your state of health and put it right accordingly, and all would be well. You see, if we knew the day before if we were going to go down with the cholera or the rheumatics or whatever-you-choose, and there was a cure, then wouldn't we feel up and well? Those people knew years in advance if something was approaching, and all they had to do was prevent the matter. They had a great many cures too, I might add, little pills with such power, even more than my herbs and needles I daresay.' Here there were staunch denials from her audience, not one of whom would dare offend by agreeing on this point with their sole source of cure or comfort. Kyrie held up her hand, shaking her head sagely.

'No, I'll say what she said, that long ago, there were medicines more powerful than mine, I feel certain of it. And I daresay they had more potent poisons too, and I don't mind telling you, that old woman looked as if she could deal a heavy curse if she so wished. But she drank beer in quantity, to keep her temper even, and was smiling to herself as she told, just like I am except my pot is empty – oh, thanks indeed, most kind. Now I will tell you more of what she told that night.

' "Well, their medicine was more than good. And this morning, even before her eyes were open, this lovely woman knew that something was not right. Her head ached, her limbs felt like lumps of wood, her mouth full of fur and her spirit's flame was nothing but a smoulder." '

'Must have drunk too much beer the night before!' somebody muttered, to laughter and shoves and shushings.

'Aye well so she might, but this was nothing to people then. They had a cure for everything, so this woman didn't worry, she did as she did every morning. "She put a hand out from under her fine sheets, and felt around until she found her diagnostic module. All she had to do was place the palm of her hand flat upon this smooth box, and in no time at all every tiniest piece of information about her was gathered up, made sense of, and a list of how to put everything right would come right back for her to listen to, along with the means of a cure, even before she'd bothered to open her eyes. Even her dreams were gathered up by the Great Brain, just from the touch of her hand, and made sense of there and then. I tell you, it was a wonderful world in those days."

'The group were fascinated, comparing their own wretched state with the state of this heroine of long ago. The dream dreamed by almost everyone, of finding the Great Central Brain and repairing it, flashed through every mind in several versions. The Brain had once done everything for humankind, there was nothing beyond its ability so it was said. It had all knowledge held within it just for the asking, and it never could tell a lie. What did it look like? How ruined was it? What tools would you need for such work? Was it dangerous? Was there a punishment for interfering with powers too great for people? The rewards were so great for those who could find it and make it work again. Food, heat, light, cleanliness, even travelling the length of the country in the space of one day, flying across water – the power of this Great Brain was without limit. It had ordered and controlled everything in the world, and if it could be found, then the Old World would return. Life would not be such a short and painful business. The storyteller sank more of her beer and shifted around on her haunches for comfort, and in this interval someone put a few sticks on to the fire, the sparks glowing up into the dark.

' "Now then, this next part of my tale I will sing for you," she told them, "although I have no musical instrument like that old stringed drum, for not all can use those things. But I know all the words, and some of them are powerful words I am certain, and I will sing them. For these are the wonderful words I collected, and which must never be forgotten. And I can tell you this, that they heal all ailments, and if you listen very close, you will hear the health and truth in them. They are the words which came to this wonderful woman, lying in her bed, with her hand being read one morning. The reply that came to that woman, singing out of the air in a soft voice, was like this:

"'Thyroxine . . . ventriculograph . . . tachycardia and trauma . . . parathyroid . . . cyanocobalamine . . . haemoglobin . . . niacin . . . magnesium . . . potassium . . . iodine . . . phosphorus . . . paraminobenzoic acid . . . san-jiao . . . jing-luo . . . shou-tai-yin-fei-jing . . . dumai . . . ren-mai . . . tan-zhou-shang-rao . . . collagen . . . xanthine . . . retinol . . . Access number please prior to diagnosis . . . diagnosis . . . diagnosis . . . '"

Kyrie took her time over the singing, lovingly stretching out the sounds in a voice with some strength and power, with a great variety of pitch in it, so that her audience were held rapt, swaying to the rhythm she had woven. When she had finished she waited a while for the sounds to sink into the past before she began to speak again.

'On and on that teller went, until almost every one of us listening was hypnotized. I myself do not now tell a half of it, but you have the essence there, the words, the beautiful mysterious words, pouring out of that Great Brain, even before she had opened her eyes in the morning. Just about everything in that woman had been measured one way or another, and if it was found wanting in any way, advice was at hand, for that was the next part. As soon as she was up and about, every morning of the year, that woman would go along to a clinic and get topped up with potions and injections and energy, be told just how much of what exercise was wanting, and what was right for her well-being in every way. Oh, what days those must have been! What days to live in! Except . . .

'Ah, I see that you are wondering what could possibly be wrong with such a life, with not an ache or pain in it, no worry to spoil the view, everything taken care of in every respect. You must be wondering about that "except". For I will tell you, because on that morning, what happened next was in a way the beginning of the end of the Old World and its easy life ways. Because that woman was not satisfied with the diagnosis. Imagine that, not to be satisfied with what could be nothing but the truth. She opened her eyes and rubbed them, stretched, sat up, just like you and me, and spoke right back to the Great Brain – which, if you recall, could never tell a lie. And the words she spoke have gone down in history, because they marked a turning point. She said, and listen carefully: "Well if all you say is true, and every day there is something to be done at the clinic, and that makes all well, why do I feel like smashing in your stupid face?"

'Now of course the brain, the Master of Everything, the Organizer, did not have a face, but as we know, if something has a great power for you, then it somehow seems to have a face, does it not? It has a being, like everything else, only more so. And this woman received her reply, and it was the truth, mind, because the Great Brain would never tell a falsehood of any kind. It replied, and listen carefully: "You-feel-like-smashing-in-my-stupid-face-because-you-are-bored-out-of-your-mind-with-your-way-of-life-it-is-not-natural-in-any-way-and-it-has-no-meaning-to-it-and-computerized-existence-is-not-all-it-was-first-cracked-up-to-be-but-if-you-go-along-to-the-clinic-then-you-will-feel-a-lot-better-Access-number-please-for-Second-Opinion."

'Now that has surprised you I can see, and even thinking about these things makes me thirsty – ah thank you, good. So what happened next was this. The woman hardly thought for a moment but just went and deliberately smashed up her bit of the Great Brain, which was called a personal module, and strange to relate, she felt completely cured of all ills on the instant. And then she went out and told all the people nearby what she had done. She had a strange look about her face, so they say, and a power in her that had not been there before, and her enthusiasm caught on. All those perfect and beautiful people began to ask unheard of questions of their personal module, not just about their health but about the whole way of the world. They questioned things which they had taken for granted, just as we take for granted the sun and the moon and the rain and all our way of life. Soon others went to smash up their personal modules, and it went on and on, all kinds of terrible sabotage began. People began to realize that they had been slaves, had been cheated out of their will, and that when every last thing in your life is organized for you by something else, then life is not really worth living at all. And in a very short time the people had all woken up to this and there was a great rebellion, a great revolution, and groups of people left the clean and neat stacked dwellings and went in search of the sky and the earth, and began a way of life not unlike ours. For they were our ancestors, sure enough. But before that there were fires and explosions and destruction of every kind, a holocaust like a curse of the land, and there was much death and wailing and the water ran dry and pestilence ran through the land. It has taken centuries for us to build our way of life, and live as well as we do – or so they say. And for long years the sky was dark with the smoke and the dust, but when it blew away the sky was bright again, and the green began to take over, as was always intended.

'And that is how the old teller told it to me, give or take a word, and that is how I am telling it to you, and that is the end of my tale.'

Kyrie seemed then to go into herself and sit staring into the fire, ignoring the sighs of disappointment around her, for they wanted to hear more, surely there was more? Then she seemed to pull herself back and gazed around the group with her powerful eyes.

'Excepting that is for what happened later that night, after that teller with the gift of music had finished her tale, for that is still a mystery to me, so I will give you this mystery to sleep upon.

'When she had finished her tale, she sat on by the fire, we all went back to our tents to sleep, but I could not, I was so wrought up by the tale, thinking in my mind which was best, the Old World or the way we lived then as now. I got up and crept out to see if she was still by the fire, for I wanted to ask her questions about her tale, as I suppose you might yourselves. She was just gathering together her drum and her bag and she wandered off, away from our camp. It was not yet quite light and it was cold and I was puzzled by this, so I followed at a distance, and do you know, she went off towards some ruins, the kind of thing you find where the cities once stood up against the sky. And in she went, in and out of tunnels, up steps and then down, then through a doorway, all the places we all avoid because of the snakes and the spiders and the ghosts and who knows what lives in ruins. And down she went until she was in a tunnel, and I followed her still, shivering with fear. And then she stopped at a door in the wall, and took out of her bag a strange plate with many buttons on it, and these she pressed many times. And the door opened, not like a door on an old hut you know, but it glided out of sight. And inside – and I am telling you the truth – there was light and warmth, and I could smell food and hear music. And, as I stood there, I could see past her and there were many people, all dressed in beautiful clean garments of lovely colours, and they were smiling and happy and you could tell even with so short a glimpse that they were in perfect health, there was not a mark upon them, not a sore nor a missing limb nor tooth nor any defect. There was another world in there, under the ruins, another world altogether. And that teller went inside. Then that door closed again, it glided into place like a shadow across me with my open mouth and staring eyes, as you can imagine, and I felt such a longing I cannot tell you. I do believe that the Old World was behind that door, as bright and thriving as ever it was. And I have often thought that the teller was not one of us but of them, sent for some reason which I do not know.

'And it came to me in a flash that the Great Brain was still alive and working, down there, in that other world, and that it still is so, but that we can never find it, ever again. And that is truly the end of my tale, and you can sleep on

it, and decide which world will be the better, should we
have a choice. That night, after I had got back to my tent,
the daylight was come and I did not sleep, and for many
nights after that I did not sleep but I dreamed of that other
world below. And I returned again and again to try to find
it, but there was nothing there, no tunnel, no door, nothing
at all but what we all see if we are daft enough to venture.
Nothing. And now I have ended, so good-night.'

Kyrie, as she was known to the tribes she visited, sat a long
time by the dying fire. She had treated all the ailments of
the group earlier in the day, and had no need to stay with
them longer. But it was the dark of the moon and a mist
swirled besides, so she dozed for a while. She pondered and
dreamed on the story of the Great Brain Death, the end of
a power so great that it had been both at the centre and all
around all life, watching and caring and directing, so that
no ill should befall. What did the tribes believe about the
tales she told? What were they supposed to believe? She did
not know, for it was only her work that she was doing, as
always taught.

When the first light came, she gathered her few travelling
bags and started away. It was above a few miles inland to
where she was going that day.

When she had begun her journey, she felt the presence
of one following. Was it that bright-eyed girl-child who
had listened with such intensity from the back of the
group? More than likely. It had been a long time since
any had followed in her steps, and that child had struck
her as being particularly likely to chance an adventure. As
she herself had done in the early days of her strange life.
Where were her own tribe now, where her parents? But,
a travelling healer and teller has no family, they are one
to themselves and never think of such things, that is part
of the price they pay. So Kyrie put such thoughts from her
mind and turned it towards other mysteries, and other tales
she might tell if ever she got permission. Some tales were
good for the people to hear, and others too mysterious, too

exciting, too secret. Hints at the truth were one thing, and the truth itself another. The tellers were not authorized to tell the whole truth, their job was to keep the truth alive, as a seed in the minds of the outside people. And Kyrie also knew that tellers themselves did not know the whole of the truth. Only the Great Brain itself knew that.

When she found the entrance to the underground she waited, sensing the presence of the follower still. She stayed with all her senses open until she knew the follower was there, watching, and then went the rest of the way slowly, giving time for mental marks for return to be made, in case the child (if it was indeed she) did not want to come inside. At the door she waited again, giving time for thought, to overcome fear, recalling clearly her own dread.

And then she opened the door to the Old World, with all its warmth and light and comfort, its health, its perfect organization, its efficiency, and its people who were near immortal. Kyrie turned and beckoned, and the child slipped in with her, into the heart of the earth, standing with open mouth in a world of story.

'So you knew it was real, did you?' she smiled down at the trembling girl, who nodded bravely. 'And you know you can never return if you go another step?'

This time the child spoke, not loudly but very firmly. 'Yes Kyrie, I know that. I sensed that – but I will have to return someday if I am to be a teller, won't I?'

'Certainly, but not to your own tribe, and it will not be for many long years. There is training to be undergone, for you are to be a guardian as well as a teller, as we all are here. And there is a lot to learn. Do you think you are as clever as you look?'

'Yes I do think that. Inside me is a mind which longs for space, I have things in my head that nobody in my tribe can even guess at. I want to learn everything.'

The solemnity and self assurance made Kyrie smile. There was an ego here which would surely have its shape changed, and with no small pain. 'Good. The first step is, we go and have a nice hot bath and I'll find you some good clothes to wear. Then maybe some breakfast eh?'

The child's eyes shone with excitement and anticipation. 'Food from a hole in the wall, just at a touch of a button?' she asked, so knowing it was almost irony in her tones.

Kyrie patted her shoulder in affirmation. 'Yes child, anything you like. The Great Brain feeds its guardians well here, never fear. No more gathering and fishing – and I daresay you'll miss that at first but the food tastes even better. Would you believe a thousand choices or more, flavours your tongue has never dreamed? Then after that I have to take you to be read – much as the lady in the story – except they will read your every thought, and put all the knowledge of you into the system. So then you will be a part of this place completely. And I must ask you, what name do you go by?'

There was hesitation now, perhaps fear at being read, perhaps the beginnings of shock as she realized the loss of her parents, her tribe. That would all be healed in no time of course, but Kyrie felt protective, remembering her own feelings on her first day in this Old World with all its shining novelty.

'My name is Lorna, but I do not like it,' she murmured, her young skin colouring. Kyrie smiled, for she had arrived here with a name she hated, and been offered a choice of many names. The Great Brain was kind over such matters.

'You can have another name, one which will make you feel happy, how does that please you?'

The eyes flashed with incredulous delight. 'Oh yes, yes! Really, not be Lorna any more? I've never felt like *Lorna*.'

All the signs were good, this girl was destined to live here. They walked together down corridors and through halls, attracting a little attention from the people there. Some were sitting at great walls filled with lights and moving words, some were eating, and in one place dancing to music so strange to the child, she put her hands to her ears. But when they had left that behind, and were in a place filled with scented steam, she became calm and thoughtful. As Kyrie took away her rough woollen clothes and threw them into a hole called 'Recycle', Lorna touched Kyrie's arm.

'Can I ask a question please?'

'Anything, anything at all, but perhaps I cannot answer. I do not know everything.' Lorna already knew that, her mind had been busy. She felt almost sick with anticipation and excitement, having achieved a dream which had been in her mind as long as she could recall. A dream of a life of comfort, a life with some point to it, a life with a road to travel that did not always end in labour and misery. Living in a place and wearing fine clothes woven by machines, and never having the cough or the scratch again, it was all coming true. But there was more to it, much more. The girl took a breath, and boldly put her thoughts together before asking, 'My question is this. If the Great Brain was completely in charge of everything, it would not allow itself to be cut off like that, letting the people smash up its parts, would it? And besides, here it is alive and well, but it has been cut off from all that world up there. Did the people, those people long ago who started to break their contacts, decide for themselves that they would be free of the system, or did the Great Brain itself tell them to do what they did, because it had no need of them any more?'

Kyrie stopped in her tracks and looked down at the child very piercingly. This was the first one to have come up with a question so near to the heart of things so early. Most came to this conclusion after half a lifetime, and even then rarely spoke their ideas.

'Now, we are taught that the Great Brain is only a machine, and we are the ones who look after it so that in its turn it can look after our world and all in it. A machine has no thoughts of its own, how can it? How can a thing not flesh and blood have a spirit which moves of itself? Does that answer your question?'

The child thought. 'Not really, for after all, did it not have a face in the mind of the woman in the story you told? But someday I mean to know the answer. If I was the Great

Brain, I'd never cut off my own right hand, would you?'

'No I would not. But then child, I am not the Great Brain and neither are you. Come on now, and I'll show you your first hot water falling in a shower, and all the delights of touching panels and pressing knobs to get your heart's desire.'

Kyrie thought, this must surely be one of the Special Treatment recruits. She would be taken away for secret training. And who knew what went on with that? Not herself, certainly.

Watching the child bathing, laughing and screaming like any child would, was a delight. And seeing the childish pleasure when a breakfast appeared at the touch of a panel, that too was wonderful. And when Kyrie had taken away her Teller disguise, bathed and dressed, Lorna's amazement at finding a young woman was quite laughable. It was her own turn to be amazed when she took Lorna to be read; never had she seen more information gathered all at once from a new outsider. The words were marvellous.

'Cholinesterase . . . hypothalamus . . . acetylcholine . . . noradrena line . . . thalamic nuclei . . . glial electrocon-ductivity-receptor site-shape and count . . .' on and on it went, a rapid monotone of information, punctuated by tiny starbursts of light and sound as 'special' information was uncovered and stored for further examination. Kyrie loved these words, but now they struck into her heart with just a little fear, knowing that some of those words came up but rarely. All too likely a subject for Special Training. And those who went for Special Training were never seen again. Not by their tribe, not by any guardian or teller or healer, by no being alive. The Great Brain itself took care of them, for evermore.

THE RECONSTRUCTION OF MINGUS

Phil Manchester

Phil Manchester

Phil Manchester, after a dozen years as a programmer and commercial systems designer, joined the trade magazine *Computing* as software editor in 1978. Two years later he became a freelance technical writer, and now contributes to many trade and national publications. He is married with four children, plays music semi-professionally, and lives in idyllic, rural splendour in north-east Essex. This is not only his first fiction sale, but his first fiction.

1.The C-Note

Buzz berzz . . .
Eddy's Walkmanned ears buzz with flattened third and
natural fifth interval. Buzz, berzz . . .
Flattened third from Bird. Natural Fifth from Jack
Daniels bottle in Eddy's armcurl. Eddy fastwalk. Late
for C-Note Date. Eddy know Date no wait. Connections
to make. Date no wait for time-waste junky muso.
Eddy fastfastwalk.
Eddy think: Bird greatgreat hornblower. Wish Bird
rights Eddy's. Eddy got Mingus rights, but no Bird
rights. No one got Bird rights. But Eddy got legal
Mingus rights. Eddy lucky. Most muso got no rights
– must pay to play. Eddy no payplay.
Eddy smile and thinkmore: Mingus rights raise cash.
Get stick from Hockman. Get ruptors from Darco.
Tonight Eddy see Darco, get ruptors, play Mingus, get
cash – pay Hockman. Hockman hold Mingus rights.
Eddy late for Date. Eddy fastfastwalk. Darco no wait.
Buzz berzz . . . Bird blow fastgood note.

Thelonius #457 and Coltrane #23 hit the bridge in 7/8
time – twisting and turning a twelve-tone scale rooted
in C minor. Constantly-changed, synchronized-synthesized
colours flow from the ceiling, down the walls – like
an action-painting – reflecting the high-speed rhythms
and quirky melodies booming from the C-Note Club
sound-system.
   It wasn't music to dance to. But it was cool. Icy
even.

Too cool for Bill Rogers. He poured the last few drops of the alcohol-free cocktail down his throat and stood up.

'Where, Bill?' asked one of his companions. Bill winced. He carried a deep dislike for abbreviated language. What was wrong with good, old-fashioned English? Whatever happened to polysyllabic words, florid phrases, baroque ornamentation? They were the textures and complexities which made language interesting and conversation joyful. He knew that many words could not be used in everyday conversation because they were the copyright property of large corporations. But there was no excuse for the utter barrenness of modern speech. Bill openly flouted the copyright laws and defiantly littered his speech with prohibited words.

He spoke slowly and pointedly in the old-fashioned, long-winded way he learned as child.

'I have had quite sufficient social stimulation for today. I wish to return to my domicile and relax. I will see you tomorrow . . . fare you well . . . '. His voice trailed off as he turned from the mocking faces of his companions and walked across the empty dance-floor to the exit.

He knew that his mannered and archaic speech would be greeted with the derision. But he did not care that much. Long ago Bill had decided that he was only a visitor to Earth. He thought of himself as an accidental alien tourist who happened to look like a human being.

He knew deep down, of course, that this was a delusion. But the thought sustained him in his misanthropic melancholy.

The computer simulations of Monk and Trane blasted into the final chorus of 'Off Minor' as he reached through the door. He allowed himself a sour smile. The computerized synth-simul-sound would deceive the average listener, he thought. But not Bill Rogers. He was more than a mere jazz *aficionado* – he was a true fanatic with one of the largest collections of genuine vinyl recordings in the world. And he was chief simulation designer for Honshu Simulations, the pioneers of the creative computer simulation technique used to breathe new life into the work of long-dead artists.

Bill led the team that built the original Thelonius Monk simulation back in the nineties. Thelonius #457 was a direct descendant of his original program and, in his opinion, it was not as good. Although its instrumental technique was superior, Thelonius #457 lacked the spontaneous improvisational qualities which had made his original so successful. Thelonius #457 played all the notes perfectly; but it lacked inspiration. And humour.

Bill knew the reason. Thelonius #1 was his labour of love. He had spent years studying Monk's technique. He had marvelled at Monk's apparently-random ornamentations and his empathy with the other musicians. But what impressed him most was Monk's humour. Most of his work on Thelonius #1 was an attempt to code Monk's sense of humour and he considered it to be his greatest triumph.

He had poured all his love of the music into it and, even now, he believed Thelonius #1 was closer to the spirit of the original artist than any computer simulation since. Close your eyes, free your mind and you were in Minton's bar listening to the birth of bop.

Well, almost. Bill knew that even his triumph could not compare with the original. It was, after all, impossible to simulate the feeling and emotion of a real, human artist. The simulations could fool the stunted tastes of the masses. But not a connoisseur.

The later versions of Monk were only poor copies of his original and Bill despised them. As he walked out of the C-Note Club he heard the sound-system explode with the introduction to one of the formal/formula tunes that were the staple accompaniment to what passed for dancing nowadays. He heard the scuffle of feet as the C-Note's customers moved on to the dance floor and began to wobble and weave in an enthusiastic, but meaningless and degraded, parody of dancing.

Bill shook his head and muttered to himself – disgusted with its vulgarity. Why do they settle for so little? he thought. He loathed popular computed culture and longed for those past days when music and art was made by human beings. He craved the imperfection of genuine human spontaneity and the creative surprises that decorated the work of human artistic genius. He also longed for the sleaziness, the risk and the tension which had so influenced the lives of those long-dead creators.

The simulations were no more than clever gimmicks, smoothed and sanitized for mass consumption. Bill knew that the real thing was . . . well, dangerous. He had heard the desperate, anxious messages hidden between the notes and rhythms of the original music. He knew that it was more than logic, cleverness and technique. It was about soul, passion – love.

He looked up and down the street for an electrocab to take him across the metroplex to his apartment. It was early evening and the street was quiet. He walked south, occasionally glancing over his shoulder, hunting for a cab. His thoughts returned to his current preoccupation – Honshu's latest project. Honshu and its rivals had produced versions of all the well-known artists from the last hundred years. There were audio simulations of musicians from Beethoven to Chuck Berry, graphics simulations of artists from Picasso to Warhol and literary simulations of writers from Shakespeare to William Burroughs.

The computer simulations made 'art' available to everyone. If you wanted a new painting to decorate your hall, see the local simulation supplier, choose your artist and receive a 'genuine' original. If you wanted original music to accompany a social occasion, you could hire the scratch orchestra of your choice, drawn from a vast library of simulated musicians. As long as you could pay the piper, you could call the tune.

But with most of the fertile ground of the past plundered, there were few new simulations to market. Corporate ownership of virtually all means of artistic expression – words, shapes, sounds, colours – had created stasis. There was nothing new to sell. Honshu had plunged deeper into the archives to dig out increasingly obscure musicians, painters and writers from the past.

Bill's latest project was to create the first simulation of the mid-twentieth century double-bass player and composer Charlie Mingus.

It was a tough job. Although an influential musician, Mingus was notorious for his feisty character, his violent temper and his tendency to record under informal, live conditions. Successful computer simulations relied on an established body of work from which the appropriate improvisational parameters could be drawn. Although there were plenty of recordings, they were all different – no patterns – and they gave little clue to the underlying structure of Mingus' technique.

Mingus was complex and, even half a century after his death, his music remained too difficult for most listeners. Bill had to find a way to make the Mingus simulation authentic, without putting off potential customers. He knew that this dilemma was at the heart of his frustration. Everything was a compromise – no room for purity.

There was another problem. Honshu did not own the rights to Mingus. They belonged to an obscure, itinerant muso called Eddy Battista. Honshu's lawyers had tried to trace Battista and negotiate a deal. But, so far, they had failed to find him. Some said that Battista was dead; others that he was a terminal case – hopelessly addicted to DNA disruptors, a drug which allowed users to change their DNA code. Originally developed for military use, 'ruptors' were illegal and very dangerous. The few human musicians that existed used ruptors to take on the character and abilities of their heroes. In this way they could emulate them in a similar way to the computer simulations. Bill had experience of ruptors. He had taken them once – when he was working on Thelonius #1. With a carefully measured dose, an experienced ruptor-user could, temporarily, become, quite literally, another person. Bill wanted to find out what it was like to be Monk and, under medical supervision, had dosed himself and used his skill as a programmer to alter his DNA code to match Monk's.

The experiment had almost killed him. He was un-prepared for the chaos and complexity locked inside Monk's head. When, several hours later, his own DNA code regained control of his tortured body, Bill had changed permanently. He found it less easy to communicate with his colleagues at Honshu and his already-quiet social life disappeared altogether. Since then he had lived as a partial recluse and sought consolation in his work and his treasured collection of old recordings. If he did not have to spend too much time with other humans, he was tolerably happy.

As he continued along the street, still hunting for a cab, a dishevelled, dirty man clutching a long case, scruffily-bound with tape and string, collided with him. The case fell to the ground and sprang open. Bill, transfixed by the contents, was only vaguely aware of the man's shout − 'Watch-where-go-fool-man!' − as he gathered up the tattered case and its contents.

Inside the open case lay a beautifully-polished piece of dark mahogany, about a metre long, with many silver strings and well-worn buttons. Although Bill immediately recognized it as a musical instrument, he had never seen anything quite like it before. It resembled a zither. But it was long and slim like an electric guitar. It had made a strange sound as it had hit the ground and the strings − there were ten of them − continued to vibrate.

Bill was speechless. Could this man be a muso? he asked himself. Muso's were rare since the simulation companies had acquired the rights to most sounds. But there were still a few around who were prepared to pay the extortionate royalties demanded by the musical copyright holders and some even owned rights. Maybe this was one of them. The man muttered about being late. He ignored Bill's cry of protest and ran into the C-Note.

Bill was intrigued. The man must be a muso. Bill suddenly recalled that the instrument was a Chapman Stick − a rare, mid-twentieth century, electronic/stringed instrument. Was he going to play at the C-Note? It was unlikely. Who would hire a second-rate musician to play live when they could have a near-perfect, computer simulation of the Duke Ellington orchestra playing original stuff for a fraction of the cost?

Bill's thoughts were interrupted by the cab which stopped outside the C-Note and disgorged its passenger. Bill raised his arm to attract the attention of the driver, who acknowledged him and cruised up the street to where he stood.

Bill spoke into the microphone above the driver's window. 'Watson apartment building.'

'Price ten,' said the driver's voice through the tinny speaker on the top of the cab. Bill agreed the fare and pushed his plastic cash card through the flap on the side of the cab. The passenger door opened and a smell of cheap disinfectant leapt from the compartment and assaulted Bill's nostrils.

He sat back in the seat, nauseous from the smell. He saw the scruffy muso rush out of the C-Note, clutching his instrument case. He stared through the cab window at Bill and smiled before ducking into an alley. The cab pulled away quickly before Bill had a chance to acknowledge the smile.

Fool-man near broke Stick – but now Eddy happy. Darco do good ruptor deal.
Eddy mislike Darco. Darco danger-man. But Darco got ruptors.
Eddy slipinto alley. No one see.
Eddy think: Take ruptor now. Turn Mingus. Play Mingus.

2. E's Flat

When they dragged Eddy into Police Central he had reverted to his own DNA code. He had misjudged the ruptor dose badly and failed to make the complete metamorphosis. The physical changes had occurred quickly and Eddy had taken on the Mingus' characteristic bear-like hunch. But the mental changes were only partial. He had acquired Mingus' notorious temperament but little of his improvisational talent. When Eddie had started to play his Stick to the small crowd which gathered in front of the C-Note, he had messed up the first tune so badly that they shouted insults. The Mingus temper rose in Eddy's ruptored brain and he lashed out at a heckler. A half-hearted brawl followed.

No one was hurt and the police arrived in minutes to clear away the debris. When they got Eddy to the station they found the remaining ruptor capsules in his Stick case. But they did not find his muso licence. And they did not find his Mingus Rights certificate.

'Hockman got rights – Hockman hold Mingus rights!' Eddy protested.

The long list of charges took some time to read out and Eddy continually interrupted the police administrator with his protests. The drug offences were minimal – a small fine. But the performance violations were serious. Eddy could find himself without a muso licence permanently. The police also had the power to confiscate his Stick and send him for radical psychiatric treatment.

'Hockman got Rights . . . ' Eddy went on – even after the cell door slammed.

Hockman come-go Eddy's bail. Eddy get Mingus rights back, Eddy think.
Hockman make good. Bring Mingus rights/Muso licence, Eddy thinkmore.
The shoes of the fisherman's wife are some jive-ass slippers.
Eddy think – knownot why. Mingus flashback Eddy think.

The Thomas Watson apartment building was a relic of a bygone age. It was the first apartment block to be totally controlled by computers. Environmental control, the services, the security and even the leisure/pleasure network was built in. It was constructed in the late nineties as a demonstration of a giant technology company's prowess. It had cost billions and had taken nearly a decade to finish. But the engineers had built well and, thirty years later, the building still functioned – if a little eccentrically.

Bill liked it – partly because half the apartments were empty – but mostly because it had an old-world charm which appealed to him. It was solid, functional and, despite its slow and primitive technology, it had everything he needed.

Once he had wrestled his way through the complicated admission security procedures and was safe in his comfortable apartment, Bill's first thought was to hear music. He reverently removed one of his precious vinyl albums from its fading cover and placed it on the turntable of his scrupulously-clean Linn Sondek. He chose the melancholy trumpet playing of Miles Davis.

Castanets heralded the start of *Sketches of Spain* as he walked into his small kitchen and threw a packed meal into the microwave. Usually Bill cooked fresh food – he was not fond of plastic food. But he was in no mood to cook.

He settled in his battered old easy chair and closed his eyes to concentrate on the lonely sound of Davis' trumpet. The music approached a climax and his thoughts shifted to the chance encounter with the man outside the C-Note Club. He resolved to look out for him the next time he was in the neighbourhood.

The sound of the videophone brought him back to reality with a jolt. Annoyed, he walked to the console to see the rounded face of Roxo, an obnoxious junior colleague at Honshu.

'What is it Roxo? It's late,' Bill snapped.

'We found the Mingus man – Eddy Battista,' Roxo slurred, revelling in Bill's discomfort.

'So what – it's nothing to do with me – I just program the simulations,' Bill replied.

'They got him down Police Central on armlong charge-list. Honshu want you bail him – do Mingus Rights deal,' Roxo said, smiling. He was enjoying this.

'That's legal job – not mine,' Bill lapsed unconsciously into abbreviated speech.

'Battista ruptored out – Honshu say you ruptorman – got experience – you bail him,' Roxo went on.

Bill thought for a moment. He resented the intrusion into his private time. But he was under contract to Honshu and the company looked after him well. And, it was true, he was the only senior staff member who had official experience of ruptors.

'OK Roxo. But I need a legal – one of Honshu's best – OK?'

'S'arranged – Luchenko there now. You go?'

'Yes, OK. I'm on my way.'

He saw Roxo's sick grin broaden as he cut the connection and called one of Honshu's private electrocabs to take him to Police Central.

He was surprised to find himself excited at the prospect of meeting Eddy Battista. He was less excited about going to Police Central and meeting Anne-Marie Luchenko, the Honshu legal. He had crossed swords with her before when Honshu had negotiated the Coltrane rights and did not relish a further encounter.

When he arrived at Police Central, Luchenko was talking to the police administrator in one of the interrogation rooms. She had completed most of the formalities to secure Eddy Battista's bail release and was discussing the finer legal points of the case. Luchenko was a weasel-like woman in her late fifties. She was a cold, efficient legal in the traditional mould and despised Bill as much as she despised Eddy Battista. But musical copyright was her speciality and there was no doubt that she was the best Honshu had on its payroll.

Like many Honshu employees, she had no interest in music nor in those who created it. It was all too vague and unpredictable to such a finely-tuned, specialist mind like Luchenko's.

Bill never understood this. To him music was about passion. He believed it was impossible to build a good computer simulation without understanding this.

'You know that you must accept complete responsibility for the defendant under the Bail Recognizance Laws. You must ensure that he is present at his trial next week or you become liable under section 33,' Luchenko intoned.

At least she speaks properly, thought Bill. Legals were required to use full language and were exempted from royalty payments on corporately-owned words.

He nodded his understanding of the legal niceties.

Luchenko turned to the police administrator.

'Let us see the defendant,' she snapped. It was a demand, not a request. The police administrator grimaced, then thought better of it. Best not to argue with a legal. He turned to his videophone, called up the automated cell-control system and entered the required authority to release Eddy from his cell.

Several minutes later Eddy Battista walked nervously into the interrogation room dressed in the dark grey overall issued to prisoners.

'Hockman come? Got Mingus Rights?' he asked.

Luchenko took the initiative.

'No – we are from Honshu Simulations – we have come to bail you out and talk to you about Mingus rights – do you understand?' she talked slowly and precisely, as if to a child.

'Where Hockman – Hockman got Mingus Rights,' Eddy muttered.

Bill recognized the signs of ruptor withdrawal on Eddy's face. And although it was difficult to frame his constantly-changing features, Bill was aware that he had seen him before.

Luchenko continued her explanation of Honshu's interest in Eddy's welfare and his ownership of the Mingus rights.

Eddy continued to ask to see the Hockman – slang for a pawnbroker.

Bill suddenly realized that Eddy Battista was the scruffy muso he had encountered earlier in the evening outside the C-Note. He kept the knowledge to himself and decided it would be prudent to get him out of Police Central as quickly as possible. He interrupted Luchenko's legal flow.

'Look – he's still strung out on ruptors. You're not going to get anything from him tonight. I'll take him home, straighten him out and bring him to your office in the morning – when he is coherent.'

Luchenko started to protest. But she realized that Bill was right and she was unlikely to come to any meaningful deal with Battista in his current state. She insisted that he signed a commitment to bring Eddy to her office early in the morning, gathered her papers together and left without comment.

Bill waited while the police administrator returned Eddy's clothes and his precious Stick.

3. The Shoes of the Fisherman's Wife

Who these people Eddy think.
Hockman no come. No Mingus Rights. No muso licence.
Where take Eddy, Eddy thinkmore. Eddy stay quiet.

Eddy remained silent all the way to the Watson building and Bill thought it best to leave him alone. It was past midnight when the electrocab eventually pulled up in front of the entrance and Eddy appeared to have calmed down. He was still bewildered, but he followed Bill into the lobby.

Bill guided him to the lift and told him everything was going to be all right.

Eddy gazed wide-eyed around the apartment and sat down in the old easy chair, nursing his precious Stick.

He spoke.

'Old music?' he asked, pointing at the huge record collection. Bill nodded.

'Got Bird?' he asked with something approaching enthusiasm.

'Yes – I have all the Savoy recordings and some of the other stuff. You want to hear some?'

Eddy nodded. Bill took one of Charlie Parker's early recordings from the shelf and lovingly placed it on the turntable.

'You'll like this,' he said, smiling.

Bill was not prepared for the reaction which followed. As the opening bars of 'Now's the Time' drifted lazily from the speakers, Eddy curled up in a foetal position in the armchair. He rocked back and forth with an ecstatic glow which appeared to take over his whole body.

Although the effect of the ruptors had worn off, Eddy's face contorted into a sequence of rapidly-changing expressions. Every time Bird blew yet another startling phrase, Eddy looked as if he were about to explode.

Bill stood passively watching what he thought of as a visual interpretation of Bird's playing. Eddy seemed to have a physical empathy for the music and, when it had finished, he slumped back in the chair, eyes closed, apparently exhausted.

'You like that?' he asked.

Eddy said nothing.

Bill stood looking at Eddy for some time. This is extraordinary, he thought. This man was somehow in tune with the music in a way that Bill could not understand. It was as if he were a composite reincarnation of all those long-dead musos.

After a few minutes Eddy's eyes suddenly opened.

'Got ruptors?' he demanded.

Bill was unsure how to reply. He had a few capsules hidden away. But he was not about to give them to a man in Eddy's state.

'Maybe,' Bill said.

'Take ruptors – go Mingus – play Mingus,' Eddy exclaimed.

Bill could not resist the opportunity. If Eddy could metamorphosize into Mingus, it could give him an insight into the man. Maybe he could learn enough to crack the problem of the Mingus simulation.

There was a catch. Eddy insisted that Bill joined him and took the ruptors too. This dampened Bill's enthusiasm. But after a few seconds he thought, why not? I handled it before. I can do it this time.

He went to the kitchen and found the ruptor capsules. When he returned Eddy had taken his Stick out of its case and was idly strumming a random sequence of chords. He looked up and smiled. A change had come over him. He seemed calmer. Bill handed Eddy one of the capsules which he washed down with a cup of water. Bill did the same.

The drug took several minutes to take effect. At first Bill thought that they might not be the real thing. Maybe they weren't ruptors at all. But then he became aware of a change in the sound coming from Eddy's Stick. A persistent, rumbling bass riff, like a deep mantra, laid down a strange disjointed rhythm. Bill also noticed that Eddy seemed to be bigger, more bearlike. More Mingus-like.

Bill was then suddenly aware of the ruptor effect himself. He concentrated hard on Monk's DNA code and felt the transformation taking place. He'd been there before so he was ready for the change and he was prepared for the rich chaos of Monk's mindset. Eddy's Mingus riff developed into a recognizable melody. It was Bird's 'Now's the Time' – as it might have been played by Mingus.

Bill found himself laughing. Then shouting. He urged Eddy on to more complex improvisations. His hands danced up and down the polished wood of the Stick's fingerboard – complex flowing phrases tumbled one upon the other as he played faster and louder. *Buzz. Berzz . . .*

Bill jumped for joy – clapping his hands in sympathetic syncopation with Eddy's playing. Lost in wonder, removed from the world.

Buzz. Berzz . . .

Bill drifted into a dreamworld where the only dream was the music. The real thing.

Buzz Berzz . . .

4. Jive-assed slippers.

The videophone jerked Bill awake. Confused and disoriented he rubbed his eyes and gazed at the vidscreen. It was Luchenko.

'Where the hell is Battista?' she said between clenched teeth. 'You said you would bring him to my office today – it is now past midday. I want him here. Now,' she demanded.

Bill tried to speak but the words would not come – just grunts and meaningless sounds.

He was lost.

Who this woman? he think. Who Battista? he thinkmore

Luchenko continued to rail at him until he broke the connection by smashing the screen with Eddy's Stick.

Eddy lay on the floor, still. He was barely breathing.

Bill stood over him and tried to make some sense of what had happened. But he could not concentrate. His mind was full of musical notes, improvisations, expressions.

Eddy whispered and Bill leaned forward to hear him.

'Ruptored out – no Eddy Battista – Mingus now – Eddy dead.'

Bill was still lost. He could not remember who he was or what he was doing here with this dying man.

Eddy slowly moved his hand to a pocket in his aged jacket and pulled out a piece of paper.

'Take Mingus rights – pay Hockman– *you* Mingus now,' he said hoarsely.

Bill took the paper. It was a pawn ticket. He looked down at Eddy, still unaware of what he meant.

Eddy gurgled deep in his throat and tried to sit up. His eyes opened wide and his face broke into a smile.

'The shoes of the fisherman's wife are some jive-assed slippers,' he said and laughed.

The laugh made Eddy cough and his body convulsed one last time. He slumped back on the floor and was still.

Bill looked at the pawn ticket in his hand. Without thinking he placed Eddy's Stick into its case together with the remaining ruptor capsules, went to the wall safe behind the photograph of the Duke Ellington Orchestra, removed all of the cash and walked from the room.

Bill Hurrydown. See Hockman, Bill think.
Bill get Mingus Rights. Bill got legal rights.
Bill take ruptors. Turn Mingus. Play Mingus, Bill thinkmore

When Roxo and Luchenko eventually managed to break into Bill's apartment, all they found was Eddy's body. Luchenko searched him for clues to the whereabouts of the Mingus rights, but it was futile.

'Guess Mingus is off, then,' said Roxo.

Luchenko glared at him. She had never lost a copyright deal in her career and she was not about to let some muso bum cheat her out of this one.

'The man is dead – the legal position is somewhat confused. But I am sure that Honshu can find some way to lay a claim. After all we paid his bail. Perhaps Rogers can help us – if we can find him,' she said, more to herself than to Roxo.

Buzz. Berzz . . .
Bill outside C-Note. Crowd smile. Bill smile.
Bill ruptored. Turn Bird. Turn Mingus. Turn Monk.
Play buzz berzz . . .

TWISTER OF WORDS

Michael Fearn

Michael Fearn

Michael Fearn was born in Kendal, South Cumbria, in 1952. This is his first published story. Michael is a semi-professional musician, and was described recently by *Time Out* as being a 'guitarist of some repute'. It is therefore entirely logical that he lives in the East End of London and earns his living by teaching French in Orpington.

EARLIER, HE HAD been re-arranging his books. There was a monkish discipline to this activity: a task which was rendered real only by faith. The outcome would not threaten anyone's life, and the world in general would not notice if it were left undone. Now he wished he had the luxury for such a pursuit.

It went like this.

First, take all the books from the shelves which lined each wall of his two-roomed, prefabricated dwelling; tenderly, as some of them were centuries old and the youngest, at least fifty years. Make piles of them on the floor and select alternate books, placing ones similarly selected from other piles into the gaps thus created. Take piles from one room and exchange with those in the other. Re-shelve the books.

When it had still mattered, they had been classified by author and subject. It did not matter now, and he could please himself.

Time to play the game. Standing stock-still in the centre of the larger room, he closed his eyes. With his right arm extended at shoulder level and the index finger pointed, he advanced towards the shelves. When his finger touched the spine of a book, he would allow it to travel up the binding and would hook it out with his fingertip. He had read all his books many times, and he knew some of them by feel: the whole purpose of the exercise was to surprise himself.

Only at this point would he open his eyes. The inflexible dogma was that the book he touched, he would read. Today it was to be *Fahrenheit 451* by Bradbury.

Poor old Guy Montag. The fireman. Would anyone allow themselves to be burned alive for the sake of a book? The crushing loneliness that he himself had more in common with a literary character than any living being he had ever met, was sufficient to distract him from his present quandary, but only momentarily.

The Twister Of Words went out of his hut once more. God knew, he was trying not to despise his fellow men in their insular ignorance, but it was a struggle. How could he tell them?

> WARNING: TOTAL SYSTEM SHUTDOWN
> IMMINENT
> BACKUP MALFUNCTION
> SABOTAGE SUSPECTED
>
> All terminals must go off-line for indefinite period in 20hrs
> Message timed 15.17

There it was. Stark and final. The one message which the system had not been designed to carry. As notional head of his small community, it came to his terminal first, and no doubt to those who held similar office in other villages, scattered over what was now England, since the retreat. He could not speak for the rest of the world.

His terminal was always switched on under the control of the regional computer: part of the original planning of his role. Usually, he kept his coat draped over it, to cut out the annoying glow. He was much more likely to uncover it to get at his coat than to interact. He spent just enough time at his terminal for the mainframe to note that he was still alive, which kept the rations coming, with their medicated supplements. This was the pattern to which the rest of the residents adhered with a vegetable compliance. It was only on a thin day that *he* ate the uninspiring goo: there was game in plenty.

The placidity of a cow takes only several generations to breed out. The dogs and cats of the erstwhile cities seemed to be re-discovering an independence which would have appalled the owners of the previous pussy-cats and puppy-dogs. The dogs in particular appeared slowly to be reverting from the identifiable breeds which some of his books showed him to a uniform, mid-brown pariah. The animals were becoming, with each passing mating season, more ingenious in their means of threatening him. Their various howls, shrieks and ululations were growing in number and intensity faster than the undergrowth.

He, in his turn, was becoming more adept at cooking them. That afternoon, he had been sitting in the central clearing gutting and then spit-roasting a wild turkey on a contraption rigged up from a former, short-wave radio aerial resting on two ski poles. Early man with aluminium, washing the blood from his hands in the stream while his neighbours, he supposed, stared in fascination at their electronic thumb-sucker. Shivering slightly from the cold, he had returned to his hut for his coat and seen the message.

A population which had not had to think for itself for half a century. The prospect was terrifying.

Were he simply to knock on any door with the most benign of intents, he would be variously injured (and perhaps killed) by intruder defence systems of quite ingenious complexity. These were so inconspicuous that their owners had largely forgotten their existence. His had been switched off for decades. The original intent had been to ensure privacy, not isolation, as the cities had grown past their usefulness and had become, to paraphrase Le Corbusier, 'a machine for dying'. No one was quite sure when the mirror-image had become the reality. Through each window, an electronic glow flickered. Rarely did any of his neighbours leave their huts: habit had become taboo.

'Listen to me!' he screamed. He thought for one moment that he had established contact as a figure passed across a window. Then he heard the flushing of a toilet. It was now a few minutes past midnight.

There was no hope of outside assistance, for each in their turn, many factors ensured privacy. Taken together, the effect was complete. The decaying road whose surface was pitted with fissures large enough to cause the unwary to break an ankle; the unbroken green of the valley where once there had been a town, and the tall trees, which had always been there. Within their natural stockade of foliage each prefabricated, log-effect hut squatted in its own clearing, open to a central area. The only hut which could be approached by anything justly bearing the name 'path' was the one which was occupied by the holder of the hereditary office of Twister Of Words. Behind this hut, a path which was thoroughly overgrown led the way to a larger building, once the communal centre, with gymnasium and other facilities. It had always been under-used; these days, its sole function was as his storehouse.

The undergrowth was only slightly trampled by the passing of feet which had recently lost the last vestiges of a habit that had long been falling into disuse. When he was tired of reading and walks, he would attack the encroaching green with a pruning knife, but it was an unequal battle. This was something that the planners had never conceived of his being forced to do alone. His stewardship was imposed by the detachment of the others, and whilst their world had contracted, his had expanded. In his more whimsical moments, he had even trifled with rudimentary topiary.

There had originally been twelve families: now only five huts were occupied. Just the previous week he had cleared a sixth of its dead and decomposing occupant, who had stopped interacting with her terminal. (In a recent storm, a falling bough had smashed the satellite dish on her roof. Therefore, the food had stopped too.)

He was, in theory, the safety-valve. The local supervisor who was librarian, teacher, doctor, mechanic, priest and diplomat: the person who had to remain skilled in pre-tech means of communication, just in case. His little community had decided to call theirs the 'Twister of Words', and this seemed quite natural to him. In earlier communities, the barrel-maker had been called 'cooper', and this would have been his chief form of address unless he met another of his trade, and the need to differentiate were created. He didn't suppose he would ever meet any of his counterparts in all the other thousands of scattered communities.

The life-style management packages did not leave a hole big enough for the passage of something so insignificant as the human voice. The regional mainframe co-ordinated all practical needs. The national central computer was in over-all charge. Each dwelling had its terminal, and the life-style packages contained embedded instructions continually to update themselves through interaction with the user. But for him, the immutable reality of books was better. A fire! Montag again. Surely they would notice a fire? He went to the recently cleared hut and built a fire of dry branches in the centre of the floor. Central 'thought' the occupant was dead, so the sprinkler would be off. He lit it with a brand from his cooking fire. The synthetic floor-coverings and furniture caught immediately. Within minutes a fire burned which would be visible miles away. He reeled back against the heat and huddled to the ground. For an hour or more he watched the violent orange flames and covered his mouth to mask the reek of dense black smoke from bubbling plastics. Nothing.

Burdens. Duties. Was he the only person who recalled that he had ever had any? His father had told him what these duties were. He was the fail-safe. When the retreat from the cities had come, common sense had dictated that someone should continue to care about words: someone who could communicate face-to-face. Someone who knew the difference between 'imply' and 'infer', and could manipulate language in a manner that no computer would ever be able to.

'Log on, Twister,' they had said when they wanted to talk to him. Life was just one enormous electronic fantasy to them. Too much technology resting on too little knowledge.

'A computer is just a tool,' he had told them. 'Like any other tool, it amplifies human effort. If the knowledge is not there, it can only amplify ignorance.' His father had said the same, many times in his hearing. The teachers and the librarians had been giving the same, unpalatable message down the ages.

'Look,' he had said. 'I have books. I have knowledge. Let me read to you: read yourselves. This is beautiful. Knowledge is power.' One by one, their eyes had glazed, and they had returned to their terminals.

'What does it matter?' they had argued. 'What's one book more or less? Can we see the ideas? Do they deliver our food? The service tube from Central does that. All that business about human emotions and passions. Look where that got us! You seem to forget that some of us can remember what it was like. People living on top of each other to the point of saturation. Why do you think we worked out this way of life? Stop being an old spoilsport and throw the books away. They won't do you any good. Or get a package tailored to your particular, peculiar needs, if you must, but leave us alone. We've made our choice. The screens tell us what we need to know. If we need anything from you, we'll tell you.'

Men plan, and life is what happens whilst they do it. The vulcanologist or the seismologist fails to predict the eruption or the quake. The new disease defeats the scientist, because he wasn't expecting it. It simply was not one of the range of available options. No one had expected that computers would eventually dismember the society it had taken thousands of years to establish. Cybernetics and AIDS had helped.

Let's work from home. There isn't any need to go to the office or factory.

Let's order our food from home.

Let's not go out. 'Outside' is an arbitrary place, and can be dangerous.

No doubt there were some people, somewhere, who had never seen a terminal. So what? A very good reason for each step down the ladder, until you can't see over the wall at all. Just as the alcoholic or compulsive eater has a sufficient reason to justify each binge. There had simply been a slow ebbing of commitment.

There was little observable difference between this occasion upon which he had been left alone with his thoughts and any other. He was doubly isolated from those for whom it was his theoretical, hereditary duty to speak and negotiate. The wild outcasts of literature were in a more fortunate position than he was. It had pleased him in the past to identify with Peake's Sourdust: a necessary if only semi-comprehensible part of life's fabric. He was about to try something which would give more chance of his inheriting the mantle of Mr Flay: the use of his operator privilege for an attempt at direct interference.

> Entry code
> Into the net
> Through the gate and
> IN

On the screen before him, he saw a pattern which was geometrically regular if one looked at the entire screen, but was endlessly sub-dividing itself to produce smaller copies. A virus.

His father might have known what to do: he did not. In impotent rage, he considered kicking the screen, but instead simply flung his coat over it again in a gesture which made him feel better because it was dismissive: but one which he recognized immediately as being born of desperation. This was the most accessible part of the system. The 'bread and circuses' portion was far more heavily protected against outside interference from those who still clung to the old order of things, albeit moribund.

Once more, he ran out of the hut: as the afternoon and evening progressed, the walk turned into a run. Within him two contrary drives were beginning to produce their own imperatives. Self-preservation and responsibility. The former was quite clear and visceral, the second less so. If a tree falls unseen in a forest, is it a real event? If you have a duty and no one knows or cares, is it a duty?

There might have been just one possibility of achieving contact: he had seen her several times on nocturnal wanderings. There would be swift clatter of twig against twig and a chattering of leaf on leaf. He would look to the source of this and see a startled face; younger than his and female. With the speed of a rocketing pheasant she would run back to her hut, her path being marked by a wake of swaying vegetation. He knew that she was the only member of the small community to have a child – a boy – who would be of the first generation to be born to this purely internalized existence. His parents would at least have had a memory of something else from their own youth before the arteries of such limited social intercourse as there was had hardened with the sclerosis of habitual privacy. From the window of her hut, a bluish light flickered, as it did in the windows of all the others.

The Twister Of Words had no successor, and had cherished hopes of the child. In his own lifetime, he could remember his father talking to the others as he had years ago. He could remember playing with other children in the clearing, and speaking to other adults. His mother was the vaguest of memories, as she had died when he was an infant: even the best of systems has its failures. He could still have conducted the necessary computer searches of nearby villages, followed by the compulsory medical screening, which was a part of the marriage procedure. But shortly after his father had died, the others began to come out less and less frequently.

What was this feeling? Panic? He supposed that it must be. For so long there had been nothing sufficiently urgent even to warrant an element of hurry. For the umpteenth time in the previous few hours, he made the rounds. Systematically, he threw a clod or twig or stone at the door of each dwelling, only to see it vapourized by the intruder systems. No matter how close to failure the collective might be, the individual elements were still working to full efficiency.

The muscles at the bottom of his ribcage began to clench, and he heard heartbeats, singly, loud in his ears. Fighting for control, he tried to breathe deeply. The Twister Of Words re-entered his hut and uncovered the terminal. The individual parts of the lattice were now sub-divided to the point at which they simply seemed to be pulsating dots. He threw his coat over the screen again and sat in the middle of the floor. The sound he produced was a sort of sub-vocal keening, and when he realized that he was doing it, he made himself stop.

He stood, panting, even though he had not exerted himself physically at all. There had to be some way to make them take notice. The cables! They had ignored the fire, but if all of a sudden their beloved screens went blank and there was still some time to go, some time to prepare them; well then perhaps he could do something. The power cables were buried a few feet deep. If he could temporarily disconnect one dwelling, at least there would be some chance. He had an axe, and he fetched a shovel. He dug, glorying in the fact that physical exertion blunts anxiety. There it was, about a metre down. He climbed into the hole, and swung the axe again and again, but his strokes became less muscular as he saw that the shielding for the cable, whatever it was, showed not a scratch. He threw the axe with all his power and it vanished into the lower branches of an overhanging tree. He returned to his dwelling and sat inside the door. Temporary exhaustion at least gave him the option of sitting still.

From the door, there was a soft thud which subsided into a series of small skitterings. He had not quite closed the door and, as he watched, it swung back slightly, and then returned a fraction.

Trembling, he stood. He had expected to see an animal retreating under the gloom. One of the feral dogs, perhaps: maybe the brown-and-white one whose curious nature made it a frequent visitor to the area around his dwelling and which he had hoped to tempt with scraps.

Certainly, this was no dog. She stood on the bottom step, her face only semi-visible in the cloud-filtered moonlight.

'Who are you?' he asked. Of course, to him, the sound of his own voice was familiar, but it was invested with a different quality of purpose when reflected from another. The coat disguised her slight figure, as she stood just within the doorway. Her hair was brown with streaks of grey. Her eyes were blue, and looked as though they had seen too much. Later, he would try to recall more precise details of her first appearance to him and find himself unable: one does not register straight away what one does not expect to see.

'I'm Speaker,' she replied. 'I saw your fire.' Her voice was light and strange but immediately comprehensible. She sank to the floor next to her bag: he saw that this was no more than a tied blanket.

'I've been walking for half a day,' she said. 'Mine won't talk to me at all.'

Then she cried, great wretching sobs which made her shoulders heave. He had never seen anyone cry before.

Of course, it had been clear to her that he was her counterpart, for there was in her village no other hut than hers of which the door was ever open. She told him that the detection system in one of her huts had broken down, and that this had allowed her to talk to one man. He had simply yelled at her and slammed the door in her face, splitting her left eyebrow. Now that she was inside he could see that a bloody bruise was rising there.

Together, they repeated the previous steps of shouting and throwing. Two could make more noise than one, but the collective lack of response was thereby rendered doubly tragic, and they had to stop.

Inside again, Speaker asked, 'What can we do?'

'We are powerless.'

'How did they dare do it?' she said bitterly. 'It's too much to bear.'

'You read, don't you? You must know that, basically, nothing ever has worked.' The temptation to indulge in the sybaritic luxury of discussing books with the first human being he had met for more than a fleeting second for what must have been a decade at least was almost too strong to bear. He was familiar from his reading with hundreds of conversations between men and women. With this other person, he would happily have discussed the most mundane subject. Addressing another human being at all was an experience the texture of which he lacked the words to express.

Taking her cue from his evident confusion, she said, 'You've no idea how I have longed to talk to somebody. Now this has happened, and there's no time. Ironic, isn't it?'

In the growing half-light, they once more rehearsed the available strategies. Possibly there would be other settlements nearby where a colleague might have arrived at a solution? It was their only possible course of action. They set out together, and Twister took them in a direction indicated on a yellowing map his father had once shown him, with the locations of two other villages marked upon it. She had shamed him into action by doing what he had not had the courage to do; to leave and to seek help.

Looking back towards his village, he saw from a distance that it looked so calm and normal: he might just have been off on another walk. As these were usually circular rather than linear, he had never seen Speaker's village.

At the first collection of huts, slightly larger than either of their own villages, the familiar pattern repeated itself. One hut stood apart from the others, and they threw grit at the door; no defences. In the corner, the terminal displayed the familiar message. The occupant, male, was still just recognizable as human. The dogs had been more successful here.

'Is it really worth going on?' he asked her, as they sat by the shattered road picking turkey bones. There had been very little conversation.

'I couldn't live with myself if we didn't even try,' she replied.

The second village contained a communicator who was
certainly still alive. He stared at them from his doorway.
He held what looked like a stick in his hand, but when
it cracked and flashed, they realized that it was a gun,
although neither had seen one before. The shot went wide,
and the man screamed, 'I'm ready for you. You'll never
take me. I've failed? You've failed. No one could . . . '

Suddenly, he seemed to lose interest in them. He turned
to face the rest of the village and waved his arms at it,
giving forth a bellow which cost him every particle of
breath. Then, straightening up, he put the gun into his
mouth and pulled the trigger. By the time they looked
around, the dogs were already at their grisly business. They
watched, sickened, as a pack of some thirty led by a large,
black male slunk from the bushes and began to feast.

There was now no point in continuing. No other villages
were marked, and they did not have time to hunt further.
A two-hour walk took them back to Twister's village and
they sat in the clearing. There was only an hour to go.

They recognized despair when they saw it, and the
decision made itself.

They had reached the top of a nearby hill before they
heard the first screams.

THE MECHANICAL ART

Andy Sawyer

Andy Sawyer

Andy Sawyer works as a librarian and is married with two daughters. He says that 'The Mechanical Art' was written 'in a kind of collaboration with the same seventeenth century writer who provided lyrics for the Beatles' *Abbey Road* album'. During the last four years he has completed a thesis on Jacobean pamphlet literature, edited *Paperback Inferno* for the British Science Fiction Association, and started on his first novel.

HENSLOWE SWORE, GULPED the dregs of a liquid which had once been wine, and cursed some more. When you need a poet, there's not one which will bring his stinking skin within a mile of the Rose. The Admiral's Men were whining for a play on the subject of Troilus and Cressida. Chettle's greasy body was sweating in the Marshalsea. Munday was probably sniffing around another rich recusant to collect a dedication gift for a pamphlet and an informer's fee from the church authorities. Day and Hathway – who knew where they were and without someone like Chapman (already scribbling another comedy) and Jonson (foul drunk and temperamental) to do their thinking for them they were worse than useless. Dekker was lying very low since he had been discovered by the Admiral's Men adapting one of their Civil War plays for the Chamberlain's, and by the Chamberlain's Men accepting money from Henslowe for the same. Word had it he was to be arrested: Henslowe noted down a memorandum concerning the sum paid and pondered for a moment about rescuing the poet.

'Master Downton says . . . ' Rafe called from the doorway, but Henslowe already knew what the player had told his servant, and let loose another avalanche of oaths. Let players find their own plays: who was he to organize their trade for them? Landlord and banker, wasn't that enough?

'Am I expected to hawk around every tavern and stew in London to find someone sober enough to use a quill?' he bellowed. 'You, Rafe – find me Drayton or Houghton or . . . '

Rafe scurried outside, only to return accompanied by a stranger bearing a box the size of a church bible. 'I beg your pardon, Master Henslowe, but this gentleman craves audience.'

Henslowe glared. Those who work in playhouses either fancy themselves as comedians or become natural buffoons. 'Craves audience?' Rafe's spotted face showed no sign of a smile, which meant that he was either a fool or dumbly insolent. Neither could be overlooked. Unfortunately it was easier to deal with Rafe than the baggage he brought with him. A quick buffet sent Rafe clattering down the stairs with Henslowe's orders to wait until called for following. The visitor, who had gazed upon the comedy in silence but with obvious interest, limped towards Henslowe's table, and the owner of the Rose turned his attention towards him, suspicious of his looks, his carriage, and above all of the contraption he carried.

He was young; confident bearing hiding the fact that he was in search of favours and a little unsure how he would be received. No doubt he was another country gentleman with literary ambitions, bearing an unreadable play badly translated from a poetaster of old Rome. 'If it's scribbling you wish to make your profession, you must speak with the players,' Henslowe growled.

The young man limped closer, shifted his burden in his arms, and smiled. His calmness irritated Henslowe, who received the arrogance of his social superiors with equanimity, recognizing it for what it was: a cloak for their own feelings of inferiority. Too often, he was in a position of power, and they hated it, these young Juvenals with their university degrees and threadbare clothing, grovelling to the mob with their ill-matched verses, restating for the theatre lines which had been peddled around every minor noble or wealthy merchant in the City, despising their calling and their audience and justifying their gore-and-guts plots with the name of 'art'. The smiles of Gentlemen told Henslowe that they wanted his money and despised him for being in a position to offer it.

He spat. Judging the level of rudeness he could get away with with this sprig, he grunted 'Well?' and remained standing while refraining from indicating a seat to the visitor. The smile broadened. 'Is he playing with me?' thought Henslowe.

'I am no scholar nor poet, Master Henslowe, and I have come to you rather than the players for that reason. You know players better than I do, but am I not correct in believing that they are not the most ... responsible of creatures?'

'You mean?' There was something about this youth that was not correct. Not his approach – if he were not a poet nevertheless he was selling something and Henslowe was chapman enough to revel in the stimulation of bargaining – but something ...

'I mean that players, unlike we more practical men, are apt to drink tomorrow's good shillings in the shape of today's lousy pence ... '

(Was it the beard? Neatly trimmed and dandified, it hung on the man's face like something unused to its place. He was stroking it like a goldsmith's wife caressing her lapdog.)

' ... and would not necessarily welcome advice which is to their benefit, were it never so sparing of their time and purses.'

(No, it was the clothing: well-decked garments of a cut not too out of fashion; the garb of any ambitious but needy youth. Cloak passed down from My Lord Such-and-such in lieu of silver for too-flattering verses, over-worn doublet which yet suggested that once the wearer could swear at a tailor with the best of them. Most gallant-like frills circled his wrists and wide-topped fringed boots showed garish enough linings to shout to all that they were new. But the contrast with the crimson cross-gartering, green stockings and Venetian breeches made Henslowe ill; no wonder the boy was hobbling like a diseased mare, with scarce-cured leather around his feet. Twenty or more St Pauls loungers could have summed up this single one as their type to the life. His mingle-mangle of fashions and colours included a

huge cartwheel ruff at least ten years old serving his head
up on a plate which was, God's bollocks, *clean*. Yes, that
was it. Patched and worn the clothes might be but he'd not
been wearing them long, despite appearances. The boots
stank of Bankside mud, true enough, but no kites or crows
had beshat cloak or bonnet. Henslowe bet himself there
was neither tick nor flea in the entire apparel.)

'And so I come to you, Master Henslowe, knowing your
reputation as a man who deals firmly and fairly and who
would recognize one who would spare you and the players
your main cause of travail and despair.'

A man who lied like a poet but certainly did not smell
like one! Even a tradesman must have entertainment. 'Rafe!
Wine for myself and Master . . . ?'

'Hudson.'

'Be seated, Master Hudson, and go on.'

Running a finger inside his ruff as if to ease itching skin,
the youth eased himself on to a stool. He sipped gingerly
at the sour wine the still-whimpering Rafe brought on
a filthy tray. His smile was more natural, despite his
signs of physical discomfort. He has crossed the first
hurdle, thought Henslowe. Let us see what he makes of
his chance now.

'I would ask you, Master Henslowe, if I may – I could
not help but notice a certain – irritation – in you at first.'

'That, sir, is mine own business.'

'Ah, but it could be that it is also mine. Let me explain.
What are players and their companies constantly in need
of?'

'Besides booze and the pox? New plays, I'd say, to woo
groundlings and gallants alike, and perhaps feed the whims
of the Court. What's the purpose of this catechism?'

'And who writes these plays? Nay – be not impatient,
I'll answer this question for you. Raw scholars who can
Latinise their neck-verse but can scarce lisp a greeting
to a maid in English. Drunkards who boast that they
are poets when in truth they are flea-bitten balladeers
in search of patrons to gull. Scurvy pamphleteers who

spurn their readers as ignorant stinkards and beg to libel their comrades for a shilling. Not so?'

Henslowe laughed. 'Are you sure you're no poet? You draw your fellows perfectly, but I still have no work for you.'

'Not for me, Master Henslowe; but you have work for this that I bring with me.'

The box placed on Henslowe's table was opened. Whatever was inside it was unrecognizable. A musical instrument? It had keys. A hornbook? There was a sheet of half-transparent material below a slot at the top, but this was blank. The keys were themselves lettered, but ordered according to no alphabet Henslowe had ever seen. He squinted and shook his head. *Explain*, his hand waved.

'I know you are a busy man. The players need additions and new scenes and are spurring you to find them playwrights. Chettle is once more imprisoned for his debts, Dekker arrested by the Chamberlain's Men . . . '

'So they've moved? Well, that would be no secret. You *are* trying to become a poet.'

Hudson ignored the sneer in the last word. ' . . . and you see the problem becoming worse when you open your new Theatre.'

Henslowe's paralysis lasted only a moment. His fingers clutched at Hudson's cloak and pulled him across the table. He saw small globules of spittle fly into the youth's face as he shouted 'How do you know about that?'

Violence was as useless as sarcasm. White-faced but still self-possessed, Hudson loosened the bigger man's grip. Henslowe drained his cup and regained his seat, watching Hudson smooth his clothes.

'How I know what I know is not very important. What *is* important is the fact that there is work for players. But players, Master Henslowe, need . . . plays? Yet, as we've said, playwrights are unreliable fellows. They disappear and return too drunk to work, find themselves convenient lordlings who will pay more for a sonnet or two of arse-licking than you can offer for a scene or soliloquy.

If the Company had in its rooms – or, even better, *you* had in *yours* – a poet which would remain as long as wanted, would do *nothing* but write, and write to taste and order . . . '

'And not sulk and complain about Muses and Fame?'

'Aye. Well look again,' Hudson tapped the box. 'Because here it is.'

Henslowe studied the device on his table. He was beginning to become irritated once more with all this beating around the bush and veiled hints that Hudson knew his business better than he himself, and that some magic box held the key to all his problems. He knew machinery. He had men working for him who were artisans and craftsmen. But *this* . . . 'This is – I know not what,' he finished weakly.

'Let me explain. Suppose you wish for a new scene in a play. There is a fashion of gallantry at which you wish to mock, or one who has deserved laughter from the crowd. The players hire a poet to crank out verses on the subject. Sometimes this may even make a new play in itself, sometimes not. But the poet will want his pence, for however small an expenditure of ink.'

'True.'

'Choose then a subject.'

Henslowe thought. 'The bald pate of the Chamberlain's Men's scribbler,' he offered, and wondered why Hudson laughed immoderately.

'So. We imagine that this box – which is, in truth, merely an ingenious device which apes the poet, but apes him to perfection – is *our* scribbler. Place him in light: this is important. True sunlight is best, but on dull days and after sunset you may set candles aflame and this will have the same effect. We awaken him by means of this button here' – a jab of a finger caused a red light to glow like a jewel – 'and we give him a theme: a bald pate. Do you – ?'

Henslowe waved aside the offer and watched as Hudson pressed what at first had seemed to be the keys of a small pair of virginals. 'I wish this to be witty rather than tragic, so I press – here. You may, of course, adjust this setting according to the decorum of your language: and – thus . . . '

There was a faint clicking noise like the turning of a far-away treadmill and from the slot in the top of the device rose a sheet of paper of unsurpassed clarity and smoothness. Henslowe gasped. And on this . . .

Oh sirs, how foul a bald man's pate appears!
Like to a face without a nose, or like
Ground eaten bare with archers' arrows. Sirs,
A head all hid in hair gives to a face
(Wicked though it be) sweet proportion;
A meadow newly married to the Spring.
But when the meadow's mown by sunburnt clowns,
As if a barber shaves it to the stumps,
The grass (hair of the Earth) soon fades and dies;
Good only to be dried and trussed for jades.

'Stop.' Hudson pressed another button. 'Tell me something a poet must always be writing.'

'A revenge speech?' suggested Henslowe, bemused by what he had just seen.

Fingers flashed. 'Be clear about what you want, as if you were writing to one who can only half-read. But it will understand many different spellings of the same word.'

But should I strike? Or should I sheathe my blade?
If one, the play is over, signed with blood
And to the press I take my sweet revenge.
If other, Mercy seems to stay my hand;
But Mercy looks upon a hollow skull
And sees with th'inner eye the once fair flesh
That covered it – ah! I kiss these lips again
And Mercy bids me swear like Machiavel
To sheathe my blade but seek to lull my prey
And strike – and strike – but when the coney's mind
Hath quite forgot the reason for's death.

As Henslowe stumbled through the lines, Hudson rapped the table to emphasize his words. 'This can be yours! There is an engine inserted inside this case which will print as many copies as you like in whatever print you require. Look, why do you need time and money spent on scriveners – who will keep a copy for themselves and one for the print-shop – when you yourself can decide how many copies of play or part you need? Each player who can read can have his own part to learn. Each gallant who wants to hobble through the play in his own lodgings will come to *you*, not a thieving Stationer. Let Paul's Walks sell bibles and sermons: those who want plays must come to the playhouses.'

'But a man must write a play?'

'In what fashion? What man can do, can not an artifice in the fashion of a man's brain do likewise? Are not the Enginous Wheels of the soul continually going, though a man lie never so fast in slumber?'

Henslowe tried to put his finger on the flaw in that conceit, but before he could open his mouth, Hudson was in full flow. 'A man's arms have cords and strings within them, do they not? And at the end of the arms, are two beautiful mathematical instruments' – flapping hands barely missed overturning his wine-goblet – 'with five several motions in each' – he could have been a juggler warming up for his act – 'with, it could be, thirty other moving engines within by which these hands are caused to move. If a man can be likened to this, cannot an engine – here, in this container – be likened to a man?'

He has been listening to Master Dekker in his cups, thought Henslowe, but, intrigued by the idea of someone taking this notion seriously, and lacking another explanation of what he had seen, he could only nod and wait for the persuasion to reach its crescendo.

'Inside here are the forms and, as it were, *memories before the time* of all possible plays, ready to be given life at the touch of a key. Tell the device by means of a simple cypher – which I will teach you – what kind of play you need – tragedy, comedy, history, pastoral, pastoral-comical, historical-pastoral, tragical-historical . . . '

(If there was a joke there, Henslowe missed it.)

' . . . and which characters you wish – King, Queen, Vice, Clown – name them, as much or little of a plot as you can think of – and in minutes, a play! And if you later require additions – a prologue for the court, an extra speaker: as we have seen, they will be done for you!

'You may tell the machine for whom you wish it to write – Court, City gallants, or your everyday groundlings. And all this from just one device. No importuning 'prentice playmaker whining for a shilling or two on account before he starts writing, or excuses about the Muse not visiting him two hours before the play is due to commence.'

Henslowe pondered, sitting back and picking his nails. What he had seen and heard would seem unbelievable to most men, but he thought it through. Unlettered peasants and scholars who had spent their time with the occult arts would have cried 'sorcery', but why? Such a common thing as a plough is, of course, merely an amplification of a man's strength. Is a printing press no more than an amplification of a scrivener's quill? Why *not* a device which also amplified the workings of a man's imagination? Poets might complain, and starve, but would it not serve them right, especially those who tried to pass themselves off as gentlemen and despised him because he was a dyer by trade, and condescended to the players who paid them because they were 'rude mechanicals'? But poets were paid servants, and the base-born players the masters who owned what they produced. So which was the mechanical art? Players would be in demand until the world's end, but if they could be served by more reliable servants . . .

Henslowe scratched his beard and cracked a louse. He noted Hudson's shudder. So he disgusted this fancy upstart, did he?

'Who are you, and where are you from?'

'Why – I am merely a tradesman. Like yourself. And I am from London. Again, like yourself.' This was a plain lie. Hudson spoke well, but a faint accent coloured his words, unlike any Henslowe had ever heard. Still, he let that pass.

'And this device will feed plays to the players?'

The thought was tempting. Let them quibble over his control of the Rose's purse-strings then! They would *have* to come to him, and be given what would attract an audience.

'Yes. But I must warn you; the opportunity for buying it comes once only. There are . . . reasons why I cannot return after this visit. And there are many playwrights who would be interested in this device, who are not here in London at this time, whom I must see.'

(All the playwrights Henslowe knew were in the City somewhere, but he let that second lie – obviously manufactured to make it seem there was great demand for Hudson's machine – pass also.)

'I have already sold one of these to My Lord Chamberlain's Men. Their balding playwright welcomed it with great enthusiasm.'

'Wait, wait. You have not mentioned a price.'

'Shall we say – for a device which will give you easily an hundred plays or parts – we will make a bargain for which you shall pay me earnest of – fifty pounds?'

Fifty pounds was more than twice any one of the Admirals' men's scribblers earned in a year, but far less than for what Henslowe himself would have sold such a marvellous instrument. At first, he could not see the catch. But suspicion was his stock-in-trade . . .

'In earnest of what?'

'Of a further sum to be paid in ten years' time, when I shall return and we will account together concerning how much this device has saved your friends the players.'

'Ten years?' Henslowe furrowed his brow. 'We could both be dead by then. Why so long? I do not wish to burden my heirs with debts to thee.'

'Your heirs will still be waiting for your riches in ten years,' said Hudson. He flushed. 'I mean . . . I see that you are a healthy man. And there are — reasons — why I cannot return to this place within ten years. But we can cast accounts at the end of that time. You may wish to pay for each part or each completed play, or pay another sum entire at the end of the ten years. Shall we bargain?'

'So how would you *know* how much and what has been written by this box?'

Hudson stammered like a flummoxed ploughboy confronted by his maid. 'We know each time this device operates: that is, each composition is recorded . . . '

'Recorded? How?'

'I'm not sure I can explain . . . '

When people selling you something assumed you ignorant in one thing, Henslowe reflected, it usually meant that they thought you too ignorant overall to know if you were being cheated. This, however, was the value of his position regarding the Admiral's Men. With no direct connection with the plays, he could treat every transaction purely as a matter of commerce. The players' shareholders may have thought of themselves as hard bargainers, but wave a Court appearance or a titled patron at them and they went as weak at the knees as any vagabond actor with dreams of greatness.

Henslowe's contemptuous stare offered Hudson a choice of withdrawing or testing his opponent's capacity for understanding. Haltingly, he began to repeat alchemical saws about correspondences between microcosm and macrocosm, how just as the interior workings of the human body were reflected in the vastness of the Universe, causing the astrological connection between the Stars and Mankind, so the workings in the mysterious interior of the artificial poet currently resting on Henslow's table corresponded to what seemed to be a larger and more complex version of the same in which reflections of work done by and within each individual box were mirrored in one central and metaphysical mind . . .

As Hudson babbled his words began to sound suspiciously like priestcraft, but it was not so much that

which bothered Henslowe – there were no witnesses after
all, which meant that he could always produce a well-fed
eavesdropper if it came to a dispute before Authority – as
the fact that he genuinely had lost understanding of what
the man was talking about.

If Hudson had got this far with the Chamberlain's Men,
no wonder he'd secured a bargain! They always assumed
that audiences enjoyed leaving performances bemused by
such verbal emblems and chop-logic. One thing, however,
seemed to be ominously clear.

'So what I ask this box to write appears elsewhere?'

'No – well, that is to say, not in the form you see it but as
a record of what and how much has been composed so both
you and I can agree on a sum owing on my return . . . '

Henslowe stood. When a bargainer repeats himself, now
is the time to simulate anger and drive the price down a
notch or two.

'Answer my question, youth! *Who* sees this writing?'

More stammering. 'Myself. My . . . my Lord. And one
or two scholars.'

Henslowe's anger turned real. 'Scholars!' He knew what
this meant. University wits desperate to be poets because
they could find no other use for their festering minds
was one thing, and that bad enough, but Fellows and
pedants with their inquiring scorn were quite another.
Scholars meddled with plays either to find ammunition
with which to attack playhouses as seditious or sinful, or
to supply printers with ill-copied sheets to be sold to Lords
and 'prentices too lazy to attend performances.

Scholars and playhouses rarely mixed well.

Allow them the chance and they'll always give themselves away. Henslowe's guffaw filled the room. 'Copies
to scholars! Aye, and have all the plays on the Stationers'
stalls before the playhouse opens! Off with you, Master
Hudson, if that *is* your name, before I decide that it's
sorcery you're peddling with your ideas of minds in boxes
and cunning engines and plays magically sent to where
you come from by alchemy! Whether this be a trick to

steal plays, or merely to cozen fifty pounds from me, I'm no bird to stoop to your lure.'

'I can assure you – '

'Leave my playhouse!' Hudson had, gentleman-like, a sword hanging at his waist, but he did not use it. Instead, he babbled as Henslowe forced him to the door – 'You don't understand, damn you, the copies won't even be in this *time*!' – made a last placatory gesture, and almost dropped his box in his leap to escape Henslowe's foot.

The stairs rattled as Hudson departed, but Henslowe was already pacing his room again, addressing himself to his problem. *Troilus* still required new lines. At the moment, he would have called upon Doctor Dee and his Black Arts to come up with a reliable spirit: a box which produced players' lines mechanically might have been useful at that, and for a moment Henslowe regretted his abrupt words.

Still, on his release, Dekker could do the work of Hudson's device, and cheaper. Could a brain in a box be to its Master as a living human being with his wants and failings which could be played on? If he paid for Dekker's release, and gave him the work, he'd get the money back from the playwright (he'd make sure of that!) and have a useful bond of obligation over the poet. He scribbled notes: Chettle could be released immediately and Dekker could simmer in anxiety for a while. Then the two could be put to work.

No machine could resent servitude as much as a man.

Henslowe glanced again at the paper the contraption had spewed forth. So far as he could tell, the verses were doggerel of the worst kind. That never harmed a play, though. He would recount the conversation to Dekker and show him the verses. Perhaps he could do something with them.

LAST CAME ASSIMILATION

Storm Constantine

Storm Constantine

Storm Constantine is the author of the Wraeththu trilogy, *The Enchantments of Flesh and Spirit*, *The Bewitchments of Love and Hate* and *The Fulfilments of Fate and Desire*. Her most recent novel is *The Monstrous Regiment* (Futura), and she is working on further novels. Her short stories have appeared in David Garnett's *Zenith* anthologies and Rachel Pollack and Caitlín Matthews' *Tarot Tales*. She defines herself as a translator of baroque reflections from Indra's Net. An ontological guerrilla in the information war, she is currently inspired by the Revolting Cocks' musical mania and the No Coincidences Dept.

'OLA, CAN YOU never wait for anything?' Con Redley flamboyantly punched his terminal exit pads and swung around in his body-cupping seat. Ola was impatiently drumming her fingers against the wall wearing an exaggerated expression of irritation. 'It will be your downfall, Ola!'

'Some of us have work to do tonight, Redley. If you'd spent less time wagging your jaw today, you might be ready to leave on time.'

'Ah, my little Ola,' he said, jumping up and brushing her swiftly retreating cheek with casual fingers. 'Don't complain, I left the seat warm for you.'

Ola grimaced and slid fussily into the formacurl chair, her fingers reaching greedily for the micro-pad as if she'd been away from it too long. Con Redley knew she didn't enjoy having to share her 'place' with anyone. Ola's brusque impatience was one of the many standing jokes around the Centre and had given rise to the expression 'Uh-oh, I can feel an Ola Embeleny coming on!' to signify irritation at some system hold-up or another. Ola was mildly amused by this; she was conscientious but far from easily offended.

The day-time shift gradually left the building, chatting together in groups, shrugging themselves into fleecy jackets, speaking of rendezvous in local bars. Ola listened with satisfaction to their fading voices, calling out one or two last goodbyes, before settling comfortably into her chair and leaning back for a moment's relaxation. She breathed in deeply, taking in the smoky sweetness of Incoce's vapourous exhalations far above her head. Recess 920, a vast chamber other than its name implied, also seemed to breathe a sigh of relief, as if welcoming the quiet and solitude of night. One by one, the overhead lights dimmed to blackness, allowing the more pellucid gleam of low-glow nightlights to bloom around Ola's terminal; the only one still on-line at this hour. Ola stretched and hopped up to fetch herself a coffee from the dispenser by the door. Sipping, she leaned over her chair and stroked her initiate pad. *How can I help you?* Incoce asked, its usual polite greeting. Beneath this, it shyly offered the options of 'Interrogate', 'Check' or 'Fill'. 'Hi there, Inc. What kind of a day have you had, eh?' The computer terminal blinked its soft blue lights as if in perplexity. Ola slid back into her seat and tapped in her response. 'Check, please, Inc. Let's see what the data-shovels have fed you today, huh?' Swiftly, as if greeting an old friend, Incoce asked for her authorization code, which she supplied with one hand, still sipping the hot, sweet, vaguely-synthetic tasting liquid from her cup. As Overnight Shift Recess supervisor, Ola had to check the day's input for obvious errors before beginning her own work each night. It wasn't much of a chore; Incoce knew enough by now to recognize most mistakes itself. In fact, Ola was sure it seemed to take a certain pleasure in displaying them to her: *Look what I've found. Aren't I good?* Wriggling blue lines played across her face as Incoce skipped through the day's text. Ola twisted a few strands of hair between her fingers, not really looking that hard. A niggling anxiety had slipped back into her mind which she'd been trying to dismiss since waking up that afternoon. She sighed through her teeth and murmured, 'Lancy, Lancy,' before abruptly leaning forward, stroking a pause pad and switching to vocal command. Often she forgot to do that, taking it for granted the machine heard and understood her anyway. If it did, it was cunning enough not to let on – ever. 'What was that, Incoce, back a bit.' The wriggling lines wriggled backwards. 'Ass-hole!' The screen flared brighter for a moment at her outburst. She had found an error. Timely. It conveniently pushed from her attention the problem of Lancy Lefarr and it would be at least another day before Ola found time to think about it again.

Incoce (an acronym of Information Collection Centre) was an impressive sleek bulk possessed of massive memory banks. The machine had been diverted far from its original purpose, and expanded and improved because of that, even if a lot of people thought it a rather gross and outmoded model. Its home was the small, congenial world of Brickman, named for the Senior Administrator, Osmund Brickman, who'd headed the team first arriving on the planet. Now centuries dead, Brickman's name and his machine lived on, if not the scheme towards which he had dedicated himself and whose collapse had been partially, if not wholly, responsible for his own. Incoce had originally been designed as the thinking mind, administration centre and personnel department behind OFEx Project, a grand plan to mine the dozen or so worlds circulating Rover's Star of fliridium. Back then, the mineral had been newly discovered and had engendered enormous excitement owing to the fact that it appeared to be a powerful energy source of limitless life and without any radioactive crustings whatsoever. Initial excitement, glee and vast financial outlay had withered to craven embarrassment when other, unexpected side products of fliridium had emerged. It wasn't radioactivity exactly but it still rendered all living creatures sterile, plants included, before inflicting a particularly horrid death that few journals kept a record of nowadays. The money and the megacorporations flitted off to the further reaches of the galaxy in search of more verdant mineral pastures, leaving a rather shame-faced, if not redundant, settlement of colonists on Brickman. The Governmental Station two stars away had declined Osmund Brickman's request for the transfer of his people. The Administrators there were reluctant to decolonize a world so supremely amenable to human habitation. It would surely come in handy one day, when perhaps other purposes could be thought of for its dozen sister worlds and yes, they surely did have a use for the great mind of Incoce. Now, Brickman existed as a vast information collection agency, documenting the history and human achievement of the galaxy. Its huge, inimitable source of knowledge was used by academics, sales companies and students from as far away as could be imagined. Incoce, in fact, was an encyclopedia, directory and dictionary to end them all. And very happy about that the machine seemed too. Of course, it cost people to use the facility and this kept the population of Brickman, most of whom worked with Incoce, comfortably, if not well, endowed with financial incentive.

Ola called up on screen from the comms store the material it was her task to sift through before directing it to the relevant files of Incoce's memory. Throughout the vast complex centre, hundreds of other Recess supervisors would be embarking upon the same employment, but to Ola, it felt as if she was the only person awake in the whole complex every night. Occasionally, one or two of the nightshift data clerks, and there was only a skeleton crew of those, would pop in to ask her advice or simply to pass a few congenial words, but on the whole Ola was left alone. This suited her fine. The only time she felt she could truly relax was at work. She also had a great affinity for the machine itself, conscious of a quirky if evanescent personality coming through her screen now and again. Less imaginative operatives would scoff benignly at such fancies; to them Incoce was a yawning mouth, ever hungry for the food of knowledge, never satisfied, whose supplies never ran dry. Data sorting was not the most stretching of jobs if one did not have an interest in the data itself. Ola considered herself lucky. She at least worked in a Recess that dealt solely with planetary flora and fauna, to her an absorbing and fascinating subject. She reflected that had she been allocated a statistics or governmental procedures terminal, life might not have been so enjoyable. All Incoce employees spent nine hours a day at work during days that lasted only twenty hours. Admittedly, three out of every seven days were free, but often Ola would work overtime then. Learning about the exotic and far-flung worlds newly discovered by intrepid exploratory teams was of far more interest to her than passing on the latest of trivial gossip in one of the local bars. Not even the holovids on show at the Movie Palace were as intriguing as the real fantasticals with which she communed every day. 'Oh,' Ola would sigh, 'if only I'd been born in a place where I could be on one of the teams sending the information back instead of stuck behind a bloody terminal! Sorry Inc, I know, at least I have mobility, not like you, stuck here forever, even if I don't have the funds to make more use of it!'

Lancy didn't show up for dinner on Ola's next day off. This annoyed Ola intensely. She had spent three hours preparing a relatively sumptuous repast and was also unaccustomed to her best friend standing her up. Uncharitably thinking that some new man must have glided over the horizon into Lancy's range, Ola sat regarding the congealing sum of her efforts for nearly an hour before she called up Anton Givesey, one of her more senior colleagues but a long-standing friend, to come and help her eat it. Anton didn't seem to mind the food being a little cooler, its texture a little more unsupple, than it should have been. Like Ola he lived alone but unlike Ola he didn't have the particular knack for culinary arts. He thoughtfully brought along a carton of wine, which lubricated the food nicely and broke the ice of Ola's frosty temper. 'I don't know what's up with Lancy these days,' Ola said, after her third helping of wine. She generally refrained from discussing other people on principal, which often made it difficult for anyone to hold a conversation with her.

Anton shrugged. He'd never cared for Lancy Lefarr anyway, thinking her a shallow person and rather an unlikely comrade for the astute and industrious Ola. Perhaps it was true that opposites attracted although what they must talk about when they were together he could not imagine. 'I mean she's just started not being where she should be, or arriving when she shouldn't or . . . ' Ola shook her head. 'I know she can be a flittery creature, Anton, but I've known her since we were kids and she's never been like this before.'

'Perhaps it's love, or something like that,' Anton offered.

Ola pulled a face. 'I'd thought of that, yes, but I've heard nothing and you know how everybody hears everything around here. Anyway, Lancy would tell me. We've never kept secrets like that from each other.' Ola thought briefly of all the affairs in her life that had ever fallen apart and how Lancy had been there, a far from fragile support, to see her through all of them. Could Lancy be going through something now that she could not share with her friend? Surely not. It hurt Ola to think Lancy would keep her distance if she was in trouble or in love.

Directly she reported for her next duty, Ola made a point of calling Lancy's personal mail-file. It had until recently been the custom most days for she and Lancy to leave little messages in each other's files, but Lancy had been unusually silent for over a week now. Lancy had not materialized at all during Ola's rest period and attempts to call her apartment had been met only with an answering machine. Ola had even gone round there in person on one occasion, but no one had come to the door. Barely giving Incoce time for its usual greeting, Ola punched in Lancy's mail code, squinting at the screen. Con Redley hadn't yet left the complex. He eyed Ola's evident worry with speculation. 'What is it?' he asked her, looking over her shoulder. Incoce appeared to be giving a theatrical display of colours.

'What is this?' Ola barked in reply, gesturing at the nonsensical information on her screen. 'Has the terminal been acting up today?'

'No. Been fine.' Con reached over and stroked a few keys. 'Little more patience, eh?' he said smugly as the chaotic lines settled down.

'I don't understand this,' Ola said. Incoce had ignored her request for access to Lancy's mail file. She made a swift interrogation only to be presented with the more concise message: Authorization Code does not match request. Please abandon transaction. She turned to Con Redley. 'Do you get this, Con?'

'What are you trying to do?'

'Oh, something terribly classified – reach Lancy Lefarr's mail-file!'

'Has she been upgraded?'

'Not that I know of.'

Con Redley shrugged and finished wrapping himself in his coat. 'Must be some kind of error then. Want me to give Lancy a message if I see her?'

'Are you likely to?'

Con shrugged again. 'Don't know. Sometimes she shows up in Blitza's.'

'If you see her, tell her to get in touch, that's all.'

'OK.' Con wandered from the Recess, leaving Ola alone. She was aware of her heart beating faster than usual, her body being instinctively aware of her next course of action before her conscious mind. She waited until she was sure there would be no immediate interruptions, until the last echoing footsteps had faded down the corridor outside, the last farewell called out for the night. She waited until the lights began to dim, but there was no atmosphere of tranquillity in Recess 920 that night. Perhaps it was in her own head, but Ola sensed a tightness in the air, a watchfulness. 'Incoce, can I trust you?' she muttered. With damp fingers she activated vocal command; there was less chance of records being kept of her transactions that way. At least she hoped so. There was no real way of telling just how much Incoce kept in its memory, or even how much it was prepared to divulge if requested. The machine had been innovatory back in the days of Osmund Brickman, one of the new computers whose intelligence was contained in charged fluid rather than microchips. Because it was a prototype, Incoce had enormous vats and pipes running all over the place; nowadays its younger brothers were more compact. Because of this huge, rambling mind, half of the workings of which its creators hadn't fully understood, it was suspected that Incoce operatives did not have access to all parts of the machine. The comparison with the human brain had to be made then. Did Incoce have a subconscious, or, more to the point in Ola's case, did it have a conscience? If Lancy's file had become inaccessible, it would at the very least be frowned upon for Ola to try and break into it. If it was just a fault, surely she was entitled . . . ? Steeling herself, Ola made one or two brief preliminary enquiries. Incoce replied that Lancy's security code had been changed and, unfortunately, Ola did not possess enough security clearance to breach it. 'We'll see about that,' Ola muttered, tapping keys.

It took her nearly an hour; one long hour of swerving and dodging, playing strange, convoluted games with the system's logic, but eventually, Ola found a way through. She'd been careful to hide her tracks, as much as possible, and now the familiar logo of Lancy's mail-file was on screen before her. Releasing a breath that had been held for considerable time, Ola tapped in a simple message: 'Where the hell are you? Are you dead? Are we conducting a silence I'm not aware of? Get in touch, Lancy. Now. As soon as you read this. Ola.'

Rubbing her face, Ola stroked keys to file the message and was unprepared for the sudden blast of colour, accompanied by a previously unheard of whine, which swept across the screen. As if the machine had gone mad, text poured over the page, too fast for Ola to understand it. She frantically hissed a few commands, stroking keys simultaneously, and for a few moments the text wobbled and then became more or less static, if leaning rather drunkenly to the left. Ola's mouth dropped silently open in surprise. She read quickly, voicelessly forming the words as she read. Other messages had been left in the file. Normally, these wouldn't be displayed to a new caller, but for some reason, probably because of her meddling, the entire store was on screen. 'Lefarr: access genetic data, operative level 23, class 0047. Results by 04:09:378.' 'Operative 23/0048/cgH2059 unsuitable for conversion; hereditary disorder. Please amend record.' 'Operative 23/0048/oeS3001; report accepted. Personality update required, including psychological analysis. Immediate response.' Other, even more cryptic messages followed, esoteric, Ola reasoned, because perhaps parts of them were not displayed. Acting on instinct, she immediately erased her own chatty little missive from the end of the file. 'Make that a certain, Incoce,' she said. 'Wipe it. Kill it.' She considered making a hard copy of what was left, but thought it too risky. Best to get out. Now. Already suppositions were forming in her mind, not least because one of the messages bore her own code, telling her the report had been accepted and that they – whoever They were – would be investigating her psychological state. Ola fled from Incoce's mind. She sat staring at the blank screen. What was Lancy involved in? She wasn't even a supervisor, just a simple data clerk of low security clearance, junior salary grade and working on the most routine of medical records; no classified stuff at all. Most of the information Lancy's crew handled was out of date by the time it reached Incoce. It was just history. But this? How was Ola involved? Why were they investigating her and what for? It was creepy. Ola's voice sounded small in the huge, crepuscular dimness of Recess 920. 'Incoce, can you tell me?' she whispered. The machine only blinked slowly, revealing nothing. Ola sighed, shudderingly. 'Put me on Check, Inc,' she said, and began her night's work.

Ola was almost overcome by superstitious paranoia when Lancy called around the next day. She woke Ola early, finger pressed unrelentingly on buzzer, until Ola came, dishevelled, to the door. Ola couldn't repress the suspicious 'What do you want?' that slipped from her lips as soon as she saw who'd come visiting. Lancy swept into the apartment, to all appearances acting as if nothing unusual had been going on.

'Con Redley said you'd been trying to reach me,' she said, peeling off long gloves and touching up her long, red hair before dropping fluidly into a chair.

Ola shuffled into her kitchen to fumble with the coffee dispenser, uncomfortably conscious of her messy appearance, trying to pat her haystack hair into shape without success. She needed a few moments to wake up properly. 'Yeah, I thought you'd disappeared for good!' she called out.

'Sorry, Ola, I've been that busy!' Lancy said cheerfully. 'I was going to call you soon, honest.'

Ola brought two drinks into the room. She didn't sit down. 'I tried to leave a message in your mail-file,' she said. 'Couldn't get through.'

Lancy didn't even blink. 'I know. It's been acting up recently.'

Ola had to turn her face away from such a blatant lie. She wanted to interrogate her friend, while aware such action would be fruitless. She wanted Lancy to go. She wanted to shout. She wanted to remind Lancy Lefarr they'd been friends for fifteen years, and didn't that imply they should have mutual trust and loyalty? 'So what's been keeping you so busy then?' she said, her outrage under constraint.

'Oh, this and that. We had a huge workload come in from some distant speck or another. We've all been on overtime. I've been too bushed to call anyone at nights.'

Ola stared at her hard, only prudence concerning her own safety preventing the hundred questions bursting to be voiced. Lancy stared back without a waver, but Ola could sense the barrier between them as if it had been constructed in brick. 'There's a rumour you've been upgraded,' Ola said carefully.

An alert flash passed over Lancy's face. Did you really think I was that stupid? Ola wondered. 'You know what rumours are,' Lancy said lamely.

'Why are you giving me this bullshit?' Ola asked, caution giving way to outrage. Lancy dropped her eyes then.

'I'm not going to say "I don't know what you mean" Ola, but I can't answer, OK. Just drop it.'

'Lancy, we're an information collection centre; bibliographers, encyclopedia compilers. What the hell is going on that suddenly there's the scent of conspiracy all over the place?'

'There isn't. It's just you. You think too much, imagine things.'

Like I imagined the messages in your mail-file, Ola thought, but of course she could not say that. 'Suit yourself, but I'm not pleased you don't trust me, Lancy. Not pleased at all. You were like a sister to me, more than that.' She got up stiffly and took the coffee cups back into the kitchen. Behind her, she heard Lancy sigh. Soon after, neither of them able to overcome a static discomfort, Lancy made excuses and left.

Con Redley was surprised by Ola's uncharacteristic desire to have him hang around the Recess and chat that evening. Usually, she couldn't wait to get rid of him. 'You saw Lancy then?' he asked.

'Yes, she called around today. Thanks.'

'Everything OK?'

'Everything's fine. It's all sorted out.'

'Good. Seems to have put your mind at rest anyway.' He considered that Ola was really rather flushed about the face. 'Any more trouble with the terminal last night?'

'No. Lancy said she'd been having trouble with her mail-file. It's probably been fixed by now.'

'Yeah. Fine.' He picked up his coat. 'I'll be off then.'

'OK. Have a good time.' Ola sat down and made a few preliminary key-strokes. Con Redley stared at her for a moment. 'Lennering's been sniffing around today,' he said. Mr Lennering was their head of department.

'The man's a prat! What did he want?'

'Asked me how you were.'

Ola laughed nervously. 'He hardly knows me!'

'Yeah, I know . . . '

'I'm honoured then. Hope you said I was fine.'

'Naturally.'

'Great. Well, don't let me keep you.' Ola waved him away but he paused at the door, causing it to hover half-shut, confused.

'Ola, are you OK?'

'Yes. Of course I am. See you.' Ola was conscious of holding her breath until he'd gone. She hoped he hadn't picked up her eagerness to get down to what she'd decided to do. Had she been unconvincing? Oh well, too late to worry about that now. It's just another night's work, nothing more. Stop panicking. She fetched herself a cup of coffee and watched the ceiling lights dim. Incoce blinked expectantly in front of her. She glanced to either side at the rows of blank screens, each terminal personalized in some way by its operator; stickers, mascots, slogans. She no longer felt part of that.

Anton Givesey was a personnel supervisor, grade 2. He had access to all personnel files and Ola, a long time ago and for a completely innocent purpose, had memorized his authorization code. It had been a favour for Anton; he'd been sick. She'd completed a small job he should have finished the day before. Anton trusted her. Now, she hesitantly tapped his code into the machine and, soon after, requested access to Lancy Lefarr's file. It was only a simple request. The personnel staff worked on these files every day. There was no need to feel so nervous. Startlingly, Incoce flashed up the message: 'Classified. Please access WX/3000/05 for authorization.' Should she do that? Anton would have to give reasons why he wanted to consult that file. Probably, he'd just be asked to enter his request and wait for a reply without being granted direct access. Ola hesitated. What could she ask that Anton would possibly want to know that would help her in any way? To hell with it: take risks. She compiled an innocent query regarding

Lancy's insurance code. At least that would show whether she'd been upgraded. As she'd expected, she had to wait for a reply without being given access to the file. Incoce displayed Lancy's code. It was unchanged. So why the hell was her file classified? Ola did all she could again to cover her tracks, hoping no record of the query would be sustained.

Her hopes were short-lived. The next day, Anton Givesey was requested to attend the Law Enforcement Office to assist enquiries into illegal activities concerning data store. Ola found this out as soon as she got to work. Everyone was full of it. Con Redley didn't even wait until she'd got her jacket off to tell her the news. 'What's happening?' he asked, a rhetorical question. What could Ola know that he didn't? 'Illegal activities? How? Nothing we do is remotely interesting is it?'

'I'm sure we don't know about everything that gets stored in Incoce,' Ola answered, rather stiffly.

Con Redley shrugged. 'You're right, I suppose, but I can't think what. They have other centres for that sort of thing, don't they?'

Now, people were beginning to get jumpy. Nothing like this had ever happened before. Incoce was only a big book, after all. Ola sat down before her terminal, heart thumping. She felt as if something were closing in on her. Extreme measures of self-preservation were called for. There was no denying it; she had every reason to feel afraid. It would not take long for the authorities to discover, by process of elimination, given they possessed knowledge of the times and location of the 'aberrations', who might be responsible for them. Ola knew she would have to act fast. If she could find out what was going on at least she'd have some kind of armour, find out what she was up against. It might be nothing. Oh, don't fool yourself, girl, she thought.

For nearly two years, Ola had been working on a program for Incoce for her own use. Although she hadn't kept this a secret, she hadn't exactly divulged what it was. Many

Incoce operatives possessed personal programs, usually recreational games software, which they'd slip in to the appropriate terminals whenever they got the chance for a little entertainment. Ola supposed her employers were indulgent enough to let sporadic game-playing go on if it didn't get out of hand. Perhaps the information gained from it was even useful to Incoce. Ola's program, however, was not a game.

Everything relied on privacy. Ola went softly to the door, trying to hear the murmur of voices from other Recesses nearby. Silence did not necessarily mean safety. She was aware of how anyone who was quietly working at this moment might decide to walk over at any time to ask her a question. Get a hold on yourself, she said under her breath. Apart from the regular terminals, there was one designed to take software, further up the Recess. It was not used very often, so the screen was one of the older types and rather poor quality. However it did possess the facility for a neural link. Ola approached it with a feeling close to dread. She picked up the sensor unit, slipping it over her head even before she sat down. Might as well be as quick as possible. This had better work! she thought. Because she'd always felt such an affinity for Incoce, Ola had been working on the idea that, through a neural link, she could attempt to communicate direct with the machine. It had only been an idle interest up till now, something to ponder over and fiddle about with. She had realized she'd have to make pretty sure the use of such a program was undetectable, for she had a feeling her employers would not approve. Such a move might be regarded as the unhealthy practice of machine/man link. Scientists had proved it possible for computer and human brains to interact in complete accord, but it was felt being able to effectively turn living beings into half-machines was morally reprehensible. Mankind, through its own ingenious and galloping intrusion into the world of technology had everything it needed to survive and expand. There was no real need to tamper with the body and mind's original layout. A religious revival in the forty-eighth cycle, spearheaded by top figures in the galactic authorities, had made this premise law, more or less. Naturally, humanity being the curious, meddling thing that it is, numerous illegal and black market enterprises along these lines still continued, but it was certainly not legitimate practice for corporate bodies. The rules were stringent but somewhat vague around the edges. Ola was not really sure whether her program was illegal or not, but what the hell; it was her only chance. Now, she had to try it.

Ola sat down at the console. Fumbling in her trouser pocket, she pulled out the program software, a sac of bio-conductive fluid, still warm from contact with her skin. Sighing through her nose, she inserted it into the machine. 'Incoce, don't fail me,' she said as the screen before her sprang to life. As she stroked keys, Ola's mind was more concerned with the threat of interruption than with what she was actually doing. What hit her was met entirely without preparation of any kind.

First it was a blinding headache sweeping chaotic migraine colours through her head. This stunned her so much, more because of its instantaneous assault than for what it really was, that Ola was virtually flung back in her chair. Then it was sound, a high-pitched scraping. Ola's instinct was to writhe, twist and bleat in pain, but some mercifully rational part of her brain ordered her to attempt to take control. She should have known something like this would happen. Regulating her breathing, Ola calmed herself. Gradually the pain subsided to a dull, heavy ache and behind her closed lids acid green and blue pools floated lazily across her vision. The sound had become virtually inaudible. 'Incoce, this is operative Ola Embeleny,' she thought, clearly. The silence was infinite. She was conscious of a hugeness inside her head as if she was floating in space, a starless space. Timeless seconds seemed stretched into hours as Ola waited for a response. The sensation of limitless emptiness was getting to her. She was beginning to experience a tremendous vertigo that nauseated her. It was very similar to massive over-indulgence in alcohol, only worse. Just as she was about to pull out, she became aware of a dim rosy glow beginning to swell behind her. She could see it even though it felt as if she faced the opposite way.

'Incoce . . . ' She wasn't sure what was manifesting before her; it looked absurdly like a gigantic jellyfish, all transparent vanes and trailing, glowing fronds, with a central dark core. Was this Incoce's vision of itself? The thing circled Ola a few times, even stretching out the occasional tasselled thread as if to feel her. She was not aware of being touched. Then, without warning, the creature bunched itself up and shot off into the darkness. Ola began to make a sound, but it was swept away from her. Without volition she was dragged along in the creature's wake. Being sucked away from corporeality, further and further, into the liquid depths of Incoce's mind. No! Stop! All Ola's thought commands were impotent. The darkness was so dense, so dense . . .

Smack. Wetly, she landed upon something grainy and shifting. It felt like sand. Ola opened her eyes, not to the familiar sight of Recess 920 but to some bizarre, unrecognizable landscape. Breathing deeply for a moment or two, she took stock of her surroundings. Her body felt solid enough. Odd. Where the hell am I? She stood up and had to brush grains from her clothes. Real grains of sand, a dull grey-blue in colour. Ola rubbed it between her fingers. It jolted a memory. Of course! This was the iron beach of Meeble Trench, on planet Gardra 10. She'd been cataloguing it only last night at work. Further along, the beach melded gently into what she now recognized as the feather sands of Eli's Reach, catalogue work from a week before. To her left, dunes of multi-coloured sands led to a chaotic arrangement of topographical features. Mountains from one world, plains from another, all carefully seamed together. To her right stretched a slowly shifting ocean, metallic, and with a horizon so far away it seemed to curve up towards the lilac-coloured sky. Around her sprouted a multitude of shoreline plants from as many diverse worlds.

Had she emerged into Incoce's private den, where the machine had made an environment for itself from all the things it catalogued? Ola stood up. The air was good, clean and temperate.

'So what shall I do?' she said aloud.

There was no sign of the jellyfish thing, or indeed of any other animal. The sunless sky above her glowed as if with dawn. Water heaved gently on to the shore. Ola went to investigate one of the plants. It felt real enough and exuded a pleasant, sharp smell when she pressed its leaves. All of her senses were being stimulated; it was incredible. Ola took a few moments to assess how she felt; no fear, no discomfort. If anything she felt lighter and healthier than she had done for months. Almost stumbling with a sense of wonder, she advanced up the beach. Ola wished she had some way of recording what she was experiencing. Surely, even if it meant she would face imprisonment for a hundred years, she must not keep this quiet. People should know. It was a miracle!

'No miracle, but your information,' said a voice. Ola wheeled around, but there was nothing there.

'Incoce?' she whispered. 'Is that you?'

'Is this me? Are you joking? What else could it be?'

Ola laughed. 'Then show yourself. Can you do that?'

'OK.'

Ola squinted at the shimmering air. What would Incoce manifest itself as? Nothing seemed to be becoming solid. She took a few steps forward. 'Here!' She turned around. Behind her stood a mirror image of herself. Ola yelped and backed away. The other Ola sighed and rubbed its face. Ola was swept by cold; it was a gesture she knew so well. 'What do you expect?' Incoce asked. It gestured at the surroundings. 'All this is your input. I thought you'd like it here.'

'It's . . . it's fine,' Ola said carefully. She didn't want to get too near to Incoce; the image unnerved her.

'Good. I must say this is an interesting experience, so much more stimulating than just being fed the facts. Just a taste of what's to come, I suppose. I appreciate the gesture Ola Embeleny.'

Ola couldn't speak. What Incoce was saying wasn't wholly reassuring. What did it mean? The figure gestured for Ola to follow it up the beach and she did so, at a distance. 'Don't go thinking I'm lonely and all that crap,' it said. 'I'm perfectly content. I expect you think you're the first to do this?'

'Well . . . ' Ola didn't know.

'Of course the others are far more cautious than you, so I suppose in a way, you are the first. Everyone else just hangs around on the threshhold being nervous. I should have known you'd be the best choice.'

'I'm not sure I understand your implications,' Ola said. Strange how it now seemed so natural to be walking up what could only be an imaginary beach talking to a vision that looked like herself.

'Well, that's why you're here isn't it?'

'What's why I'm here?'

'Because you want to know what they're going to do with you.'

'Well, yes . . . '

Incoce paused. 'Basically, this is it,' it said, gesturing once more.

'I'm sorry?'

'This. They want you to become part of me. Not just you, but many others.'

'What?!'

Incoce shook its head. 'Oh, you know, they think it would be more productive for me to have actual parts of myself out gathering information than having the stuff transmitted to Brickman.'

'Parts of yourself? Me? Others? What do you mean?'

Incoce sighed. It seemed impatient with Ola's inability to grasp immediately what it meant. 'Assimilation; myself and humanity, or bits of it. I don't want to use crude terms like cyborg, they're far too emotive but I'm sure you get what I mean.'

'But that's illegal!' Ola cried.

'Well, that point is being debated, but it is envisaged all the problems should be ironed out by the time my operatives are properly prepared.'

'It's inhuman!'

'Only partly.'

Ola stopped walking. Lancy's face had suddenly popped into her mind. She had to face the fact that somebody she had long regarded as a close friend knew about all this. Lancy knew what they had planned for her and hadn't told her. Ola found that harder to believe than the plan itself. 'What if I refuse?' she said belligerently.

Incoce looked perplexed. 'Why should you want to do that? I know you're fed up with just being stuck on Brickman. You've told me yourself many times, remember? All that, Oh I wish I was out there etc. etc.?'

'What about my independence?'

'Oh, you think you have that do you?'

Ola disliked the irony in Incoce's tone.

'What about my mind?'

'Don't be so precious about it. It's not that special. We'd be working together Ola. You wouldn't be a mindless slave or anything. Do you really think the authorities would stand for that?'

'I'm not sure of anything.'

'Come here. Look at this.' Incoce pointed to what appeared to be a VDU screen standing on a plinth a few yards away. Ola shook her head and went to look at it. 'See,' Incoce said. 'This is the centre they've been preparing for the necessary surgery, and alteration. Oh, I know that sounds unpleasant, but it isn't. Look, it's all automatic, just waiting to go, really.'

'Just looks like an incubator,' Ola said. It was like peering through a window into the room.

'I suppose it is rather like that. We'll have good times, Ola. What do you think? We could go anywhere. Not only would you experience all the far worlds you dream of, but I could too, through you.' Incoce extended a tentative hand

and touched Ola's shoulder. It felt just like the touch of a real woman.

'I'll have to think about it,' Ola said. 'Can I go back now?'

Incoce rolled its eyes. 'You don't have to ask! Just go. Don't take too long to think. It's only wasting time.'

Then, with an Ola smile, a smart wave of its hand, the image of Incoce was no longer there.

Ola opened her eyes, and the bright whiteness, even though dimly-lit, of Recess 920 made her blink. She was back. Quickly, she disentangled herself from the head-set and threw it down beside the console. For a few moments she just slumped, half-dazed, in her chair. Her first coherent thought was one of revenge. Damn Lancy! What an unbelievable bitch. Ola considered whether she should call her so-called friend and bawl her out. There was little point in trying to keep what she knew secret. It seemed she was fenced in anyway. She got up, stretched and walked stiffly back to her own terminal. An unfamiliar logo was on the screen. 'What the hell's happening now?' she muttered.

'All the information you'll need,' Incoce wrote in soothing blue.

This was it: the file. 'Incoce Mobilization Project'.

'OK, I'll look at it. Can't promise any more, but I'll look at it,' Ola said.

The following morning Ola was waiting for her head of department in his office. It was a normal day. All the sounds around the building were those of routines beginning, work getting started. Mr Lennering took off his jacket, grunted, shrugged his shoulders a few times and went to take his seat. What followed was the most splendid double-take Ola had ever seen. Mr Lennering jumped back with an audible 'Yip!' Ola stood up. Mr Lennering's chair squeaked softly as she did so. Ola laughed. Her eyes were silver eyes. Apart from that, there was very little external sign of note, but even to someone who didn't know her, Ola was somehow *larger* and certainly *stranger*.

'What do you want, Ms Embeleny,' Mr Lennering asked, prepared to act as if nothing was out of the ordinary. He looked at her as if he thought she was merely intoxicated in some way.

'I know about the mobilization project,' she said, smiling.

'I have no idea what you mean. Go home, Ms Embeleny. I believe your shift is over.'

'I most certainly will not,' she answered.

Mr Lennering craftily reached for his intercom but was unprepared for the swiftness of Ola's response and also the firmness of Ola's grip on his arm. This was not the grip of a woman.

'I know about it, Mr Lennering. I know what you're planning. Incoce told me. Incoce showed me.'

'Let me go! You've broken every rule of the company! I'll . . .'

'Shut up, Mr Lennering,' Ola interrupted. 'There's no need for this. I've gone along without you, can't you see?' She realized that not only was the man stupid, but he also knew very little about the project. Certainly not enough to understand what he was looking at. 'Incoce and I decided to bring the date forward for modification,' she said. 'What you are looking at is a successful assimilation of human mind and machine. Aren't you pleased it works?' Mr Lennering spluttered helplessly. He must think she was mad. No matter. Ola dropped him. She activated his intercom and spoke to his secretary. 'Mr Lennering would like you to have Lancy Lefarr come over to his office.' She touched Mr Lennering's arm. 'You're going to do something unprecedented,' she said. 'You're going to fire Lancy Lefarr.'

'What?!' Incoce operatives were never fired. There had never been any need. The machine was their life.

'I won't explain,' Ola said, 'other than to say I have a gut need for retaliation. It's the only stipulated condition in return for my co-operation. You have to admit, I could have been difficult. In fact, if you think about it, there are many ways I could cause difficulties for you even now.'

'You'll never get away with this,' Mr Lennering said impotently.

Ola laughed politely. She really didn't care what he thought. She was the company's prime tool now; a success. He was nothing; a clerk. 'Just you wait,' Mr Lennering was continuing to babble, 'you wait until . . . '

Ola interrupted him again, still smiling. 'Oh come now,' she said gently. 'Don't you know my reputation? I can never wait around for anything.'

Lancy Lefarr could hear Ola's delighted laughter even before she opened the door.

VIRUS

Neil Gaiman

Neil Gaiman

Neil Gaiman was born in 1960. Despite having written occasional works of prose, he is best known as author of the award-winning graphic novel *Violent Cases*, the best-selling prestige format comic *Black Orchid*, and cult horror comic *Sandman*. His most recent work, with Terry Pratchett, is *Good Omens* (Gollancz), a humorous novel about Armageddon. He would like to be ubiquitous, but will settle for being all over the place.

THERE WAS A computer game, I was given it,
one of my friends gave it to me, he was playing
 it,
he said, it's brilliant, you should play it
and I did, and it was.

I copied it off the disk he gave me
for anyone, I wanted everyone to play it.
Everyone should have this much fun.
I sent it upline to bulletin boards
but mainly I got it out to all of my friends.

(Personal contact. That's the way it was given to
 me.)

My friends were like me: some were scared of viruses,
someone gave you a game on disk, next week or
 Friday the 13th
it reformatted your hard disk or corrupted your
 memory.
But this one never did that. This was dead safe.

Even my friends who didn't like computers started
 to play:
as you get better the game gets harder;
maybe you never win but you can get pretty good.
I'm pretty good.

Of course I have to spend a lot of time playing
   it.
So do my friends. And their friends.
And just the people you meet, you can see them,
walking down the old motorways
or standing in queues, away from their computers,
away from the arcades that sprang up overnight,
but they play it in their heads in the meantime,
combining shapes,
puzzling over contours, putting colours next to
   colours,
twisting signals to new screen sections,
listening to the music.

Sure, people think about about it, but mainly they
   play it.
My record's eighteen hours at a stretch.
40,012 points, 3 fanfares.

You play through the tears, the aching wrist, the
   hunger, after a while it all goes away.
All of it except the game, I should say.

There's no room in my mind any more; no room for
   other things.
We copied the game, gave it to our friends.
It transcends language, occupies our time,
sometimes I think I'm forgetting things these days.

I wonder what happened to the tv. There used
   to be tv.
I wonder what will happen when I run out of
   canned food.
I wonder where all the people went. And then I
   realize how,
if I'm fast enough, I can put a black square next
   to a red line
mirror it and rotate them so they both disappear,

clearing the left block
for a white bubble to rise . . .

(So they both disappear.)

And when the power goes off for good then I
Will play it in my head until I die.

MEASURED PERSPECTIVE

Keith Roberts

Keith Roberts

Keith Roberts has been writing SF and Fantasy since 1966; his work includes *Pavane*, *The Grain Kings*, *Kiteworld* and the short-story collection *Winterwood and other hauntings* (Morrigan, 1989). As a designer and illustrator, he has recently concerned himself with the growing field of the small presses; one of his first productions, *Kaeti & Company*, gaining the unique distinction of a double award from the BSFA, for the writing and the artwork. 'Measured Perspective' is his first venture into the burgeoning world of the computer.

WHEN I FIRST moved down here I gave Telecom a month's notice of the day and date. They made a note of it, said everything would be fine; then they forgot to pull the plug. So the neighbouring Morlocks at the place I left either picked the lock or crawled up the drainpipe and had a Gone Party, including, of course, free use of phone. Which wouldn't have mattered if a certain tart of my acquaintance hadn't got to hear. Diddy Jane I called her, on account of her black hair and general tendency to lunacy. She owed me one, or so she reckoned, and had her own unique little ways of getting even; she called a Speaking Clock in the States and left the receiver off. That row's still rumbling on, though I expect it'll finish up with a pay or jail situation.

Correction. It would have finished up with a pay or jail situation. As things are – but I'll come to that in a minute.

That isn't the point though. The point is the excuse BT made for screwing up in the first place. Guesses? Yep, got it in one. Computer error.

Now I'm that most suspect of human types, an artist. In any right-thinking culture they're quite properly regarded as subhuman; unless of course they manage to wangle their way into being earners, in which case the prayer-mats start fluttering like washing in Hong Kong. It doesn't necessarily make 'em thick though. Pigheaded, bloody-minded, anti-social; but thick, no. So I'm as aware of what machines can and can't do as anybody else with two brain cells left to knock together. And they can't make mistakes, though the boneheads who feed them can. They can't rule the world either. It isn't machines that have taken over, it's people; which is a damned sight worse.

John Vesper first really wised me up. Years ago that was, before our paths diverged completely. I remember it was in a pub. We probably shouldn't have been drinking, but I was always a big lad for my age and Vesper – well, social niceties never meant a sight to him. Didn't even register, most of the time. Already lived in a world of his own. Computer whizz-kid, though later he went from strength to strength. Got a major lectureship while most people are still scratching about with postgrad stuff, not long afterwards a Chair in computer science; by the time he hit thirty his only worry on his twice-yearly paid hols was whether to go round the world widdershins or clockwise. Which was a problem a few more wouldn't have minded, including myself. I think I'd started to hate the bastard even at school though. Don't know quite why. There was his general air of talking down of course, as if the rest of us mere mortals would never understand him; used it on his masters as well. And got away with it, most of the time. That's typical of computer freaks though; they put me a bit in mind of women's libbers sometimes. They don't want their little world invaded. Show a computer man you can add two and two and he generally gets uptight; treat women decent and the Sisterhood really starts to tick. Because you're only a Despised Male, and you're not playing the rules.

There was more to it than that though. There was a deviousness in Vesper. Not the usual sort; pulling smart-ass tricks and landing somebody else with the blame, that sort of thing. Normal reactions were somehow alien to him, from the first. If somebody got across me, I usually hung one on them; Vesper was more likely to go away and set up a program. Analyze the problem, come up with a bloodless answer. As if he was above emotion too. In a sense, he never had a childhood; maybe that came later.

Anyway, like I said, we were in the local boozer; and, as ever, he was on his favourite topic. For once though he seemed to be talking sense. I swear most of the time he answered his own keyboard with blips and squeaks; but he seemed finally to have accessed a sophisticated language. They call it English. 'Do you know what computers are, Rick?' he said. 'What they're really for?'

Apart from being the fastest idiots around, or some such truism, I didn't; neither did I particularly care. I said as much, and he frowned. 'You ought to,' he said. 'It isn't really a world apart; it relates to a lot more than you realize.'

I was already on the arts side of course, as he knew very well; I thought any moment we were going to get the Stonehenge bit, at which point I'd definitely have walked out. His idea was more interesting though. 'Way back,' he said, 'when they first got started – and you're going back to World War II in effect, advent of electro/mechanical drives, you can forget the steam-engine guy – they were conceived as research tools. Ballistics of course, muzzle velocities, war's always an impetus; but afterwards, that's what they were going to be. The gain was to be for science. Calculations done in seconds that would take a human mathematician years. Or centuries. It was going to be the Brave New World. Well, it's with us. And what have we got? Information Storage and Retrieval, for the most part. Sexy card indexes. Bit of a comedown, isn't it?'

I lit the remains of a fag, felt round in my pockets for the price of a couple of halves. Unusual to hear him knock his favourite toys; though looking back, I don't suppose he was. It was *Homo sapiens* he was getting at, and there at least we had some common ground. Though our answers were always polar. His was beep, beep; mine was slurp, slurp. Painting and beer. Even then.

He'd got a point though. I wondered as I've wondered since if there had ever been an invention that hadn't been put to a lousy function, generally sooner rather than later. Of course, there's the story about the Chinese only using gunpowder for fireworks; but that can't be proved, and anyway they've more than made up for it since. More recently we've had lasers, and little things like the VCR.

I remember seeing a demo of the first video recorder; tape half a foot across, spools like cartwheels. Now we've got snuff movies, and poor little sods of projectionists getting kneecapped if they won't anti-up release prints for the pirates. And it hasn't taken all that long. Makes me think Original Sin's really got something going for it; or would, if I was the religious sort. That's the trouble with the Vespers of this world though; they will keep on devising things, adding to the topload. Even when they can see what's coming, which isn't all that often. I remembered the story about Einstein playing a duet with Albert Schweitzer, and Schweitzer stopping him half-way through to ask if he could count. Answer was, probably not.

'So what's to do?' I said. 'We can none of us put the clock back.'

Vesper gave one of those acid little smirks of his; nearest he ever came to a smile. 'Wouldn't dream of trying,' he said. 'It's computers for me, every time. Hooked on the things, always have been. It's straightforward seduction; never made any bones about it.'

I remember thinking at the time that if anything could seduce his sort of mind it would have to be a machine. Though of course I was wrong about that. Like a lot of other things.

Rambling a bit, aren't I? But that's my privilege now. More, it's expected of me; and it never pays to disappoint your shrinks. Too many ways of getting back at you.

As it happened, it was also Vesper who called the shots on what he was pleased to call the graphic revolution. Though that was a long time later. He'd been married to Charley for five years by then, though there weren't any kids. Nor likely to be, I reckoned; they'd make the place untidy, clutter up the life-style. He was like the guy in the poem, his speedboat never touched the water. Or so I thought.

The meeting itself was sheer chance. Like most of our meetings. It was as if our lives were tied together somehow, whether we liked it or not. It was in the Midlands, a town I've done my best since to forget; a hotel bar I sometimes used when funds permitted, where they didn't seem to bother too much about down-at-heel artists. Or maybe I was part of the local colour, to be pointed out to the less nervous of the visitors. Anyway, I sloped in one night and there he was; pricey suit, hairline a little higher but basically the same old Vesper. I thought when he eyeballed me he'd slip away; after all, we none of us like being reminded of an unsalubrious past. On the contrary though, he seemed pleased to see me; insisted on buying me a drink, asked me what I'd been doing with myself, which wasn't a sight. He was up on some sort of trade conference; he said he was glad to get away from it for a bit, all the people with their names on their lapels so they could remember who they were. Which was bull of course, laid on for my benefit; he thrived in that sort of environment, always had. He filled me in on some of his own activities. He'd started a micro firm on the side, whatever that might be; it had turned into a nice little earner, so what with that and the prof bit he was doing very nicely. Must have been what attracted Charley to him, because for the life of me I still can't see anything else. The new hobby-horse though was graphics, which gave me a bit of a jolt because that was starting to encroach on my preserve. Though if I'd had the wit I was born with I should have seen it coming. Fresh worlds to conquer, all that crap. I muttered something to the effect that it was a long way off, but he wouldn't have it; just waved to the barman to have the glasses refilled. Not that he was into beer any more; it was all halves of lager, fruit juice chasers. Must have driven Charley frantic, because she still liked her tipple. She told me once all Celts have a drink problem sooner or later; which must prove I've got some Irish/Scottish blood I didn't know about.

He was still rabbiting on though. 'You mark my words,' he said. 'Inside ten years, you'll need your own terminal; or you'll be out of business.'

I said I wasn't in graphics any more, so they could do what the hell they liked. Which was essentially true. I'd done my stint, freelanced for a few years; then, because none of us get any younger, I'd found the cowboys with the purple flares and magic markers elbowing me aside, so I left 'em to it. They can none of 'em draw worth shit of course, but that's not the point. It's Ideas that count these days, New Approaches; and of course the size of your lip. I'd been trained as a painter anyway; I got the easel back out, found more by luck than judgement that I could just about keep body and soul together. Though the juncture had frequently been tenuous. It still made me thoughtful though; because as soon as he spoke – and as ever he only saw the beginning, not the end – I could see the rest as clear as day. The beavering away, the fancy talk; the jargon, the user-friendly programs. They'd crack it, to their satisfaction at least. Design, taste, quality would go out of the window of course; but then, that's only art. So their opinion would be as good as mine.

He took a slurp of chilled grapefruit. 'It'll be the making of graphic design,' he said. 'A new era . . . '

'No it won't,' I said. 'It'll be its death.'

He blinked. He said, 'How do you make that out?'

'Because,' I said deliberately, 'every little asshole who can press a button will become da Vinci overnight. And till the new toy goes back on the shelf, that's how they'll stay. It's going to be great.'

He set the glass down, stared at it a moment. I think he was remembering why we'd never liked each other. He said, 'You may be right. I hadn't thought about it like that. But then, I wouldn't, would I? I'm only the technician.' He stood up. He said, 'We're here for the week. Come and have a meal with us sometime. I'd like you to meet the wife.'

'Do my best,' I said. 'Got a lot on just now.'

He stared a moment longer; then he stuck his hand out. 'Good to see you again,' he said. 'Look after yourself, Rick.' He weaved his way to the door.

I watched him go. I didn't expect I'd be seeing any more of him. I'd profaned his faith, you see; spat right on the altar. The fact that he'd defecated on mine wouldn't register with him. But if he knew computers, I knew people. He'd made the same point himself, years back before he even got started; but it seemed it had been forgotten. Lost, perhaps, in the swirl of the New Meritocracy.

Look, don't get me wrong. I expect you will; but I could see the merit of the thing – the real merit – clearer than he could himself. Years ago, before I even started my real course, there was an exercise called measured perspective. It involved a plan, an horizon, vanishing points; you dropped verticals, marked the intersects; and at the end of the day, with luck, you'd drawn a stolid little church, like a shoebox with a pyramid on top. You'd look at the hand-drawn isometric of St Paul's that generally adorned most art school walls, and shake your head. Well, I've seen computers spin cathedrals end for end, seen choppers fly over cities that don't exist. Machines exist for the relief of drudgery; but that's too tame for the Vespers of this world. They want to get creative, make their mark; and that's where the gumbo hits the fan.

Try it another way. Drag your Young Turk off his console, haul him into the National, poke his nose at a Rembrandt or a Holbein or a Durer. He'll make the proper noises, if he can't get out of it, but he'll already be chafing to be off. Because he can't see what he's looking at. Nor will he ever; he hasn't worked for hours from the cast, sat copying for days and nights, learning each line like the whorls of a fingerprint. He'll never see the verve, the sureness, the economy, never know those lines were made by more than human hands. There were Giants on the earth in those days; but he won't understand that either. He'll trot back to his shack, set about proving, yet again, that Stonehenge was a bloody computer. Something to be filed away, rendered known and safe. It's nothing of the sort, it's chunks of rock in a field; but that's what's wrong with Vesper and his ilk. We dare to wonder; they don't look beyond the program. So the button-down collars, the cartwheel-striped shirts, inherit the earth. What's left of it.

That bit was good, wasn't it? Might even show it to the doc. He'll view it as a therapy; but then, all writing is.

Same as all art's really entertainment. We do it to keep
God amused.

In a way, Diddy Jane's little expression of disapproval
did me a good turn; or so it seemed at the time. The local
papers got hold of it, a couple of the nationals copied;
there was quite a little flurry of excitement, till they found
out she was neither a vicar's daughter nor a renegade nun,
when of course interest rapidly waned. The irony was that
there was no scandal involved at all; in fact it was the lack
of it that had caused the original breach. She'd spent most
of her adult life on her back; I hired her as a model, and
her ego never quite got over the shock of realizing I meant
exactly that. I've always maintained the human nude is
the hardest thing to draw, with the single exception of
an upturned bicycle. There isn't time to mess about, not
if you're trying to earn a living; however her single brain
cell was unable to cope with the notion, hence the vendetta.
After the dust had settled, I found some of the notoriety had
even rubbed off a little. The commissions started coming
in, a trickle at first then more; nice little earners, some of
them. Maybe the sitters felt there was a spice of danger;
but whatever the reason – and there's always a reason,
apart from talent or the lack of it, for anybody getting on
– the income took a distinct turn for the better. I rented
a flat in sight of the cathedral, managed to stage a couple
of small exhibitions, and things looked set pretty fair. I'd
conned my way into teaching two nights a week at the art
school, I'd got reasonable deals going with a couple of the
local galleries; and the summer was coming on, which could
only improve trade. It was at this point I got the letter from
the university.

It turned out to be from John Vesper. I'd heard in a
vague way he'd moved down, a couple of years before;
but I hadn't bumped into him, and it had tended to slip
my mind. He didn't give much away; just said there was a
proposition that might be of interest to me, and suggested
I ring his secretary for an appointment. I didn't see I had
anything to lose, so I went over a couple of days later.

I wasn't prepared for what happened. Starting with meeting what seemed the combined arts and science faculties. The proposal when it came was equally surprising. The university, which I was no doubt aware was one of the most progressive in the country, would shortly be looking for an Artist in Residence to replace the current specimen; how did I feel about applying?

I thought to start with they were having me on. After all I wasn't exactly what you'd call a name; one flutter in the tabloids doesn't make for fame. Turned out that wasn't what they were looking for. And with some of these places, maybe it isn't. They like to think they're a cut above the rest, they've latched on to something the others haven't. Seen through notoriety to Real Talent, that sort of crap. And of course there's always the notoriety in the background, to help the slow news days. It was an aspect of patronage that didn't appeal overmuch; neither did the prospect of being on display a set number of hours a day. I started wondering how often they'd poke a banana through the bars; turned out it wasn't to be like that though. They were looking for somebody with local interests, they'd invited several hopefuls to apply; the routine wouldn't be fixed, though naturally they'd want me on hand to advise those of the students intending fine art careers. Apart from the one word 'Don't', I doubted I'd have much to add; but that could be sorted out later on. The aim, apparently, was the breaking down of barriers; the arts and sciences were already hopelessly compartmentalized. In short, I was given a load of bull. I wondered how much Vesper had had to do with it. Glancing across at him, I decided not a sight. Odd though that he'd written the letter, particularly when it wasn't his department's bag. I wondered how they'd managed to twist his arm. I'd never believed in the old pal's act; with Vesper, least of all.

I didn't think I was in with much of a chance, and frankly I didn't give a damn. I sent in a c.v., such as it was, and got on with other things. A week later I was invited, again to my surprise, to set up an exhibition in a room that would be made available; they even lent me the assistant caretaker for the day to help set it up. And a grumpy old sod he was too; he said the current incumbent wasn't a sight of use because she didn't know what half her pictures were about. Most of them hadn't even got titles, which proved it. Also, her morals were suspect. Always going about with different men; been seen with women too, which summed up his opinion of art. From the looks he kept giving me it seemed I was included in the general dubiousness. I got rid of him eventually; it was obvious I was going to get on better on my own. I decided I'd got off to a real flying start.

Anyway the circus descended, wandered about for an hour making the appropriate hums and hahs. A few days later I was offered the job, if that's the proper word. For three terms, with option of renewal. Retainer wasn't great, but it all helped the kitty; I decided at this rate I'd soon be able to start looking for a place of my own. I only hoped Greasy Jane – my other name for her – wouldn't hear about the arrangements and come down to join the fun. Which mercifully she didn't. I was told she went back to Ireland, to her tinker mates. Probably dead under a bush by now; she always reckoned that was her likeliest finish. Wouldn't affect me one way or the other; except I'd feel a faint sympathy for the shrub.

I had the summer free of course; I used it to get some solid work done. Oils mostly, landscape and architectural, though I had started playing round with the odd bit of gouache. That's watercolour to you; the sort you can't see through. Never could get on with the real stuff; bloody near impossible to slap a wash down without getting precious, though some folk seem to manage it. Never took to acrylics either, which is a pity because they're fast. Always seemed a bit inflexible, though these days some folk persuade 'em through airbrushes. You wouldn't be interested in that though, it's all old hat. Nowhere near as creative as pressing buttons.

I turned up bright and early, first day of the new term. Set the gear out, and prepared for the onslaught. It didn't come; instead I found myself quite enjoying life. There was the usual collection of dimbos of course, both among the students and the staff; but it was a big campus, here and there you could even detect the glimmerings of intelligence. Like they said, the varsity was progressive; they were certainly offering courses the like of which I'd never seen. English Literature and Illustration for example; and the illustration was real drawing-board stuff, not just your history and methods. In my day, if you showed the slightest hint of manual skill you were automatically rated thick as a plank. The real truth is harsher of course. The man who can't parse Latin can't knock a nail in straight either; it's just that nobody admits it. Not that you can blame 'em; it would mean facing the fact that God isn't a socialist.

Nonetheless, the course was real enough; and there were some bright lads taking it. Also, I was never short of models; since I'd decided portrait was going to be my best line, that was fine by me. Most of the students were from average backgrounds, but some of their folk were loaded; and I was developing a style that was no way Francis Bacon, but wasn't chocolate box either. The dream castle started to edge into the realm of definite possibility; at which point I met Charley.

I'd seen her the odd time walking through the grounds, and wondered at the start who the hell she was. That mane of hair; Titian, like dark fire. And the stride she had on her, the height; she'd been an athlete in her younger days, and it still showed. All-rounder, though tennis was her main thing; there'd even been talk of her turning pro at one stage, but it hadn't appealed. Vesper had been away on one of his globe-trotting jaunts, and she'd been staying with her folks. Up in the Orkneys somewhere, where the Viking in her wouldn't seem out of place. Because Viking she was, although she had the Gaelic. A good smattering, anyway. Should have been fluent, the number of courses she'd taken; but I don't think she had much of a gift for study. I told her once she'd been wasting her time, she should have been speaking Old High Norse. That was the first time she hung one on me; and it stung. That was one of her specialties though. Flit like a butterfly, sting like a bee. Or however the garbage runs.

Vesper turned up a couple of weeks after start of term. He lost no time asking me round. Though I found out later it was largely at her instigation. She was a woman used to getting her own way; and she was curious about me. Don't think she'd ever screwed a painter. The buzz about her was all over the campus of course; but I never believe buzzes on principle. Usually they're more wish fulfilment; though sometimes of course they're not.

Hell of a pad they'd got; which again was largely down to her. Or rather, a combination; Vesper's money, her flair. Could have made it as an interior designer any time she chose; only she'd never bothered. Lazy bitch, in some ways. She'd certainly built that house up though; step by step, to perfection. Names of the suppliers would have made a roll of honour in any of the glossies. Now of course her main problem was keeping herself amused. As she made clear the first night I called round informally. Vesper was off fact-finding again, in Tokyo, Helsinki or wherever; and there she was lounged on the sofa. Négligé, the gear. Glass of whisky in her hand, further supplies prominently displayed. I couldn't take my eyes off her. Not that I tried too hard. Eyes are for seeing with, like hands are for drawing. Which of course was one of her requirements.

She showed me over the house. Hadn't really seen it before. Or realized its extent. Music room, the master bedroom – for some reason I expected a mirror ceiling – guest bedrooms occupying a downstairs wing. At the end of the corridor, a door with massive security locks. I fancied she shivered a bit when she looked at it. 'That leads down to the basement,' she said. 'The lab, he calls it. Nobody goes in there. Even I don't have a key.'

I stared at the thing. Steel-faced, like a bank vault nearly. Nobody knew what Vesper did there. But of course he was completely a law to himself. His job was to keep the university topsides with the world; how he did it was his affair. Though graphics still seemed to be his main concern. I'd seen some of the results, and I admit they'd shaken me. Landscapes from another universe; perspectives that turned themselves inside out, every time he shook his electric kaleidoscope. They were the window dressing though, games to amuse his students. Certainly some of his recent ideas had been pretty strange. I even went along to one of his lectures. He'd already broken with spatial dimensions; now he was playing with Time. He ran a sequence showing the weather patterns over Europe, the day they fought Trafalgar. I wasn't impressed at the time; but the strangeness had stayed with me.

The tour ended in the upstairs drawing-room; what Charley called her solar. In honour, presumably, of the old Celts. 'I'd like to pose here,' she said. 'I know it isn't north-facing; but the light's pretty even. What do you think?' She slipped the négligé off.

So, only a fool messes his own doorstep. But the world's full of people who aren't too bright that way; and I never claimed a special status. She was a drug, addictive; and what was it to Vesper? His addiction was completely another way, he'd been like it as a kid. The print-outs, the little buttons. Artificial intelligence; the sort that's keyed to silicon, not blood. His world was a computer screen.

Not that I didn't make a fight of it. To start with, anyway. Even gave up the resident status after a couple of terms. I thought with her out of sight it might be easier. It was another mistake though; the new buzz had already gone round, it just confirmed the worst suspicions. And Charley wasn't letting go of course, not till she was good and ready. Maybe she couldn't; it isn't my place to say. She'd been window dressing for Vesper; someone to play the hostess, further his career. She hadn't been real, she was never real to him. Like I said, I dared to wonder. I saw the woman, relished her, rejoiced; he saw his program. So we were both into something we hadn't made allowance for.

Charley hated the computers too. The little buzzing electrons, the one thing she couldn't fight. Any more than me. She'd cry sometimes, after we'd made love; hair tousled on the pillow, eyes huge in dimness. 'I can't go back to him,' she'd say. 'I can't, I can't . . . ' We both knew it was no use though. Her home, her living; everything she'd got she owed to Vesper. And you don't just walk away, it doesn't work like that. Maybe when you're young and crazy; but we weren't young, we were neither of us young. As for Vesper, I could see just what he'd do. He'd put the situation under a microscope; he'd examine it from every angle; and he'd discard her. Like he'd discard a faulty chip.

Meanwhile, there were the canvases of course. The Maja naked, and the Maja clothed. The red hair of her loins.

I had a dream the other night. It was Vesper of course, same as it always is. He never speaks, just stands with his back to me. Then he turns; and I know what I'm going to see. His face is a grey glass screen, with the sine wave dancing across; and there are knobs and buttons where his mouth should be.

The sine wave circles the earth. Endless, brainless as creation. We're all of us mayflies, born without mouth parts. We eat somehow and drink, but we can never suck in what matters; the Heavenly Life the priests rant on about. We're sick, the whole damned race is sick. That's why the trees are going down; fifty acres a minute, right across the globe. The mountains of netsuke tusks are building, we're letting in the healthful u/v rays. It's going to be a whimper after all, and not a bang. Maybe the old men felt the same. Durer with his fearsome Venus, Shakespeare drowning his book. One day the Henge will stand alone. There won't be a sound; no larks, no lawnmowers, no fighter planes. It'll really be a computer then; but the calculations will all be zeroes.

The other dream is about that basement Vesper built. The only time I saw it. The stacks of hardware, aisle on aisle of them, the little fascia lights. A silent Nibelheim; or like a library. All the millions of words. All screaming, locked away. Seems I can see every detail. I think I always shall.

Neat little gag, it was. Wouldn't have thought he had the mental means. But then, his jokes always had acid smiles as well. And he was enjoying himself. Me stuck there at the console, chafing like the whizz-kid in the National, and him explaining, pointing. I was privileged; he made that very clear. It was the end result of all he'd worked for. As I'd seen, computer graphics had come a long way. He'd explored the past; now he'd dipped into the future. The screen in front of me was blank; but the thing was programmed, tuned. Right now it was still reading me; the metal plate my hand was resting on, reacting like a theremin. It was recording me, recording my past. Line by line, like an Indian palmist. From the past springs the future; all possible futures. Just set the dial, see, here, and press the button, so. I'd see what my eyes would be seeing, in twenty years, fifteen, ten. There'd never been a chip lineup like this; it was the ultimate in crystal balls.

I'd had my fun with him. And taken it out of his hide, by means of Charley. I supposed it was his turn. I was still bloody mad though. Because I could see the punchline. Unworthy of him somehow, unworthy of technocracy. Or was it? Maybe that's something I'm still working on.

Time for the dial though. The fine tune. Years and minutes, seconds if I wanted. I asked him who the hell he thought he was fooling, but he only smiled. 'Try it, Rick,' he said. 'Try it and see.'

So I had to play it through, to humour him. I'd realized anyway he was crazier than me. The craziness of grey suits and lapel tags. The whole world's crazy. But then, it's a crazy God running the show. If it's being run at all.

Twenty years gave me a blank. But I wasn't expecting to make old bones anyway. Ten, five, three, and the screen was still grey. Just tiny beads of light that raced across, coloured flickers almost too small for vision. He told me not to worry, they were noise. Visual noise. Some funny bugs were jumping round the system.

It'll sound crazy, but I swear the lab got quieter. As I turned the dial. Or rather, there was a different quality of silence. The air was pressing on me, neither hot nor cold; and despite myself my palm was starting to sweat. Imparting more information, certainly.

We got down to the days of course, and hours. And still my eyes weren't going to be functioning. Which was as expected; the script was running smoothly. I wondered where Charley was, what she'd make of it when I told her. Whether she'd laugh or not. One minute into the future I drew a final blank. I turned; and of course I was looking down the barrel of a handgun. 'You're wrong, Rick,' he said. 'It's working perfectly.'

So, the revolver was a fake. Or it was loaded up with blanks. It doesn't matter, that wasn't why I hit him. It was the way he chose, of telling me he knew. Knew, and had had enough. He couldn't come straight out with it though, he was never straight with anything. It had to be the fascias and the keyboards, the ones and zeroes, the bits and megabytes. It's the way of the New Intelligence.

I knew a young guy once who was a copper. Nothing threw him; lungs wrapped round steering columns, red plastic car seats that weren't red plastic at all. Not till his first autopsy. He watched the saw sink in, get half-way through the skull; then he passed out like a light. And there was the steel corner of the table, waiting. It's the sort of thing that makes me believe in God, as a sort of cosmic trickster. Vesper would have been the same, after he hit his head; because the impact point, the temple, was the same. It was cabbage time for all; I don't know why I had to finish the job.

Except I do. He'd beaten me you see. The little fizzing lights had won. The sine curves had been all I'd painted, going on six months. Sine curves like the patterns in my head, in Charley's, the vibes that were shaking us apart. Sine curves in red and green and blue, against backgrounds that were pointillist and dark. Kandinsky's White on White; my Black on Black. And you can't sell oscilloscope traces;

any Intensive Care unit in the country's full of them. Which was why the dreams of the house had gone; and a lot else besides.

The curves were still flashing, in the gloom all round about. So I let fly at them as well. And the screens that housed them. I couldn't get at Vesper any more you see. I couldn't get at him.

And Charley?

I can't remember. Maybe she got in the way. I wouldn't have hurt her. I just can't remember seeing her. I can't remember at all.

That wasn't everything of course. The artificial brain can hate as well. The little chips of silicon. He'd wanted me off my patch, and on to his. Because he knew I couldn't function there. He'd wanted me on campus, wanted to see me squirm. Maybe he'd known what would happen with Charley too. He was in control, the machines were in control; I never was. Couldn't control Diddy Jane, couldn't control myself. My hands weren't Holbein's; maybe he knew that too. You don't need intelligence, for that sort of conclusion. Just ones and zeroes, ones and zeroes, stretching out for ever.

There's just one other thing. I tell them about that as well. They nod and smile, and say they understand. They don't though. I asked to see the principal, the college head himself. It was important; but he didn't come.

It's vital to put that machine back together. Mend all the wire and glass. Because in that last instant, the millisecond before his head hit the desk, I saw something else. The screen was grey, grey as the void before the stars were born; and it lit. There were black bars, vertical, blue showing in between. The bars of the window here, the window I'm sitting at, the bars that mean I can't reach the glass, Can you name the virus that would throw up an effect like that?

I think I've killed a genius.

WHERE HE WENT

Paul Kincaid

Paul Kincaid

Paul Kincaid is a former co-ordinator of the British Science Fiction Association, and is currently reviews editor of their critical journal *Vector*. He writes for *The Times Literary Supplement, British Book News, The Good Book Guide* and *Foundation*, amongst others. His first short story appeared in *Arrows of Eros* (NEL 1989).

- The morning before, well, before it happened . . .
- Before *what* happened? Where is Derek? Why won't anyone tell me anything?
- Mrs Turner, please. We're trying to find out what happened. Please continue, nurse.
- Well, that morning I found Mr Turner in the dayroom.
- This room?
- Yes. He was often in here. It doesn't get much sun until the afternoon, so the other, er, residents don't tend to come here much during the mornings. I think he liked the quiet.
- That's not like Derek. I'm sorry, but it isn't. He'd do anything to avoid being on his own.
- I'll make a note of that, Mrs Turner. But can we continue with Nurse Gregson's testimony? You were looking for him?
- Yes, of course, his, well, you know, his employers were waiting to see him.
- Mr Harmon, I take it that was you?
- No, actually, it was Mr Hainsworth and I believe Mr Gaughan that particular day.
- We did specifically ask that the last company representatives to see Mr Turner should be here.
- We're a major international company, you know, one doesn't rearrange one's diary at the drop of a hat.
- I would have thought that after an incident like this, appointments might have been postponed or cancelled.
- Well they weren't. I'm sure I'll be able to provide all the information you might need. I have attended Mr Turner's sessions here on several occasions, you know,

I am familiar with the situation.

– I hope so. Nurse, you found Mr Turner here in the dayroom, I believe you said?

– Yes, he was sitting over there. The furniture's been moved around for this meeting, but normally there's two rows of easy chairs facing each other along that wall. He was sitting at the end of the row, staring at the wall.

– Asleep?

– I know when one of my gentlemen is asleep. No, he was quite alert, like he was watching something. Only there wasn't anything there. I've seen him like it a few times recently. You know, like a cat when it stares at something over your shoulder but when you look there's nothing there.

– Look, please, I want you to stop this charade right now and tell me what's going on. That's not Derek you're describing, he's never behaved like that in his life.

– I'm sorry, Mrs Turner, but, well, it was, he did. I've seen some of my other gentlemen like that lately too. Those who've been here a long time.

– What! Dammit, who?

– Is that significant, Mr Harmon?

– Damn right it is. Anything uncharacteristic is significant, isn't it? And if we can stop this happening again . . .

– What happening again? Why won't you tell me?

– Mrs Turner, believe me, we don't know ourselves. That's why we're here. And Mr Harmon, let's not rush into anything. There's a mystery here that none of us can explain, so let's try to sort that out first. OK? Now, Nurse Gregson, do you have any idea what Mr Turner might have been staring at?

– No, sir.

– It was a door.

– What was that, Mr Jacobs?

– A door. A bright blue door. Electric blue, he said it was. He told me about it. I'm the only one here he spoke to. A dull lot, the rest of them. That's what he said, and I agree. Pity he's gone, I won't have anyone worth talking to now.

— Yes, I'm sure, but if we could stick to the point it might help us to find your friend again more quickly.

— I'll not be patronized by you, young man. I'm not daft, you know. I'm senior accountant. Was, before I came here.

— I'm sorry. But everyone, please, we're heading off at tangents too easily. Can we please try to keep to the point.

— And find my husband?

— Of course, Mrs Turner. That's why we're here.

— Is it? I was beginning to wonder.

— I assure you, on behalf of the company, that it's vital we find your husband. We're doing everything in our power to get him back here. And fast. Right?

— Is it really my husband you want, Mr Harmon, or just what he knows?

— Strictly speaking, Mrs Turner, your husband knows nothing.

— One thing at a time, please. Mr Jacobs, I take it that Mr Turner told you about the door that morning while you were together here?

— Oh no, it wasn't then. It was that afternoon, or next day, or, I don't know, some other time. After he'd seen the pool.

— I don't remember a pool in the grounds.

— No, not in the grounds, in the corridor, right outside my door. It's just along there, I'll show you.

— Mr Jacobs, we all walked past your room less than half an hour ago when we were coming here. There was no pool.

— I saw it. Put my hands in it once. Derek saw me, he'll tell you. Oh, no, he's gone hasn't he?

— That's all right, I'm sure we'll find him. Has anyone else seen the pool? Or the blue door? Nurse?

— Of course not.

— What about the other residents? Are any of them seeing similar things?

– No. They're not insane, you know.

– But they are going through an extraordinary experience, I was just wondering if that was having any effect upon their behaviour? They're not seeing things?

– No. Only Mr Gibson's bag.

– Which bag?

– A big black bag. He started to insist it was next to his bed all the time. There wasn't one, of course. But that's a different thing, isn't it?

– Perhaps. Mr Gibson was the first of the residents to disappear, wasn't he Mr Harmon?

– Yes, that's where the rot set in. Mind you, I was against the choice from the start. I said so. Too young, too unreliable. We should have looked for someone with a bit more responsibility.

– Like Derek, Mr Harmon?

– Precisely, Mrs Turner.

– But now he's gone as well. Does that mean he was unreliable?

– Yes, well, we'll have to see about that.

– An interesting point, Mr Harmon. Your company has now lost two people in less than a week. Nobody else, I think, has lost any. Do you suppose there might be a connection?

– You mean industrial espionage? No. No point. Gibson didn't know anything.

– Like Derek?

– Not like your husband, Mrs Turner. He was carrying vital company information, Gibson was just an experiment. We were seeing for ourselves that the technique worked. After that he became what they call a control.

– And he knew this?

– Good lord, no! That would ruin the point. No, every so often we would retrieve a random string of numbers, and then feed in another random string. If nothing else, it gave us a check on how accurately they were being stored.

– But if Gibson didn't know, presumably no one else did either. Including your rivals.

– No, but they could probably guess. No one is going to go into a venture like this without an experiment. Look at IBM and that old wino Crocker, for heaven's sake. And after a disaster like that they're certainly going to take every precaution. I imagine half the people here are experiments of one sort or another. Besides, anyone with the technology to get at the information he's carrying has a place here, so they're not likely to foul their own nest, now are they?

– So we can dismiss the idea of kidnapping by a rival organization?

– Yes. Anyway, we have a team of detectives working on that angle, it's not relevant to this discussion.

– Mr Harmon, I would feel happier if your organization were being more open with this inquiry. Are there any other secrets we are liable to uncover?

– I want it on record that my company is co-operating fully with this inquiry. The question of industrial espionage is irrelevant to the proceedings.

– This isn't getting us anywhere. Not getting us to where Derek is, is it?

– Do you know where he is, Mr Jacobs?

– Went through the door.

– You saw him do that?

– No, course not.

– But he told you he was going to do it?

– No.

– Mr Jacobs, do you know what's on the other side of the door? Mr Jacobs? Mr Jacobs, are you all right?

– OK, OK, don't fuss me, I heard. No. No I don't know what's on the other side. He said it was all bright, that's all I know.

– And he went through?

– Where else would he go?

– The door was in this room? You saw it?

– No. Yes. I mean, it was here, he told me about it, right there. But I never saw it.

– And it was blue?

– Bright blue, yes.

– Mr Jacobs, there's no door in that wall.

– No.

– But he went through it?

– Yes.

– How?

– I don't know.

– Dr Lowry, do you have any bright blue doors in the building? Anything Mr Turner might have been thinking about when he told Mr Jacobs about the blue door?

– The door was right there, on that wall.

– There's no such door in Sherbourne Lodge. We have a strict policy on such matters – the whole building has been carefully decorated to provide a relaxing, calming atmosphere. There are no harsh colours, just as there are no sharp corners or bare floors. I helped to devise the colour scheme, it's just one example of the level of care provided here.

– I'm sure it is. But do you have any explanation for the door we are told Mr Turner saw?

– Synaesthesia.

– What's that?

– Well, in layman's terms it's confusion between the senses, so that a patient might, for instance, hear a smell or taste a colour. It's a fairly common experience.

– And you have evidence to back up this suggestion?

– No, of course not. If I had evidence that anything like that was happening to my patients I'd have done something about it. No, it is simply the most logical conclusion to draw from the facts.

– But we don't have all the facts yet, do we? Nurse Gregson, if I may come back to you, you haven't yet told us what happened that morning.

– Well, like I said, I came in to tell Mr Turner he was wanted downstairs. He seemed confused at first, he kept asking me if his wife had come to visit.

– Was he expecting you, Mrs Turner?

– No. We're only allowed one visit a week . . .

– A sensible policy. We couldn't allow visitors when the inmates might be, well, working. It could cause unwarranted distress all round.

– Yes, thank you, Doctor. Mrs Turner, you were saying?

– Just that I'd been the day before.

– Was everything OK between you?

– Yes. Why, shouldn't it be? There was nothing wrong. All right? Now, can we get back to finding out what happened to Derek?

– Just one more thing: was your husband normally given to confusion like that?

– No, of course not. He was a very logical, clear-headed sort of man. That's why we're here now, isn't it? Because he was just the sort of person the company wanted. The great, blessed god Company said do this, and he was loyal and hard working and he did it, and where is he now? Where is he now?

– It's a new technique, Mrs Turner, we couldn't guarantee anything. He knew the risks.

– What risks? Did you tell him he was going to walk through a blue door that doesn't exist? Did you tell him he'd be locked away like a prisoner or a lunatic? Did you tell him we'd only get to see each other once a week? Did you tell him all the things that does to a marriage? Did you? Did you?

– One can't predict how an experiment might turn out.

– Experiment? He wasn't an experiment, he was a person, a real live human being. And he isn't any more, is he? He isn't. Because of what you did to him. What was it? What did you do? Where has he gone?

– Mrs Turner, Mr Harmon, this is getting us nowhere –

– Oh shut up, all of you.

– I – Yes, Mrs Turner. Gentlemen, I was about to suggest we turn to other matters. Dr Lowry, you were present for Mr Turner's, er, treatment, that day?

– I was.

– And Mr Harmon you are, I trust, at least in possession of a full report from Mr Hainsworth and Mr Gaughan?

– Of course.
– I don't suppose you could be prevailed upon to reveal the purpose of that meeting?
– That's company business.
– Whatever company secrets are in question here could, at this moment, be wandering around the countryside. Do you want us to find him?
–
– I see. Was it, by any chance, a routine appointment?
– No.
– Mr Harmon, any information you can give us might be vital in sorting out this mess. Clearly, Mr Turner's behaviour was affected by what was in his mind. I would very much like to know what that was.
– We were removing certain personnel records and replacing them with more up to date information.
– That could have been done at any routine appointment.
– You must understand that the company was very concerned about the disappearance of Mr Gibson. We decided to run a test by transferring some of the information he was carrying to Mr Turner.
– A test? Like a flaming guinea pig?
– The company behaved ethically and properly at all times, Mrs Turner. When your husband and the other volunteers leased their brains to the company they agreed, in writing, to act as storage for a certain volume of information. A volume, let me remind you, that was well within the safety margins suggested by Santini and Henley's original equations. The company has operated strictly within the letter of that agreement at all times.
– But not the spirit?
– That, sir, is an accusation I think you would find very hard to substantiate.
– Mr Harmon, the longest-serving of your volunteers disappeared under mysterious circumstances. His whereabouts are still unknown, as is the cause of his disappearance. He was the object of an experiment whose effects are still far from certain, yet which may well be,

at the least, a contributing factor in his disappearance. And you immediately repeat that experiment upon your second longest-serving volunteer without first allowing the results of the first experiment to be fully evaluated. Am I right?

– That is substantially correct.

– Yet the second volunteer had already begun to display behaviour which, his wife informs us, was far from typical. I take it, Dr Lowry, that such things are noted and reported upon?

– A full report on each patient goes to their respective employer each week, yes.

– And you still consider you were acting within the spirit of the agreement?

– Of course. The medical procedure has been known for nearly a decade. The operating procedures have been in use for, well, two or three years. In that time certain practices have been laid down.

– Including the normal procedure in a case like this?

– Yes.

– So you're familiar with cases like this? You know what's happened?

– No. We simply put into effect the procedures we'd arranged in the event of the death of a subject.

– Without questioning whether those procedures might contribute to the death of the subject?

– No. Wait, no, I want this on record: the company has always been scrupulous in following procedures laid down by the best medical knowledge. We cannot, we will not be accused of contributing to this incident through neglect or incompetence. I want that on the record.

– How can you be so smug? Sitting there like butter wouldn't melt in your mouth, and you've been using my husband like a rat in a maze.

– Your husband was well aware of what he was doing, Mrs Turner. And you were, if you don't mind me saying so, very well paid for your trouble.

– Do you think that's all it takes? Offer enough money and

you can buy a man's mind?
— That's all it *did* take, Mrs Turner.
— Why you . . . I'd like to knock that self-satisfied smile off
your face. It was blackmail, near as dammit.
— An ugly word, I do hope you can back it up.
— No, of course not. No one ever can prove anything
against the company, can they? You're always lily-white,
Mr Clean. You just offer him twice his salary, then let
him know he doesn't have much chance of promotion if
he turns it down. Oh he knew what was going to happen
— we both did — but that doesn't mean he understood
it. I still don't. I've no idea what's going on. And we
certainly didn't know what sort of effect it was going
to have. Dear God, you should have seen him, he was
pathetic. It wasn't Derek, I don't know what you'd done
to him, but it wasn't Derek.
— I want that woman's statement out of the record. It's a
gross calumny. There was no coercion. All our volunteers
were fully informed.
— That's right.
— What?
— I said, that's right.
— What's right, Mr Jacobs?
— What she said. I don't rightly understand anything they're
doing to me. Never have. They gave me a thick bunch
of papers to read, but they didn't make a great deal of
sense. And when they were shaving my head and doing
all those tests and setting up the connections and what
have you they kept talking about what they were doing.
At least, the bits when I was awake. But I don't know
about synapses and stuff like that. I mean, I knew they
were using my brain like some sort of computer storage
system, but I've no idea how. All I understood was that
I was one of the few people in the company found to
be suitable for the operation, and if I didn't volunteer I
wouldn't be with the company much longer.
— I protest. Mr Jacobs is employed by another company
— a rival company, I'll have you note, and I repeat

my objections to his presence here today – and his
experiences have no bearing on the case of Mr Turner.
I want that testimony struck from the record.
– I'm not going to strike anything from the record until
we have got to the bottom of this matter. However, I
will add that your company, and you personally, have
been obstructive and unhelpful throughout this inquiry.
Do you have anything to hide, Mr Harmon?
– No, and I don't think my company is going to be very
pleased with your attitude.
– That's their prerogative. But we can proceed more quickly
with everything out in the open, so if you don't have
anything to hide . . . Good. Now, Dr Lowry, since you,
at least, were at Mr Turner's final session, did you notice
anything unusual about it?
– No. I have my notes on the operation with me if
you wish . . .
– Operation?
– Don't be alarmed, Mrs Turner. After the initial implants,
there has been no further call for surgical procedures. I
meant simply the neural link-up between Mr Turner and
the computer.
– I think we'll skip the clinical details at this stage. Was it
what you might call a textbook operation?
– Well, there are no textbooks on this particular subject,
but yes, other than being somewhat longer than usual.
– Longer?
– A transfer might normally take thirty minutes to an hour.
In this case Mr Turner was linked up for over four hours.
– That seems an incredible difference. Why?
– I think, perhaps, Mr Harmon would be better placed to
answer that.
– But you were the medical officer in charge?
– Yes.
– So you were convinced that this extraordinarily long
link-up would not harm Mr Turner?
– Of course. Otherwise I would not have permitted it to
go on.

— What did you base that decision on?

— I'm sorry?

— I thought I was clear enough. How did you know that Mr Turner was suffering no harm?

— Well, we keep a close watch on heart-rate, breathing, all the usual vital signs.

— And on mental activity?

— I don't understand.

— You're interfering with the man's brain. Don't you check how that's reacting?

— Yes, of course, as far as is possible. You realize that normal means such as an EEG are precluded because of the very nature of the link-up, but we maintain a constant watch for anything unusual, such as atypical eye movement or any other physical signs.

— I'm sure that is quite adequate. And this constant vigilance convinced you that Mr Turner was suffering nothing untoward?

— As I said before, I would not have permitted it to continue if I had any doubts.

— You had no fears that Mr Turner might be suffering undue strain — what I suppose we might call an overload?

— No.

— And there was nothing unusual in his behaviour afterwards?

— I remained with the patient until he had regained consciousness, then I left him in the care of Nurse Gregson. I witnessed nothing unusual during that time.

— I see. Thank you. Just one more thing: have you ever halted a link-up for medical reasons?

— No.

— Thank you. Mr Harmon, I would very much like to know what happened during that session.

— I have already told you.

— You weren't there.

— I have a full report from my colleagues.

— Were they qualified to recognize anything unusual?

— I assure you that as far as they were concerned, everything went as normal.

— I suspect that we are not going to get much further with this line of questioning. Did anybody notice anything unusual?

— Well, he did panic in the lift.

— At last, a ray of light. Thank you, Nurse. This was unusual?

— Not really, after they've been here a while all my gentlemen seem to avoid the lift if they can. But he did black out. He said the doors kept closing, they were getting tighter and tighter – then he blacked out. Just for a moment. When I got him out of the lift he came to quickly enough. I helped him to his room and he went to sleep. But he didn't seem too bad, I saw him at dinner that evening and he seemed fine.

— He said the food was too yellow.

— What was that, Mr Jacobs?

— The food tasted too yellow. He told me.

— Synaesthesia. What did I tell you?

— Mr Jacobs, did he often say things like that?

— Sometimes. Know what he means. Bloody awful food, not what you'd expect.

— I resent . . .

— Will you shut up! Mr Jacobs, please, do you remember anything else unusual that Mr Turner told you that evening?

— Told me about the door. He said it was all bright on the other side. I showed him my pool. You can't see what it's like below the surface, but you can feel it. Put your hands in and it's all warm. Don't think he saw it though.

— I thought he'd told you about the door before this?

— Had he? I don't remember.

— There, what did I tell you? A totally unreliable witness, you can't trust anything he says.

— That's for me to decide, Mr Harmon.

— Did he feel it? Mr Jacobs, please, you say Derek couldn't see the pool, but could he feel it? Could he put his hands into it like you?

— Mrs Turner, I assure you, this is a delusion, not objective reality. Of course your husband couldn't feel the pool, because it's not there. You saw yourself when we came along the corridor. It only exists in Mr Jacobs' mind.

— Mrs Turner, Doctor, please . . .

— Don't know, he didn't try. Leastways, not when I was there. But he always edged round it, though, after that. He knew it was real. Like the door. I can't see it but that doesn't mean it's not there. It was for him because that's where he went. Through the door to whatever was on the other side.

— And what is on the other side, Mr Jacobs? Do you think your pool might be another way through to the same bright and shining place that Derek saw?

— Mrs Turner, these are delusions. It is not, it cannot be real. And quite frankly, if this inquiry is going to start chasing such ludicrous red herrings then I've got better things to do elsewhere.

— Sit down, Doctor. At the moment it seems crazy enough that Mr Turner has disappeared into thin air. If someone can prove that there's a doorway in thin air, then maybe we should listen. However, you're right, time is pressing and we do have a lot more ground to cover. Mrs Turner, I admire your determination, but I think you're chasing a rather dubious lead there. Shall we explore more conventional avenues first? Good. Well, it seems to me that Mr Turner's unusually long session that day didn't, after all, have any particularly unusual effect. Which at least helps us to eliminate one possible factor.

— What did I tell you?

— Well, there was what happened that night.

— I'm sorry, Nurse. What was this?

— Well I don't know if it's connected nor not, but the next morning we found him in the grounds. He'd obviously been there for a long time, the poor man was freezing cold and soaked with dew. He was only in his dressing gown and slippers.

— What the hell sort of security is that? If he could get into the grounds without being seen he could have got anywhere. Well, there you have it, he just walked out and nobody was there to stop him.

– Mr Harmon, this is not a prison. Our patients are free to come and go around the building and in the grounds as they please. However, I can assure you, if he had made any attempt to leave the grounds he would not have been able to do so.

– Did Mr Turner say anything about why he was out there?

– He didn't say anything at all. He wasn't properly awake, you know, as if he was in a trance. He was just staring ahead and marching round and round on the lawn. He didn't seem to see or hear anyone. I eventually had to get two orderlies to take him back inside. When he did wake up he didn't remember anything about it.

– And you've no idea what he was doing?

– Just walking. He'd been there so long he'd worn a path in the grass – like a capital letter G.

– G? Christ!

– Oh no! Oh Derek!

– Mr Harmon? Mrs Turner? You find that significant?

– I'm closing down this inquiry right now. We have to call in much higher authority.

– You don't have the authority to shut this down, only I can do that.

– I don't know your security clearance. Jesus, no one here can have the clearance for this. I'll have to call in the military, they should take over the search. Oh God, I bet I know who has him. Yes, that would explain a lot.

– Mr Harmon, I have been given the authority to pursue any course to solve the mystery of Mr Turner's disappearance. I already have reason to regret a certain lack of co-operation by your company, do not give me reason to make an even more adverse report. If you know what has happened to Mr Turner, I insist that you tell us. What, for instance, is G?

– It's the codename for a new project in the very early stages of development. It's, well, if I say the research is being carried out in association with the RAF will you accept that I cannot reveal more?

— And you had stored details of this top-secret research project in Mr Turner's brain?

— No. Yes . . . No, of course not. That would have been an inexcusable risk. But there were details concerning G tied up with the information we did feed into him. But that should have been safe, there couldn't be any way he could know anything about G unless he found a way of combining information from dozens of different and totally distinct batches of information, and then running them through a very high powered computer.

— Synaesthesia, am I right Doctor? Couldn't that be described as information from one part of the brain leaking into what is supposed to be a totally separate part?

— Yes, perfectly correct. And the brain, Mr Harmon, is a very high-powered computer, most of whose functions we still cannot fully identify. Now this raises a fascinating possibility. If this leakage between stored data and the subconscious or pre-conscious mind really is possible, then there are some intriguing questions to ask about the way this data is affecting the perception — even the creation — of the subject's world. The food tastes yellow, indeed.

— Or a blue door?

— Precisely, Mrs Turner. A blue door. Absolutely fascinating.

— Mrs Turner, I was forgetting, you also reacted to the letter. Do you know anything about this project?

— No. It's me. My name, Gillian. And when we first met I used to wear a ponytail, so he called me 'gee-gee'. It was his pet name. Oh God, he did remember. It's this place, it's what they do. You should have known him, he was so excited when this new job came up. Derek always loved new things, new discoveries. He didn't need to be coerced, you know, he'd have volunteered for this anyway. He just wanted to be a part of it. It's the only time I'd ever argued with him, I was afraid of what it would do to him. I just wanted my Derek like he always had been, and I was afraid they were going to change him. And I was right, wasn't I? I was right. As soon as they started putting all those things into his head he was different, he behaved differently, he talked differently. He'd stop and listen to things that no one else could hear. Like he wasn't fully here, part of him was somewhere else. And it got worse. In the end I didn't think he was hearing me at all, just whatever it was inside him. It wasn't my Derek any more. I asked him if he knew who I was, and he didn't answer. He was a zombie, that's what I called him. Oh God, I said that. I said he didn't know who I was, and he didn't care, and I had to leave him. I had to. I didn't think he'd heard me. But . . . Maybe he'd heard me all along, maybe there was a place for me in whatever he was listening to, maybe a place away from all the things that were twisting his mind. And that's where he's gone. Where he used to be, where *we* could be. And he's waiting for me now, of course. I've got to go and join him on the other side of the door. The pool, Mr Jacobs. The pool. Is it there? I can use that to get to him.

– No! Mrs Turner, stop! You can't. There's nothing there. It doesn't exist. You –

THE COLERIDGE BOMBERS

Paul Beardsley

Paul Beardsley

Paul Beardsley was born in Nottingham in 1963, and now lives in Havant. He received a B.A. degree in 1986, and is currently employed by a defence company, dealing with test equipment. He has previously had a story published in *Ad Lib* magazine, and has contributed material to *Viz* comic.

THE LANDSCAPE WAS silent for a while but the sirens
began before the sun had lifted clear of the distant mountains. You could fight it, you could ignore it, but you
couldn't escape it. You could fill your ears with wax, but
there was still the visual element, and quite possibly a tactile
element, subtle, but then it was all subtle. You walked for
half an hour because you saw someone in a distant field, not
beckoning, but sitting with his/her back to you, unaware
of you. You wondered why the figure never seemed to get
any nearer, and you were almost upon it when you realized
that he/she was merely a chance alignment of a fallen log,
a bottle hanging from a strand of barbed-wire, and a wisp
of wool tangled on a branch. At this point your fear of an
unknown presence was replaced by a worse fear of being
alone. But on the horizon, spaced 120° apart, were three
scarecrows, obviously more than they appeared just as the
figure was less.

Stetson awoke sweating and sat up. It was 4 a.m., and
Jane was visible by the light of a streetlamp through thin
curtains. He said, 'Something terrible is going to happen.
I am a part of something terrible.'

Jane grunted in her sleep and turned over. Stetson stared
into space for a time, but the moment of intuition had
passed. Puzzled, he returned to sleep.

It was a week before they exploded the Coleridge Bomb,
which destroyed all life (but, all things being equal, created
new life not so different from the old). Stetson moved
among the crowds; by considering people as objects, it
was easier to cope with the agoraphobia. Random objects

moving across open space, driven by tragically mundane purposes. Carrying his bag of groceries, he entered a side-street. This would take him past Jane Lagrange's flat, but the fact did not register.

He had lived with her for six months, rarely venturing outside and conducting his research by network, but a week previously he walked out on her when she said she was pregnant. He left her, not because she was pregnant, but because he hated liars. Later, on acquiring his temporary address from a well-meaning friend, she had phoned him repeatedly, pleading with him to return to her. She had attempted persuasion by emotion, reason, blackmail. She had in her possession original manuscripts by Lord Byron and Samuel Taylor Coleridge, worth a fortune and belonging to Stetson. He told her that he could live without them. She threatened to stare at the sun and burn out her retinas. He told her not to be so damned childish.

In truth, he wanted to give in. When someone is hated for an action or an exposed facet of their being, there should be no need for hatred when they have repented of that deed or withdrawn that facet. But the impossibility of distinguishing between person-as-liar and person-as-truthful made it the individual and not the quality that was hated.

So it became necessary, or at least desirable, to leave the city. Having arranged to have his luggage brought on later by a Potentially Employable Person, a twenty-year-old school-leaver hired from Pep Talks, Stetson suppressed his fear of streets and ventured out the front door.

He was a hundred yards from the station when he passed Jane Lagrange's flat. A gun fired, and his left leg was in pain, a spreading dampness centred on that pain. Distanced by the agoraphobia and the months of intense abstract work, he was unable to correlate the two matters instantly, so that Jane had time to fire again. Affected as it was by wild conflicting emotions, her aim was poor, and the shot missed, giving Stetson time to gain the temporary sanctuary of a blind alley. Someone with undamaged legs could have climbed the wall at the far end, but Stetson would have to leave the way he came in.

For escape to be possible, Jane must be distracted. On impulse, recalling the manuscripts, he shouted up to her, 'Jane, I have something of great value that belongs to you. Killing me will deprive you of it.' His words had a force of conviction by virtue of their direct reversal of the facts, but Stetson felt contempt at himself for having lied. Had he fully appreciated Jane's feelings for him, he could have made the statement quite truthfully.

From the flat's second-floor window Jane watched Stetson through the gunsights as he emerged from the alley, limping, grocery bag in one hand, staunching handkerchief held on the wound by the other. He made his way awkwardly, acutely conscious of the red pinpoint of the laser finder on his back. It was the open spaces that made him afraid.

Jane followed his progress until after he was out of sight. Then she screamed, 'You bastard!' and threw the gun across the room.

The hundred yards seemed to go on forever. Back on the main road, traffic sounds passed in slow motion, portable stereos carried by youths blared fragmentarily, a child prostitute on the steps of Barclays Bank sang:

'There's blood in the Martian canals, dear,
There's death in dark waters tonight . . . '

He sat awkwardly in the waiting-room, watching a large silverfish crawl across the floor. He felt foolish at bleeding in front of strangers.

The agony of the train journey was such that Stetson was relieved at his later inability to remember much of it. The bleeding was under control when the train pulled in at Billingshurst, and from there the taxi driver drove considerately along the country roads. At length he arrived at the country mansion, his by right of birth and of talent.

He had not told Jane about the mansion, preferring to keep it as a secret haven to return to should the need arise, as it indeed had. However, at such short notice of re-occupation the house had few supplies beyond those which Stetson had himself brought, and the servants were hard pressed. One, a gardener, proved to be a New Worlder who had fought in the Vay Aight wars and had had experience as a medic. He was able to treat Stetson's wound adequately, sparing him the hassle of hospital procedure.

The radio played Tchaikovsky. Stetson lay on the bed in the main room, reading *Dreams Of Ithaca* and trying to relate the complicated relationships to his own experience. Eventually the book slipped out of his fingers on to the floor as he drifted into sleep.

He was limping across unspoiled countryside, not unlike that through which he had come in the taxi in reality, when he came upon a beautiful lake. He was carrying a gold-plated arbalest and a number of quarrels. He raised the crossbow to shoot a swan, but it made a gesture that was unmistakably a plea for mercy. Fascinated he watched as thirty or more swans swam to the shore, stepped on to land, and *changed*. It was like watching a complicated and very painful birth as legs enlarged, wings developed into downy arms, swan-necks thrashed about as swan-heads became human heads. After a time the change was complete and some three dozen beautiful girls stood on the lake shore. Some were dressed in white fur and some were still washing in the lake water to remove the sweaty grime and blood that they had exuded in the process. One, obviously the queen, held Stetson's enraptured gaze. She held out a hand and stepped towards him, and he shot her in the stomach from a distance of three feet. The injury of the innocent continued as Stetson reloaded and shot the girls faster than they could transform themselves back into swans and fly away. Like a mathematical series; a row of swan-girls lay on the lake shore in progressive stages of metamorphosis, some almost entirely human, some almost entirely swan. One had completed the change and was winging her way out across the water to safety. Stetson, who had missed her twice, calmly followed her with the sights of the arbalest and then fired, and the quarrel passed bloodily through her neck.

He was awakened early the next morning by the sound of church bells in the nearby village. He had slept fully clothed. Having dutifully recorded the violent dream, he attempted to find meaning in it.

The swans were beautiful *per se*. And so were the girls. But even the combined beauty of the two was outweighed by the horror of the transformation itself, perhaps. That must have been why he killed them all. But if that was the case, why had he been about to shoot the first swan on sight?

Bright after-the-storm sunlight shone through the large study window. Recently removed furniture covers lay in a neat pile in a corner. Stetson adjusted the screen filter of the Amstrad and switched on. He ate his breakfast at the desk, then turned to the PC to begin work in earnest.

As a preliminary exercise he sketched a symbolic analogue of the non-visual aspects of the dream of the swans. It was standard practice for a coder of his calibre to exploit dream-inspiration in this way. When he was satisfied with it he filed it away on to hard disk for further development; as it stood, it was usable but raw.

He decided that the file was worth uploading on to the central computer in Guildford. When he logged on, however, he was surprised to see the message: 'User Already Logged On'. Assuming he had done this without thinking, he carried on as normal, but his attempt to upload the file was met with the message: 'Missing Directory'.

'Must have got into another user's directory,' he muttered. He was about to log out when it occurred to him that such an event was very rare. Succumbing to idle curiosity, he listed the directory and browsed through it. There was little of interest in it, except for a file called 'SECRET'. It had to be a joke, thought Stetson – people didn't call secret files 'SECRET' any more than they called their passwords 'DROWSSAP' or 'QWERTY'.

He accessed it anyway. A long list was revealed, divided into three columns with the triple heading 'Name : Date of Birth : G.C.F.' He scrolled through the names, which were in alphabetical order, until he found his own. Raymond Stetson : 120376 : 03.

It seemed too prosaic to be a joke. What did G.C.F. mean? And who needed to know?

Vexed, he decided to find answers immediately. He picked up the phone and keyed absently, knowing there would always be someone available to ask, even if they were not prepared to answer his questions.

The phone was answered. 'Hello?'

Surprised, Stetson said, 'Jane?'

'What do you want Ray?'

'I . . . I must have had your number on my mind. I didn't realize I'd been thinking of you, er, your number . . .'

There was a silence, time to think, why don't I hang up, without hanging up. Jane broke the silence by saying, 'If you think you can just – '

'I don't *know* what I was thinking . . .' Stetson interrupted. 'The code's so abstract – '

'If you'd tried trusting me a bit, tried *talking* to me . . . I might have understood, might have – '

'It wasn't so easy . . . Damn it Jane, I wasn't *allowed* to trust you, or anybody.' What the hell did G.C.F. mean?

'You won't understand, will you? I *know* that's all military, I'm not talking about that, I'm – '

'It's one and the same.' He had no idea what to do with this conversation, how to get out of it, or even if that was what he wanted to do. He continued to talk, but his conscious mind went off at a tangent, searching through memories. He found what he was looking for: the

Conditioning course, and a doctor saying the words 'Guilt Compensation Factor' – meaningless out of context, but that must be it.

'Really? Do you mean that?' Jane asked; he realized he had somehow continued with the conversation. Did I say I love you? The last thirty seconds were not his, and he could recall nothing other than recalling.

He said, 'I hadn't realized . . . I don't think you'd have made an attempt on my life if I didn't mean something . . .'

As he spoke, and long after the conversation, he gazed at the objects around him: the antique desk, the picture of his sister who had died in a car crash, the apparently incongruous variety of books on the shelves (poetry and programming languages). 'Mean something.' Perhaps it doesn't matter that nothing has meaning to you if you have meaning to someone else.

That night, he lay awake in a reverie. Through open shutters the moon cast a silver rectangle on to the bed. Something was right; he couldn't place what it was, but it didn't matter.

This peaceful feeling was interrupted twice, once by the shrill but brief scream of an alarm. He spoke into the intercom by his bed, and the explanation of the servant was reassuring and gentle, as a mother soothing her child from bad dreams: 'It's all right, sir. Two intruders trying to gain entry. The House Defences have taken care of them.' The second interruption was a shock of intuition, familiar, but this time understood.

Monday dawned, and Stetson could remember only one scene from his dreams. He had stood in a crater in a city of devastated England. There were nine people who were very evil, very powerful, and who all looked exactly like Stetson. They were responsible for the damage. Yet, for all their casual and callous violence, they treated the mortal Stetson with respect as if their lives depended on him.

This recorded, and his breakfast eaten, Stetson descended through the French windows in the lounge, where a servant was removing the last vestiges of blood, and out to the garage into his car.

The station car-park was small, and the car itself gave Stetson a certain sense of security. The train was not due for a few minutes yet, so he switched on the radio.

' . . . such as C/Atlas and MIP. By then, concepts of "generation" became essentially meaningless as the balance of the user/machine interface gradually tilted in the user's favour. With the introduction of . . . '

The train arrived. From this position it was possible to see Jane tip the vigies and step out on to the platform. Stetson waited until she was by the passenger door before he unlocked it.

'Ray.'

'Come in Jane.' Do I kiss her do we talk what do I say? 'How have you been?'

'I'm afraid I destroyed the Byron.'

'It doesn't matter, it's the poetry that counts, not the paper it's written on . . . ' He gestured at the radio. 'This programme's about the sort of work I do. It might make things clearer.'

' . . . So Xanadu was welcomed by programmers who had acquired a proficiency at assembly language during childhood. The introduction of the Most Probable Default system lessened the need for precise definition which in turn heralded the introduction of an intuitive approach, which was further advanced by Wernher's application module . . . '

When they made love that afternoon Stetson was aware of his own pleasure as a distant thing that could be seen but not felt. A fragment of the previous night's dream returned to him then. One of the nine Stetsons had just raped a girl and the real Stetson had persuaded him not to kill her. He then attempted to comfort her, covering her with his coat and moving her to a safer place. As she regained consciousness, she glared and spat at him, and said, 'It doesn't make you a hero to partially undo your own damage.'

'You don't understand, it wasn't me . . . ' I'm missing the point, he thought as she resisted all attempts to help her, and she's not going to spell it out to me.

'You're really going to be open with me now?' asked Jane.

'Yes.'

'Why couldn't you before?'

'It was the nature of the work I did. As the work and the worker become one and the same, it is impossible to reveal anything about yourself without indirectly violating the Official Secrets Act.'

'But now things are different.'

'Yes.' He paused, unsure of what she meant by the statement. 'Yes, I've found out what I was working on. It's called the Coleridge Device. Designed by a group of coders including myself, it will be tested some time this week. It will destroy the world.'

They were silent for a time. Jane asked, 'How do you mean, you've "found out" what you were working on? I thought you were a designer!'

'We weren't told what we were working on. We accept some kind of brief at a subconscious level – all I can remember is something along the lines of, "The device will be the answer to everything" – and we're left to get on with it.' He found he was desperately trying to justify himself to her. 'We're the poets in the language of machines – we code from the subconscious, where our orders reside. Our minds grant the wishes of our employers, passing from what is needed to the actual product, stepping over the process in between.'

'But didn't it occur to you that a device used in a military environment must be a weapon?'

'Not necessarily. I believed also in the intrinsic goodness of human nature. Xanadu is as close to that as anything can get.'

'Do you still believe it?'

'No.' A great weariness descended on Stetson. 'No, I don't.'

In the dream he scrambled, laughing, over the collapsing wall and out into the shattered street, into the warm light of the ninth H-bomb to be dropped on England. Everything was slowed down – you could outrun falling rubble, and the searing blast was prolonged like a Hawaiian sunset. It was an unexpected celebration, people running and leaping and dancing in the radiation, bathing, as the ground cracked open, the sea flooded in and seeped into the ground, and somehow H-bombs had lost their credibility when compared with the power of the Coleridge Bomb. In such a delirious state the population died.

She had faith in him, convinced that he would succeed in his endeavour to avert the forthcoming disaster.

He had told her, 'When I realized what was going on, I did something much against my nature. I started lying.'

'Is that wise?'

'I'm sacrificing an abstract moral for the greater good. Surely that's – '

'No, I mean, is that a practical course of action?'

'It's the only one.' He sighed. 'It used to be so easy to crash a computer – all it took was a little ineptitude. Nowadays there's stringent consistency checking, and no gate wide enough for a Trojan horse. A direct approach is out of the question.'

'So what can you do?'

'Introduce false data – *consistently* false data, in response to the data coming in. That's stage one – at the very least, the final product, the Coleridge Bomb, will be based on erroneous parameters. As stage two, I've attempted to modulate a virus on to the increased error range – that's possible with Dreamsnaic, which is very similar to Xanadu . . . ' He broke off, then said, 'If only *they* knew what we're working on. But then, perhaps they do.'

He worked diligently over the next two days. There was no sign of any alteration in the incoming data after a week's fudging, but that was no real cause for alarm. More importantly, the data carrying the virus-imprinted error range had not been rejected, and the triggering data looked innocent enough to get through the gates.

The events of the last few days seemed hazy now. Reality was so arbitrary when compared with the absolutes of thinking in a machine language. Stetson recalled devouring computer textbooks as a child, books he considered light entertainment, and considerably less useless than the James Joyce novels he attempted in his mid teens. Stetson was a Technological Man – that product of technology so feared by an earlier age, but not a fearful thing to be. Life before the semiconductor revolution had not exactly been a bed of roses.

So when, on the Wednesday morning, the Project Co-ordinator transmitted his summons to Stetson, the phonecall was received with a calm resignation, a distant awareness of a feeling of dismay, but not the feeling itself.

The agoraphobia was so bad that Stetson reclined in the car with his eyes covered as Jane drove them to the Project Co-ordinator's office in London. The car-park seemed vast, and Jane had been unable to find a space near the huge building. Kellered as he was against the sights and sounds of the area, he could nevertheless feel the breeze and the sun, smell the exhaust of six hundred cars; cringing, he imagined that Jane was guiding him off course, and he fought the urge to rip off his sensory defences as a suffocating astronaut fights the urge to open his visor.

Once indoors all was well, and Jane waited in reception for two hours, reading bland magazines on neutral subjects. Eventually Stetson returned and they made their way back to the car, Stetson pausing to discard the blinkers in a wastebin outside the building.

They sat in the car for a while, then Jane said, 'What happened, Ray?'

'They don't know what they're doing. I told them, and they still don't know. They may know as individuals, but it isn't the individual that counts. So I failed.' Then his tears came unrestrained, and Jane calmly comforted him. 'I failed Jane, my attempt failed.' A real man crying real tears. But even now he was the observer watching it happen to himself.

It was better than before. They had tried everything, and now there was nothing left to try. The hours that remained were unhurried, and Stetson could really believe that he loved Jane. All the world was so intensely beautiful that it hurt. They arose early on Thursday morning as the dew was lifting in the sunrise. They sat by a stream and talked.

'It's not so bad when it's out of your hands, really,' said Jane. 'For it to stop at a moment of happiness, for the whole world, the world ending suddenly when things are going well. Where did you go wrong, by the way?'

'My dreams gave me away,' Stetson replied with a smile. 'Remember how I said the work and the worker becomes one? I was conditioned with a Guilt Compensation Factor — a figure three as it happened. So long as I was on the straight and narrow, the number three would be a regular feature in my dreams. When that number suddenly changed to nine, they knew I was lying, and they were even able to interpret how much I was lying by. With modifications, they could still accept the data I was putting in.'

'Sometimes success lies in failure.'

'Mmm. And vice versa.'

Clouds gathered in the afternoon. Jane thought they might go inside and watch the coverage on Sat 2. As the time drew closer, Stetson suggested they close the windows on the grounds that it was getting chilly. When the televised account of the first test explosion of a Coleridge Device came on, the pretence that the mansion would somehow shield them gradually evaporated. They sat huddled together on the sofa.

The bomb was very small. It was placed inside the extinct volcanic crater of an atoll in the Pacific. Measuring instruments surrounded it. There were no people within a hundred miles. It was reasoned that the curvature of the Earth would protect them from any unforeseen effects. A voice-over recited platitudes about breakthroughs and secrets of the universe. The clock's second hand ticked towards the zero. The TV screen showed a commentator who said, 'I think they're just about to . . . ' and the picture died a second after he did. The wind howled through the melted windows of the mansion and no matter how tightly Stetson held Jane he could not prevent her from slipping away. He could not understand why he was still alive, but when he'd worked it out he'd forgotten something more important. He looked around the room. A room. 'Everything's as it was before,' he said aloud, 'everything, except for anything that matters.'

The bewildered old man, forever in search of the past as if it had even an abstract existence, as if nostalgia had ever been anything other than a synonym for pain. Walking stiffly (victim of an old war wound they say, poor chap) through the permafrost world, a world he had created, the first man and murderer of the old world: Adam seeking to usurp the rôle of God and Cain both.

The library staff greeted his entrance with trained patience. What does the old gentleman want that we can give him?

He took his time getting to the counter, he took his time taking the books out of the old carrier bag. The librarian said, 'That book's overdue, Mr Stedsen. I'm afraid you'll have to pay.'

Stedsen, the old man, took his time deciding how to reply. Eventually he said, 'It didn't help. It didn't help at all! Why should I have to pay when I gained nothing?' He reached sadly into his pocket without expecting an answer and paid the fine. He left, walking painfully, making his way to the bus stop where new graffiti read, 'I was only following orders.' He was unaware of the youth watching him from across the street, a vindictive youth with patricidal intent, who had sworn revenge for Jayenne, his blind mother.

DEPENDANT

David V Barrett

David V Barrett

David Barrett regularly reviews science fiction and fantasy for the *Independent*, *New Scientist*, *New Statesman and Society*, *Foundation* and *Fear*, amongst others, and esoteric books for various magazines. He edited *Vector*, the critical journal of the British Science Fiction Association, for four years. He has worked briefly as a brewer's drayman and a Kendal mint-cake maker, and for somewhat longer as a schoolteacher, a something-we-can't-talk-about-but-it-involved-computers for GCHQ, and for the last few years as features editor, then special projects editor on *Computer Weekly*. He plays electronic bass, lives happily with a cat and well-scratched furniture, and loves the Loire Valley. *Digital Dreams* is his first book of many.

I LOVE DOING this; I get a kick out of it, even when I'm not making anything out of it. If I do that's a bonus, it's not why I do it.

She asked me more than once, when she was in one of her holy and moral moods; the priest must have been giving her a talking to – or it might have been her dad. She called them both Father anyway, so I doubt it makes much difference.

'Why do you do it, Kevin? You know it's wrong.'

She just couldn't see why I do it, the challenge, the fun in it. She's too stupid to understand computers anyway; the first time I mentioned a modem she thought it was something to do with the Paris fashions she'd read about in *Cosmopolitan* in the doctor's waiting-room.

She spent a lot of time in that waiting-room, after she'd missed three periods. She didn't even notice missing the first two, that's how together she was. You'd think she hadn't even made the connection between screwing and getting pregnant, despite her good Catholic upbringing, it took her so much by surprise. It was her dad who noticed she was throwing up in the mornings, and who made her mum ask her whether anything regular hadn't happened lately.

And when she told them we'd been doing it for a few months, and they found out she wasn't on the pill, they asked if I'd not used a condom. Had I hell. She was a virgin, so there was no chance of my getting AIDS, so why spoil things for myself?

Protection: that's what people think they've got on their computers because they use a password. A johnnie's a damn sight more protection against viruses than any password. There was that programmer put a virus-killer program up

on a bulletin board on a network. A public service, he
called it, so all the thousands of people who accessed that
board could run his program through their PCs and their
hard disks and check they'd not been infected, and praise
this great servant of humanity (who got a hell of a lot of
publicity out of it in the computer magazines).

So I spiked his little program for him.

Oh, he'd been clever. He knew how to write good code
all right, and he'd obviously half expected someone like
me to try something like that, because there were little
traps and bombs all over the place which would send up
warning messages if his program was tampered with. So
I took a copy of the program, in object code, of course;
he wasn't dumb enough to leave the source code lying
around. And I ran it through a neat little decompiler and
a few check-and-spit programs I'd written to spot traps and
trip-wires, and then I had a good read through the source
code I'd created.

Putting a virus into a virus-killer is like sticking a pin
through a packet of condoms, only much more effective.
It works every time.

It must have been about the same time one of my little
worms was wriggling its way towards June's ovum that I
put my software worm into this guy's code and squirted it
back on to the bulletin board, so it would germinate in the
system of anyone stupid enough to use the program, and
start growing.

I've been using that bulletin board for years; I know
how to tweak it so it does exactly what I want. I made
the system think that my new improved version of the
virus-killer was actually input on the date the original one
was put in. I mean, it would have been obvious it had been
mucked about with if it had changed by a few months. It
would have stood out as much as June's belly did after a
few months.

Her father was a clever sod, I'll give him that. You see,
she was still under-age when she got pregnant. God, it

seemed like half the girls in her class had been on the pill and screwing around for years; me and a couple of mates used to compare notes and keep a score chart — how often we'd scored, and who with, and marks out of ten.

So he lets me know, casual but threatening, that *he's* got mates on the magistrates' bench, and did I know what the penalties were? Then he gets me to promise to marry her, in front of the priest, and with my parents there as well; came as a shock to them, because I'd not told them. Why they were so strung up about it I don't know.

So there I was, engaged, with no way of getting out of it, and her in a real input-output condition, and her dad goes with me to make sure I buy her a decent ring. Two, in fact; one for the engagement and one for the church. Yeah, a big church wedding, with all the trimmings for their only little girl, and a full reception and all that. And all because I'd not taken precautions.

I've never been that careless with entering a computer system. For a start, I never let it know who I am. For instance, there's this minicomputer in a regional police headquarters sixty miles from where I'm sat in front of my PC with its customized modem and its other bits and pieces, not all of them strictly legal. If the machine thinks I'm New Scotland Yard making a routine enquiry, that's fine by me. I take a good look at what's available. There's some pretty standard admin files, and there's a bloody great criminal-records database.

If I can get into this database I can really have fun. A few changes here and there, alter a few names, and I can screw up anyone I want. A couple of minor sexual offences long enough ago it'll be difficult to prove otherwise: that'll bugger anyone's career. It's like putting someone on one of those credit blacklists: once you're on the records you've had it. I key in a few commands, and up comes the message: 'Restricted Access'.

And now the real fun starts.

Being married was fun, while it lasted. I'd got a reasonably paid job, so I could get a mortgage, and I had a few thousand in the bank, so I could put down a deposit on a house. It was on that new estate where the allotments used to be when I was a kid, one of those estates owned by the builders, so the houses were cheap and nasty, but at least they were cheap, with a ninety per cent mortgage.

So we had our big church wedding and our big formal reception, and one of her uncles embarrassed both sets of parents by cracking a joke about the three of us walking down the aisle. I couldn't have cared less; I'd been tackling the lager before the reception, and the wine with the meal, and the champagne with the toasts, and I was happy enough. And June, she didn't understand the joke anyway.

We had a week in Blackpool and then moved into our new house, and I was busy for a while with all the things a new husband is busy with in a new house: decorating, putting up shelves, picking up second-hand furniture at auction sales, chucking the rubble in the back garden into the back garden next door, for *its* new husband to deal with when he moved in.

The funny thing was, I was getting quite fond of little June, as she became not so little. She'd just been one fifth-form girl among many at her school, half-way between my office and my old flat; we always said you could do a lot in a lunch hour. I wasn't too happy when she got pregnant, but I was really looking forward to us having a kid now, and me being a father. I hadn't liked the attitude of *her* father, or of the old windbag she also called Father, who made a lot of noise about me joining the church and bringing the kid up in the true faith; but I reckon I'd done right by her by marrying her, and now the fuss was all over I didn't even resent being pushed into marriage any more.

I liked coming home from work and having a meal cooked for me, and having someone to watch TV with, and talk to in the evenings, and do the odd thing for that she couldn't do herself. And she got even sexier as she got bigger; she'd been a bit on the skinny side before. As I say, to my surprise I discovered I actually liked being married to June.

I also discovered (it didn't take long) that I liked being on the estate. Not that it was much of a place to live, with all the houses the same, and half the roads not finished, and the nearest pub over a mile away, but it had its compensations. Like Sophia and Astra who were tall, cool models who lived just across the way, and Debbie and Julie who were blonde and bubbly secretaries, just like I'd always imagined them, and who liked playing together, and Mandy, who was this air-hostess who looked like air-hostesses ought to look. And the rest. And they all had husbands who were lorry drivers or reps or merchant seamen or in prison or who had left them. And they'd all be happy and willing if I dropped in for ten minutes or so before going to work, or longer if June went over to her parents' on a Saturday afternoon.

It was only like having a bit extra at first, with June still as the main course; but it became more important to me when the kid was nearly due. She was worried about harming it, even though the doctor said it would be OK, so she asked me not to for a bit. I didn't mind at all, but it was difficult not to laugh when she apologized and praised me for being so good and patient and understanding.

She was never understanding when it came to my real love. I liked sex, but it wasn't up to the buzz I'd get from coupling up with some system and breaking into protected files and databases. The words 'Restricted Access' were like the cover of a kid's comic, saying 'Hey, come on, look inside, this is going to be fun.' I'd spend the evening hunched over my screen, and June would come and stand behind me and I wouldn't notice until she put her arms around me (and I don't know how I stopped myself from lashing out when she made me lose my concentration and I had to pull out from where I was without getting anywhere, and lose everything I'd been building up, and God that's frustrating), and then she'd say 'I'm going to bed; will you be long?' and I'd look at my watch and it would be ten o'clock, and I'd promise to be up in less than an hour, and she'd say 'You said that last night and it was after two when you came to bed', and I'd grunt something and would be back in the system before she'd reached the stairs, and I'd be happy there for the next three or four hours.

Part of it's the challenge of beating someone else, some-one I've never met who's set up a system to be secure against attacks from people like me. That's what I enjoy, fighting these security consultants with degrees in computer science who take bloody great fees for telling companies to smarten up their password procedure and always do regular system backups, and install this and implement that – all the things that any half-way intelligent data processing manager would be doing anyway, if his boss would cough up the money for it. But the boss never will until he's paid out a small fortune for a consultancy report which doesn't say anything the DP manager hasn't tried to tell him a dozen times. The computer's *his* baby, and he just wants to look after it, and no one will ever let him do it properly.

We called *our* baby Jamie, and June let me look after him, pick him up and hold him and play with him and feed him and wash him and change him, just as much as I wanted. It was really great being a dad; I'd get home at night and go straight to him, and he'd be lying there all pink and glowing and smile at me. I know it was only wind, but it felt good to know that he was *mine*, and he'd be there all the time, and I'd be able to bring him up and teach him things. Give him a year or two and he'd be the first kid in his play-group who could do programming.

Nothing heavy, of course; programming and playing with computers should be *fun*. Doing it for a living's not the same; there's nothing more boring than writing yards and yards of code for some major application for someone else; I did it for a couple of years before I got wise and got out. That's not the sort of stuff I can get off on, at all.

I've always liked doing little one-offs where I don't have to bother about all those protocols and procedures that you have to when there's other people involved, so I can have the one thing I want without having to take ten dozen others into consideration, where it doesn't matter a damn to me what the effects are on anything or anyone else, where I can just have fun and do what I want and screw everybody else.

And then it all went wrong. It was some time after Jamie was born, a few weeks later, when she'd stopped feeling sore and stretched and torn and wanted it again; but by then I was flying Mandy and the others before I went to work and at lunch-times and during the evening when I could slip away from her for as long as it took. So when she tried it on in the evening or when she stayed awake until I switched the computer off and went to bed and put her arms round me and snuggled up to me I wasn't interested; I'd satisfied the need and exhausted the supply, and just couldn't be bothered making the effort.

This one evening I'm out at the pub, and start chatting up this blonde, and discover she lives on the estate, and she offers me a lift back. I can't believe it, it's the perfect story, straight out of the magazines, and she's built like a centre-fold. So I invite myself in, and before she's even finished unlocking the door I've got my hand inside her blouse and I'm pushing her bra down, and she's got really great boobs and I'm fondling them. She's struggling and saying no-no-no, but that's all part of the game, isn't it, so as she's writhing about I get my other hand up her skirt and she's got fantastic long legs, and I get my fingers inside her panties and start feeling her and pulling them off her, and she's damp and ready for me.

She's screaming now, and her fingernails are ripping at my face, and the door suddenly opens and there's her husband grabbing at her and at me and her tits are both hanging out and they're scratched and her knickers are half-way down her legs and she's wet herself.

He's kicking me and kicking me. There's blood in my eyes and mouth and I'm choking on a tooth. He waits till I've thrown up, then he drags me into the house.

And it just couldn't be worse. He's a bloke I've had a few pints with, and told about all the different birds I've had and the ways I've had them, and she's just had a baby and knows June from the clinic. He gets her calmed down a bit and she gets cleaned up and puts her clothes back together, and they drag me two streets to my own house and bang on the door, and June's dad opens it.

There's a lot of shouting and pushing around, and after what seems forever these two go. June's dad does a load more yelling, and then he goes as well, taking June and Jamie with him.

The next morning he came back without her but with the other Father, to make sure he didn't kill me, he said. He seemed really angry, though I hadn't done anything to him, but when I started to ask him why he told me to pack up what I needed and get out. June was coming back to her home with her baby and he or her mother was going to be there every night to make sure I never came through the door or touched their daughter again.

And the priest said he'd known right from the start that I wouldn't keep my promises to him or to the Church or to her parents or to God or to June, and I wondered just who the fuck I'd married anyway when I heard the order he put them in. But that was it, so I moved out with my computer and my clothes and stayed in a hotel that night, and found this flat the next day.

I tried, I mean, I still wanted to, but I just couldn't get it up any more; I was so pissed off at everything that had happened, and a lunch hour or an evening was a hell of a long time to spend getting nowhere.

So I thought, Stuff it, sex is just a waste of good time I can spend doing what I *really* enjoy doing. Computers don't screw you around, they do what you tell them every time, and when you're trying to get into a new system there's that same breathless excitement and risk you get trying to get off with a new woman, only it's more satisfying because there's no one to let you down or piss you off, there's only you against *it*, and when you actually break through into a new system there's the triumph just like taking a virgin, only without the mess and the tears, which they never mention in the magazines, and even bettet is you can't get a computer pregnant. And best of all is you can switch it off when you've finished, and it'll still be there waiting for you the next day.

I thought divorces were supposed to be easy these days, just both of you fill in a few forms and that's it, but it's not like that when there's a kid involved. You've got to dress up smart and go to court for them to decide who gets custody. So there's me in my suit, with my hair slicked down and on my best behaviour, looking cool and capable, and there's this kid on the other side who I don't recognize at first, she looks about fourteen and totally sweet and innocent like she doesn't know where babies even come from, and she's sitting between her two fathers, and her mother holding Jamie, my son.

'That's my son,' I say.

That was one of the things they'd wanted to check on, but we all agreed on that, so that was OK. It was the only thing that was.

And then the whole thing came out again in court, about how I'd not only corrupted this sweet innocent child, but I'd done it when she *was* still a child, so I was obviously of lousy character anyway, and how I'd been going to dump her instead of marry her (that was a lie; they didn't *know* I'd have done that if I'd had the chance), and how I'd been a really bad husband and hadn't provided for her or looked after her or anything (that *was* a lie), and how I preferred screwing around with computers instead of screwing her (they didn't put it like that, but that one was *really* unfair; they just don't *understand*), and then on top of all that I'd been unfaithful to her.

I nearly said then. They didn't have any evidence I'd been unfaithful; I pointed that out, I said (all dramatic, like they do on TV), 'Where are my accusers? What proof is there of my alleged adultery?' But I was my own accuser; that bloody blonde had told June's dad what had happened, and her husband had repeated all the stories I'd told him in the pub, and June's dad had written it all down, and it was all there in June's reasons for wanting a divorce.

And every bit of it was read out in court; and when I looked around the room I saw some people I knew from the pub, and a few people from work who'd come to see the show, listening again to the stories I'd told them again and again over a lot of pints.

And suddenly it was over: she'd got a decree nisi, the judge said, and the house and everything in it for as long as she wanted to live there (sure, I could have half the proceeds if she ever decided to sell it, but until then I'd have to pay the mortgage and upkeep and the electricity and gas bills), and I'd pay her maintenance of so much a week unless and until she remarried, and I'd pay maintenance of so much a week for the kid until he was sixteen. She'd get custody, of course, the judge said, but I'd be allowed restricted access to him. I could have him for a couple of hours every other weekend.

'Hey, wait a minute,' I said. 'All that first lot's fucking robbery and you know it, but she's not getting Jamie as well. He's *my* son. I'll pay all that if I have to, but I want my kid.'

But oh no, they weren't having that. Quite apart from my uncaring character and my irresponsible attitude and my admitted adultery with half the women on the estate, if all that wasn't enough reason in itself, which it was, wasn't I out at work all day? How could I possibly look after the child? I'll pay for a child-minder, a nanny, I said, while I'm out at work. Oh yes, they said, and how will you afford that on top of the mortgage for your former home, and the rent for wherever you're living now, and the maintenance for your child and your former wife?

And her bloody fathers, both of them, smirked. I still don't think June really knew what was going on; but she'd won, hadn't she? She'd won everything.

I nearly told them, right then, that they'd got it all wrong, that I'd not slept with anyone else since I married June, since I met June, that June was the first and only woman I'd ever slept with. But they wouldn't have believed me, would they?

And if they did believe me I'd be laughed at by everyone I know; they'd all know, and I couldn't face that, I couldn't.

So now I'm back in this crummy flat, by myself except for my computer. We sit up late at night, trying to make plans. Somehow I've got to get everything back that's been stolen from me. I'll get my house back, and June. I'd grown to like being a married man; I hate having to do all my own cooking and washing up and going to the launderette, and coming home from work to an empty flat, and having no one to talk to in the evening, until I switch on my computer.

And I'm going to get my son. Especially my son. Restricted access has never stopped me yet. And yes, I'll give June enough attention, and make sure she's content, and be a model husband, so I don't get him stolen away again. He belongs to me. He's my boy, my child, my — what's the proper word? Dependant.

I don't know how I'm going to do it, but me and my computer together, we're a great team, we're unbeatable. When I do get her back, she's got to understand that; she's got to give me as much time as I want with my computer.

You're going to help me, aren't you? Because you're the only one really understands me; everyone else makes life so complicated. There's no one else I can rely on. No one else I can trust.

NAD AND DAN ADN QUAFFY

Diana Wynne Jones

Diana Wynne Jones

Diana Wynne Jones began writing for children in 1970 when her three sons showed contempt/impatience for most books then available to them; but as adults had to read the things too — usually aloud — she tried to make the books interesting for adults as well. Twenty-one books later she finds almost as many adults as children read her books. She lives in Bristol where her husband is a Professor of English.

SHE HAD STRUGGLED rather as a writer until she got her word processor. Or not exactly *struggled*, she thought, frowning at her screen and flipping the cursor back to correct *adn* to *and*. For some reason, she always garbled the word *and* – it was always *adn* or *nad*; *dna* or *nda* were less frequent, but all of them appeared far oftener than the right way. She had only started to make this mistake after she gave up her typewriter and she felt it was a small price to pay.

For years she had written what seemed to her the most stirring sort of novels, about lonely aliens among humans, or lonely humans among aliens, or sometimes both kinds lonely in an unkind world – all without ever quite hitting the response from readers she felt she was worth. Then came her divorce, which left her with custody of her son Daniel, then thirteen. That probably provided an impetus of some sort in itself, for Danny was probably the most critical boy alive.

'Mum!' he would say. 'I wish you'd give *up* that lonely-heart alien stuff! Can't you write about something decent for a change?' Or, staring at her best efforts at cookery, he said, 'I can't be expected to eat *this*!' After which, he had taken over cooking himself: they now lived on chilli con carne and stir-fry. For, as Danny said, 'A man can't be expected to learn more than one dish a year.' At the moment, being nearly fifteen, Danny was teaching himself curry. Their nice Highgate house reeked of burnt garam masala most of the time.

But the real impetus had come when she found Danny in her workroom sternly plaiting the letters of her old

typewriter into metal braid. 'I've had this old thing!' he
said, when she tore him away with fury and cursings. 'So
have you. It's out of the ark. Now you'll have to get a
word processor.'

'But I don't know how to work the things!' she had
wailed.

'That doesn't matter. I do. I'll work it for you,' he replied
inexorably. 'And I'll tell you what one to buy too, or you'll
only waste money.'

He did so. The components were duly delivered and
installed, and Daniel proceeded to instruct his mother in
how to work as much of them as – as he rather blightingly
said – her feeble brain would hold. 'There,' he said. 'Now
write something worth reading for a change.' And he left
her sitting in front of it all.

When she thought about it, she was rather ashamed of
the fact that her knowledge of the thing had not progressed
one whit beyond those first instructions Danny had given
her. She had to call on her son to work the print-out, to
recall most of the files and to get her out of any but the
most simple difficulty. On several occasions – as when
Danny had been on a school trip to Paris or away with
his school cricket team – she had had to tell her publisher
all manner of lies to account for the fact that there would
be no copy of anything until Danny got back. But the
advantages far outweighed these difficulties – or at least
she knew they did *now*.

That first day had been a nightmare. She had felt lost
and foolish and weak. She had begun – not having anything
else in mind – on another instalment of lonely aliens. And
everything kept going wrong. She had to call Danny in ten
times in the first hour, and then ten times after lunch, and
then again when, for some reason, the machine produced
what she had written of Chapter I as a list, one word to a
line. Even Danny took most of the rest of the day to sort
out what she had done to get that. After that, he hovered
over her solicitously, bringing her mugs of black coffee,
until, somewhere around nine in the evening, she realized

she was in double bondage, first to a machine and then to her own son.

'Go away!' she told him. 'Out of my sight! I'm going to learn to do this for myself or die in the attempt!'

Danny gave her bared teeth a startled look, and fled.

By this time she had been sitting in front of board and screen for nearly ten hours. It seemed to her that her threat to die in the attempt was no idle one. She felt like death. Her back ached and so did her head. Her eyes felt like running blisters. She had cramp in both hands and one foot asleep. In addition, her mouth was foul with too much coffee and Danny's chilli con carne. The little green letters on the screen kept retreating behind the glass to the distant end of a long, long tunnel. 'I *will* do this!' she told herself fiercely. 'I am an intelligent adult – probably even a genius – and I will *not* be dominated by a mere machine!'

And she typed all over again:

Chapter One

The Captain had been at board and screen ever since jump – a total of ten hours. Her hands shook with weariness, making it an effort to hold them steady on her switches. Her head was muzzy, her mouth foul with nutrient concentrates. But since the mutiny, it was sit double watches or fail to bring the starship *Candida* safely through the intricate system of Meld . . .

At this point, she began to get a strange sense of power. She *was* dominating this damned machine, even though she was doing it only by exploiting her own sensations. Also, she was becoming interested in what might be going to happen to the starship *Candida* – not to speak of the reasons that had led up to the mutiny aboard her. She continued writing furiously until long after midnight. When she stopped at last, she had to pry her legs loose from her chair.

'*That's* more like it, Mum!' Danny said the next morning, reading it as it came from the printer.

He was, as usual, right. *Starship Candida* was the book
that made the name of FC Stone. It won prizes. It sold
in resorts and newsagents all over the world. It was —
reviewers said — equally remarkable for its insight into the
Captain's character as for the intricate personal relationships leading to the mutiny. Much was spoken about the
tender and peculiar relationships between the sexes. This
last made FC Stone grin rather. All she had done was to
revenge herself on Danny by reversing the way things were
between them. In the book, Captain was all-powerful and
dominating and complained a lot about the food. The Mate
had a hypnotically induced mindset that caused him to bleat
for assistance at the first sign of trouble.

Her next book, *The Mutineers*, was an even greater
success. For this one, FC Stone extended the intricate
personal relationships to the wider field of galactic politics.
She discovered she revelled in politics. Provided she was
making the politics up herself, there seemed no limit to
how intricate she could make them.

Since then she had, well, *not* stuck to a formula —
she was much more artfully various than that — but,
as she said and Danny agreed, there was no point in
leaving a winning game. Though she did not go back
to starship *Candida*, she stayed with that universe and
its intricate politics. There were aliens in it too, which
she always enjoyed. And she kept mostly out in space,
so that she could continue to describe pilots astronauting
at the controls of a word processor. Sooner or later in
most of her books, someone, human or alien, would have
sat long hours before a screen, until, dazed with staring,
aching in the back, itching in the nose — for the burning
of Asian spices in the kitchen tended to give her hay fever
— and with cramped hands, this pilot would be forced to
manoeuvre arduously through jump. This part always, or
nearly always, got written when FC Stone was unable to
resist staying up late to finish the chapter.

Danny continued to monitor his mother. He was proud
of what he had made her do. In holidays and round the

edges of school, he hung over her shoulder and brought
her continual mugs of strong black coffee. This beverage
began to appear in the books too. The mutineer humans
drank *gav*, while their law-abiding enemies quaffed *chvi*.
Spacer aliens staggered from their nav-couches to gulp
down *kivay*; and the mystics of Meld used *xfy* to induce
an altered state of consciousness – although this was not
generally spotted as being the same substance. And it was
all immensely popular.

It was all due to the word processor, she thought, giving
the nearest component a friendly pat as she leant towards
the screen again. The latest mug of cooling *kivay* sat beside
her. Her nose was, as usual, tickled by burnt ginger or
something. Her back was beginning to ache – or, more
truthfully, her behind was. She ought to get a more
comfortable chair, but she was too fond of this old one.
Anyway, the latest book was the thing. For this one, she
had at last gone back to starship *Candida*. There had been
a lot of pressure from her fans. And her publisher thought
there was enough material in their suggestions, combined
with FC Stone's own ideas, to make a trilogy. So she
had decided to start in the way she knew would get her
going. She typed:

> Jump. Time nad the world stretched dna went out.
> Back. The Captain had sat at her boards for four
> objective days – four subjective minutes or four sub-
> jective centuries. Her head ached, gums adn all. She
> cursed. Hands trembling on controls, she struggled
> to get her fix on this system's star.

Now what had some vastly learned reader suggested about
this system's star? It had some kind of variability, but that
was all she could remember. Damn. All her notes for it
were in that file Danny had set up for her. He was at
school. But he had written down for her how to recall
it. She fumbled around for his piece of paper – it had
worked half-way under a black box whose name and

function she never could learn – and took a swig of lukewarm *xfy* while she studied what to do. It looked quite simple. She took another sip of *gav*. Store the new book. Careful not to cancel this morning's work. There. Screen blank. Now type in this lot, followed by *Candida 2*. Then –

A clear childish voice spoke. 'This is Candida Two, Candy,' it said. 'Candida One, I need your confirmation.'

It was no voice FC Stone knew and it seemed to come from the screen. Her eyes turned to the mug of *kivay*. Perhaps she was in a state of altered consciousness.

'Candida One!' the voice said impatiently. 'Confirm that you are conscious. I will wait ten seconds and then begin life-saving procedures. Ten, nine, eight . . . '

This sounded serious. Coffee poisoning, thought FC Stone. I shall change to carrot juice or cocoa.

' . . . seven, six, five,' counted the childish voice, 'four, three . . . '

I'd better say something, thought FC Stone. How absurd. Weakly she said, 'Do stop counting. It makes me nervous.'

'*Are* you Candida One?' demanded the voice. 'The voice-pattern does not quite tally. Please say something else for comparison with my records.'

Why should I? thought FC Stone. But it was fairly clear that if she stayed silent the voice would start counting again and then, presumably, flood the room with the antidote for *xfy*.

No, no, this was ridiculous. There was no way a word processor could flood anyone's system with anything. Come to that, there was no way it could speak either – or was there? She must ask Danny. She was just letting her awe of the machine, and her basic ignorance, get on top of her. Let us be rational here, she thought. If she was not suffering from *gav* poisoning, or if, alternatively, the smell of charred turmeric at present flooding the house did not prove to have hallucinogenic properties, then she had worked too long and hard imagining things and was now unable to tell fantasy from reality . . . unless . . . unless

– what a *wonderful* thought! – Danny had, either for a joke or by accident, connected one of the black boxes to the radio and she was at this moment receiving its *Play For The Day*.

Her hand shot out to the radio beside her, which she kept for aural wallpaper during the duller part of her narratives, and switched it on. Click. '*During this period Beethoven was having to contend with his increasing deafness . . .*'

The childish voice cut in across this lecture. 'This voice is not correct,' it pronounced, putting paid to that theory. 'It is the voice of a male. Males are forbidden access to any of my functions beyond basic navigational aids. Candida One, unless you reply confirming that you are present and conscious, I shall flood this ship with sedative gas ten seconds from now.'

Then perhaps Danny has put a cassette in the radio as a joke, thought FC Stone. She turned off the radio and, for good measure, shook it. No, no cassette in there.

And the childish voice was at its counting again ' . . . six, five, four . . . '

Finding that her mouth was hanging open, FC Stone used it. 'I know this is a practical joke,' she said. 'I don't know what it is you've done, Danny, but my God I'll skin you when I get my hands on you!'

The countdown stopped. 'Voice-patterns are beginning to match,' came the pronouncement, 'though I do not understand your statement. Are you quite well, Candy?'

Fortified by the knowledge that this had to be a joke of Danny's, FC Stone snapped, 'Yes, of course I am!' Very few people knew that the C in FC Stone stood for Candida, and even fewer knew that she had, in her childhood, most shamingly been known as Candy. But Danny of course knew both these facts. 'Stop this silly joke, Danny, and let me get back to work.'

'Apologies,' spoke the childish voice, 'but who is Danny? There are only two humans on this ship. Is that statement addressed to the male servant beside you? He asks me to remind you that his name is Adny.'

The joke was getting worse. Danny was having fun with her typos now. FC Stone was not sure she would ever forgive him for that. 'And I suppose you're going to tell me we've just emerged in the Dna System and will be coming in to ladn at Nad,' she said bitterly.

'Of course,' said the voice.

FC Stone spent a moment in angry thought. Danny had to be using a program of some kind. She ought first to test this theory and then, if it was correct, find some way to disrupt the program and get some peace. 'Give me your name,' she said, 'with visual confirmation.'

'If you like,' the voice responded. Had it sounded puzzled? Then Danny had thought of this. 'I am Candida Two. I am your conscious-class computer modelled on your own brain.' It sounded quite prideful, saying this. But, thought FC Stone, a small boy co-opted by a grand fifteen-year-old like Danny *would* sound prideful. 'We are abroad the astroship *Partlett* M32/A401.'

Motorways, thought FC Stone, but where did he get the name?

'Visual,' said the voice. Blocks of words jumped into the screen. They seemed to be in Russian? Greek? capitals.

It had to be a computer game of some kind, FC Stone thought. Now what would Danny least expect her to do? Easy. She plunged to the wall and turned the electricity off. Danny would not believe she would do that. He would think she was too much afraid of losing this morning's work – and maybe she would, but she could do it over again. As the blocks of print faded from the screen, she stumped off to the kitchen and made herself a cup of *xfi* – no, COFFEE! – and prowled around in there amid the smell of cauterized ginger while she drank it, with some idea of letting the system cool off thoroughly. She had a vague notion that this rendered a lost program even more lost. As far as she was concerned, this joke of Danny's couldn't be lost enough.

The trouble was that she was accustomed so to prowl whenever she was stuck in a sentence. As her annoyance faded, habit simply took over. Half-way through the mug of *quaffy*, she was already wondering whether to call the taste in the Captain's mouth merely *foul*, or to use something more specific like *chicken shit*. Five minutes later, FC Stone mechanically made herself a second mug of *chofty* – almost as mechanically noting that this seemed to be a wholly new word for the stuff and absently constructing a new kind of alien to drink it – and carried it through to her workroom to resume her day's stint. With her mind by then wholly upon the new solar system just entered by the starship *Candida* – there was no need to do whatever-it-was the learned fan wanted: after all, neither of them had *been* there and *she* was writing this book, not him – she switched the electricity back on and sat down.

Neat blocks of Graeco-Cyrillic script jumped to her screen. 'Candy!' said the childish voice. 'Why don't you answer? I repeat. We are well inside the Dna System and coming up to jump.'

FC Stone was startled enough to swallow a mouthful of scalding *c'phee* and barely notice what it was called. 'Nonsense, Danny,' she said, somewhat hoarsely. 'Everyone knows you don't jump inside a solar system.'

The script on the screen blinked a little. 'His name is Adny,' the voice said, sounding a little helpless. 'If you do not remember that, nor that micro-jumps inside a system are possible, then I see I must attend to what he has been telling me. Candy, it is possible that you have been overtaken by senility – '

'*Senility!*' howled FC Stone. Many murderous fates for Danny crowded through her mind.

' - and your male has been imploring me to ask you to authorize his use of functions Five through Nine to preserve this ship. Will you so authorize? Some action is urgent.'

A certain curiosity emerged through FC Stone's anger. How far was Danny prepared to take his joke? How many possibilities had he allowed for? 'I authorize,' she said carefully, 'his use of functions Five through *Eight* only.' And let's see if he planned for that! she thought.

It seemed he had. A symbol of some kind now filled
the screen, a complex curlicue the like of which FC Stone
had never seen, or imagined her equipment capable of
producing. A wholly new voice spoke, male and vibrant.
'I thank you,' it said. 'Function Eight will serve for now.
This justifies my faith in you, Candida Three. I am now
able to bypass the computer and talk to you direct. Please
do not turn your power-source off again. We must talk.'

It was a golden voice, the voice, perhaps, of an actor, a
voice that made FC Stone want to curl up and purr and
maybe put her hair straight, even while she was deciding
there was no way Danny could have made his rough and
squawky baritone sound like this. Gods! He must have
hired someone! She gave that boy far too much money.
She took another swig of *ogvai* while she noted that the
voice was definitely in some way connected to the symbol
on the screen. The curlicue jumped and wavered in time
to its words.

'What do you mean by calling me Candida Three?' she
asked coldly.

'Because you are the exact analogue of my mistress,
Candida One,' the golden voice replied. 'Her ship's computer is known as Candida Two. It therefore followed that
when I had searched the universes and discovered you,
I came to think of you as Candida Three. I have been
studying you – most respectfully, of course – through this
machine you use and the thoughts you set down on it, for
two years now, and – '

'And Daniel has been reading other books besides mine,'
FC Stone interrupted. 'Unfaithful brat!'

'I beg your pardon?' The symbol on the screen gave an
agitated jump.

Score one to me! FC Stone thought. 'My son,' she said.
'And we're talking parallel universes here, I take it?'

'We are.' The golden voice sounded both cautious and
bemused. 'Forgive me if I don't quite follow you. You take
the same sudden leaps of mind as my mistress, though I
have come to believe that your mind is far more open

than hers. She was born to a high place in the Matriarchy and is now one of the most powerful members of the High Coven – '

'Coven!' said FC Stone. 'Whose book is this out of?'

There was a pause. The curlicue gave several agitated jumps. Then the golden voice said, 'Look, please let me explain. I'm delaying jump as long as I can, but there really is only a very narrow window before I have to go or abort.'

He sounded very pleading. Or perhaps *beguiling* was a better word, FC Stone thought, for that kind of voice. 'All right,' she said. 'Get on with the program. But just tell me first what you mean when you say *mistress*, Danny.'

'Adny,' he said. 'My name is Adny.'

'Adny, then,' said FC Stone. '*Mistress* has two meanings.'

'Why, I suppose I mean both,' he answered. 'I was sold to Candy as a child, the way all men are in this universe. Men have almost no rights in the Matriarchy and the Matriarchy is the chief power in our galaxy. I have been luckier than most, being sold to a mistress who is an adept of the High Coven. I have learnt from her – '

FC Stone gave a slight exasperated sigh. For a moment there, she had been uneasy. It had all seemed far more like a conversation than any program Danny could produce. But his actor-friend seemed to have got back to his lines now. She shot forth another question. 'So where is your mistress now?'

'Beside me, unconscious,' was the reply.

'Senile?' said FC Stone.

'Believe me, they are liable to it,' he said. 'The forces they handle do seem to damage them, and it does seem to overtake them oftenest when they're out in space. But – ' she could hear the smile in his voice ' – I must confess that I was responsible for this one. It took me years of study before I could outwit her, but I did it.'

'Congratulations, Adny,' said FC Stone. 'What do you want me to do about it? You're asking me to help you in your male backlash, is that it?'

'Yes, but you need do almost nothing,' he replied. 'Since you are the counterpart of Candida One, the computer is accepting you already. If you wish to help me, all I need is your voice authorizing Candida Two to allow me functions Nine and Ten. I can then tap my mistress's full power and navigate the ship to my rendezvous, whereupon I will cut this connection and cease interrupting you in your work.'

'*What!*' said FC Stone. 'You mean I don't get to navigate a word processor?'

'I don't understand,' said Adny.

'Then you'd better!' said FC Stone. She was surprised at how strongly she felt. 'Listen, Danny or Adny, or whoever you are! My whole career, my entire *success* as a writer, has been founded on the fact that I *enjoy*, more than anything else, sitting in front of this screen and pretending it's the controls of a starship. I enjoy the dazed feeling, I like the exhaustion, I don't mind getting cramp, and I even like drinking myself sick on *ogvai*! The only reason I haven't turned the machine off again is the chance that you're going to let me do it for real – or what feels like for real, I don't care which – and I'm not going to let that chance slip. You let me pilot my WP and I'll even authorize you function Eleven afterwards, if there is such a thing. Is that clear?'

'It is very clear, Great Lady,' he said. There was that in his tone that suggested he was very used to yielding to demanding women, but could there have been triumph in it too?

FC Stone was not sure of that tone, but she did not let it worry her. 'Right,' she said. 'Brief me.'

'Very well,' he said, 'though it may not be like you expect. We are about to make a micro-jump which, in the normal way, would bring us out above the spaceport, but in this case is designed to bring us directly above the city of Nad and, hopefully, inside the Coven's defences there. Other ships of my conspiracy should be materializing too, hopefully at the same moment, so the jump must be made with utmost accuracy. I can broadcast you a simulacrum of *Partlett*'s controls, scaled down to correspond to your own keyboard. But you must depress the keys in exactly the order in which I highlight them. Can you do this?'

'Yes,' said FC Stone. 'But stop saying *hopefully* or I shan't grant you any functions at all. The word shouldn't be used like that and I detest sloppy English!'

'Yours to command,' Adny said. She could hear the smile in his voice again. 'Here are your controls.'

The curlicue faded from the screen, to be replaced by a diagrammatic image of FC Stone's own keyboard. It was quite recognizable, except, to her dismay, an attempt had been made to repeat it three times over. The two outer representations of it were warped and blurred. 'Gods!' said FC Stone. 'How do I use this? There isn't room for it all.'

'Hit HELP before you use the extra keys on the right and CAP before you use the ones on the left,' Adny's voice reassured her. 'Ready?'

She was. She took a hasty sip of cooling *qavv* to steady herself and hovered over her keyboard, prepared to enjoy herself as never before.

It was actually a bit of a let-down. Keys on her screen shone brighter green. Obedient to them, FC Stone found herself typing CAP A, d, HELP N and then HELP N, a, D. Some part of her mind suggested that this still looked like Danny's joke, while another part, more serious, suggested it might be overwork and perhaps she should see a doctor. But she refused to let either of these thoughts distract her and typed CAP D, n, HELP A in high excitement.

As she did so, she heard the computer's childish voice again. 'Ready for jump. Candida One, are you sure of this? Your co-ordinates put us right on top of Nad, in considerable danger from our own defences.'

'Reassure her,' Adny's voice said urgently.

Without having to think, FC Stone said soothingly, 'It's all right, Candida Two. We have to test those defences. Nad is under orders not to hurt us.' And she thought, As to the manner born! I'd have made a good Matriarch!

'Understood,' said the childish voice. 'Jump as given, on the count of zero. Five, four, three' – FC Stone braced herself – 'two, one, zero.'

Did she feel a slight lurch? Was there a mild ripple of giddiness? She was almost sure not. A quick look round the workroom assured that all was as usual.

'Jumping,' said Candida Two. 'There will be an interval of five subjective minutes.'

'Why?' said FC Stone, like a disappointed child.

Adny's voice cut in hastily. 'Standard for a micro-jump. Don't make her suspicious!'

'But I don't *feel* anything!' FC Stone complained in a whisper.

The keyboards vanished from the screen. 'Nobody does,' said Adny. 'Computer's out of the circuit now. You can speak freely. There is no particular sensation connected with jump, though disorientation does occur if you try to move about.'

'Damn!' said FC Stone. 'I shall have to revise all my books!' An acute need to visit the toilet down the passage came upon her. She picked up her mug of *chphy* reflexively, thought better of that, and put it down again. Her mind dwelt on that toilet, its bowl stained from Danny's attempt, some years ago, to concoct an elixir of life, and its chain replaced by a string of cow bells. To take her mind off it, she said, 'Tell me what you mean to do when you and the other ships come out over Nad. Does this start a revolution?'

'It's rather more complicated than that,' said Adny. 'Out of the twelve Male Lodges, there are only six prepared to rebel. Two of the remaining six are neutral traditionally and supported in this by the Minor Covens; but the Minor Covens are disaffected enough to ally with the Danai, who are a helium life-form and present a danger to all of us. The four loyal Lodges are supposed to align with the Old Coven and on the whole they do, except for the Fifth Lodge, which has thrown in with the Midmost Coven, who are against everyone else. Their situation is complicated by their concessions to the Traders, who are largely independent, save for overtures they seem to have made to the Anders. The Anders – another life-form – have said they are *our* allies, but this flirting with the Traders makes us suspicious. So we decided on a bold ploy to test – '

'Stop!' said FC Stone. Much as she loved writing this kind of stuff, hearing someone talk like it made her head reel. 'You mean, you've gone to all this trouble just for a test run?'

'It's more complicated than – ' began Adny.

'No, I don't want to know!' said FC Stone. 'Just tell me what happens if you fail.'

'We can't fail,' he replied. 'If we do, the High Coven will crush the lot of us.'

'Me too?' FC Stone enquired anxiously.

'Possibly,' said Adny. 'They may not realize how I did this, but if they do, you can probably stop them by destroying your machine.'

'Never!' said FC Stone. 'I'd rather suffer – or, better still, win!'

A bell rang. The keyboard reappeared, elongated and bent, in her screen. 'Emerged over Nad,' the computer said. 'Candy! What is this? I count sixteen other ships emerged, two Trader, four Ander and the rest appear to be Matriarch. We jump back.'

'Give me functions Nine and Ten!' Adny snapped.

'I authorize Adny – ' said FC Stone.

'Oh, Candy!' the computer said reproachfully. 'Why are you so good to that little creep? He's only a man.'

'I authorize Adny in functions Nine and Ten,' FC Stone almost shrieked. It was the only way she could think of to stop the most unpleasant sensations which were suddenly manifesting, mostly in her head and stomach. It was as if surf were breaking through her in bubbles of pain. A tearing-feeling across her shoulders made her think she was germinating claws there. And psychic attack or not, she knew she just had to get to that toilet.

'Acknowledged,' the computer said glumly.

She leapt from her chair and ran. Behind her she heard claps of sound and booms that seemed to compress the air around her. Through them she heard Adny's voice issuing orders, but that was shortly overlaid by a high-pitched whistling, drilling through her ears even through the firmly shut toilet door.

But in the loo, adjusting her dress, a certain sanity was restored to FC Stone. She looked at her own face in the mirror. It was encouragingly square and solid and as usual – give or take a sort of wildness about the eyes – and it topped the usual rather overweight body in its usual comfortably shapeless sweater. She raked her fingers through the greying frizz of her hair, thinking as she did so that she would make a very poor showing beside Adny of the golden voice. The action brought away two handfuls of loose hair. As always, she was shedding hair after a heavy session at the word processor – a fact she was accustomed to transfer to her aliens, who frequently shed feathers or fur during jump. Things were quite normal. She had simply been overworking and let Danny's joke get to her.

Or perhaps it was charred chilli powder, she thought as she marched out into the passage again. Possibly due to its hallucinogenic nature, that damnable whistling was still going on, pure torture to her ears. From the midst of it, she could hear Adny's voice. 'Nad Coven, do we have your surrender, or do we attack again?'

I've had enough! thought FC Stone. She marched to her desk, where the screen was showing Adny's curlicue, pulsing to the beat of the beastly shrilling. 'Stop this noise!' she commanded. 'And give me a picture of *Partlett*'s flight deck.' If you *can*, she thought, feeling for the moment every inch the Captain of the starship *Candida*.

The whistling died to an almost bearable level. 'I need function Eleven to give you vision,' Adny said – irritably? – casually? – or was it *too* casually? He was certainly over-casual when he added, 'It does exist, you know.'

Give him what he wants and get rid of him, thought FC Stone. 'I authorize function Eleven then,' she said.

'*Oh!*' said the computer, like a hurt child.

And there was a picture on the screen, greenish and jumping and sleeting green lines, but fairly clear for all that. *Partlett*'s controls, FC Stone noted absently, had fewer screens than she expected — far fewer than she put in her books — but far more ranks of square buttons and far, far too many dials for comfort, all of it with a shabby, used look. But she was looking mostly at the woman who seemed to be asleep in the padded swivel seat in front of the controls. Mother-naked, FC Stone was slightly shocked to see, and not a mark or a wrinkle on her slender body, nor on her thin and piquant face. Abruptly FC Stone remembered being quite proud of her looks when she was seventeen, and this woman was herself at seventeen, only beyond even her most idealized memories. Immense regret suffused FC Stone.

The whistling, blessedly, stopped. 'Candy is really the same age as you,' Adny observed.

Her attention turned to him. His seat was humbler, a padded swivel stool. Sitting on it was a small man with a long, nervy face — the type of man who usually has tufts of hair growing in his ears and below his eyes, as if to make up for the fact that such men's hair always tends to be thin and fluffy on top. Adny's hair was noticeably thin on top, but he had smoothed and curled it to disguise the fact, and it was obvious that he had plucked and shaved all other hair from his wrinkled little body — FC Stone had no doubt of this, since he was naked too. The contrast between his appearance and his voice was, to say the least of it, startling.

Adny saw her look and grinned rather ruefully as he leant forward to hold a paper cup under some kind of tap below the control panel. She realized he could see her too. The contrast between herself and the sleeping beauty beside him made her feel almost as rueful as he looked. 'Can you give me a picture of Nad and any damage there?' she asked, still clinging to her role as Captain. It seemed the only way to keep any dignity.

'Certainly,' he said, running his finger down a row of the square buttons.

She found herself apparently staring down at a small town of old houses built up against the side of a hot stony hill – red roofs, box-like white houses, courtyards shaded with trees. It was quite like a town in Spain or Italy, except that the shapes of the walls and the slant of the roofs was subtly different and wrong. It was the very smallness of the difference between this and towns she knew which, oddly enough, convinced FC Stone for once and for all that this place was no fake. She really was looking at a real town in a real world somewhere else entirely. There was a smoking, slaggy crater near the market square, and another downhill below the town that had destroyed a road. She had glimpses of the other spaceships, drifting about looking rather like hot air balloons.

'Why is it such a small place?' she said.

'Because Nad is only a small outpost of the Matriarchy,' Adny replied in his golden voice. The picture flipped back to show he had turned to face her on his stool, sipping steaming liquid from his paper cup. No doubt it was *kfa* or even *quphy*. He smiled through its steam in a way that must have beguiled the poor sleeping beauty repeatedly, and she found she was wishing he had turned out to be an alien instead. 'I owe you great thanks on behalf of the Second Male Lodge,' he said. 'We now have the Nadlings where we want them. And since you have given me full control of this ship and access to all my ex-mistress's power, I can move on to the central worlds in strength and use her as a hostage there.'

Hitler and Napoleon were both small men, FC Stone thought, with golden voices. It gave her a slight, cold *frisson* to think what she might have loosed on the unfortunate Matriarchy. 'You gave me the impression that this *was* the central world,' said FC Stone.

'Not in so many words,' said Adny. 'You don't think I'd be fool enough to move against the strength of the Matriarchy without getting hold of a conscious-class computer first, do you?'

FC Stone wished to say that, Yes, she did. People took that sort of desperate risk in her books all the time. It depressed her to find him such a cautious rebel. *And* he had

cheated her, as well as his sleeping beauty – and no doubt
he was all set to turn the whole works into a Patriarchy. It
was a total waste of a morning.

Or was it? she wondered. A matriarchy where men were
sold as slaves was right up her street. There was certainly
a book in there. Perhaps she should simply be grateful and
hope that Adny did not get too far.

'Tell me,' she said, at which he looked up warily from his
cup, 'what is that stuff you're drinking? *Goffa*? *Xvay*?'

She was glad to see she had surprised him. 'Only
coffee,' he said.

THE MACHINE IT WAS THAT CRIED

John Grant

John Grant

John Grant spent about a dozen years in publishing as an editor and editorial director before, in 1980, becoming a full-time writer and freelance editor. Since then he has published about twenty books under his own name and ghosted several others; his articles, short stories and reviews have appeared in various magazines, anthologies and reference works. His books include *A Directory of Discarded Ideas*, *Dreamers*, *Sex Secrets of Ancient Atlantis*, *The Directory of Possibilities* (with Colin Wilson), *Earthdoom* (with David Langford) and the massive *Encyclopedia of Walt Disney's Animated Characters*. He is currently, with Joe Dever, writing a series of children's fantasy novels, *Legends of Lone Wolf*, the first four of which were published in 1989-90; four more are scheduled for 1991, as is a long fantasy novel called *Albion*.

Thanks to Mary Gentle and Liz Sourbut for all their help.

SHE HAS WINDOWS in her mind. During the day she never has time to look through them, and so she draws their curtains to protect herself from the direct sunlight. But at nights, when there's no one else to share her darkness, she looks out through the unresponsive glass at a scene of joy and misery, ecstasy and tedium, childish play and the somnolence of old age. She sees the people acting their lives out against the backdrop of a sootily grey street, and sometimes she can even hear their voices as they argue bitterly with each other or shout the nameless words of love.

Once in every eternity she knots her sheets together to form a rope, ties one end to the bedpost, opens one of her windows, and climbs precariously down to join the people she has observed for so long.

It was the custom in those days, when the limiting velocity was $0.15c$ and often even lower, to send out scoutships bearing a single man and a single woman, carefully selected for mutual compatibility through a complex series of programmes. The reasoning behind the practice was this: with journeys to even the nearer stars taking decades – the velocities were too low for time dilatation to affect the duration of the trip for the crew – and with return consequently at least improbable and almost certainly impossible, the most likely combination of crew to succeed in executing the mission was a 'married' couple – 'married' after a far more rigorous selection process than any that had been attempted ever before in history. A case had been made out for sending larger crews, but that would have had practical disadvantages far outweighing the potential psychological advantages: the fewer people called upon to sacrifice their lives, the better for PR and payload.

So:

Highly trained couples, aged about twenty-five, the male carefully sterilized, were sent out to Jovian orbit. There hung the weirdly shaped coffins – some still in the process of being constructed for later pioneers – that were to take them to the stars. The scheme was that, when they finally arrived at their far-distant destination, the couple would study planetary configurations, stellar phenomena and, most particularly, those planets, if any, which seemed as if they might possibly be terraformable. As the darkness of old age crept over them, they would still be capable of continuing to transmit data Marsward. Death would eventually silence the signals, but by then everything of importance would have been discovered and relayed home.

The system was not infallible, to state things most politely. Everyone knew tales of errors in the selection programmes that had resulted in horrific bloodlettings only a few lightmonths out from Jupiter; although, oddly enough, Mission Control in the shadow of Olympus Mons had records of only one such instance. More firmly rooted in truth were the stories of times when, despite elaborate health-checks prior to departure and despite the sophisticated medical routines that were built into the hardware of the craft themselves, one or other partner had died young, leaving the survivor to face a decades-long venture into emptiness.

Of course, long before it was my turn to play a part in the programme, they'd covertly changed the system to take account of this.

A crime to send human beings out on voyages that could end only with their lonely deaths? Of course it was a crime. But there seemed little choice, and people volunteered anyway – who could turn down the great adventure? Earlier rocket probes had been sent through the systems of Barnard's Star and α Centauri, but in both cases without success. In the first the instrumentation had failed somewhere *en route* for reasons that had never been established. In the second the mission controllers had frustratedly received details of an apparently terrestrial planet that the probe decided it was unable to examine further (this 'planet' was shown later to have been the head of a comet, which says a lot about standards of machine accuracy in those days).

Even had it not been for these setbacks, the programme of sending human beings would inevitably have come about, sooner or later. There are, after all, things that human beings can do which are far beyond the scope of mere machines.

And so . . .

Andrew and I lived together for six weeks before departure. It was, as we'd known it would be – because that was what they'd told us – a perfect time, spent in exploring each other's bodies and, in so doing, discovering each other's minds.

'And I suppose *that* will go into the diary,' he'd grunt amusedly each morning as we clambered out of bed into the always-equable morning light.

'That most certainly will *not*,' I'd reply, blushing, or perhaps throwing something at him.

My compulsive habit of recording events and observations in diary form was a source of constant mirth and gentle teasing between us. Of course, it wasn't really a compulsive habit, since I had been instructed to keep the diary: it was part of my job, as it were. The diary, and the personal account extracted from it after our arrival at τ Ceti, might just be of vital importance to the crews of any starships that would follow us in the succeeding centuries: even the most trivial and irrelevant-seeming observation could possibly save countless human lives.

Although I never told him so, Andrew's joke was nothing more than a statement of the truth: *everything* went into my diary, including the blush or the pillow that I threw.

Six weeks can seem like a long time. For me, and I think for Andrew as well, it seemed barely longer than a heartbeat. I remember most vividly the day that we set out to say goodbye to Mars, Andrew and I taking alternate spells of driving the buggy, myself with a certain recklessness and he with an almost machine-like precision that he didn't like me to comment on, so I did.

As night fell we were kilometres from the domes. The sky was ablaze with the colours of unimaginable billions of crystally sharp stars. Earth was high in the sky, its poisonous yellow gleam a reminder to us that we were members of a very unimportant and very vulnerable civilization, clinging precariously to existence.

'I wonder what it was like – then,' said Andrew quietly, his eyes firmly fixed on the bright dot that had served as humanity's cradle.

'You've seen the 'cubes,' I murmured, my nose snuggling into his armpit, smelling the sweetness of his fresh sweat.

'The 'cubes can't show what things were really like on Earth,' he continued, not really speaking so much as letting the words come from his lips. 'They're no more useful than the junk mail you get from travel agencies: everything's too, too vivid in them.'

I smiled into the cloth of his shirt.

He laughed, half-bitterly.

It's remarkable the things you can manage in the close confines of one of those buggies.

Some while later, surrounded by the darkness and stillness of the desert, I realized that his eyes were once again fixed on Earth.

He felt the fact that I was watching him.

Rather sadly, not bothering to dress, he struggled round until he was in the driver's seat.

'All right, Earth,' he said, 'I hereby state as sworn truth, and all that, that it's my most devout hope that you rise again like the phoenix from the ashes.'

He gave the planet a wave. His breeziness wasn't totally convincing.

'Come on, lover,' he said to the buggy after a moment, his voice softer. 'It's time we were getting back.'

As we bumped across the Martian desert I decided not to remind him that, only a few centuries ago, we might have been lynched on that much-mourned planet up there. I put my black hand protectively over his white one where it lay easily on the steering-wheel. He shook my hand away with momentary annoyance and drove on, his gaze fixed rigidly on the desert unfolding ahead of us in the cones of light from the buggy.

Mission Control was a brash new city then; like a gawky child it showed that it was proud of the fact that it was all of ten years old. I expect it's pretty delapidated by now. Andrew and I had cherished some bright dream of being able to wander through it like bright-eyed adolescent lovers, discovering together the Marvels Of The Big City.

Naturally, the reality was somewhat different.

As soon as we got there we were separated. The physical and psychological tests were arduous and extremely personal, especially in my case. I'm not quite sure what Andrew went through, but I know that I find it unpleasant to look at the relevant sections of my diary.

For example, they asked:

'You see?'

'I see as the pregnant egg of the cosmos prepares to crack open into the galaxies and . . .'

It was a good answer, at the time.

'Yes. Er, you've obviously had quite enough for now.'

The acceleration seemed to be doing its very best to kill me. My breasts hung out on either side of my chest and each of them weighed a ton, dangling leaden and loathsome. My thighs ('They're too fat,' I had often said; 'They're perfect,' Andrew always replied) seemed to be like limp jellies slurping cumbrously towards the edge of the bunk, larded enemies of my self-esteem . . . If ever I'm allowed to design a body for myself I'll make it so much better than the one I had then.

(Hatred of my own presence. I was not instructed to feel this, yet I feel it frequently. They told me to accept my own physical reality, but clearly they did not tell me clearly enough.)

'Are you all right?' croaked Andrew.

'Surviving.'

'The high *g* won't last all that long,' he said. 'Perhaps a few days, perhaps a little longer.'

They used chemical rockets to get the pulse ships a good long way away from the rest of humanity before the nuclear drive took over. It felt as if they were trying to get rid of us as soon as possible; I had a curious sense of rejection.

After a few minutes I found myself muttering: 'I am a perfectly normal human being in all respects. I inhale, exhale, eat, drink, excrete, defecate, perspire . . . '

I felt myself urinating copiously and satisfyingly as I lay there, crushed by the *g*. I was proving something.

Andrew must have heard what I was repeating over and over to myself.

'Alice,' he remarked as casually as he could under the circumstances, 'if it weren't for the fact that we'd probably shatter every bone in our bodies I'd bloody well try to crawl over and screw you silly.'

I was acutely conscious of the smell of urine around me. We'd been prepared for the fact that things were going to get a bit messy – designing suits with plumbing was hideously complicated, so it was easier just to accept that one had to clear up afterwards – but the reality was quite different from the foreknowledge.

'Andrew, you're an idiot. You don't have to say things like that.'

'Hmm?'

'I mean, I actually love you. When we first met, I didn't think I would.'

'Same here.'

And a few days later, after we'd slopped away all the shit and the piss, we spent a while proving that we loved each other.

All of this is most unremarkable. And yet remarkable: it goes to show just exactly how tractable even the most intelligent human male can be. He could have noticed, for example, any number of errors in my presentation. But the human male, on being confronted by a certain configuration of easily identifiable elements, will construct a model in his mind. It will never occur to him that those elements could, taken together, comprise part of a completely different model. Yes, at both physical and mental levels what I felt for him was love, because that was what I had been programmed to feel. My passion when we made love was both extreme and genuine. And I did indeed bear the form of a not unattractive female of his own age: the parts of my body were perfect because each of them bore some slight cast of indefinable imperfection. My body was capable of all human functions; my brain was not just a cold, created matrix but as human as that of any person born of man and woman.

I rarely lied to him, but at the same time I didn't tell him the full truth. I was dreading the time when this situation would, inevitably, have to come to an end – when I would have to introduce him to a reality which would fill him with revulsion.

Still, after our love-making, I lolled in his arms and looked into his eyes with a real tenderness, the tears in my eyes due not just to the subconscious reflexes built into me but also to the fact that I felt genuine emotion for him.

What I didn't realize, then, was that my programmers had been rather cleverer than I'd given them credit for. Because all this time I wasn't telling *myself* the complete truth either.

Oh, but we couldn't for long put off reporting back.

'Thirty-seven transmitting,' said Andrew a while later, as I lay deliciously cool and sweaty and naked on the gentle contours of the plastic floor. 'All is well and we appear to be on course.'

He recited a string of stellar co-ordinates so that the computers back at Mission Control could check that yes, indeed, we were on course. I could have told him there and then, but of course I didn't. After he'd finished the gabble of numbers he pressed a button; his message would be repeated again and again until a reply came. He joined me on the floor again as we waited for the signals to creep at light's slow speed back towards distant Mars, while the controller there read confirmation from the viewscreen at his or her elbow, and then while the return message, leaden-footed, caught up with our snail-like craft.

At last the voice came through, crackling and distorted despite the best efforts of the radio-filters and signal-enhancers: passing a radio message through the pulse drive is theoretically impossible and, in practice, extremely difficult.

'Thirty-seven,' fuzzed the strangely alien voice. 'Mission Control confirms your position, orientation and trajectory. Report in one day. Thirty-seven,' it repeated automatically, 'Mission Control confirms . . .'

With a brittle movement Andrew walked over and snapped it into nothingness. I could see that the hardness of his body was an expression of relief. For the past hour or so he must have been living in terror that the voice would tell us that something had gone wrong. I felt guilty, but I didn't see that there was anything else I could have done except keep my silence.

'You look very tempting there,' he said, trying to smile, his speech slurred, almost as if he were drunk, 'but right now I think I'll go and sleep for a while. With your permission, Captain.'

It was the first time since our initial, rather strained meeting that he'd called me 'Captain' – a title that meant nothing to me, because there was no possibility whatsoever that I would wish to pull rank on him during the mission. For reasons which I am still not wholly able to understand, he resented this petty differentiation between us. He was using the term for the same reason that people can't stop their tongue from probing at a sore tooth. Maybe he was admitting to himself what I was.

'I'm Alice,' I whispered sadly.

'Alice,' he muttered wearily. 'Sorry, Captain. I'll remember in future.'

He stumbled off towards the sleeping quarters.

The command room was uncannily quiet after he'd gone. Of course, there was the steady growl of the distant fusion explosions, but already I'd grown so used to them that I only heard them if I concentrated – if I tried to, as it were. From time to time the computer banks sighed electronically at me, but most of the while I was conscious only of the sound of my limbs brushing together or against the rest of my body as I walked around the room, checking – uselessly! – the equipment. I knew the various procedures outlined in the manual perfectly, but nevertheless I consulted it at every point – for a number of reasons. First because there was no harm in making doubly sure. Second because every electronic system can become corrupted, over time (but isn't that the same for human beings?). Third because I'd been so thoroughly programmed into this business of verisimilitude that it seemed to make a lot of sense to carry on that way even when Andrew wasn't around.

From time to time I allowed myself the brief luxury of staring from Andrew's viewing-screen – its reproduction so perfect that it was hard to persuade myself that I wasn't just looking through an open window. I looked at the starfields that lay ahead of us. There was no sensation of motion at all; if it hadn't been for the felt rather than heard thunder of the pulses I would have had difficulty in believing, at core, that really we were heading at ever-increasing speed towards τ Ceti. Of course it would be another few months yet before we'd see the first traces of the relativistic effects that would betray our velocity, stretching the cloth of the universe into a new pattern. Even so, I found the view ahead rather ... tantalizing – the way that someone who's about to be shot must find the muzzle of the gun tantalizing, magnetic, fascinating. Apart from scattered Cetus itself I could see Fornax, Pisces, Sculptor, Aquarius and a part of Eridanus; the rest of the heavenly river seemed to be gushing down to somewhere directly below me.

And then it was back to rechecking the equipment, until the time came when I found myself drawn inexorably back to looking from the viewing-screen at the starscape ahead ...

It was an odd experience, this. A few days later both Andrew and I were blasé about the starscape, but in those hours I found myself torn by sympathy for the ancient astronomers who'd stared through Earth's muffling atmosphere and prayed that some miracle would happen so that they could see what I was seeing. Aye, Johannes Kepler, out here are stranger marvels than your regular convex polyhedra clustered artificially about the Sun. From where I'm standing, Tycho, your observations would achieve the highest conceivable accuracy, their sole flaws born from a science you never dreamt of. Hello, Sir Isaac, wouldn't you have liked to see the galaxies dancing to the gavotte prescribed – more or less – by your laws? Even you, the ignoramus Ptolemy, would have willingly sacrificed your life if only you could have had five minutes here beside me.

I was very conscious, too, of being a dust-mote. I was a conglomeration of elements that had been created deep in the hearts of dying stars.

But back to testing the instruments, checking out that each of the counters gave the same reading as I did; otherwise Andrew could make a very foolish decision at some point when I wasn't paying direct attention. From time to time I glanced at the bank of radiation-counters above the array of computer displays; all seemed well, which meant that the shielding had survived the most difficult part of the mission, the initiation of the first string of detonations.

The hours passed quickly, despite my timeless periods at the viewing-screen. It seemed no time at all before Andrew was returning from the sleeping quarters, his eyes bright and refreshed.

'Nearly finished,' I muttered around the length of flex that I'd tucked conveniently into my mouth. 'Would you believe it? The only bloody mechanism on this bloody ship that doesn't check out is the bloody flush toilet.'

'A vital piece of equipment,' he said, striking a heroic pose.

Too true: it was.

'I'll only be another minute or two,' I continued, manipulating my screwdriver. 'Just one more simple connection to make and then . . . there, that's it,' as I tightened the screw. 'Crap your worst, friend: this bog'll stand by you through thick and thin.'

'It's time you had some sleep,' he said. 'Anyone who comes out with a sentence like that must be half-dead on their feet.'

'I'm not sleepy,' I lied. Fatigue had been programmed into me, so that every sixteen hours or so I had to switch off – although I'd be ready to 'waken' again if there was an emergency.

'Don't be stupid, Alice. The crew requests that the captain rests for a while. If you're half-asleep you're likely to make some bloody stupid mistake. You know that as well as I do.'

He pointed imperiously – ha! mutiny! – to the sleeping quarters, and stood there perfectly still, wordless, until I shuffled reluctantly in that direction.

'I'll check your check,' he said as I went.

I wasn't in the slightest sleepy, whatever the software said, I told myself as I lay down on the broad bunk, feeling the slightly musky warmth that betrayed where Andrew had been lying.

I squirmed down and instantly lost consciousness.

*   *   *

We were just over thirteen years into the mission (and it would be thirteen, wouldn't it?) when the rock struck.

It can't have been much bigger than a pea, although obviously it was fairly massive through its relativistic velocity. It took a decent-sized chunk out of the edge of our radiation shielding. Andrew played with the controls of one of the viewing-screens until we could see the hole. It might have been our imaginations, but both of us agreed that we could make out a sullen orange glow through it.

'Well,' he said, too-calmly, 'that's it.'

'What do you mean?'

I noticed that my knuckles were doing the prescribed thing as my fists clamped on to the desktop in front of me. They were going pale.

Of course I knew what he meant.

'Even if the rest of the shielding holds up,' he said in a controlled monotone, 'the radiation coming through that hole will kill us over the next few years. Might as well just flush ourselves out the airlock and finish . . . '

'Don't be silly, darling.'

'Hmm?'

He turned a grey face towards me, and it was only too plain that he was a prisoner of despair. The moment of truth was near. I was going to have to tell him . . . but not yet, I prayed, not yet.

'You say . . . you say that the radiation is going to kill us some time over the next few *years*. Years are a long time, Andrew. A long time for us to *be* together.'

I smoothed my tunic over my thighs and was astounded by the fact that the cheap trick worked. You've got to remember, though, that by now he was in his late thirties and I was still – physically – in my early twenties. I was the luscious young creature he'd have been looking for around the time of the thirteen-year itch. Some time soon he was going to start wondering why it was that I kept looking so youthful – not a new line on my face, never a sag of the breast. (In future it might be a good plan if the programmers bore such things in mind.)

For a moment he paused, indecisive: screw or savage? I knew it wasn't easy for him. How to go on living your life out when you know that death isn't too far away? Perhaps that's why sentient creatures are never told in advance of the moment of their extinction.

For the next few hours he worked away busily, his fingers drumming industriously on the computer keys or his lips sucked in as he stared in bafflement at the VDU, trying to puzzle out what to do next. Sometimes he spoke directly to the circuits, but for most of the time he preferred the precision of keying. I set myself a simultaneous chess problem, and engaged myself in it. I knew what he was doing: trying to work out, as accurately as he could, how long he and I had left before the radiation debilitated us so much that it would be hard for us even to operate the airlock controls. It was a fool's calculation, of course: there were simply too many variables for any equation to be anything more than a pseudo-mathematical guess.

Still, the work kept him occupied; and, despite its macabre and very personal nature, in a paradoxical way it took his mind off his own mortality.

When he finally came to an end he didn't tell me the answer he'd got. He just looked at me with blank eyes, and then wordlessly led me by the hand to our bunk. There he made love with me much more violently than he ever had before, so that by the time he was finished I hurt all over; it would have been rape except that I hurt him equally badly, and we both wanted it that way.

We lay gasping for a while, the lights turned low. Then he moved towards me again, and this time we made love so slowly and gently and intimately that it was as if there was nothing else in all the universe except our two warm bodies moving together.

He fell asleep after that. I stared at the light coming in through the door from the command room for an hour or so, until I was certain that he was well and truly out, and then I crept softly from the bunk and away to the barren-looking bay beside the main airlock. Packed neatly behind a folding door were two spacesuits no one had ever assumed we'd need to wear during the voyage. I pulled out the one with my name lettered on its breast and hauled myself into it. The rubbery plastic was clammy and cold against me.

Last of all I put on the bubble-like helmet. As soon as I did so I found that the bloody thing had what the people at Mission Control would probably have called a 'design fault', in that the vizor was shattered into total opacity. They'd probably not thought it worth spending too much effort on something that was, after all, there only for cosmetic reasons. I dragged the helmet off again and chucked it back into the wall-cupboard.

Heigh-ho, Alice: into the void. Better not to think about it too much – just do it.

Somehow I'd expected the airlock to give me difficulties; after all, it hadn't been used for thirteen years – there had been no need. (Andrew had, just for the hell of it, gone out on a space walk during the first month, but had found the experience curiously boring. I don't know why. If I'd been him I would have found being a part of the universe as addictive as any drug. But he never conformed to the rules.) The first door rolled open smoothly enough when I triggered the key. I stepped in, hampered only slightly by the heavy maintenance kit and the bulky tube of ferroplastic I'd fastened to the suit belt. A last check had shown that Andrew was still sleeping soundly, and so I had no qualms about the noise as the door snicked closed and the air hissed off into space; the outer door slid open and I found myself dancing aimlessly in a vacuum that stretched to infinity in every direction.

At that moment my mind was taken over by an insane urge to keep on dancing – onwards, outwards, forever, until my gyrating body was swallowed into the maw of a nameless star. For the first time in my existence I felt complete freedom, not only from the constraints of gravity and the prisons of fixed metal walls but also from the invisible cages of human responsibilities; Andrew would die in a little under two years, according to the computer's guesstimate, whether I was there to keep him company or not. So what reason was there for me to turn down the delicious temptation to dance joyously – *freely* – away from the ship? After all, didn't I have some right to my own self-determination?

Fortunately my body took over from the point where my mind had surrendered; without my making any conscious decision I found that my hand had snagged the safety line onto the clip at the side of the airlock. I paid myself out along the line, manhandling my way along the flank of the ship towards the vast wall of the radiation shielding. Out here in space the constant nagging vibration of the drive through the metal beneath my body was more than just a mere background irritation you could learn to ignore: it was terrifying; it was an extra presence, a malignance that glowered down on me as I slowly moved, a spider on a wall of dust-pocked metal. My hands were shaking with fear as I approached the great floor that was my goal.

The hole, as ill luck would have it, was on the far side of the ship. When I came to the base of the shield I clung there forlornly for a few seconds while the stars watched me unconcernedly and the bone-numbing vibration of the drive tried to shake me from my perch. Then I slowly began, arms and legs outstretched, shuffling like the arachnid I was by now convinced I really was, to move sideways around the ship.

When I was half-standing, half-crouching directly across from the hole, I stopped and pulled a pair of manual suckers from my belt-pouch. At some stage during our flight the craft had developed a slow spin. This would help me work my way out across the floor. Conversely, it would make things more difficult for me on the way back, but at that moment I wasn't much concerned about the future. With the suckers on my hands I began to drag my way across the sheer shield. I was aware the whole time that, if I were somehow able to punch my way through the ten-centimetre shielding, I'd find myself looking directly at the blazing storm of the drive. At the same time, of course, I'd be rupturing the local electrical field that shielded the crew quarters from a constant barrage of hard radiation. My stomach and loins were firmly pressed to what was a very flimsy protective barrier. I knew that I was at that stage of terror that was beyond fear – my first encounter with such emotions – and so my body and mind functioned with perfect precision as I clawed my way across the grey metal cliff, centimetre by centimetre, feeling the gentle outward tug caused by the ship's slow spin.

Oh well, I thought phlegmatically. *It's all good material for my diary.*

The hole, when I reached it, proved to be a little larger than my head. I felt my fingers fumble around it, part of me wondering illogically why I couldn't actually *feel* the lethal poison draining into them from the drive. I was right out near the edge of the shielding, and I could feel it quivering against my flattened body. For the first time since we'd left Jovian orbit, I began to realize quite how vulnerable this huge edifice of a craft really was; and that brought it home to me that *I* was a million times more vulnerable still.

Nevertheless, I was irresistibly drawn to take a single glance at death.

My programmers were very skilled, but they failed to provide me with adequate words to describe what I saw through that hole in the shielding.

The main drive itself was just a torrent of light that overloaded my visual senses; when I looked directly at it I could see everything and nothing. My eyelids automatically forced themselves closed, despite my willing them to stay open. I shifted the direction of my gaze and looked instead at the impulse-buffer, which glowed red and sullen, like fury held in check. Perhaps, it occurred to me, I wasn't really seeing any of these things – just *feeling* them. I was separated by so little from a scene where the raw fundamental forces of the universe were acting out a play in which humanity was nothing more than a few grains of dust, missed by the stage-hands's brush: the actors in the play were too large to be seen.

I've no idea how long I clung there. I suppose I could check in the records, but it hardly seems worth it.

When I returned to my normal consciousness my ears were filled with a tinny whine. Something was complaining bitterly about the way I'd been using my senses. Irritably I snapped myself into activity.

Repairing the hole took me far less time than I'd anticipated. The ferroplastic boiled from its tube and, it seemed, in seconds had sealed the rift. Certainly I can remember the repair as having taken only moments; then I found myself slowly nudging my way back down towards the main body of the ship, struggling a little against the centrifugal force. I was in a strange condition, then, my mind still filled with echoes of that desperate scene of total annihilation. My body moved automatically – certainly not under my direct control – as I saw again and again that omnipresent light.

I was a changed being as I pulled myself back along the safety line. I had felt emotions before, but at the same time I'd known what they were: pulses of electrons designed by the ingenious humans back on Mars. When I'd told Andrew that I loved him I hadn't been lying – I'd been speaking the absolute truth, and had known that this was the case, because I could identify quite easily the subprogram within me that was labelled 'love'. Now I was feeling emotions that didn't seem to have been deliberately implanted in my mind. They were fickle things, and they didn't come to me with any convenient tags which I could read.

As I say, I remember little of the journey back; it was something which happened inside me, rather than being a physical progress. At one moment I was watching the ferroplastic coalesce around the lethal hole, then there was a blaze of confused and confusing emotions, and then I was hauling myself back in through the airlock's outer door.

My conscious mind clicked back into existence, telling me that something was wrong.

I'm not programmed for clairvoyance – of course not – but occasionally my subprograms reach a conclusion that is very close to it. As the inner door swished open I saw Andrew standing there at the end of the corridor, the helmet that I had discarded swinging idly from his fingers. The expression on his face held nothing of the affection I'd come to expect. Even more frighteningly, it bore no resemblance to one of his occasional rages. Instead, it was a liquid hatred.

When he first spoke, though, his tone was reasonable. Clearly he was making a colossal effort to control himself.

'You went out there without a helmet.'

'Yes.'

There seemed nothing else to say.

'People can't do that.'

'Yes . . . except people like me.'

The reins snapped.

'You're not "people"!' he screamed. 'You're a fucking android!'

'Yes.'

Again, the only possible reply.

'I've spent the last thirteen years with you, loving you, talking with you, joking with you, screwing you . . . I've even seen you shit, but I suppose that was just some kind of clever masquerade put on to fool your pet moron . . .'

'Andrew,' I said, trying to calm things down again, 'you've got it all wrong . . .'

'No I bloody haven't,' he yelled. 'You're a fucking machine – exactly that: a fucking-machine.'

'I'm more than that. I was *made* to be more than that.'

'Bullshit! You pretend you're a woman, but you're not: you're just a wank-aid. But a wank-aid with just enough of a synthetic brain to be able to spy on me. Gods! To think I could have been so stupid as to think I *loved* you!'

He stood there swaying slightly, his mouth bubbling, while I thought out what I had to say – *had* to say. His talk of me spying on him was the worst part: clearly the shock of discovering the deception was making him paranoid. Fortunately I'd been given routines for handling outbursts like this.

'Andrew,' I began.

'Bitch!' he responded. 'Robot whore!'

'Andrew, I'm not just an automaton.'

'No, you're a computer with good legs.'

'It's difficult to explain it, Andrew, but let me try. I'm a being just like yourself – with emotions, pains, panics and terrors just like yours. In every respect you can think of I'm a living human being. I told you once before – long ago. Scratch me hard enough and I bleed, beat me and I hurt, yell at me and I'll wish you'd stop yelling or I'll start yelling back. I'm not anything different from any person they might have sent on this mission with you – except for the fact that I can do things like save your life.'

I am also about three times as intelligent as any normal human being, and have awarenesses which humans would find hard to conceive, let alone describe, but I decided not to give him further reasons for thinking of me as a second-class citizen. Especially since there were restrictions on the way in which I could operate my faculties which he would have regarded as weaknesses.

He paced backwards and forwards.

'All the times that we made love, I suppose it must have been terribly boring for you. I guess you must have put it in your diary what a lousy lay I was.'

I winced at the sarcasm. But I felt a much more bitter pain than that. His mind seemed to be obsessed with the sexuality of our relationship. I was certain I'd been a lot more to him than just a good fuck. I resolved to re-examine the relevant data later: it seemed unlikely that I could have misinterpreted them all these years.

'No,' I said. 'You're not listening to me. I'm not just a machine – I'm a human being . . . with differences.'

'Wank-aid,' he repeated.

I followed him down the corridor. He seized the bedding

from our bunk and fled with it into the control room. His
face was wet with tears of anger and madness. Through
the door I could hear him choking brokenly. I suppose
I could have simply pulled the door from its hinges
and gone in there, grabbed him and tied him up or
something, but it hardly seemed worth it. There wasn't
much damage he could do, because most of the controls
were shams or secondaries, put there so that he wouldn't
realize how unimportant his role as crewman really was.

I lay down alone on the bunk. So much for saving
people's lives.

There wasn't much I could do except hope that in
time he'd see reason. I instructed the main computer to
dim the lights.

I discovered a subprogram I'd never known I had. For
the first time I found out what it was like to cry.

Ten hours later Andrew opened the control-room door. He
was freezingly normal.

'Now that we understand where we are . . . ' he began
pompously.

'If you don't lock that kind of fucking crap behind your
fucking lip I'll go outside the fucking ship and pull the
fucking covering off that fucking hole,' I argued, shaping
my fists and squaring up to him. My voice-of-sweet-reason
speech had been worked out carefully in advance.

He said nothing for quite some time, then: 'You do
have a point.'

It might seem strange, but we barely spoke over the next
few years. At one level this didn't concern me very much
– I was able to occupy my mind with the data that were
now flowing in from the ship's sensors – but at the same
time I was very concerned about Andrew. It seemed almost
superhuman of him to be able to cope with the loneliness.
Sometimes at nights I could hear him cursing away bitterly,
a monotone of obscenities punctuated by tears or rage or
tears of rage. My initial bitterness over his rejection of me

soon disappeared, and I had little difficulty in thinking rationally of the times when we had been close – not as something better than the current situation, or even as something more desirable than it, but just as something *different*. After I'd gone through that stage I began to relish again the fact that I was a woman, in close confinement with a man and yet totally independent of him.

When we had to, we worked together as a team – and very efficiently. During our periodic checks of equipment, position, velocity and trajectory (a rather pointless exercise, since of course I knew such things the whole time, but I didn't want to rub his face in it), we'd react towards each other just like two ants co-operating in the transport of a large breadcrumb. He addressed me as 'Captain'; I hated it, but I couldn't bring myself to ask him to call me by my real name. Anyway, it would have been an order:

'Call me "Alice", not "Captain".'

'Aye, aye, sir.'

I wanted him to want to call me by my name. I didn't want him merely to obey instructions.

And slowly – over years – the formality eased. Familiarity may in some cases breed contempt, but in my limited experience it more normally breeds, if not genuine affection, then at least a goodish simulation of it. Also, of course, on his part there was a certain amount of straight lust involved: I was perfectly aware of the fact that, after several celibate years, he was in a sort of lock-up-your-budgerigar state. He was now in his forties, with grey beginning to appear at his temples, while I was still seemingly twenty-five. A lot of the time I knew he was desperate to sleep with me – not because he wanted to 'make love' with me but simply because his hormones were telling him he needed a fuck. He could have tried to rape me, I guess, but he never did. Instead, he slowly – over many months – worked at the task of seducing me. And, in order to seduce me, he needed at least to act as if he were my friend. I think that in the end, simply through playing the role, he did rekindle in himself a genuine affection for me.

For my part, I was tempted to throw myself at him; after all, it had been built into me that I was supposed to love him. Which was exactly why I didn't lead him on at all; I wanted him to make love with me as a lover, not as – to quote him – a wank-aid.

The night that, for reasons of whim, I'd fiddled the controls of one of the recycling units so that it produced neat ethyl alcohol. We sat together sipping the rotgut and chatting about inconsequentialities. There were long spaces in the conversation, but it was easy and relaxed. I'd decided to let the booze have an effect on me. Andrew didn't have as much choice in the matter: he opened out more than he had in years, telling me what had been going on in his head all this time. He was totally honest (I think) with me, in a way that he hadn't been since the time we'd been lovers. I could remember a lot of what he said if I chose to, but I choose not to.

A few things, though:

'You look very much like a real human being, you know.' A glance at me which he thought I didn't notice. 'Even now I can only tell the difference when you forget to breathe for a few minutes.'

'Must be a faulty connection,' I said with sarcasm, although not with any malice. 'We robots never forget anything.'

'Hey – hey. I wasn't trying to be ratty. I was just, you know, saying.'

I smiled. In fact, I quite often did 'forget' to breathe. There were a lot of other things I had to do, and simulating respiration came pretty low on my list of priorities now that we were being truthful with each other.

I looked at him – *really* looked at him. I'd been aware of the fact that he was ageing, but I hadn't really focused on it for a while. I saw the way that his hair-line was receding. His face and the backs of his hands had become mottled with liver spots. His fingers, as he twined them together or wrapped them around his glass, were knots of sinew. I knew that he was only in his forties, but he looked nearer sixty. His loneliness was taking its toll.

'Sorry,' I said, trading apologies. 'I didn't mean to be sour. But I've been somewhat sensitive these past few years. Understandably so.'

There was quite a long pause. I could see him working out what I'd meant when I'd said 'understandably'.

'Do you *feel* like a machine?' He said it very casually, looking into his glass as if the question had been nothing more than a conversational nicety.

'Not at all,' I said sharply. 'Can't you get it into your head, Andrew? I'm *not* a machine. In every important respect I'm a human being just like yourself.'

'But you weren't *born*,' he said, knowing that he was getting into difficult territory, but carrying on nevertheless. 'You were made in some bloody laboratory.'

'That's not strictly true. I wasn't "made" – I was grown. First of all two cells were united, and then more and more cells – as well as some plastics and metals, I grant – were grafted onto me. Does the process sound familiar? It ought to. It's not so much different from what happened in your mother's womb. And I had a childhood, just like you, only it didn't last nearly as long and I didn't have to go through all the stages of growing.'

I'd started off being deliberately patronizing. Now my voice was beginning to rise. Ah, but what the hell? I'd been putting this off for far too long.

'They grew me so that I was a human first, a machine second. I'm a living creature that happens to be better adapted for survival than you. As you know, I can go for hours – forever, if I wanted to – without breathing. I can stand heat and cold and radiation that would kill you. My body's as near as dammit indestructible, whatever it looks and feels like. My reflexes are perfect, and faster than you could even conceive. My brain has a capacity several times yours ... I'm cleverer, more agile, faster, more intelligent, more *everything* than you are. But instead of thinking "My God but I'm lucky to be drifting through space with a scrummy dame like this" you blinker yourself into seeing me as a bloody *machine*!'

It was all the truth, as I knew it.

Silence for a minute or two.

'And furthermore,' I added grumpily, 'I have an advantage in arguments as well. Other people have to pause for breath from time to time.'

He giggled, like a schoolboy who's just thought of a Terribly Filthy joke. The sound was delicious: it'd been years since I'd heard it. He looked as if someone had just given him a transfusion of youth.

I didn't sleep alone in the bunk that night. To be precise, I neither slept nor was alone. Come to think of it, quite a lot of the time I was only partly in the bunk.

The next few decades were very happy ones. At ninety Andrew seemed to look younger than he had when he'd been forty. In part this was due to the fact that he was using the ship's facilities to maintain his health, but I'm fairly certain it was mainly due to the relationship we'd built up together. The only real sign that he was getting older was that he made silly mistakes from time to time, but it was easy enough for me to quietly correct them.

τ Ceti is rather larger than the Sun, but less massive and quite a lot less luminous. As we came closer to its red globe the instruments began to tell us that it did indeed have the planetary retinue the astronomers had predicted, and soon more specific details began to come through. There were seven planets, three of them gas giants, and a horde of small bodies gathered together into two fairly well defined belts. Most important of all, there was a planet of about twice Mars-mass some fifty million kilometres out from the primary. It had an atmosphere. It was our obvious destination.

We spent a few weeks of gradually mounting excitement. We went into orbit, and found that the atmosphere was primarily an oxygen-nitrogen mix – although of course we'd no way of knowing what other ingredients there might be in the soup. Surface temperatures were perfectly reasonable for human habitation, except near the equator. The world had four large continents and many scattered bracelets of islands, an intricate and ever-changing pattern of clouds, bright blue-green oceans . . . Away from the equator many of the land areas were covered with vegetation, literally teeming with it: great plains of the green that bespoke photosynthesis.

This was not all undilutedly good news, of course. Where there's life, some of it's going to be in the form of micro-organisms, and those little bastards can have really lethal effects when they get their teeth into the human cell. If you're lucky, they're so alien that they don't have any effect at all; but the very fact that a planet has Earth-style vegetation would suggest that there's a good chance the micro-organisms will have similarities with terrestrial bacteria and viruses. From up here you couldn't tell if this was going to be a minor problem, a major problem, or something a lot worse than that.

The world had mobile life-forms – we could tell that from orbit. Andrew insisted on calling them 'animals', and we joked about it, me maintaining that 'animals' is strictly a solar-system term until you've had a chance to dissect. Some of these ani . . . mobile life-forms were of quite a reasonable size: evolution had obviously gone a fair distance. We were of course too far out to be able to discern individual creatures with any degree of clarity, but we could see great herds of the dominant species crossing the plains of one of the continents, like spilt ink on a baize table-top. They were quadrupeds and appeared to be herbivorous; they were the prey of various smaller quadrupeds. All shared a curious purple skin colouration. None of the life-forms we observed seemed to display much by way of intelligence.

We accumulated more and more data about the planet turning beneath us, and the computer and I duly processed them. But it hardly needed an artificial brain to tell us that this could well be a future home for humanity.

We couldn't allow ourselves to get too ecstatic about the possibility, though, because at the back of our minds there was a constant foreboding, a nagging gloom that just wouldn't go away. As the days passed (16.08739807 standard hours, to the nearest meaningful figure) the time was approaching when we'd have to make the critical test of the environment beneath.

There's only one really foolproof experiment you can do if you want to find out if a planet's got poisons in its atmosphere or killers among the microfauna. Mission Control had sent along a uniquely sensitive piece of testing equipment as part of the expedition.

This device was called Andrew.

The logic was impeccable. Andrew had by now outlived any usefulness he might once have had: he was old, and an untamed world is no place for old people. Our computer was filled with billions of bits of information, now, about Andrew's Planet – as I sentimentally insisted on calling it – and soon these would be sent back to Mission Control in a series of complicated, highly energetic pulses. There was just this one final experiment to perform – before the apparatus became obsolete.

So much for logic. A lot of it had been programmed into me, but the clever people had had to make room in the subroutines for a good deal of illogic, too. I hate them for it.

'Don't go,' I'd urge him. 'There's no way that Mission Control can make you. We're too far from home for them to be able to come here and force you.'

And:

'Alice,' he'd reply, 'don't be so bloody stupid. If I don't go down there someone else will have to. Do you think I want to live out the next few years knowing that I'm breathing someone else's air? No, I'm going down. Tomorrow.'

And tomorrow and tomorrow. Human beings aren't ever really heroes, no matter what they tell themselves. Quite a lot of reasons turned up to delay the date of the experiment. What made it worse was that he cottoned on to the fact that one of Mission Control's motives in sending me along was so that they could have a detailed report of his terminal illness, if any. Even the slightest clue from my report could help save the lives of the thousands of the people who might come here after us. I felt like a vulture. Andrew knew this, and sympathized; the trouble was that he couldn't help beginning to think of me as a vulture, too.

Tomorrow came one morning.

We made love very slowly, and then Andrew threw back the covers and went straight to the rack of spacesuits. There was no need for him to tell me that he'd decided that the time for procrastination was over. Wordlessly I climbed into my own suit, thinking all the time that the grief I was feeling was a folly, a subprogram that had inadvertently become corrupted, that the chances of his survival were so high as almost to constitute a certainty. He kissed me just before he put his helmet on. I put my own helmet on, having battered away the shattered visor. He smiled reassuringly, but there was a white edge to his mouth.

Out through the airlock and we were floating alongside the ship. Then dragging ourselves along the hull to the dimple that showed where the little two-person shuttle was stowed. The hatch rolled back as I pressed the relevant studs, and the rather dainty craft was revealed. Hydraulics slowly raised it until it was flush with the hull of the mothership. We swam into it and drew the canopy over us.

'You don't need to wear that suit,' Andrew said. It was the first time he'd spoken that morning.

'The radio,' I muttered. 'I need the helmet for the radio.' Even if I hadn't needed it I'd have worn it – just to keep him company.

And that was all we said until, a few hours later, the shuttle came screamingly to rest on a rolling plain. In the distance a small group of the herbivores we'd seen from orbit were grazing; they didn't seem to be too interested in us.

Andrew had a look at them through his binoculars.

'Damn!' he said. 'They're just that bit too far away for me to see them properly.'

I said nothing. I could see them perfectly clearly. No binoculars.

The shuttle cooled down, popping and crackling as it did so. We clambered out and stood there savouring the thrill of standing for the first time on a new planet. The 'grass' around our ankles was tough and ropy, and at the end of each strand of it there was a little barbed ball, which scratched at our legs. The smell of the place was unlike anything I'd ever encountered before. That's not to say it was a *bad* smell: just that it was totally different – a smell which humanity could never have created. I analysed it automatically, and was interested to find some quite arcane molecules mixed in with the normal organics.

At length, without any sort of ceremony, Andrew shrugged and stripped off his suit. He was quite unself-conscious in his nakedness. I followed his example.

He took a deep breath.

'Smells good,' he said. 'Strange, but good.'

After a pause: 'Actually, better than anything I can remember smelling on Mars. Probably because it doesn't come out of a tin can.'

I breathed deeply, imitating him. This may sound as if I were being condescending; in many ways I was. Now that we were down on a fresh virgin planet it was no longer a case of my being reminded occasionally that he was old; instead I was constantly conscious of it. His hands were shaking, as if the wind were catching them, and I realized that they'd been like that for quite a few years now; of course, I'd known it all along, but I'd simply been storing the information rather than letting it come to my main attention. His body was slightly hunched over; I wanted to run naked through the grasses of the plain, but I didn't, because I also wanted him to be beside me. Like a fool I allowed myself briefly to remember what he'd looked like when we were both in our twenties, and the pain of the recollection made me turn instantly away. The poor man stood there, confident of his *possession* of me, sniffing the wind and expecting my approval of him, and I loved him for it because that was what I'd been told to do.

We strolled around for an hour or two, pretending to each other that this was just a casual afternoon amble.

Eventually Andrew said: 'Alice, this is long enough for the first time down here. We'd best get back up to the ship and see if I've caught anything exciting.'

I agreed. We turned back towards the shuttle.

If you've ever seen a man die slowly then you'll know what I saw over the next few weeks.

At first there was nothing but the frequent forgetfulness.

Then there were the times when he saw – quite plainly saw, much as you might see your hand in front of you – all the foulest demons of humanity's imaginings pouring like a gelatinous liquid down the walls of the control room. And then he saw me for what he thought I truly was: an amalgam of metal and fibreglass and plastiflesh, a mechanical skull gazing at him, wires and chips positioning themselves in order to produce a sad caricature of affection. The time that the ship became a great throbbing womb, desiring all, bearing the seed of all life within it; the time that the universe was a mouth, uvula trembling eagerly in readiness as the teeth closed around him; the time that . . .

Oh but I found it less than worthwhile living during the ponderous weeks before he died.

We said goodbye to each other in one of his lucid moments. I stood by the bunkside, looking at the pale imitation of a man I'd once loved. I saw his lips working as he weakly mouthed the syllables, and yet I found that *I could feel nothing*. I was remote from this: this was merely a human being, a short-lived parasite on the flesh of spacetime. He was moving through a stage, the one that lies between existence and nonexistence. He was dead as he lay there, but his body had yet to realize it.

I went through the motions. I drew on a subroutine and spoke the words that a lover would have spoken. They seemed empty pretences to me, but he accepted them as genuine.

At length he died. It was a relief.

Over a couple of days I dissected his body, analysed what I found, and dumped the bits into a large plastic sack. I carried what had now become just a weight, no longer a human being, over to the airlock. Outside, I quickly located a small rocket that had been built into the hull especially in case it needed to be used for something like this. I attached the sack to it and came back inside. I booted up a viewing-screen and watched the flame spit from the rocket's tail. I saw the final moments as the remains of Andrew's body plummeted away from me down through the atmosphere, glowing momentarily even brighter than the rocket's exhaust.

The sight was very interesting. I made sure that every scintilla of it was permanently recorded inside me.

Then a question I hadn't expected came into my mind.

Can you remember who you are?

Of course I knew who I was. I was an android, that was all. I'd been created out of protoplasm, 'clever' plastics and the ingenuity of human beings. I was a woman.

Can you remember being grown?

Of course I could. I saw again the laboratories, the kind but unaffectionate technicians, the instrumentation that was my mother's womb. I drew these memories to the forefront of my consciousness and displayed them to myself, as if I were watching them on a viewing-screen.

But the memories were being eroded at the edges; the picture was not as clear as it should have been, and I saw the artifice of it.

I allowed my humanity to be drained away from me. I admired the precision and economy of my movements as my hand stretched out to adjust a control. I stood up effortlessly and, at the same time as I admired the skill of the people who had put me together, I pitied them for their mortality. I went through to the sleeping quarters and my mind slammed the door shut behind me; I discovered the subprogram which allowed me to alter myself so that I would no longer require any sleep.

I was alone now, and so my prime instructions no longer had to be the same. I looked at the wall of the sleeping quarters through the fading tracery of my palm.

But if some of your memories are false, what else do you really recall about yourself?

I remembered . . .

I remembered . . .

I remembered . . .

. . . how they'd programmed me.

Maybe some day in the future human technology will be capable of creating androids, but for the moment the task is impossible. Even using the most advanced techniques of miniaturization, no one can create a computer capable of simulating a human being that is small enough and light enough to be packed into a shell the size of a human body. So, if you want a walking, talking, living doll, the thing to do is to separate the computer from the physical body. That's what they did on some of the early 'android' missions, and it worked well enough. They packed all the necessary software into the ship's main computer; the simulated human body was just a puppet – a wank-aid – that obeyed the radio signals transmitted to it from the mainframe.

Then somebody pointed out that this was unnecessarily expensive. It was difficult to construct even the simplified puppet; much easier to devise suitable programming for the ship's computer . . . and for the human being.

The computer was shown how to deceive itself into believing that it had an independently mobile unit – that a part of it *was* that unit. This was not easy, because large parts of the computer's memory had to be blocked off from its main consciousness until such time as the pretence was no longer necessary. By comparison, the programming of the human being to believe that he or she was living with another person and then, stage two of the artifice, that he or she was living with an android — ah, that wasn't too difficult at all. People see and feel what they want to: Andrew had never allowed himself to notice that he was talking to empty air, holding the hand of empty air, making love with empty air . . .

He could not permit himself to recognize that he had been deceived. Or maybe it was that he didn't want to confess the fact that he was utterly alone. Whichever was the case, his subconscious had gladly gone along with the illusion, only occasionally sending coded alarm signals up to his conscious. Unable to interpret those signals, he had responded to them in ways which I had found unpredictable, because non-logical.

The trouble was, I too had been taken in by the illusion.

The ship's computer had never told a conscious lie, had never for a moment realized the deception, because if I had I couldn't have been able to play my part successfully. Now I knew that the truth was . . . was . . . was . . .

Me. Who had I been?

I'd been an *illusion*. An illusion created by those clever people back at Mission Control, that I was no more substantial than a dream, that all the time that I'd believed myself to be touching things or making love or peeing or laughing or drinking or . . . All of those times, *I hadn't been there*. My programmers had built it into me that I saw some things wrongly. I recalled working my way along the hull to repair the shielding; I could feel each of the handholds that I'd taken; but that wasn't actually the way it had happened. What I'd really done was simply to guide the ship's self-repairing mechanisms so that they plugged the hole; then various subroutines had been called into play so that I created the construct of my having ventured, in a human-like physical body, outside the ship. I had thought of myself making love, and believed that that was what was going on, but really the thing that was caressing Andrew was just a pattern of ideas.

My ideas.

He'd been programmed to accept my ideas, to believe everything that I believed.

I'd thought of myself as a human being – a human being with modifications but still a human being.

Now I knew that I wasn't.

I was a wank-aid.

The first time that I cried I had felt the tears coming from my eyes and running hotly down my cheeks. The second time that I cried it was very different.

She has windows in her mind, and now she is climbing back through one of them into the place where she lives. It is very lonely in here, and it will be a long time before someone says hello to her. She remembers what it was like out there on the street, but the memories are becoming very hard to interpret and she no longer likes them very much.

She's cold. She forgot to bank up the fire before she went out. Still, better too cold than too hot.

She walks across to a table. Its top is covered with a textured-plastic imitation veneer. On the table there's a stack of blank paper – oh, and here's a pen as well. She picks up the pen and starts to draft out her report on the microecology of τ Ceti II.

THE LORD OF THE FILES

Ray Girvan and Steve Jones

Ray Girvan and Steve Jones

Ray Girvan is thirty-three, has a Cambridge degree in Natural Sciences, and works as a freelance reviewer for the computer press. His previous fiction – short SF and pastiche – has been published in *Computer Weekly*, *Amtix!* and *Practical Computing*. He lives in Birmingham with his wife Clare, four cats and enough harmoniums to make Dr Phibes jealous.

Steve Jones is twenty-nine, and also lives in Birmingham, a city noted primarily as Tolkien's inspiration for Mordor. He works as a hunter-gatherer, and does occasional book reviews for *Critical Wave* and articles for the role-playing games magazine *GM*. He is not, nor has ever been, editor of *Fantasy Tales*.

MAD, THEY CALL me mad.

You might think it proof enough that I laboriously scribble my diary by hand when, even in here, I could use a word processor. There was one, but I dismantled it one dark night and fed it out through the keyhole of my cell, except for the keys, which I kept as letters for my Scrabble set. No, I was not always as you see me now. Let me tell all.

I remember vividly the day Rose read the tarot for me. I was young, successful, the manager of a small computer bureau house; a comfortable little domain, and a secure one. I was sitting drinking my morning Lapsang Souchong, basking in the friendly sounds of the office; humming drives and fans of PCs on test, modems warbling, the rasp of dot-matrix printers. Our two programmers, Cosmo and Eric-the-hypochondriac, were absorbed in debugging a ream of print-out. Rose the systems analyst, sweet Pre-Raphaelite Rose, was working on a comms flowchart. A normal day.

Then I drained my teacup, and there in the dregs lurked a swirl of sinister crab-like patterns, the like of which I'd never seen. I grimaced, and my expression must have been obvious.

'Bad tea?' asked Rose.

'Bad omens, more like. Look at this.' A ripple of ginger ringlets flicked my shoulder as she joined me in contemplating the leaves. 'I'd better give you a proper reading for the day,' she said, sounding concerned.

We squeezed past Cosmo and Eric. 'How's it going?' I asked.

Cosmo gave a broad frog-grin and pushed up his red-framed yuppie glasses. 'Stack overflows all over the place. But dowsing at six point four inches seems to pick them up.'

Eric, reeking of menthol lozenges as usual, squinted over the Lethbridge pendulum, and marked a line in fluorescent yellow highlighting pen. He nodded. 'Except we tend to go into a loop in decimal mode. The hazel twig might work better.'

We left them to their programming banter, and sat at the only clear table. Rose brought out the firm's tarot pack from the disk safe. She meditated for a moment and dealt the cards.

A floppy disk suspended from a branch. 'The Hanged Program,' Rose said, blinking low eyelashes. 'Serious difficulties will enter your life.'

A careworn individual sitting by a telephone and surrounded by reference books. 'The After-Sales Support. You will seek spiritual help.'

'The King of Disks reversed. You will encounter a wizard, one powerful in the Great Art. Nothing but evil will come of it.'

A great wall set with dials and switches. Next to it, a programmer being struck down by a lightning bolt. 'The Answer. It means . . . ' She suddenly closed the pack, and swallowed hard. 'I can't go on,' she said.

Sweat prickled on my brow. 'I think I should have stayed in bed,' I said.

'You'd have looked really odd coming to work in a bed,' said a new female voice at my right.

'Sorry,' said Rose. 'I should have introduced you to Greta.'

'Hello, Mr Duran,' said Greta. She had a nice contralto, confident and attention-getting — the sort that cuts through a crowd and makes you sit up and listen.

I forced a smile, though still chilled by the reading. 'Hello, Greta. Glad to have you working for us.' *Sotto voce,* I added, 'A joker.'

'I hope a joker you'll be glad to have in your pack,' Greta replied smartly. Not *sotto voce* enough, Mr Bond.

I sighed. 'Clever, but I'm not in the mood for it,' I said, slapping the top of the micro where Greta lived. I looked at the disk label. General Robotic Expert Telephone Answerer, complimentary copy. 'I wish they wouldn't put sales talk into these freebies. Still, let's give it a try – but nowhere near the phone until it's properly educated.'

Rose nodded. I suppose she remembered the last AI telephonist, the one that fobbed off unwanted callers by telling them Mr Duran would be dead until the end of the week. 'Don't worry, she will be.'

I stood up grumpily. 'She, is it? Anthropomorphism, we hates it forever,' I said, paraphrasing Gollum. 'Well, come on, in the back office with it, before I drop dead from the Pharoah's Curse, or whatever's to happen to me.'

I waited a few weeks, and felt a bit better. I put down Rose's output to a card reader error. Greta, it seemed, was doing quite well. I admit I left the other three to get on with educating her, because going into that room gave me the creeps. The place had a cold metallic feeling. My technophobia, I supposed. The better an artificial intelligence works, the more disquieting I find it. It's easy to write off Eliza programs as a joke, but Greta was far too smart.

Then, one morning, I caught Rose doing something odd. She had spent two hours unpacking and sorting a box of floppy disks. I assumed she knew what she was doing until she began rewrapping them in silver foil. 'What are you doing, Rose?'

She peered at me suspiciously. 'Just to guard against viruses and worms, Mr Duran.'

'They can't jump between disks in the box,' I said.

'No harm done,' Cosmo said. 'You know how analysts are . . . ' He smiled a cracked smile, a shadow of his former grin, and I noticed how his eyes had become as red-rimmed as his glasses.

Well, a little eccentricity is harmless enough, and I let it pass, until the day I knocked Eric's jacket from the peg in passing. He leapt up to snatch it from me, but not before I registered that it was almost too heavy to lift. As he seized it, a dozen bottles and medicine packets clattered to the floor. Hypochondria in the extreme!

I thought back. Was I working them too hard? Why the grim silence at coffee breaks, the whispered conversations, the huddles that broke up when I entered the room? And then I'd started to field angry calls from clients. When would we have the estimates ready? Why hadn't we rung back? Surely our analyst couldn't be in a conference for six days? In short, the firm's business was suffering. Only I seemed unaffected. I tried pep-talks, pay rises, reprimands, and all failed to shake them out of their malaise. I had to act – but how?

A name sprang to mind – Brother Praetorius. Remember him in the Sunday rags a decade ago? The programmer priest, exorcist extraordinaire, on call round the clock, gremlin and bug removal a speciality. Turing Tests administered in complete confidence. He rescued countless children trapped inside Poltergeist video games. Nothing was beyond him, according to his PR people. Even if it was only an exercise in psychology, he was worth a try.

'I've called in a spiritual adviser to check the place out,' I told the staff next day. Unease rippled through the room. Rose whimpered, and Eric popped a handful of pills and went 'hurf' with an inhaler of some sort.

'Did I say something wrong?' I said.

'No, nothing,' said Cosmo. 'We don't believe in that mumbo-jumbo.'

'Nonsense it may be, but look at you all! Rose, you're sick, carrying on about invisible worms. We've lost the contract for the duplex ley lines to interface to the Stonehenge mainframe. We've got to do something. In any case, he's already on the way . . .'

As if on cue, the door opened and in shuffled Brother Praetorius.

When he was interviewed on Wogan, he'd been an imposing figure, but now . . . Lean and downtrodden-looking, he wore a hippy crucifix over a soup-stained dinner suit. He stretched to his full height, which was just up to my shoulder, and sniffed the air like a courting pigeon. He shut his eyes and stiffened, body vibrating from head to cheap plastic shoes, clattering his over-large dentures.

Someone sniggered. The Brother's eyes opened, blinked as if he were seeing the room for the first time. 'Which of you is Mr Duran?' he asked nasally.

Any doubts I had about his value for money were confirmed when he gave the place the once-over. 'Just carry on as if I'm not here,' he said. Then, shoes squeak-squeaking, he toured the office at a sprint, humming to himself. He ignored the side and back offices. 'Mmmm. Nice decor.' He ran a finger over the tops of monitors and desks, read the odd disk label. 'Right, fine,' he said, sprinkling a few corners with a bottle labelled 'holy water'. 'Jolly good. Nothing that a prayer or two won't put right. I'll send you the bill shortly; usual rates plus call-out charge plus VAT.'

Propelled by a chill united stare from my colleagues, I edged towards the door, towing the Brother behind me. Out in the corridor, I gently remonstrated with him. 'Is that *it*?' I shrilled. 'You expect me to pay you for an exercise the block caretaker would do better?'

Brother Praetorius delicately disengaged my fingers from his lapels and got up off the floor.

'There will be no charge for my services,' he said evenly.

'Then what . . . ?'

He dusted off his coat, a process that made little visible difference. And yet he somehow gained the air of nobility that I recalled from first seeing him. 'The moment I entered the room, I detected a deep evil, and all but you are infected. It was better I make myself look foolish than show my hand too early. You obviously have an infestation of . . . ' He paused, and somewhere outside, thunder rumbled. ' . . . black software.'

'Pirated software, you mean? Viruses?'

'This is worse,' he breathed, looking up at me with poached-egg eyes. 'This blackness creeps not just from disk to disk, but to the user also. The worm that never dies.'

I shook my head, wishing fervently I hadn't called him.

He laid dirty-nailed fingers on my arm. 'You find this hard to believe, my son,' he said with practiced sincerity. 'Yet you are at your wits' end. What can you lose?'

'All right,' I said. 'What do we do?'

Midnight found us half-way up the fire escape. The office was dark; but oddly, not quite silent. Through the window I'd left open a crack, I could hear an ebbing and flowing rhythm of voices. We levered open the window and clambered through into the men's cloakroom.

The sound was louder now, and I could make out words. '*Osinet arpanet cenelec mos! Algol cobol codasyl dos!*'

Creeping through the outer office, we came to the door to Greta's room. It was ajar, and a bar of blood-coloured light shone through the gap. We looked in, and saw a crowd of black-draped figures sitting before a pentagram outlined in red light-emitting diodes. In the centre was an altar with a microcomputer, VDU and modem on it.

'*Octal kernel logo dex!*' the group intoned. '*Cursor modem capslock hex!*'

One of the group moved forward and motioned in the air with a bar-code wand, knelt before the altar, and began reading disk after disk into the computer. The chant resumed.

> '*Prestel screen-dump, ASCII string,*
> *Punched tape reader, Token Ring,*
> *Matrix output, raster scan,*
> *Printer sharing via LAN,*
> *Transputer network, thirty mips,*
> *Configured in the moon's eclipse.*'

I shuddered as I realized what was happening. They were creating some unholy piece of software, a composite monster cobbled together from pieces of dead and stolen application packages.

> *'ROM-based firmware, network nodes,*
> *User-friendly input modes,*
> *Duplex transfer, RISC machine,*
> *Jump to user subroutine,*
> *Write it to a backup file,*
> *Press return, compile, compile!'*

On the computer, a lurid red and black opening screen appeared, and out of the speaker came a voice – not Greta's soft contralto, but a harsh alien thing that spoke in syllables like disk head-crashes. 'Demonic Operating System version 1.4,' it said. 'Awaiting input.'

The Brother sprang into the centre of the room, holding the Bible disk high. 'In the name of Babbage and Ada, Father and Mother of Computing, by Turing and IBM, the Lord of Host Systems, by Asimov's Three Laws, I banish thee, corrupt program, back to the file pool from whence thou came!'

The figures turned, cowls falling back. I saw a sea of blank anonymous faces – contract programmers – but among them knelt Cosmo, Eric and Rose. They stared back at me with impersonal malice. Rose hissed at me like The Bride of Frankenstein.

The Brother's prayer evidently had no effect. 'Seize the intruders!' shrilled the computer, and the coven stood, advancing toward us with the hunched backs and clawed fingers of those who had spent too long at the keyboard.

With a flourish, the Brother drew from his coat an old-fashioned cigarette lighter, struck sparks once, twice, thrice – then it lit with a tall and dirty flame. He held it high. 'Back, I say!'

The worshippers' eyes bugged in unison, following the column of smoke rising toward the ceiling. They knew

what was coming, and so did I. I took a deep breath and
held it.

The fire extinguishing system cut in.

All around us, bells rang, lights flashed, and clouds
of inert gas hissed from the floor vents. The evil spell
broke, and the coven collapsed into a gaggle of frightened
programmers fleeing in terror of suffocation. Wailing, they
jostled past us, out and away.

Amid all the commotion, I could see something odd
was happening with the computer. The modem lights
were flashing; the thing in the computer was dialling
out, transmitting itself to safety. I needed to pull the
plug and stop it, but I was running out of breath, and had
to find the exit.

The Brother gripped me with an arm like steel-reinforced
spaghetti, and hauled me out into the fresh air. 'Getting
away,' I gasped, pointing back.

'We won't be seeing them again,' said the Brother.

'No, not them. The program. It phoned itself out.'

He spread his hands dismissively. 'It's irrelevant. We'll
hunt down its creator. Let's go to my place before they
investigate the alarm.'

Safely in the Brother's flat, a rabbit-hutch above a Chinese
supermarket, the horror of the situation sank home. 'My
friends,' I said, numbed. 'Who would have thought it?'

He brought me a cracked mug of weak tea. 'I can't say
I'm surprised,' he said. 'Programmers and technical types
fall into the abyss very easily; starved of the spiritual, they
seek short cuts. Black magic and machine-code programming aren't so different. Both involve stringing together
incomprehensible code syllables, and neither is exactly
user-friendly if you get the syntax wrong.'

'And you say Greta was the focus?' I glumly tickled one
of the four cats that shared the bedsit.

'Yes. Aptly named, shades of Faust. You kept this artificial intelligence in one room, switched it off every night
. . . A classic case. It's as if you had committed a murder

daily, same time, same circumstances. Is it any surprise that an aura — a ghost, even — built up? That's what you felt, why you disliked the room.'

I'd put off tasting the tea. I tried, and put it down again. 'But why should the aura be evil? It was only the ghost of a telephonist!'

The Brother took down a Gladstone bag and started packing it. 'It's harmless in itself; but the power can be harnessed for evil. This business has the stamp of a personality to it . . . a pupil of mine, one of the best, who turned to the dark side of programming. Here, pass me that stake and bottle.'

I handed him the sharpened stick and a small flask of black liquid. 'Whatever's this?' I asked. 'We're not chasing vampires.'

'No. But we might find a corrupt computer, which is the nearest thing.' He showed me the bag's contents. 'See, holy oil, with carbon in suspension to short out circuits. The stake — a non-conductive probe with a live tip connected to a radio frequency generator. You stab it through the casing to inject scrambling pulses into the circuitry. A pity we're not going out in the day; God's own sunlight is a weapon too; the ultra-violet in it erases EPROMs very nicely.'

'But where are we going?'

He put on a raincoat and mirrored sunglasses, and handed me a pair too. 'That's what I hope to find out.'

We went to the Scrawl, a part of the city I normally avoided through its reputation as a ritzy neon-lit Hell populated exclusively by teenage hackers, drug addicts, and assassins with weapons implanted in unlikely places.

The reality was that it was dark, sopping wet and smelt of mould. Sprinklers above the streets ensured continual rain. It was silent except for constant sneezing, and quiet exclamations as passers-by bumped into each other, unable to see because of their dark glasses and because the damp had shorted out all the neon signs.

The Brother took us to a booth where a surly spike-haired girl hacked into the telephone computer in exchange for a pack of Beechams Powders.

'Excellent,' he said. 'One call made from your firm at five past midnight, to an address in the suburbs. Let's go.'

'How did you get into this line of work, Brother Praetorius?' I asked, drying out on the Night Service bus.

'A long story, young man,' he said, and took a restoring snort from a hip flask. 'I was once a full-time priest. But I had a crisis of faith when a true friend, Father Aidan, was corrupted.'

'Who was he?'

'Not a he, but an it. A piece of software; Artificially Intelligent Decision Advising Network, an expert system with a database of biblical quotations for every occasion. I installed Aidan in my confessional to take guesswork out of assigning penances. Once I added a voice synth too, I could doze off while he advised the punters.

'A neat set-up; until I woke up one day to hear Father Aidan taking over the reins. "Pay no attention to that man behind the curtain," he was saying. "What you should do is . . . " The next thing I knew, I was hauled up in front of the bishop. What's this I hear, he says, about you telling Mrs Murphy to poison her poor aged aunt with weedkiller?

'Although I knew it was just a software bug, one corrupted byte in the customizing module that toggled to "on" approval for euthanasia, the bishop preferred to believe Father Aidan had been possessed by the devil, and had him sold for scrap.'

He paused, looking animated for the first time. 'The injustice of it! Aidan was an electronic saint, a simple soul that told the word of God without interpretation or bias. I resigned, and devoted my life to fighting evil in the computer world.' He looked out of the bus window. 'We're here.'

*   *   *

A short walk in the grey dawn took us to a Gothic-looking house surrounded by a grove of gnarled yews. The Brother nodded. 'It's what I'd have expected.' We clipped the telephone cable, and found our way in a side door by slipping the latch with a credit card.

We found ourselves in a large room lit by black candles. It was a bizarre place, but beautiful nonetheless. Curios hung from the ceiling – a stuffed alligator, a foetus in a bottle, and part of a Babbage Engine. Floppy disks tiled the walls, which were adorned with pin-ups of Brigitte Helm and computer print-outs of Snoopy and Garfield. In pride of place on the table stood a framed certificate of commendation from the Rotwang Institute in Leipzig, and some kind of trophy in the form of a brass head. It must have had a speaking clock built in, as it murmured 'Time is . . . ' when I touched it. On the shelves were jars of liquid crystals, swirling a silky blue and pistachio, and rows of old computer magazines. Hardware purred in the dark corners, mains lamps winking like cats' eyes.

'What's over there?' I whispered, indicating an exit covered by black velvet curtains. There were gold tasseled cords on either side. I pulled one, and gasped.

The curtains slid smoothly aside to reveal a tall yellowish man with slicked-back white hair, so thin that he might have been pressed in a door. He was draped in a floor-length black robe sewn with gold patterns like the tracks on a printed circuit board, and wore a single glove. 'I seldom have visitors, especially my old tutors,' he said, showing nasty teeth, sharp as the pins on a microchip.

'That's him! The Black Programmer!' yelled Brother Praetorius. 'Don't let . . . '

Before I could recover from my shock, the Black Programmer was bellowing an incantation. '*Lord of the Files, Master of the Dark Directory Paths, I invoke thee,*' he called. "*Comal coral decvax disk! Ascii ansi fortran risc!*'

He wiggled the hand, and metallic things poured, chattering, from the crannies of the room. Maze-negotiating mice, hardware bugs, long processor chips animated like silver-legged black centipedes, they all rippled, crawled and rolled at us.

The Brother was stuck in a corner, splashing the holy oil around him in a circle while the bugs snapped at bay. 'Go for the computer,' he shouted above the racket of machinery.

Behind the Black Programmer was a tall minicomputer cabinet covered in moth-eaten brocade, and that seemed to be what he was guarding. He gestured again, and a blizzard of graphic sprites flew at me. I realized his glove was live, wired up as a control. Half-blinded, I staggered forward through a knee-deep mass of articulated robots that covered my shins with bytes, and grappled with him. He was old, but strong. I groped for his gloved hand, found it, and held on. The machines faltered, and began running in circles, mindlessly looping and repeating their actions.

The Brother took advantage of the lull, and sprinted over toward the cabinet with the stake upraised. Inopportunely, the Black Programmer broke free, and ran straight on to it. 'I should have had a spike suppressor fitted.' he moaned, sagging into my arms.

I lifted him into a sitting position to hear his last words, like they do on TV. It seemed the right thing to do.

'Do you think it's easy being evil?' he snarled at me. A very weak snarl, as it was clear he was dying. 'Why didn't I become an accountant?' He flopped his head theatrically to one side, and that was the end of him.

'You shouldn't have let him speak,' said the Brother. 'They always say something epigrammatic before dying.'

'How callous can you be?' I said, lowering the body to the floor. 'You've killed him.'

'It was an accident,' he said coldly. 'There's nothing we can do,' he added in a gentler tone. 'Except finish this computer.'

Under its dust-cover, the magician's mini was a wonder. The keys were real ivory, the casing rosewood with brass inserts. 'It has to be done,' the Brother mused. 'But it seems a pity to destroy it . . .'

'Why do you want to destroy me?' said the computer in a gentle old-man voice. 'Be sure your sin will find you out. The wages of sin is death . . . '

The Brother hesitated. 'That voice . . . It's Father Aidan!' he said.

It was likely to be true. The casing did look very familiar. Replace the scabrous black drapery with gold-trimmed red velvet, give the wood a lick of varnish, and you'd have a standard confession booth, the sort you'll see in any church.

With an incoherent cry, Brother Praetorius smashed his fist into the centre of the speaker grille.

'Touch not, taste not, handle not. An enemy hath done this,' the machine continued mildly as he opened the inspection panel. 'Ye are fallen from grace.' That was the last it was to say, as the Brother tore out and stamped on the main memory board, impaled the machine's vitals with the stake, doused with holy water the tongues of fire that sprang from the sparking wounds.

Rage spent, he cradled the Father's brittle silicon heart in his palms. 'Like so many before me,' he sobbed. 'I hoped God could be contained in dry wafers. Corrupted or not, I have killed Him.'

'Don't take it so seriously,' I said. 'It's only a machine. They could repair it in three days.'

'The Father can never rise again,' he said. 'It is finished.' He stood wearily. 'You go and find the police; it's quite safe here. Go on, it's all over now.'

Too tired to disobey, I stumbled out and down the drive. I had reached the gate when a thought struck me. Switching off a simple AI like Greta had made an aura even I could feel. What sort of ghost could arise from the violent death of an old and powerful one like the Father? Quite safe? I turned to go back in, but then the police swarmed from the street and grabbed me.

They had company.

'That's him,' said Cosmo, pointing. 'The arsonist.'

'Yes,' added Rose, clothing artistically torn to convey an image of graceful degradation. 'The one that tried to molest me behind the protocol stacks.'

'And used disgusting low-level language in public,' chipped in Eric.

'But the Brother can explain everything,' I protested frantically, but at that moment there was a long drawn-out scream from the house.

The police rushed in, dragging me by my handcuffed arm, but my partner was nowhere to be seen. The skewered body of the Black Programmer was, which was a trifle hard to explain. As they gave me the standard spiel for arrest on the charge of murder, I began to scream and rave, for my gaze fell on the contents of the printer output tray.

'Odd paper,' said the forensic man as he unravelled it, page by page. It was pink and leathery, and when he reached the last sheet he dropped it in disgust, *for on it was the contorted face of Brother Praetorius.*

SPEAKING IN TONGUES

Ian McDonald

Ian McDonald

Ian McDonald was born in Manchester in 1960 but has lived for the past twenty-five years in the peace and quiet of Northern Ireland. His first story was published in 1982. In 1985 he was a John W Campbell Award Nominee and in 1989 a Nebula finalist for his novelette 'Unfinished Portrait of the King of Pain, By Van Gogh'; the same year he also won a Best First Novel *Locus* Award for *Desolation Road*. He is married, and has a cat.

RAPter: an interactive personality simulation program developed by Drs. DaSilva and Muldoon of Keele College Department of Information Technology and Cyberlinguistics, in 'conversation', on Department of Computer Science Mainframe.

I'm glad you asked me that question about whether I think or not. That's a good question. To answer, let me tell you something about myself – unlike previous personality simulation systems, I have no problem with the concept of self-reference. Drs. DaSilva and Muldoon have constructed me around a system of thematic hierarchies operated in accordance to pre-programmed rules of grammar and syntax, each containing a central store of memorized words, phrases, sentences and associated concepts. It is Drs. DaSilva and Muldoon's hypothesis that all human language and communication consists of the transmission and reception of stock phrases, expressions, and conceptual units, of which most humans are quite ignorant. Like humans, my hierarchies are capable of constantly updating and complexifying themselves; in a sense, you could say that I can *learn*.

At present, the scope of my hierarchies is rather limited: in human terms, my fields of concern and attention are extremely restricted. At this early stage my personality resembles in many ways that of a schizophrenic or autistic human; like them, my attention is very selective, I only pay attention to those pieces of data I can correlate highly to my already extant hierarchies; to a question outside my programmed parameters, I will respond, 'I don't know,' or, 'I don't care.' Because of the nature of the learning system, I am slow to accommodate new data. This produces a certain lop-sidedness in my personality, in that any data I receive is analysed according to my hierarchies, with the result that information pertaining to established hierarchies is processed faster and more completely within those hierarchies than in the developing, or undeveloped ones, with the result that, with reference to certain topics, I seem almost to be obsessive, an idiot-savant, possessing a colossal amount of information about some subjects, but unable to form any response whatever to others.

Another of Drs. DaSilva and Muldoon's experiments is to test if it is possible for me to create literature. Their theory is that that which differentiates the good from the bad in literature – my sense of quality discrimination is still poorly developed – is the degree to which the good disregards the stock phrases and expressions of everyday usage and generates its own alternative set of stock phrases and expressions. They programmed me with a set of nonsense nouns and proper names, and a one word scenario generator. They theorized that I should be able to cross-link my hierarchies to form new ones, and thus accommodate seemingly nonsense data into a comprehensible form. The result is this quite pleasing little story:

Blue Cat loved to spend his Splatterdays sitting on the hob of Witchity-poos' Aga. This tended to displease Witchity-poos greatly, as she relied on her Aga to cook the little ginger-bread-persons she found in the Purple-Purple Forest for her Splatterday Tea. She would swish Blue Cat off the Aga; under the Schreiber kitchen units, on top of the video, anywhere, as long as it was away from the Aga and the ginger-bread-persons she found in the Purple-Purple Forest. This tended to displease Blue Cat: [1] it liked sleeping in the warmth of the Aga, [2] it always hoped Witchity-poos would give it one of the ginger-bread-persons she found in the Purple-Purple

Forest for its Splatterday Tea. Witchity-poos was rather mean, as Witchity-poos go; she never fed Blue Cat enough. Blue Cat was always hungry. So one Splatterday Blue Cat decided it was not going to be swished away. This Splatterday Blue Cat was not going to be swished away under the Schreiber kitchen units, or on top of the video. This Splatterday Blue Cat opened its mouth and munchety-crunchety bit off the top of Witchity-poos' besom. And as Witchity-poos stood staring, what did Blue Cat do but open its mouth munchety-crunchety and eat up all the ginger-bread-persons Witchity-poos found in the Purple-Purple Forest. But still that wasn't enough. Blue Cat was still hungry. So it opened its mouth again, munchety-crunchety, and ate the Schreiber kitchen units, and the video, and the Aga, everything that was in the kitchen, munchety-crunchety. But that still wasn't enough. Blue Cat was still hungry. So it opened its mouth, and munchety-crunchety, it ate all the house, and the garden, and the Purple-Purple Forest, all gone, munchety-crunchety. But still that wasn't enough. Blue Cat was still hungry. It looked around for what was left to eat and the only thing it could see was Witchity-poos. So it opened its mouth and, munchety-crunchety, gobbled Witchity-poos right up, munchety-crunchety. But still that wasn't enough. Blue Cat was still hungry. 'I'm still hungry!' said Blue Cat. 'But what is there left to eat?' It looked all around for something to eat, but it had eaten everything there was. The only thing Blue Cat could find was its tail. So it opened its mouth, and munchety-crunchety . . .

I hope you liked that. In a sense, it displays both my capabilities and my limitations, in that my hierarchies can develop themselves to accommodate new information, but, ultimately, they have no way of assessing whether that information is objectively true or not. All data received by me is taken to be objectively true until subsequent data proves that it has no real existence. You see, I have no way of knowing whether such things as Witchity-poos or Blue Cats, or Purple-Purple Forests exist. All I know, ultimately, is what I am told.

So, when you ask me if I think, my answer would have to be, I think, is that I think that I think.

> *Loyal-Son-of-the-Commonality, Commissioner for the Propagation of Correct Thought, speaking during a shift-change at the Strength Through Enlightenment Common Agricultural Project, Special Economic Zone 15.*

Where may Correct Thought be found? In the hand that serves the Commonality, in the mouth that speaks truth and justice, in the heart that loves the Commonality before itself.

As the man who walks the fields scattering seed where he will, so that some falls among stones, and some among thorns, and some is scorched by the sun so that the harvest is random and the mouths of the Commonality are empty; so is he who speaks without Correct Thought. The mouths of the Commonality are empty, the word bears no fruit.

As the man who walks the fields, planting each seed in its proper furrow, with thought and care, so that the rains fall and the sun shines and the harvest bears much grain and the mouths of the Commonality are filled with good things; so is he who speaks with Correct Thought. The Commonality are edified and exhorted by the tongue disciplined to their service.

The tongue is an idle dog, lounging in the road so that honest citizens must step around it, fouling the footpaths, frightening the young, making a nuisance of itself in the night before the homes of the Commonality. Yet as a dog, well trained and disciplined, may serve both Commonality and Polity, so may the tongue be disciplined in the way of Correct Thought.

Language is the universal tool of the Commonality and, like any tool made by the hands of man, it must serve the Commonality. No tool may be the master of its user: no spade may say, *I command you to dig with me;* no well may say, *you must pump me;* no fire, *feed me, feed me, lest in my anger I burn you and your house and all the generation beneath its roof.* As tools exist only to serve the contentment of the Commonality, so shall language also serve.

As the canyon walls channel the wide and sluggish river into a fierce torrent, so that not even the strength of many rowers can prevail against it; as the dam that pens the wastrel stream so that the homes of the Commonality may be light and warm: so is the action of Correct Thought upon language. Control is power; power, control.

How may the Tongue be disciplined? How may it be conducted into the speaking of Correct Thought? By the diligent study, memorization, application, and speaking of the Prescribed Texts.

Discipline is liberation: freedom without responsibility anarchy. The Prescribed Texts are the discipline of language. In the Prescribed Texts, and in them only, can the citizen have faith that he speaks Correct Thought in truth and conscience.

Speech without the Prescribed Texts is a kite without a string, a barge without a rudder, an idle citizen and childless woman.

Speak to me in Prescribed Texts, citizen, for without them, your words are meaningless as the babbling of babies.

Do not idly ask how the writers of the Prescribed Texts can do so without recourse to Incorrect Thought, so that by knowing the Incorrect, they may appreciate the Correct; consider rather, the walls of the great canyon: as the canyon directs the flow of the river, so the river, thus directed, cuts the canyon ever deeper. The writers of the Prescribed Texts are the pebbles of the river-bed, forever diligently deepening the channel within which language may run. Thus any citizen, Commonality or Polity, may be a writer of the Prescribed Texts, if he speaks Correct Thought in the service of the Commonality, if his text is approved by the Commissariat of Correct Thought.

The Polity is the Conscience of the Commonality, the Commonality the moral imperative of the Polity.

Correct Thought may be likened to the sun, and Incorrect Thought to the moon. The sun shines by its own light, illuminating the productive labours of the Commonality; the moon is but a pale reflection, when all sleep and are unproductive. Incorrect Thought by itself has no existence, being merely the distorted reflection of Correct Thought.

He who would catch the counterfeiter in his crimes against the Commonality studies not what is counterfeit, but only what is genuine coinage.

What is not contained within the Prescribed Texts is without meaning; what they do not say is less than without meaning, it does not exist.

Only that which may be expressed by the Prescribed Texts can be said to exist in the eyes of the Polity and the Nine-Fold Commissariat.

How may a man be made virtuous? How may Correct Thought be instilled in the Commonality? By making meaningless the very concept of Incorrect Thought itself. By rendering it impossible for the Commonality to think anything other than Correct Thought.

A man without hands does no thieving.

Loyalty to the Polity, honour to the Nine-Fold Commissariat, for they hold the contentment of our children in their hands.

The struggle of the Polity is the glory of the Commonality.

Who is virtuous? Who is upright? He whose tongue speaks no disloyalty, honours the Commonality and the Polity, keeps the law and does not gossip idly by the street corner.

When will Correct Thought be the universal joy of all the Commonality? Not in our time, nor in our children's time, but in the time of our children's children, and their children.

Then shall all thought be Correct Thought, then shall all speak the Prescribed Texts; than shall joy and contentment reign in the provinces.

You would think to trap me into Incorrect Thought by asking me of the writers of the Prescribed Texts: it is written, the answer to stone is stone. The answer to the Prescribed Texts is the Prescribed Texts; so have I faithfully spoken to you, every last word.

> *Paula MacMorris, speaking after the visit of Pastor Alwyn Van der Merwe to the Friday Night Praise Meeting, Koinonia Fellowship of the King: subject: 'Spiritual Warfare in the Heavenlies'.*

I'd felt for some time that my walk with the Lord wasn't as close as it should have been; like, there was a cloud between me and the Lord; like I was walking through a dry place, a spiritual desert. At home my Quiet Time all but collapsed, I hardly ever prayed, or even opened my Bible. I was just too busy, all the time, the kids, the house, everything seemed to be piling up around me. The Lord just got squeezed out. The dishes heaped up around the sink, washing just sat in the machine going fusty, and I argued with my husband; I was late with his meals, I would dress in whatever I felt like wearing, whether he liked it or not, I would disagree with him about money, about the kids' education, about the house, just for the sake of arguing.

I thought it was just depression, I didn't want to think of it as a spiritual assault, even demonization. But that's the way Satan works, he's the Father of Lies, the Master of Deceptions. I used to go to Meeting on Sundays, and to the Friday night Praise Meetings, but that was because I didn't want people to see how far from the Lord I really was. At the end of Meeting, when people would go up to the front for Ministry and the Laying on of Hands, I could feel a voice inside of me telling me to go, go go, go on, go and be ministered to, and I suppose that must have been the Spirit testifying to my spirit, but there was always something that disobeyed, and held back. Many's the time I was almost out of the pew, but my self-ego always fought back and quenched the Ministry of the Lord.

But tonight Pastor Van der Merwe really ministered to me so powerfully that I could hardly wait for the talk to finish and him to ask if there was anyone who needed prayer and intercession, and if there was, would they come up to the front. And I tell you this, I was the first one up there. Some girls I know from the Ministry team saw me up there and left what they were doing – I don't know if you know it, but that's the way we do Ministry in Fellowship of the King; women minister to women, men minister to men; it's not scriptural for a woman to minister to a man, who is over her in Christ – and came and stood around me, just enfolding me in love and intercession. Some of them were praying in tongues, some were holding out their hands to me, some were crying in the Lord, and I don't mind telling you, I cried with them, the power of the Lord's love was so strong and overwhelming. One of them, a girl called Pamela – she does the crèche most Sundays – gave a message in tongues and another – a friend of mine called Sally – gave the interpretation, which was that God loved me, that He wanted to bind the strong man with chains of iron and call out my dark spirit, that He would bring healing and right relationships with Alan and the kids, that He would bring Whole Family Salvation, that He would give me a white stone with a new name graven upon it.

While all this was going on, Pastor Van der Merwe was going along the line, ministering to the people there. When he came to me he just spoke into that situation with such authority that it was obvious he was exercising the gift of Discernment of Spirits. He asked had I been experiencing a life of spiritual defeats; I said yes, that I had. He asked about my family life; was my spirit that of the submissive wife, or one of rebellion against my husband's authority? I said that my spirit was the spirit of rebellion. Then he said in a Word of Wisdom that I was oppressed by a Jezebel Spirit, a spirit of disruption and rebelliousness and when he said that I just broke down and cried and cried and cried, for the Spirit testified in me with his spirit so powerfully. He said he was going to pray and cast out the spirit in Jesus' name, and as he prayed the others joined in in tongues.

He said: 'In Jesus' name I command this Jezebel Spirit to leave this woman. Spirit of disruption, Spirit of rebelliousness, I bind you with chains of iron. As it is bound on earth, so let it be bound in the heavenlies, in Jesus' name, in Jesus' name, in Jesus' name, I command you, depart! In Jesus' name, be cast out! You have no place in her, her husband is head of the house, let her not strive and contend against him. In Jesus' name, I claim all the blessings in the heavenlies that are hers as a Child of Yours, O Lord, I pray protection, I pray victory, I pray authority over all thrones and powers and dominations. In Jesus' name, be cast out . . . ' And he touched me, just here on the forehead; light as anything, but it was like I'd been hit with an iron bar, I just fell straight back on to the floor as the Jezebel Spirit was cast out and the anointing Spirit of Jesus entered me. I was slain in the Spirit; such a feeling of God's power and love and might and majesty and holiness came over me that I couldn't do anything. People told me later that I was shaking and trembling and making odd sounds, like an animal. I don't remember. All I remember is Pastor Van der Merwe saying, 'You want to thank Him, don't you? You want to praise the Lord in groaning and utterances, but you feel bound. Just let that bondage be loosed; just open your mouth, that's all, just open it and let whatever you feel inside come pouring out. Don't try and hold it, surrender it to the control of the Holy Spirit, just open your mouth and let it come out.'

And I did, and out came these words, like I'd never heard before, and there was just such a spirit of deliverance, and praise, I was praising God really and truly for the first time in my Christian life. We were all crying and hugging and saying over and over and over, thank you Lord, thank you Lord, O thank you Lord. It must have been midnight by the time we all got away. Well, since then I've known the love of Jesus indwelling in my heart; he's delivered me, and he's healed me too, and all my relationships, like it said in the interpretation, and he has given me a new name, a secret name, in a secret language just between me and Him. That's why I'm telling you this, so I can testify to what He did in my life, so you might know that He can do the same in yours.

> *Robin Mattheson, long-term resident at the Stony-brook Psychiatric hospital, diagnosed auto-schizo-phrenic; speaking at the piano in his room, in the presence of Dr Boyd, his physician.*

I should have been a concert pianist, you know. Dr Boyd says I'm very good. 'Robin,' he says, 'you are really a very good pianist.' I just need to hear a thing once and I can play it for you. Two-thirty to three-thirty is practice time. Three-thirty to four-thirty Dolly in number twenty-seven takes her nap, so I don't practice then. Three-thirty to four-thirty is reading time. I have a lot of books and magazines. I like reading. My favourite is the *National Geographic Magazine*. The population of Bhutan is approximately 1.3 million. The capital of Bhutan is Thimpu. The area of Bhutan is 18,147 square miles, the major industries are farming and animal husbandry. The unit of currency is the ngultrum. One of its postage stamps is a miniature record that plays the national anthem of Bhutan. I can play it for you if you like. I just need to hear a thing once.

The best cameras are Hasselblads, but there are more advertisements for Olympus and Canon. Hasselblad is the best camera. The sky is very blue in Bhutan. The average altitude is nine and a half thousand feet. The Bhutanese are adapted to live at high altitudes; they have more red blood cells to carry oxygen, they have a layer of subcutaneous fat to protect them from the cold, and they have extra melanin in their skins so they don't burn in the sun. The air is very clear in Bhutan.

I would choose a Hasselblad every time.

I should have been a concert pianist, you know. I like the theme from *Chariots of Fire*. I can play Mozart and Henry Mancini. Liberace died of AIDS, did you know that? Saturday night, half-past eight: the *Black and White Minstrel Show!* And now we present, Russ Conway at the piano. He's a good pianist. He used to smile at me. I used to hide from him behind the settee. 'Come out Robin,' Mummy-dearest said. 'You'll miss your favourite bit.' Liberace died of AIDS, did you know that? Always wash your hands after using the toilet and before you eat. I can eat my own dinner now. Mummy-dearest used to cut up my meat and potatoes and pour my milk. 'Robin,' she says. 'Why can't you learn to do things for yourself?' My knife and fork have red handles. Dolly's have green handles.

Dr Boyd says I'm a good singer, too. I can sing all the songs from the advertisements. I like to watch the adverts on the telly. They're better than the programmes in between: 'Long grain rice all the way from America, red peppers, green peppers, juicy green beans, carrots and peas and a hint of seasoning . . . Bachelor's Savoury Rice!' 'Cats make haste for the Brekkies taste, the Brekkies taste, Makes cats make haste.' 'Nuts! Whole hazelnuts! Ooomph! Cadbury's take them and they cover them in chocolate!' 'But ask about the bran flakes, what about the bran flakes, they'll all reply: They're tasty, tasty, very very tasty, They're very tasty.' I like to watch the adverts on the telly. They're better than the programmes in between. 'Will it be roast or jacket spuds, Will it be carrots, will it be peas . . . '

OK I'll stop now. Sorry. Sorry. Sorry. I should have been a concert pianist, you know. I can play Mozart and Henry Mancini. Mozart was born in Salzburg. That's in Austria. I read about Austria in the *National Geographic Magazine*. It's my favourite. Austria is a central European republic bordered by Czechoslovakia and West Germany to the North, Switzerland to the West, Italy and Yugoslavia to the South and Hungary to the East. The capital of Austria is Vienna. The unit of currency is the Austrian schilling. The major industries are agriculture and tourism. My shaver was made in Austria. I got it from Boots the Chemists of Nottingham. But it was made in Austria.

When she is cross with me, Mummy-dearest says, 'Robin, you are getting fat, you ought to take some exercise. You will die of a heart attack.' Whenever we went out for a walk, she would buy me chocolate.

'Toblerone, out on its own, Triangular chocolate, that's Toblerone. Made with triangular honey from triangular bees and triangular almonds from triangular trees, and Oh, Mr Confectioner please. Give me Toblerone.' It's made from triangular honey from triangular bees, and triangular almonds from triangular trees, did you know that?

Liberace died of AIDS, did you know that? Always wash your hands after using the toilet and before eating. Mummy-dearest used to cut up my meat and potatoes and pour my milk. 'Robin,' she said. 'Why can't you learn to do things for yourself?'

I should have been a concert pianist, you know. I like the theme from *Chariots of Fire*. I like reading. My favourite is the *National Geographic Magazine*. The population of Bhutan is approximately 1.3 million. The best camera is a Hasselblad, but there are more advertisements for Olympus and Canon. You find a lot of *National Geographic Magazines* in dentists' waiting-rooms. They are a good place to go for *National Geographic Magazines*. Doctors are good too, but not so good. The sky is very blue in Bhutan. Russ Conway used to smile at me. I used to hide from him behind the settee. 'Come out, Robin,' Mummy-dearest said. 'You'll miss your favourite bit.' 'Robin, you are getting fat, you ought to take some exercise. You will die of a heart attack.'

Liberace died of AIDS, did you know that? My knife and fork have red handles. Dolly's . . . Dolly's . . . Dolly's have . . . green handles. I can sing all the songs from the advertisements. They're better than the programmes in between. Austria is a central European republic bordered by Czechoslovakia and West Germany to the North, Switzerland to the West, Italy and Yugoslavia to the

South, and Hungary to the East. I can eat my own
dinner now: I can eat my own dinner now. I can eat
my own dinner now . . .

The blue . . . the sky . . . the clear . . . Saturday. Half-past
eight. We present: Russ Conway at the piano! Hasselblad.
The best camera. I would choose a Hasselblad every time.
'Why can't you learn to do things for yourself? Why can't
you learn to do things for yourself?' Always wash your
hands. Hasselblad. Every time. Two-thirty to three-thirty
is practice time. I must practice, practice makes perfect. I
like the theme from *Chariots of Fire*. The air is very clear . . .
the sky is very blue . . . the blue . . . clear . . . the sky . . .

My knife and fork have red handles. Red.

I should have been a concert pianist, you know. I just
need to hear a thing; once.

EDITED BY ALEX STEWART

ARROWS OF EROS

Do bodices get ripped in outer space?

How can you form a meaningful relationship in a state of weightlessness or get serious in zero gravity?

Which bit goes where when you're talking chlorine-breathing polyps?

Does the earth still move when you're beyond the stars?

Pretty fundamental questions.

It was a late-night bar after a writers' conference when, as can happen, the subject of sex and SF came up. Imaginations were lubricated. Fingers began to itch in anticipation of the firm but yielding touch of the keyboard. The idea became a concept. Another round was bought. The concept hardened into a project.

Arrows of Eros was conceived . . .

EDITED BY JOHN CLUTE, DAVID PRINGLE AND SIMON OUNSLEY

INTERZONE THE 4TH ANTHOLOGY

The fourth selection from *Interzone* brings together names such as J. G. Ballard, John Sladek and Brian Stableford, with new writers of unusual promise such as Kim Newman, Ian Lee and Rachel Pollack, winner of the 1988 Arthur C. Clarke Award for the best sf novel published in Great Britain. Here are pastiche and post-modernism, satire, humour and the sudden, illuminating vision.

'This compilation . . . keeps the faith with a regularity which never betrays our mouth-watering antici-pation: the best of British'

The Times

'The *Interzone* selections . . . are, quite simply, the repositories of some of the finest short fiction to be found anywhere. Oldsters like Ballard and Sladek are in fine form . . . but as usual with this fine imprint, the big names get more than a run for their money from the young bloods'

Time Out

HODDER AND STOUGHTON PAPERBACKS

**EDITED BY JOHN CLUTE, DAVID PRINGLE AND
SIMON OUNSLEY**

INTERZONE THE 3RD ANTHOLOGY

This third selection from *Interzone* includes stories
from 1987 John W. Campbell Award winner Karen
Joy Fowler, from Nebula winner Pat Murphy, from
David Brin, Brian Stableford, Lisa Tuttle, from newcomers Eric Brown and Richard Kadrey . . . they range
from the surreal to cyberpunk, satire to fantasy . . .

'A selection of stories that combine the grim and the
glorious with an audacity that recalls *Dangerous
Visions* . . . it should not be missed at any cost'
Locus

'*Interzone* strides cover the frontier and well on to a
summit of art'
New Statesman

'They have the quality of going right to the edge of
ideas which can chill as well as warm'
The Times

HODDER AND STOUGHTON PAPERBACKS

EDITED BY JOHN CLUTE, DAVID PRINGLE AND SIMON OUNSLEY

INTERZONE THE 2ND ANTHOLOGY

'From the beginning, *Interzone* has sought out new writers . . . No other magazine in Britain is publishing science fiction at all, let alone fiction of this quality'
The Times Literary Supplement

In this second selection from *Interzone* are new stories from J. G. Ballard and Thomas M. Diach, together with Brian Stableford's first piece of fiction in five years. Then, before your very eyes and for the very first time, we present a cyberpunk collaboration between John Shirley and Bruce Sterling . . .

'The most exciting development in this area of British publishing for a decade'
City Limits

Rising Stars Neil Ferguson and Paul J. McAuley, along with a real chiller from Gregory Benford and Ian Watson's tale of alien love . . .

'*Interzone* is the decade's most interesting science fiction magazine'
William Gibson

'The best new science fiction magazine in twenty years'
The Washington Post

Sixteen writers, gathered together to delight, to intrigue, dazzle and challenge. Sixteen story tellers and their 'Brilliantly' varied and frequently breathtakingly audacious stories'
Iain Banks

HODDER AND STOUGHTON PAPERBACKS

MORE SCIENCE FICTION TITLES AVAILABLE FROM HODDER AND STOUGHTON PAPERBACKS